Adam Gurowski

Diary 1863-'64-'65

Adam Gurowski

Diary 1863-'64-'65

ISBN/EAN: 9783337184537

Printed in Europe, USA, Canada, Australia, Japan

Cover: Foto ©Raphael Reischuk / pixelio.de

More available books at **www.hansebooks.com**

DIARY:

1863-'64-'65.

BY ADAM GUROWSKI.

TRUTH IS THE EYE OF HISTORY.

POLYB.

WASHINGTON, D. C.:

W. H. & O. H. MORRISON.

1866.

Printed and Stereotyped by
McGILL & WITHEROW,
366 E Street, Washington, D. C.

TO THE MEMORY OF

General JAMES S. WADSWORTH,

OF GENESEO.

Der Geist durch welchen wir handeln ist das Höchste.

[GOETHE.

WASHINGTON, *February*, 1866.

NAMES MENTIONED IN THIS VOLUME.

PRAISE.	HALF AND HALF.	BLAME.
Andrew, Gov., of Mass.	Agassiz	
Ames, M. C.	Academicians	
Ashley, M. C.		
Alexander II, of Russia,		
Augur, Maj. Gen.		
Ashton, Hubley		
Boutwell, M. C.	Beecher, Ward	Belmont, Banker
Brown, Gratz, Sr.	Burnside, Maj. Gen.	Blair
Butler, Maj. Gen.	Bates	Buell, Don Carlos
Burlingame, Anson		
Brownson, O. A.		
Bingham, M. C.		
Blondeel		
Barreda, (of Peru)		
Banks, Maj. Gen.		
Blaine, M. C.		
Bright, John		
Carey, Henry C.	Chase	Curtiss, George Tick.
Casey, Maj. Gen.		Cowan, Senator
Cobden		Cox, M. C.
Coney, Gov.		Carlyle, Th.
Curtin, Gov.		
Coffey, Titian		
Conkling, Ros., M. C.		
Cushing, Navy Officer		
Colfax, M. C.		
Clark, Senator		
Canby, Maj. Gen.		
Chandler, Senator		
Davis, Winter, M. C.	Doolittle, Senator	Davis, Senator
Darwin		
Dayton, (in Paris,)		
Dix, Maj. Gen.		
Dana, Charles A.		
Dahlgren, Colonel		
Everett	Evarts, Lawyer	

Eames, Lawyer
Farragut   •
Fremont
Fessenden, Sr., and sons
Foster, Senator
Guthrie, James   Greeley, Horace
Ganson, M. C.   Gillmore, Maj. Ge...
Grant
Grimes, Senator
Grow, Ex-Speaker
Griffin, Maj. Gen.
Gooch, M. C.
Henry, Professor   Harris, Senator
Hunter, Maj. Gen.   Harlan, Senator
Howard, Maj. Gen.   Hooker, Maj. Gen.
Hale, Senator
Holt, Judge Advocate
Howard, Senator
Humphreys, Maj. Gen.
Hancock, Maj. Gen.
Hamlin, Vice President
Johnson, Rev. Dr. Walker
Kelley, M. C.

Lyon, Brig. Gen.   Lincoln
Lyons, Lord
Longfellow and son,
Lowell, Colonel
Mill, John Stuart   Meigs, Maj. Gen.
Morrill, Senator
Morrill, M. C.
Morgan, Senator
Martin, Henry
Marcy, Gov.
Morton, Gov.
McPherson, Maj. Gen.

Phillips, Wendell
Pope, Maj. Gen.
Porter, Admiral
Purcell, Archbishop
Potter, Judge, (Wis.)

                            Rosecrans, Maj. Gen.
                            Raymond, Henry
                            Russell, Lord
Stevens, Thad., M. C.   Sumner, Senator
Schofield, Maj. Gen.

Franklin, Maj. Gen.
French, Maj. Gen.

Hopkins, Bishop
Hillard, George, of Boston
Hay, Major (Florida)
Hughes, Archbishop
Halleck, Maj. Gen.

Ketchum, Banker
Keyes, Maj. Gen.
Louis Napoleon
Lamon

Maximilian, of Austria
Marble, Man.
Meade, Maj. Gen.
McClellan, Maj. Gen.

Naglee, Maj. Gen.
Nicolay,
Powell, Senator
Pendleton, M. C.

Richardson, Senator

Seward
Saulsbury, Senator

Smith, Maj. Gen., (Baldy)
Speed, James, Att. Gen. - 296 -
Smith, Goldwin
Stanton
Sedgwick, Maj. Gen.
Sheridan
Stoeckl, De
Sherman
Schenck, Maj. Gen.
Thomas,
Thomas, Adj. Gen.
Trumbull, Senator
Tassara

Wilkinson, Senator
Wade, Senator
Wadsworth,
Warren, Maj. Gen.
Wilson, Senator
Worden, Commodore
Whitman, Walt
Ward, Lieut., Navy
Winslow, Commodore
Wilkes, George

Thompson, George

Welles, Secretary of the
    Navy
Whiting, William.

Scott, Lieut. Gen.
Sykes, Maj. Gen.
Seymour, Gov., N. Y.
Sandford, Diplomat

Taney, Chief Justice
Ticknor, George, Boston

Voorhees, M. C.
Weed, Thurlow
Wood Brothers,
Winthrop, R. C., Boston.

The two former volumes contain the same proportions of blame and praise as prevail in this volume.

CONTENTS.

JANUARY, 1864.

FEBRUARY.

MARCH.

APRIL.

MAY.

JUNE.

JULY.

AUGUST.

SEPTEMBER.

OCTOBER.

NOVEMBER.

APPENDIX.

DIARY.

DIARY.

OCTOBER, 1863.

Meade's great manœuvres—and subserviency to McClellan—Grant brought forward by Stanton—Sewardiana—Romanism in a General, etc., etc., etc.

October 19. — Military wiseacres — Halleck, Meigs, and *tutti quanti*—throw out a bait for the gullibility of the gulping public. But facts and data give evidence against the wiseacres, or the *bonnets de coton*. Meade, they say, had an order to retreat, or, to make it more poetical and gullible, Meade had an order (of course from Carnot-Jomini-Vattel-Halleck) to concentrate his forces and his lines, which Meade executes—of course, in the most "masterly" manner, &c.— and—*then Lee followed.*

Facts and data. On the hour and on the day that he sent out to *reconnoitre* on his right and on his left, Meade had not yet moved his head-quarters from Culpeper Court-House. Generals Buford, Gregg, Kilpatrick, who made the *recon-noissances*, everywhere found Lee's army already moving, advancing—everywhere they met strong columns of the enemy—principally so at Madison

2

Court-House on Meade's right. Lee moved before Meade had received and begun to execute the order (?) to "concentrate his lines." Lee *might or might not have had the intention to come between Meade and Washington.* If Lee intended to carry out that desperate manœuvre—he being well aware that Meade outnumbered him two to one—then he had the fullest confidence in Meade's somnolence—or in something else and worse. Such a manœuvre must have been a death-knell to Lee's army, if the Federals had only a good non-commissioned officer for commander. In such a case Lee ought to have been allowed to come between Meade and Washington. Then Meade could execute a *volte face* as easily as on a peaceful drill, push Lee on Washington, (where about 30,000 men were in the defences)—put Lee's army between two fires—and not a rebel could escape. (Look at the map, and at the distances and differences in the positions.) About one day, or, at the utmost, thirty-six hours of double-quick marching, would have separated the two armies. NO more. Meade would have been treading on Lee's heels—and this literally, not figuratively.

Even if a McClellan had been in command, Lee could scarcely calculate on two days' march in advance, and even therewith he could not escape his fate. Lee's movement was a desperate one, and he risked it only after having at Williamsport and since, taken Meade's full measure.   As for Jomini-Halleck and Lincoln, Lee knew their mettle of old.

October 19.—Nine millions are paid by those exempted from draft.   This makes 30,000 exempted.   On the whole, it is not much in itself, but too much, in proportion to the number of the drafted.

October 20.—Meade fronts Bull Run, and finds no enemy before him or in his rear—of course not.   Lee seems not decided to gratify us by making a false move—in his position, a crime. That is *our* domain.   Now the wise double-treble headquarters (Meade's, Halleck's, etc.) establish that Lee, after having taken Meade by the nose, after having frightened Washington out of its senses, and terrified the country, has retreated to the, or behind the Rappahannock, burning all the bridges behind him; (but the burned bridges are not on Lee's road, but on that one on which our armies move.)   If so, Lee has accomplished his object.   He pushed Meade from the Rappahannock back to Washington, and destroyed the bridges and roads by which alone Meade could pursue him.   In such a way, under the nose of a *homunculus* commanding the bravest army, and double in number that of the enemy, Lee quietly disposed of the fall campaign, gave it a quietus, and made any further immediate movement impossible to us.   That is manœuvring.

October 20.—*Mr. Decembriseur* evidently seems

to wish to pick a quarrel with us about the tobacco bought in Richmond on account of the French government. Well, he may try it.

October 21.—Lee suddenly disappeared, and the President ordered Meade to find out Lee's whereabouts, and not subside "into positions, and expect." The President had better order Meade to bed, and put *a man* in his place. So ends this most shameful campaign; shameful for us, glorious for Lee. Such a display of incapacity as given to the people by Meade, such a "masterly" generalship as his, equals the worst times in France under the marshals nominated by the Pompadour.

Thus, by order, and not by choice, Meade moved from his "carefully selected positions," and found that at least two days previously Lee began his retreat, and thus baffled Meade's "masterly preparations" to receive the rebels. What a cruel deceiver this Lee is!

October 21.—As I expected, the West is concentrated under Grant. That is the fruit of Stanton's insistency, and of his visit to St. Louis. Stanton's patriotism and judgment restored to activity Grant, who was virtually shelved by Lincoln's, Halleck's, Blair's re-electioneering conspiracy.— (See Vol. II.) Rosecrans will go to making prayers. Rosecrans has military capacity, but is ruined by his Roman Jesuitic fervor. When, in the battle of Chattanooga, his lines had been broken by the enemy, Rosecrans fervently prayed, but gave no orders; nevertheless Joshua's spirit descended not upon him.

October 22.—Lee gone, and for at least three weeks he may do what he pleases—send a part of his army against Burnside, or play any other trick. The President ordered Meade to find out and fight Lee. Meade did not carry it out; so I hope the next order will be to Meade to go and join McClellan. Such is the ardent wish of the best men in the War Department. Meade looks not like a man *qui a des batailles dans son ventre,* but he looks like a Jesuit.

October 25.—Lincoln and Seward answer the Barcelona Democrats. Seward holds the pen and says: "that Lincoln incidentally promoted the cause of humanity." He means emancipation. All my accusations against Judas Iscariot Seward are justified by himself.

October 26.—Grant establishes his headquarters in the field. Brave Grant! O, why has not Grant the command of the noble and fated army of the Potomac!

October 27.—All quiet, and only the quacking of politicians is audible. As Lee is gone and beyond reach, Meade blows, puts on airs, and *displays any amount of martial activity.* In this campaign not only all the military rules have been violated, trodden in the mud, but all the rules of common sense. Meade did it probably to show that one could be found even lower than

McClellan. And as Meade is in direct communication with McClellan, as he recognizes Mac for his Chief, and reports to him all his movements, so probably Meade executed Mac's, and not the President's orders. Weeks ago I warned Stanton about this treasonable intercourse between Meade and McClellan.

October 28.—Always at work on the defences of Washington. This uneasiness about Washington is the greatest homage paid to Lee and his troops. Of course, if Halleck is to direct the defence, a drove of cattle may storm and carry all the works.

October 29.—Chase makes a speech in Baltimore. It has the flavor of a presidential candidate. Oh! we shall see to it Chase, or rather events will see to it! But then when Chase is attacked by such a one as Blair or by the Blairs, he becomes dear even to me.

October 29.—I was right (Volume 2d) to say that McClellan's influence ruined Fitz John Porter. Fitz John was quite another man at the beginning of the rebellion. He changed when McClellanism got hold of him. Here is an evidence to-day discovered by me. Early in 1861, during the revolt of the traitors in Baltimore, (all of them would-be aristocrats and would-be gentlemen,) Porter was sent to Pennsylvania to organize and take the command of some *impromptu* levies, and to march with them on the Baltimore traitors. Porter received his orders directly from the War Department. A few days afterwards General Scott, (that northern incubus,) ordered Porter not to organize and not to move; and to this Porter answered that his duty was to obey the Department and not General Scott. It would have been well for Porter and for the cause if, in the fall of 1861, and then in Virginia in August, 1862, he had had similar feelings of discipline.

October 29.—Accusations and counter-accusations between Halleck and Rosecrans. I am certain that Halleck has been muddling. Meade, *sub rosa*, complains of Halleck. In this case *l'un vaut l'autre*.

October 30.—No one will be able to trace out all the various *Sewardiana*. From one in whom I have implicit confidence, I learn that early after Sumter Seward sent an agent south to tell Jeff. Davis, "that if it could depend upon him, (Seward,) no blood would run, as he was ready to let the South go."

NOVEMBER, 1863.

November 1.—Mr. Lincoln is fully aware:

1st. That Meade is very little, and less than very little as a commander.

2d. That his, Meade's, *clique* and advisers are even worse than were the surroundings of McClellan.

3d. Mr. Lincoln knows all about Meade's double-dealings; knows that Meade flatters him, Lincoln, and offers *obedience* to McClellan; and, nevertheless, Mr. Lincoln stands by Meade, because of Halleck, and of a deputation of Philadelphians, who threaten to give the State to McClellan if Meade's feelings are hurt. Thus all efforts of that brave patriot Stanton, to prune the army at the top, come to nothing.

November 2.—Good news. Butler appointed to Fortress Monroe, etc. The White House shakes before public opinion and before the coming Congress, and so appeals to *men* and *patriots* for support. Butler is no joker, no sham, but a most thorough proconsular reality.

November 4.—The people is recovering its sound judgment, and almost all over the country the copperheads or Democrats overpowered at the polls, and the elections triumphant for us. Andrews of Massachusetts, of course, again Governor. The people does not support Lincoln's shiftless, heartless, incapable (Stanton excepted) administration, but the people stands by its own great, lofty, sacred cause, and kicks the copperheads.

November 5.—Finally Meade (not like Marlborough) *s'en va en guerre*, to search what he does not wish to find. Meade has more than 80,000, and Lee about 40,000; so Meade, schooled by his master McClellan, cannot fight the enemy.

November 6.—Meade has taken rations for ten days. When he has eaten them up, then he will stop in his martial ardor, wait for new rations, or return. And Halleck has gone West to confuse all.

November 6.—Seward makes a speech at Auburn. Full of paternal forgiveness. He, the good christian, declares that he stands at the door *expecting* the *return of the prodigal son, ready to introduce him to the vacated seat in the paternal house.* But oh, Seward! your prodigal son is worse than Cain, is a traitor, is worse than a highway robber and midnight murderer, is recking with the blood of brethren whom he treacherously slaughtered! The slaughtered good sons are of no account to the biblical Seward.

Further, Seward, schooled by Weed, upbraids the rebels for having forced Lincoln to emancipate the slaves at the ratio of 10,000 a month. Oh, how the biblicist hates emancipation! Still further, Seward impresses the necessity of the re-election of Lincoln by reasons dynastic rather than republican. The New York *loyal* Press—duty bound—is silent on these biblical escapades of Seward, as it was silent on the "incidental emancipation" in the letter to the Democrats of Barcelona; *per contre*, the *New York Herald* and the *National Intelligencer*—a well-assorted team—idolize Seward.

November 7.—Seward's worshippers and clients assert, that moved by Seward's devotion, Lincoln will step aside, and give Seward his support for Presidency. Fillmore thus humbugged Webster to the last, and cheated the great Dan.

November 8.—What are Chase's claims for the Presidency? He wished to let the Cotton States go; he showed no statesman-like foresight when, in April, 1861, he made the first loan of ten millions, being offered fifty millions by the more long-headed bankers. A very small difference between Seward's diplomatic sixty to ninety days, and Chase's ten millions. Then, he was continually either bamboozled, or twisted around the fingers, or baffled by Seward. Chase is honest, but pompous, and lacks knowledge of men—a knowledge never to be acquired by pompous characters. With all this, Chase is a thou-

sand times more fit for a President than Lincoln
or Seward.

November 9.—The *belated* hunt after Lee begins
well, but may end in smoke.   Meade and his
McClellanite advisers are not the men to force
Lee to fight if he does not want to do it.

November 10.—Always soldier-like, Lee has
already published his report of the September
and October operations against Meade.   Meade's
report, if he may write any, will never see day-
light.   What I said in the first days of October
is justified by Lee's report.   We lost more in
prisoners than did the Rebels.   Lee understands
his business; he marches, manœuvres, fights, and
writes his report—we drink whisky.   Oh! why
is this Lee a traitor!

November 11.—As yet no fight, and there will
be none.   Meade under Lincoln, is like a boy
whipped by his father, and sent in search of
stolen cattle.

November 12.—At last the report of the Titanic
days at Gettysburg is published.   Wadsworth
again honorably mentioned, but not in proportion to his or to his division's deserts.   For several hours Wadsworth's division sustained the
whole brunt of the onslaught, and the rebels
numbered three to one.   But Wadsworth is not a
courtier to the head staffs, or to reporters—he
has none of the latter on his staff; further, Wadsworth is not of the West Point clique, but simply

a patriot.   In this report Meade glides over the never-to-be pardoned crime at Williamsport.

November 13.—Sedgwick destroys a rebel division, and Meade stands by—gaping, instead of pushing the enemy, terror-struck by Sedgwick's splendid blow.   But Meade religiously follows the example of his idol, McClellan. Meade subsides, and the victory is barren for the ends of this Meade-Lincoln-Halleck would-be campaign.

But to win fruitless victories is the special capacity of West-Pointers on both sides—in our and in the rebel camp.   Lee as little understood how to transform into routs and defeats his victories at Fredericksburg and Chancellorsville, as were unwilling and unable to do it, McClellan after Antietam, or Meade at and after Gettysburg.   And thus the superhuman bravery and toughness of the soldiers in both the armies comes to naught.

November 16.—Now we quietly subside, and only the buzzing of presidential intriguing interrupts the lull.

November 16.—To believe the malcontents, and above all, copperheads—Democrats—no one is honest in this administration.   It is not so. Seward, for one, is thoroughly honest, considered from the money and gain points of view;   so emphatically is Stanton and Chase and Bates. There are only unsustained, slanderous rumors

against Welles and his assistant in the Navy
Department.

But after all, time may unveil many things
now hidden, and no wonder if we find very rich
those who *ought not* to have made money in any
way whatever. True honesty seems to be at a
discount, and many things contribute to create
this low morality. Millions are squandered,
money pours out through all fissures of the
national structure. Thus corruption fills the air,
and the current, almost irresistible, carries many
away, who, but for the temptations lavishly
thrown in their path, would have remained
honest. Public opinion, unprepared for such a
condition of society and affairs, is relaxed and
uncertain. In American polity and society,
poverty was rather a dishonor. And in
the normal condition of-American society this
judgment on poverty was just. Every kind
of labor found a market and buyers; speculation
and the use of one's intellectual powers were
untrammelled, and had before them immensities
of space; therefore in ninety-nine cases out of
one hundred, poverty was the result of shiftless-
ness, and wealth the harvest of skill and of
capacity. But though all this was natural and
logical, it contributed mightily to relax the
public judgment and conscience. Smartness,
cunning, and worse, when successful, became
accounted for honesty. If a man got rich, people became accustomed to pay him a certain

consideration. And if any doubts arose about the ways and means by which he got rich, indulgence naturally had the upper hand. After a little chill the doubtful was accepted as smart, and all was right. And now when the means to become rich *per fas* and *nefas* thickly bristle in one's way, few resist temptations. Aristideses, etc., are rare, very rare phenomena, and as to the rest see Jesus and the public woman. Nevertheless, the number of those who could use their position to make money but who remained honest, is very considerable, and I confess to be rather agreeably surprised thereby. And to conclude: more honesty prevails than in any other country and government; I can prove this at any time, facts, dates, and the history of most European governments in hand.*

November, 17.—The execution of the draft has created irritation, but has been carried out. The only drawback is, that the exemption became too easy for the rich, and thus many hundreds and thousands of the so-called gentlemen, that is, loafers of various social grades, escape the military service. The originators of the draft are

---

*My checkered political existence, especially in Europe, generally brought me into companionship with persons who in various ways had lost or were losing their respective patrimonies. Curious and entertaining is now the observation and the study of persons, who rapidly, as by a charm, throw off the garb of poverty and acquire not only competency but more or less wealth.—*Note June*, 1865.

the West-Pointers; above all, McClellan and his crew. It originated with them in the hatred of the volunteers, who in this war are the noblest offshoot of free institutions; it originated in the blind and infamous aspirations of McClellan and his crew to found a military preponderance in the American social order. It was intended to take away from the respective States the power to create armies, *to take it away*, and to concentrate it in the hands of the administration. It would have been the first step to the ruin of the Republic. After McClellan's fall, the project was taken up by the McDowell's, the Meigs', and such ones; and the civilian patriots, such as Stanton, Wade, Wilson, and other Senators and members of Congress became converted to the necessity of the draft. *Tout compte fait;* volunteering has given more and better soldiers than the draft, and the indifference and lukewarmness in volunteering is generated by the stupendous faults of Lincoln and Halleck and by McClellan's military conduct.

November 18.—If lobby-men, contractors, and all similar individuals could be put on the rack, what curious revelations they would make.

November 19.—I hear men belonging to, or in the strictest sense originating from, the people— I hear them speak with contempt of the masses, and of the philosophical comprehension of democracy in its elements and in its principle. I never felt such a contempt for *parvenues* as when listening to these villifiers, who assert that the masses are vile and mentally miserable. Truly such are the masses in the democratic party, composed mostly of the coarsest, roughest, most uncouth—mostly Roman Catholic immigrants, those products of that mental and physical degradation and desecration of man which prevails in Europe. The South fights and murders to permanently establish such an order here, and is therein supported by northern Copperheads, Democrats, and Conservatives. And if the more enlightened masses of the American people become confused and are led astray, the fault is with these upstarts who, issuing from the people, faithlessly betray the trust laid in them by the people. These sham beacons and politicians win the public confidence, and then, instead of enlightening and pointing out the true path, for the sake of various expediencies by which they alone profit, they confuse the common sense and sound judgment of that large public, who devotes its time to its respective businesses and occupations, and who rely upon the shams for advice and leadership.

So it is with the question of Lincoln's re-election. The confusion created in public opinion by the above-mentioned political upstarts is so great that even the more honest, and many from among the thoroughly honest patriots, having no confidence in Lincoln, nevertheless become carried away by the *shibboleth* of the falsely evoked expediency.   And when the masses are thus confused, betrayed, brought or pushed into the wrong path, the upstarts turn upon them and ironically exclaim, "look at the workings of your democratic principle."

November 20.—The funeral festivities at Gettysburg—"*misceantur sacra profanis*," as the great master of ceremonies at this sacred national rite is Lincoln's most intimate friend—a slave-catcher, money substractor, and president of all low loafers, blacklegs, gamblers, and the like offal.

November 21.—Everett, the orator.   The patriotic part noble and warm.   As for the rest, too classic, too enslaved to the so-called classic form, an attempt to imitate Pericles.   Copperheads, traitors, democrats will never forgive Everett for being a patriot.   Already the *World* again pours upon Everett its muddy, stinking froth.   Everett takes a broad ground against the sympathizers with treason, and of course such organs of treason as the *National Intelligencer* malign the patriot. Giving an account of the campaign, Everett glides over the crime at Williamsport; the comparison of Wellington and Waterloo is not at all just to Wellington, who rushed and followed Napoleon, and who never could have committed such a crime as Meade committed at Williamsport.

Lincoln spoke, with one eye to a future platform and to re-election.

November 22.—Meade puts on airs as if *seriously* he was intending to do some harm to the rebels. "Meade has matured his plans," say the Meade men. Oh! exactly *a la McClellan.* The disciple of the "young Nap." wanted six weeks to mature his plans, and during this time Lee has sent Longstreet west to fight Grant and Burnside. *Ohé! bourique ohé.*

Stanton is exasperated at Meade, and if he could only act, Meade would have been relieved long ago. But Lincoln! Meade consoles Lincoln by saying that *if* the good weather holds out, he will carry out his well-matured plans. Poor weather! it was for months clear, bright and invigorating, but Lincoln's, Halleck's, and Meade's brains remained opaque, muddy and debilitated. How in every step Meade imitates McClellan! Like his model, Meade appeals to IFS. Grant alone is independent of *ifs.*

November 23.—Lincoln's re-election will ingrain an immense amount of coarse vulgarity into the people, as four years of bad example will act terribly.

November 24.—I am curious if the Senate or the House will ever investigate the way that most of the military appointments are made. Above all, the appointments of Brigadier and Major Generals. For one general deserving his promotion, there are at least five zeros and worse. All kinds of influences are at play, minus capacity. When Lincoln is pushed into a

corner by daring demanders—male or female—
then a general is created. And the country's
honor and blood pay for it.

November 26.—Grant again victorious. No *ifs*
with Grant, and Meade and his clique stick in
the—to them congenial—mud.

November 28.—The news from Grant and from
his army more and more glorious! And Mc-
Clellan-Meade was to move last Monday; already
the vanguard was in motion ; then came a little
shower, then the movement of the vanguard was
countermanded, then Meade waited for fine
weather, then the fine weather came not, etc.,
etc. No one can better serve McClellan so well
as Meade.

November 30.—The politicians are at work like
moles, to counteract each other and to undermine the respective presidential candidates.
This game and spectacle would be amusing, but
that the destinies, nay, the life of a great and
noble people are at stake.

DECEMBER.

December 1. — Our victories, it seems, are always unproductive, are not pursued. In due time some evil spirit stops them, to give the rebels time to recover. As Halleck claims to have Grant under his orders, as the recent victory in the West subsided, Halleck is our evil and the rebels' rescuing spirit.

Halleck-Meade again outmanœuvred Lee, and our army—retreats. Oh! why am I so good a prophet? But prophesy is very easy with Meade as it was easy with the McClellans, the Franklins, etc. Predict the greatest blunder, the greatest absurdity close to treason, predict helplessness and imbecility; the McClellans, the Franklins, the Meades, and their Frenches, Sykes's, Naglees, etc., are certain to commit it all and you are a prophet.

December 2.—Congressional scouts and skirmishers already at work. Scouts and skirmishers are office-seekers, lobby-men, contractors, etc. Some of the contractors deserve to be quartered, but a great many of them are wronged, almost ruined, by the red-tapeism and the imbecility, the narrow-mindedness and the scurrillous conceit of some of the Departments. Most of such cases within my knowledge must be credited to the Navy Department—no wonder—and to the Quartermaster's office—*Intendance generale des Armées.* This likewise no wonder.

Further, the politicians. Gnats and musquitoes. And of all shadowings and range. From a Thurlow Weed up to a Greeley. Oh, what a discordant buzzing!

Kopf und Verstand vergehet mir schier.

Intriguing going on in the most approved style. Oh, politicians! Oh, race of hell!

December 3.—A new Congress! Treason. and the rebels strongly represented by the copperheads, the McClellanites and the Democrats. Treason will be rampant and defiant in the Woods, the Voorheeses, the Pendletons, Powells, and all of them. And to think that all this sacrilegious desecration is the work of Lincoln's double-dealing nature, aided by the Blairs, Sewards, Thurlow Weeds, etc. But for Seward and Weed, this worse than a copperhead, Horatio Seymour and his tail, would not have been elected in New York. Wadsworth would have been Governor, and with him a galaxy of patriots would have been elected to Congress. And the same in other States; but now the country is stained, and treason is in high glee.

 Happily for the honor of the people and for its interests, Congress has the old phalanx; the patriotic, devoted, truthful, courageous, self-sacrificing majority left from the 37th, is alive in this Congress. These men will remain true to the great principle, faithful to the people, to the country, and faithful to themselves.

December 4.—Meade reports about his doings. He went to find out about Lee's health, found it good, and—returned, and dutifully reported to the headquarters, to the White House, and to McClellan.

The quill-drivers attached to the army, who get whisky and inspirations from the generals, and *menaces of expulsion* from Meade, inform the public that Meade successfully carried out a successful *réconnoissance*. Will the people likewise mix with whisky this humbug of *réconnoissance,* and gulp it?

December 5.—In its mental one-sidedness the small church of abolitionists already hurrahs for Lincoln. This church can do much harm, as, after all, the faithful are as honest and pure as one-sided. I wonder not at Beecher, but wonder at Wendell Phillips, who is not of that small parish. I wrote to him.

The next presidential epoch imperatively demands bumps of energy, constructiveness, organization; and neither Gall nor Spurzheim would have been able to find a trace of the above qualities in Mr. Lincoln's skull.

December 6.—By their coolness and equanimity, the real patriot politicians evoke my astonishment—nay, my *admiration*. Whatever may be the losses — fruits of Lincoln's policy and Meade's *strategy*—they exclaim, "*we are a great people and can stand all that.*" The caucus for the Speaker's election agitates the politician patriots more than the latest dishonor and the bloody losses occasioned by Meade's incapacity and Lincoln's pertinacity. Even Greeley, who never comes when there is any danger for the people, or any grand, vital question before Congress, Greeley came to Washington to look about the Speakership. *Ex uno omnes.*

Greeley against re-election—so he told me himself. I record, and we shall see if he holds out.

December 6.—Mr. Lincoln writes a letter to a meeting in New York. Oh! the letter writing is so easy, but the acting up to one's written phrases is so difficult! Mr. Lincoln never yet acted up to his letters, whether written by him to the right or to the left.

December 6.—Wadsworth—always the high-minded citizen, the devoted patriot. In my presence he very severely admonished a young man, and his connection by blood, for not having reported an officer who took money from contractors. Wadsworth sent two thousand dollars to the Libby Prison prisoners, and nobody knows it; I had to promise to him to keep it secret from the newspapers.

December 6.—It is the fashion to praise Mr. Lincoln's so-called *admirable* scent and prescience of the popular sentiment and aspirations. Quite the contrary is the truth. Mr. Lincoln never did anything in advance of the people's wish, never showed any prescience. Lincoln acts when the popular wave is so high that he can stand it no more, or when the gases of public exasperation rise powerfully and strike his nose—and they admire him!

December 7.—It seems that the West-Pointers of the Meade class and creed have not learned tactics and the appropriate use of arms. In thick forests they dismount cavalry, armed with short carbines, and use it against infantry armed with rifles of long range. Of course our brave boys are slaughtered. So, the son of Longfellow the poet, was very dangerously wounded. This young Longfellow is an honor and a consolation to his father—the boy rages for fight.

December 7.—Jomini-Carnot-Corinth Halleck scattered in small bodies our troops all over the South, above all, on the right of the Mississippi; and thus it is that the rebel Kirby Smith, with about 13,000, occupying a central position, keeps at bay three small loyal armies scattered on the circumference. Not one of these small bodies is strong enough to fight the rebels single-handed;

but if united, they could easily crush the forces of Smith. And this condition lasts for weeks, nay, for months. And how can one witness such incapacity and not shower maledictions upon the great American Cabinet strategian!

December 8.—Speaker elected—Colfax, a true and devoted patriot, not a shifter, not a low politician. Copperheads and the representatives in Congress of the Southern creed beaten at their first attempt to raise their heads and spread their venom. The old phalanx victorious.

December 9.—President's message—characteristic of the man. Certain good intentions, with the admixture of Seward, and Blair's notions about the limits of the powers of a President, and therefore these powers overstepped. A confusion between the President's powers and the war powers of the Congress, as conferred by the Constitution. Out of this confusion comes the impossibility to act. And the proclamation corresponds to an *Oukase*—all confusion. The validity of the proclamation, and of the oath prescribed by it, are submitted to the judicial decision. And if a Taney and such ones invalidate all, what then? A tenth part of the voters are to organize a State—altogether against the paramount principle of majority. And when the remaining nine-tenths oppose, what then? Rule of the bayonet for the support of the one-tenth. And the Africo-American to be free, but without any guaranty whatever for his freedom. And all this is very transparent: it is to have sham States for the presidential election.

December 10.—The *radical* and the so-called *loyal* Press hurrahs for Lincoln. Nothing else could be expected.

December 11.—Wadsworth returned from the inspection of the liberated Africo-American settlements along the Mississippi, down to New Orleans. Stanton sent Wadsworth, as Stanton, when untrammeled by Lincoln or Halleck, almost always selects the right man. Wadsworth's report is admirable.* He exonerates the Government and the loyal party from the accusations of neglect and of heartlessness thrown on them by the slave worshippers, and their organs, the simon-pure democratic press all over the country, headed by the *Herald*. The mortality was not a result of neglect, but of the agglomeration of slaves running away in search of freedom, and of the utter impossibility of organizing them at once, and distributing them through better and healthier localities. All such causes, horrible as they are, are nevertheless transient, and Wadsworth found them already a great deal

---

* Wadsworth advised what was to be done pending the war, and therefore the question of suffrage is not touched in his report. But as Wadsworth urged the necessity of arming the freedman, that he might repel the assaults of robbers, guerrillas, slave hunters, and slave drivers; so, of course, the war being over, Wadsworth would have claimed for the Africo-American the right of suffrage as the legal defence against his, the "*niggers*," inveterate enemies.—*Note Sept.* 26, 1865.

ameliorated. And if a man in this world is to be believed and trusted, Wadsworth is the man. Before the runaways started in search of freedom, of refuge, and of bread, they had been already starved on the plantations, starved under the eyes of, and by their so-called patriarchal masters, and by their masters' *better halves*. Wadsworth found the Africo-Americans docile, and craving to be instructed, to be directed; but he likewise found the terror of the slaveholder so ingrained in the slave, that without a strong watchfulness and protection, the slaveholding whip might easily drive the poor Africo-American back into chains. Wadsworth advises the government to educate the children, and to do it without any loss of time, and to distribute arms among the older generation, that it may thus be self-sustaining and enabled to repulse any encroachments on its rights. This report is by far superior to that made some time ago by a commission, who spoke of psychology, etc., but not of common sense. When Wadsworth left, Adjutant General Thomas (of whom he speaks very highly) agreed to Wadsworth's suggestions, and began to distribute arms among workmen on plantations.

December 12.—Wadsworth's opinion is that Lincoln will be re-elected, and be it so, as an unavoidable necessity to preserve the country and the cause from the curse of all curses: that is, from McClellan and from his supporters.

Wadsworth is not a Lincolnite, and never goes to have "a talk with the President." He advised me to be prepared to swallow this bitter pill. Strange!

December 12.—The "loyal" and "intelligent" press is still ecstatic over the President's message. And I am certain that this admired proclamation oath and the one-tenth will never work at all. Logic and law condemn the whole sterile scheme. It will be a still-born child. I cannot imagine such a wonder as a State organized on that *Oukase*, and admitted by Congress.

December 12.—The Weehawken, one of the best monitors, foundered before Charleston. It looks as if Seward must have been prophesying success in some of his Seward-like diplomatic effusions. A disaster always comes on the head of the like Sewardiana.

December 12.—Halleck's elaborate report about military operations says nothing new, but, *sub rosa*, insinuates that after all, he, Halleck, is a great man. Some indirect, and, therefore, as unsoldier-like as unmanly, accusations against Meade for the crime at Williamsport, and for having left Lee alone and undisturbed in August and September. If Halleck were only one thousandth part of a Carnot, he would have long ago either crushed Meade, or accused him forcibly and openly of the above military crimes. But Meade is still in command, saving Lee to please

McClellan, and Meade will still cost the country scores of thousands of precious lives.

. *December* 13.—It seems that public opinion in England begins to turn in favor of right and justice, that is, in favor of the North. The masses, honest and true, have been always in the right track. It is the mean, snobbish, would-be enlightened or leading class in England that seems to wheel round. But now how many claim to have effected this change?

In primis: Seward claims that his State papers have changed the current of English opinions.*

How many Englishmen have read those masterly papers?

2d. Sumner assures us that his private but extensive correspondence worked wonders in England.

3d. An Evarts, who was sent by Seward to England, (*vide* Vol. II,) and in seven weeks dined out forty-five times—Evarts asserts that between

---

*I have it *from the most trustworthy and almost direct authority* that Mr. Seward fully convinced Mr. Johnson and some members of the Cabinet of the following *indubitable fact*—England or rather the English government abstained or desisted from any armed interference in favor of the rebels, thanks —————— to the *powerful, boundless influence exercised by Mr. Seward on Lord Lyons!!!* This absurdity is so gross that any refutation is superfluous. Lord Lyons will be astonished to learn it, as will all those who know that nobleman. And Russell, Palmerston and the English Cabinet in turn influenced directly by Lyons indirectly by Seward! All this is strictly believed in high quarters.—*Note Sept.*, 1865.

the *poire* and the *fromage* he brought England to her senses.

4th. Virtuous Whiting mildly insinuates that since the English had the happiness to listen to his persuasive reasonings, and have been exposed to the fire of his sweet, insinuating manners, a change for the better in the public opinion has been manifest.

5th. Beecher maintains that his stirringly, boldly, and broadly-asserted claims to Anglo-Saxon consanguinity in shams, that his invocations and fine flattery, did the work.

Beecher is nearer to the mark than his competitors. Beecher alone in some way approached the great heart of the genuine English people, and whatever may be its raceology and other scientific shams, the heart of every people beats always for right and for humanity.

The other compounds of English society—the aristocrats, the snobs, the would-be somebodies —were brought to their senses principally by the Porters, the Farraguts, the Wordens, and all those heroic and devoted sailors. I say this with all due respect to the peerless talents of the Sewards, Evarts, Whitings, Weeds, etc.

December 14.—Jeff. Davis in his message, and Halleck in his report, speak of staffs; but Jeff. Davis seems to know far more about the subject than Halleck.

Halleck tries to patronize Grant, and refutes imaginary accusations against Grant for disobedience to orders.   But, O, Halleck, nobody ever thought of accusing Grant; you have dreamed, (after champagne,) or hatched it out in your pacific headquarters!—all this to have occasion to patronize Grant, who is above your patronage.

Halleck's demand for 423,000 cavalry, and the thrashing he got from Rosecrans, crown Halleck's report.

December 14. — Charleston not yet taken; Dahlgren* at war with Gilmore; Dupont and

---

*History will determine at whose door to lay the failure before Charleston.   The volumes of the Diary point out the cardinal reasons, but besides many secondary ones exist.   Accusations and counter-accusations are plentifully made.   Admiral Dahlgren must be listened to and—believed.   At the darkest hour in April, 1861, when treason in Washington was paramount, when Buchanan, Maury and the other traitors in the Navy and in the Washington Navy Yard not only deserted to the enemy, but attempted to spread treason, to demoralize and disorganize the numerous personel and the workmen, Dahlgren's patriotism and energy stopped the demoralization and maintained order. Thucydides -Greeley ignores this fact.   And here let me correct my own negligency and attempt to preserve to the nation's and to history's gratitude the name of Ward, Lieutenant of the Navy, who on the Pawnee commanded the Potomac Flotilla in the summer of 1861.·   Every one remembers how shamefully at that epoch cowardice, represented through engineerism this cardinal product of West Point, was dominant in the military councils in Washington.   Both banks of the Potomac bristled with rebel batteries; Washington was blockaded, but the military wiseacres and the engineers (first West Point graduates) *dared* not to interrupt and to chastise the rebels.   With his little flotilla—three small vessels—Lieutenant Ward asked the support of a battalion of infantry to attack and to silence the most annoying rebel works.   Engineers and wiseacres, Scott at the

half of the Navy denounce the monitors as more
or less a failure; the other half stands by
Ericsson, and there is a general confusion in the
Navy Department.   For some reason or other,
the Navy department shows a kind of narrow-
mindedness and one-sidedness painful to witness.
Instead of as broadly as possible throwing open
a field for the almost inexhaustible creative and
inventive powers of the Americans, the Department narrows and contracts these powers to one
single invention.   Monitors may be excellent,
but other kinds of iron-clads may be as excellent,
and very much needed in the present struggle.
Our Navy has no rams, and the rebels have them
constructed here and in England.   Aside from
the heavily-sailing *Monitors*, other iron-clads of
increased velocity could be of service for defence
and offence.   We ought to have had a numerous
fleet of rams, of light draft, able to enter the
creeks, rivers, and all inland waters, to thus
clean them of rebel pirates.   The country
abounds with inventors and mechanics, the most
skillful in the world.   Our sailors, from the
admirals down to the cabin-boys, are heroes, and
nevertheless the rebels have the glory of the
initiative with iron-clads, with rams, etc.   If the
rebels had at their command such intelligent
mechanics as the North has where would be our

---

head, refused the support.   Ward attacked so to speak, single-
handed, and fell, a sacrifice to treasonable pusillanimity.—*Note
Sept.* 25, 1865.

fleets? It is not sufficient to be honest as a chief of Department; insight, promptness of decision, knowledge of the various subjects, and enthusiasm, are as imperatively necessary as is honesty. The Farraguts, the Porters, and their numberless compeers in the Navy, by their enthusiasm, by their energy, and enterprise, make up for the somnolence and pedantry of the Department, and they alone nobly redeem the nation's honor.

December 14.—The Democrats in Congress follow the leadership of Wood, and very naturally. Wood impudently and brazenly speaks out what others have in their rotten hearts.

December 17.—Mr. Lincoln answers to the Union League, that he has never read Blair's treasonable speech. The worse for him if he has not. Weeks ago Mr. Lincoln told the same story to Kelley, the brilliant and patriotic orator, and Kelley sent a copy of the speech to Mr. Lincoln, who thus had time and occasion to become acquainted with the doings of his Cabinet's pet spaniel.

December 19.—I am certain that no investigation will be made into the various miscarried operations and military crimes committed by Meade during the last four months, and so brilliantly crowned by the Mine Run blindfolded counter-marchings. If Meade and his staff have studied the country—and I am certain, at least, that Humphreys has—and if French bungled or

4

disobeyed, then French ought to be court martialed on the drum, and down with him. Warren behaved well, but was unsupported. McClellan's offal surrounding Meade wished Warren to be worsted. So by his generalship Meade wantonly murdered about 3,500 of the people's best children, and now the hero proudly retires under his tent, and—all is forgotten.

December 20.—The small Church, the things called patriotic politicians, and the rank and file behind them, are all satisfied. All find things going smoothly, and thank God that it is not worse. Very philosophical, stoical, and even christian. "Never mind the losses and the imbecility, never mind the Lincolns, the Sewards, the Hallecks, or Meades; the people are strong, and will in the end overcome all." So I believe too, and so believe such men as Wade, Grimes, Boutwell, Fessenden, Stanton, Wilson, Chandler, the Morrills, Clark, and the phalanx of genuine patriots in Congress, etc., phalanx leading the Congressional majority. Not one of them doubts the people's devotion, power, and capacity; but all of them wished from the start as they wish now—that the people's sacrifices might not have been so wantonly used and squandered by imbecility, by bad faith, and by incapacity.

December 21.—The Congress starts on the radical footing, and its earnestness and honesty seem to be firmly asserted. This Congress will be a worthy successor to its predecessor, my favorite 37th. But the "loyal" press evidently undervalues this Congress, as it undervalued and never gave its due to the 37th. Is it clumsiness, opaqueness, narrow-mindedness, or something worse, that are thus evidenced by the loyal metropolitan (New York) press? It deserves to be looked into and analyzed.

December 22.—The great shifter, the great political shuffler, Abraham Lincoln, some day or other will turn up a radical. If this country is to oscillate between Chase and Lincoln, and no other men are to deserve public confidence, then let the Americans at once send a deputation to Europe, and bring some princely loafer, a Coburg, a Hapsburg, etc., and have an end of it.

December 22.—In a speech in Cincinnati, Burnside said that all the military successes are due to officers and soldiers. Bravo! Burnside. This makes up for many of your blunders; not, however, for Fredericksburg, although you have been there McClellanized, and, above all, Franklinized. *The officers and soldiers did all*—that is the key-note throughout my *Diary*. When the storm is over, they will all find. that I am likewise right in my other key-note, that not Lincoln, not the administration, (Stanton excepted,) saved the country, that not the press directed and enlightened it; but all was done by the people; by the nameless in the villages, in the army, in the navy, and then by the Congress, whose majority was and is the incarnation of the people's spirit.

December 23.—The West-Point Halleck-Meade clique try to exculpate Meade's or French's criminal, nay, even infamous blunders at Mine Run, saying that they, the generals, *do not know the country*. *Not know the country* is to be the whitewash of the wantonly spilt blood! O you wiseacres, West-Pointers, sham captains! Not know a country in a region where for nearly three years the all-enduring Potomac army has wandered up and down between the enemy and the Potomac. Wanderings—led by you—and you had not the time to study and to know the country? Even calves would by this time have become acquainted with every path, bush, stream, marsh, and hedge in that region. Oh! your empty skulls ought to be shaved, your ears cut off, and your brazen brows branded, and then you ought to be given over to Barnum, you commanders and staffers in G street, in Georgetown, or in the camp!

December 23.—Whatever Mr. Lincoln does is done either by half, or is confused and generates confusion. So it is with the proclamation-oukase of oath and of amnesty. But all amnesties must have a term, and such a term expiring, the effects of the amnesty expire with it. Lincoln's amnesty is indefinite, also for eternities. Governors of States and judges are included in the amnesty, and governors and judges are the greatest criminals ; the governors legally, officially, called the people to insurrection and treason, and the judges, the highest power in the American polity, the judges consecrated treason.

December 24.—Wendell Phillips attacks the proclamation, and his attack is that of a philosopher and a statesman.

December 24.—The partizans of Chase puff him up as a paragon of financiers. The strong nerves and sinews of the people, its vitality, its faith in itself and in its capacity to make use of the inexhaustible resources of the country—that is the great financier; not Chase with his national banks.

December 25.—*Christmas.* More and more orphans and desolated homes, more hearths under cold ashes, and more broken hearts! And still on, on presses this sublime people; and hope, and the triumph of truth, and the palm of victory dawn over the gory fields, over the mourning and the despairing. Blood has generated right; the martyrs have saved humanity.

Fortes creantur fortibus.

That is the Christmas gift to mankind of the American people.

December 26.—If Mr. Lincoln's proclamation should or could become definitely the law, then the freedman remains abandoned to the *good-will* of the planter and of the incurable slaveholder.

And the small church sings hosannahs, and the *clear-sighted* press applauds with all its might. The serious patriots in Congress, although ignored by the Press, alone appreciate the proclamation as it deserves to be appreciated.*

---

* Events awfully, mournfully realize my words. The so-called, and by flunkeys, traitors and copperheads applauded, reconstruction policy now in full blast, leaves it to the reconstructed rebel States to decide upon the social and political *status* of the freedman, of the Africo-American. Leave the fate of the lamb to the hyena! Nine hundred and ninety-nine out of a thousand of the whites in the slave and rebel States are the deadly enemies of the Africo-Americans. The whites, be they chivalry, planters and sham-aristocrats, or be they poor-whites, clay-eaters, etc., are permeated to the core with the most idiotic and pestilential prejudices against the Africo-Americans, and those prejudices are now intensified into an unrelenting hatred on account of the unshaken, and by blood and martyrdom avowed, loyalty of the "niggers" to the Union. The Africo-Americans have won and conquered their rights of equality with the whites, and won them in such a noble manner as is yet unrecorded in the annals of the human race. During the civil war, the Africo-Americans not only have been true and loyal to the Union, though all the time exposed to the most goading and cruel persecutions by the rebels, but they remained loyal and devoted to the defenceless families of their deadly enemies. All over the revolted region their record is pure and unstained by any act of murder or cruelty of the St. Domingo fashion. And how have the rebel whites behaved and how behave now the subdued rebels towards the Africo-Americans? * * * The whites, once open rebels and now hypocrites, entrench their idiotism and their hatred behind the lie *that the intellectual inferiority of the nigger disqualifies him from enjoying equal social and political rights with the whites.* The "nigger" had intellect enough to discern that loyalty to the Union is a virtue as well as a benefit. The rebellious white

December 27.—Camp diseases, and, above all, the measles, play havoc in the armies, and principally in the Potomac Army. Measles are generated by rotten straw. In the history of wars, seldom can be found an example of an army kept so much in camps as is the Potomac Army, and for this thanks to the wisdom of its McClellanites. Since its organization in September, 1861, this army has spent in camp two out of every three months. Of course this waste of time in camp is not to be applied to besieging armies, from the Greeks before Troy down to Grant before Vicksburg. McClellanites never will learn that the camps kill or disable more men than battles do even in winter.

December 28.—New Brigadier and Major Generals are to be created. God grant that capacity and services be the mould! May only Mr. Lincoln not cast generals from materials of his own choice and notions.

December 29.—In that disgraceful affair of Mine Run, where Warren was sold, French behaved like—but the facts speak. General

man recognized and bowed to treason, perjury and murder. Before Congress meets the reconstruction policy will brew such complications, that Congress will find it easy to inaugurate a more thorough and a genuinely humane policy for the salvation of the whites and of the Africo-Americans. That is my hope. Cheerfully I adopt Greeley's credo: universal suffrage and then universal amnesty. After universal suffrage not only Lee and such ones but even Wirz, Jeff. Davis and his gang may be pardoned.—*Note Sept.* 10, 1865.

Humphreys, Chief of Staff, and who knows his business well, had given to French full and complete details about the *terrain* where French had to march, and, besides, furnished him with a truthful guide.   But French snubbed the guide, took whisky, and, with all his corps, wandered about the woods—and French still commands a corps, and Meade sustains French—undoubtedly on account of their common McClellan worship.

December 29.—The newly-baked academicians are lionized—Seward and Sumner as showmen. Of course.   But the academicians overbearingly thrust their noses into the administrative affairs of the War Department.   I hope Stanton will pull and twist their academical noses.

December 30.—Sumner, to be sure, has very studious habits and tries to study, to investigate, to post himself up (Americ:) on the questions before him.   But he makes rather too much of a vain display of the minutiæ of research, and this display becomes nauseous to his colleagues.   A little pinchbeck erudition is not to be compared with genuine, well-digested scholarship.

December 30.—The committees in the Senate ought to have been changed and modified.   Of course, Fessenden is a born—so to speak—chairman of Ways and Means, and no abler, more conscientious, and laborious man could be found. But Wade ought to have had another committee, and, generally, the committees ought to have been recast.   The *patres* have made a blunder.

December 31.—

Nihil est ab omni parte beatum.

So ends this 1863. Oh! dying year! you will record that the American people increased its sacrifices in proportion to its dangers; that blood, time, and money were cheerfully thrown into the balance against treason—inside and outside. And brighter hopes dawn, and the salvation comes in LIGHT.

JANUARY, 1864.

Your mission is great, O 1864! and I hope you will fulfill it. I see the powers of hell on the wane, democrats, copperheads, McClellanites, as furiously agitated, as Satan is in the eternal fire. I see the freedman, the Africo-American, take a stand among the defenders of right, and by his blood consecrate his accession to manhood. I see the Africo-American justify what I, and better than I, expected from him. I see demons and beslavers wincing in their agonies because neither they nor the opaqueness of official leaders could weaken, dishearten, and palsy the people. I see that my trust in the people and in the men of the people is well founded, and therefore I greet thee heartily and cheerfully, 1864!

January 1.—Reception in the White House. There they parade in splendid array, the *starred* ones! misnamed generals. Marses who very well know how not to do it. Halleck, the mighty do-nothing Commander; Meade, the dis-

organizer of victory,* and the man of manœuvres, they and their adjuncts. All of them
bats, not eagles.

January 2.—The three Blairs—not Horatii—
have all-together hold of Lincoln, because they
work for re-election. And inspired, directed,
and taught by that trio, Lincoln sneers at the
radicals. B. Wade told him that but for the
radicals, he (Lincoln) would be nowhere.

And the worst is, that in this way Lincoln
is sustained by the radicals against their will and
wish. Wait a little, O you Blairized Lincoln,
you will go to the radicals on your knees!

January 2.—A Siberian night! Certainly
many soldiers frozen, and many frozen limbs in
the army, and Halleck, Meade, and the *how-not-
to-do-it* generals warmly stretched in their beds.
Their strategic brains may freeze, they are good
for nothing; and all their limbs put together, if
frozen, would not make up for the finger of a

---

* The reach of Meade's generalship at Gettysburg can be condensed into a few lines. During the days of this terrific struggle,
our centre was repeatedly attacked and stormed. Our right was
even slightly pressed in. All this time our left remained almost
unengaged. In his attacks on our centre, the enemy repeatedly
drew on his reserves and exposed his flanks to our left. The
generals commanding our left, repeatedly asked from Meade an
order to fall on the exposed flanks of the enemy. Meade as
repeatedly resisted the prayers of our generals. So much for the
hero of Gettysburg; so much for Meade's generalship.—*Note
May*, 1865.

common soldier. Oh, how ardently I wish the mothers, sisters, and wives of the people under arms might for a moment become hyenas, tear to pieces our leaders, and thus avenge their children!

January 3.—The radicals, the purest men in Congress, begin to cave in, and to be reconciled to the idea of accepting the re-election of Lincoln as an inevitable necessity. They say that the outward pressure is very great. The masses are taken in by Lincoln's *apparent* simplicity and good-naturedness, by his awkwardness, by his vulgar jokes, and, in the people's belief, the great shifter is earnest and honest. The stern and clear-sighted radicals expect to be able to bind Lincoln by pledges to change his Cabinet and his *entourage.* Lincoln may promise it,. but is he a man of his word? Could he exist without Seward, Blair, Lamon, Halleck, Nicolay, and the like? I doubt it; they are so congenial to him. I cannot imagine Lincoln surrounded by earnest and honest men.

January 3.—Will the "loyal" press have this year a better understanding of events than it had in the past? Will that press better comprehend, and be more just to the 38th than it was to the 37th Congress? Or, will the press remain as of old, opaque, narrow, selfish, and petty?

January 4.—Inspired by Halleck, Lincoln refuses to appoint Rosecrans to Missouri, because pro-slavery Schofield* is not agreeable to the Senate. It is out and out Lincoln. If Rosecrans' appointment is an urgent necessity, what words to brand Lincoln's action?

General Thomas's† report of the operations before Chattanooga in September is superior to any military report hitherto published on both sides. He seems to combine in his person the capacity of a commander and officer of the staff. And he sends it instantly after his operations ceased, not procrastinating in the McClellan and Meade fashion. The "clear-sighted" Republican metropolitan press does not notice General Thomas's report. Of course, the report is simple, almost perfect, no clap-trap in it, and thus it is above the appreciation of that press.

---

*Such was the prevailing opinion concerning General Schofield. But even if an unbeliever in the righteousness of emancipation and equality, General Schofield is neither a copperhead nor a general and patriot after the McClellan fashion. General Schofield is one of those Union generals who dealt the deadliest blows to the rebels. General Grant, whose impartiality and modesty increase in proportion to his well-earned fame, told me that if the war had lasted about six months longer, Schofield and Wilson (cavalry) would have developed martial qualities of the first order—as captains.—*Note June, 1865.*

† The victory of Nashville, by which General Thomas destroyed the rebel army under Hood, emphatically secured Sherman's great march throughout the South. Had Hood not been destroyed, either Sherman would have been obliged to turn back and meet the rebel, or at the best the rebel army would have hung on Sherman's rear and stirred up to a desperate resistance the populations of Georgia and of South Carolina.—*Note August 15, 1865.*

January 5.—Could Lincoln have as much energy as the people has devotedness, secession would soon be crushed.   Undoubtedly secession is in its last stage, and even its superhuman efforts are a proof of it.   Sentimental, well-intentioned foreigners advise peace, forgiveness, and all the like morbid sentimentalism.   I wonder not at Gasparin with his Genevese notions, nor at Cochin who is a Roman Catholic; but Henry Martin, the first historian of our epoch, to be so sickly tender!   If this great and noble people is to have peace, the breed of southrons, falsely called Hotspurs, and in reality lawless banditti, must be crushed out, must disappear.   The young southern generation is savage, murderous, brutal, ignorant, arrogant, conceited, and is morally and intellectually debased.   Never existed a worse, a more corrosive social cancer, than that youth grown and brought up in the absolute negation of whatever is just, dutiful and honorable.

January 6.—After the suppression of the rebellion follows the reconstruction* and reorganiza-

---

* The reconstruction policy is the order of the day. An *experiment*, says President Johnson and his direct supporters. Very well. Experiment is the opposite of an absolute truth and principle; experiments are the media to discovery, to find out and to ascertain a truth, a rule, an axiom. Experiments therefore may easily cut both ways. When the Congress meets experiments may turn out to have been a series of mistakes, and it is doubtful if these experiments will establish a good rule.

tion, a task by far more thorny and difficult than
the suppression; a task peremptorily requiring
the highest faculties of a man, of a legislator, of
an American statesman.   But, even crediting to
Lincoln all the good and amiable qualities
claimed for him by his friends, certainly he has
not shown an atom of organizing or administrative capacity, and has never shown the nerve of a
pilot firmly holding the helm, and mastering the
storm.   The problem to solve for the next presidential term, is to organize the awful chaos in
which treason and rebellion will leave the
South. ·

And Wendell Phillips throws his eloquence
for Lincoln.   I called his attention to the organi-
zatory *racuum* in Lincoln.   When such beacons
as Wendell Phillips are carried away, they confuse those below them.   Emancipation and

---

Congress "will have the benefit of the experiments, and so will
the honest, loyal northern people and the public opinion." In
law and logic Congress alone has the right to decide this whole
matter.   *Cujus est condere ejus est abrogare* says the Roman
jurisconsult.   The two Congresses (37–38) made all the laws for
the treatment of the rebellious regions : the *condere* relates to
the statutes then made, therefore the *abrogare* exclusively
depends upon Congress.

In itself this question of reconstruction, or reorganization, or
whatever be its name, is of such weight, thoroughness and grandeur, that individual inmission will turn out to be powerless in
its settlement.   With their inmoveable logic, events will take
the question in hand; that is, it will settle itself on the basis of
eternal principles and be cemented by the absolute eternal
right.—*Note October* 1, 1865.

abolition of slavery are very good; but to become beneficial to the emancipated and the emancipator, abolition must be carried out on a broad system of immediate social, legal, and economical organization. Not a particle of any such notion can be detected in Mr. Lincoln's actions; and what is worse, Lincoln sufficiently shows his distaste for men of clear insight, of lofty aims, and of firm purpose.

January 6.—O cives! cives! quærenda pecunia primum est;

Virtus post nummos.

I internally exclaim, meeting in all directions these sharp, greedy, cunning lobbyists, money-makers, Lincolnites; these supporters of the administration through thick and thin, through mud and blood!

January 7.—American diplomats in Europe became degree by degree intrinsically estranged to the events at home.* They lost the scent. However, Dayton in Paris stood the storm better and is not washed away. Dayton maintained his

---

* The old, grand, pompous, but at times even majestic diplomacy vamoses, as vamose all the good and bad things, manners, customs, traditions and behaviour anchored in the past. Now-a-days, diplomacy is a poor, and often a contemptible trade and servitude. The noblest and loftiest gifts of mind, of heart, or the most soaring and creative imagination become compressed, neutralized and destroyed. A man of genius when a diplomat, may easily become a ruin like Pæstium and only superhuman vitality can save him, as is saved Tassara, the Minister from Spain in Washington.—*Note June* 16, 1865.

ground with a Seward and Lincoln, as well as with the vile *Decembriseur* and his ministers. But it can be said that not one of the American diplomats prevented any danger. Not one averted any storm, or was able to put an end to the pirato-belligerents, to their armaments, and to the aid and comfort given to the rebels in Europe and in European possessions. The Turks, the Japanese, and the Chinamen are the only powers who took a firm and decided stand against the pirates. Even Russia, notwithstanding all demonstrations of amity and sympathy, has not by any proclamation forbidden the rebel pirates entrance to her ports.

The American diplomats had almost no influence on the public opinion in Europe. The friendliness of the European masses to the American cause issues from the sound feelings of the unsophisticated people; it is generated by the inborn hatred of oppression and slavery, and by the utter scorn of that fallacy called race-ology. Peoples scorn such sham science and sham distinctions.

Most of the despatches of our diplomats are spiritless, monotonous, petty, and dragging. Incense for Seward's nose at times comes from London, Brussels, Vienna, etc. Some diplomats misrepresent and misunderstand the genuine European spirit, because they do not come in contact with it, afraid to commit their diplomatic dignity and step beyond the little, narrow diplo-

matic and saloon atmosphere; others imbibe
from bankers and slavers narrow notions of the
credit and the inexhaustible resources of their
own country, and believe that the financial
vitality of the American people depends upon
the exchanges (bourses) of London, Paris,
Amsterdam, Frankfort.†

---

* As Minister to China Anson Burlingame showed himself to
be as noble and high-minded a statesman, as in his previous
political career he was a brilliant and warm-hearted orator and
patriot. Burlingame inaugurated a new policy to be observed
not only toward the Chinese but toward all the old Asiatic
Governments and States. For nearly four centuries the absolute
aim of the so-called Christian and European Governments has
been to treat the people of the far East like barbarians—to
wrest by brutal force from their governments whatever could be
wrested, treading down all, even the most elementary, notions
of right, justice and humanity. Hindostan and China have
been the bloodiest victims of this European sham-Christian
civilization. The English have been prominent leaders in this
policy of inhuman robbery. Burlingame inaugurated the
co-operative policy, whose aim is to strengthen the Chinese Government in the exercise of its administrative and judicial power
in cities and districts inhabited by Europeans, instead, as was
formerly the case, of robbing the Chinese of lands and of jurisdiction. Burlingame put an end to the rapacious mercantile
misrule hitherto paramount in the official relations with the
Chinese people and Chinese authorities. Further: Burlingame
partly abated the coil of the misrepresentations and had faith so
prominent in the relations and accounts of the missionaries, who
are not at all needed by the Chinese. To crown all: Burlingame will promote the establishment of a college in Pekin to
form American pupils for the American public service in China.
Happy Burlingame, he had the initiative; he acted without
instructions from home.—*Note Nov.* 19, 1865.

January 7.—Oh how devotedly the Lincolnites are at work to secure Lincoln's nomination! How much lies and flattery are scattered broadcast among the people! Like sheep the country press falls in and follows.

I may be mistaken, but the honest, patriotic radicals will be caught. They believe that if re-elected, Lincoln will change his Cabinet. Small minds dread any change in their *entourage*. Further, if Lincoln is re-elected on account of the good services of his administration, then the Cabinet aided him; therefore the Cabinet ought to remain if Lincoln remains. And we all feel that, Stanton excepted, all the rest, more or less, deserve to be sent, at the best, to the incurables.

January 8.—Lincoln is the baker of generals. It is proverbial that when he cannot get rid of importunate wives, sisters, etc., he makes their men generals. And so do others, and there is the soft point with the Senate. Most of the Senators have their *protégés*, and thus one hand washes the other. However, some Senators (mine) constitute exceptions to the above rule.

January 9.—General Meade and staff corruscate their glory at receptions, among the Academicians and in warm parlors; the army frozen in mud; Lee, the undaunted, with his rebels menacing Maryland. And our army is about 80,000 men, and Lee's not 50,000, and Halleck in his warm office makes combinations *how not to do it*, and Meade bravely concentrates his forces and

shows *how not to execute it*, and Stanton and the
patriots in Congress are exasperated and attempt
to make an end of such Meades and others, and
they cannot move Mr. Lincoln, who is as great
as Allah, and prefers the army to be ruined by a
Meade rather than endanger his own chances of
re-election in Pennsylvania by the removal of
that mentally and bodily diseased chieftain.
And a deputation composed of old women and
toothless men from Philadelphia waited on Lincoln to sustain Meade, and to menace Lincoln
with the wrath of their Philadelphian con-
stituents, as brainless, as toothless, and as
impudent as the deputation. And Lincoln did
not kick them out of the people's house, but
caved in. And all is right, and Meade remains
undisturbed for the greater security of Lee, and
the glory of McClellan.

Whatever I hear from and about Grant and
the generals in the western army, all of them behave differently from Meade, and are altogether
the opposite of our Potomac McClellanised
heroes. I mean Meade and his clique. It seems
to be the curse of the Potomac army to be the
prey of intriguers.

January 10.—Reconstruction is the order of
the day. But if no better generalship than Halleck's or Meade's takes hold of our armies,
reconstruction is very far off. Catch the hare
and then make a pie. Lincoln is very sanguine
for his one-tenth idea, and the Blairs and Sewards

stand by him.   One-tenth combination gives presidential votes.   There is *des Pudels Kern.* The stern and earnest patriots in both Houses, men such as Wade, Fessenden, etc., wish to keep this whole question in suspense, rather than see it pressed and thus bring it to an issue between Congress and Mr. Lincoln.   The press is in its true character—it sees to the end of—its nose.

January 10.—The copperhead victories in 1862 —Seward and Weed co-operating—deprived the House of many sterling patriots.   But some of the new members, such as Blaine of Maine, Ames of Massachusetts, General Garfield, Major General Schenck and some others, to a certain degree compensate the losses.   Boutwell from Massachusetts is worth a legion.   The representatives of the rebels in the House will gain nothing.

January 12.—Every day I more positively find confirmed the fact that Mr. Lincoln is not the man, is not the choice of the majority in both the Houses.   The reason is obvious.   The best men in both the Houses see face to face, and observe Lincoln and his workings.   They know his length, his breadth, his mind, his nerve, and his cerebellum.   And these men had and have no personal urgings or aims; their only scope is the good and the triumph of the people's cause. The people at large does not know Mr. Lincoln, but judge him by his nick-name, and by what greedy politicians and newspapers write and spread about him, and the people attributes to him all the success (whatever it may be) obtained during these three years. The people is generous, and credits to Lincoln what is the result of its own, that is, of the people's sacrifices and devotedness.

The same erroneous notion about Lincoln is generally current in Europe. One of the reasons is, that even the most progressive Europeans cannot comprehend any action, development, etc., without a chief, or captain, *modo* Carlyle. I spoke of it in former parts of the Diary. Further, the American press, above all the New York or metropolitan is now, as it always was, the cardinal agency in confusing and deluding the people's judgment at home, and the public opinion in Europe. The small country press echoes and imitates those it considers to be the great masters of the trade. And it must be noted that, in contradistinction with the continent of Europe, the press in America, the great and the small, is a trade; the loyal press looks one-third to principles, and the rest to pecuniary gain.*

------

* At the close of the war not only most of the leaders and owners of the principal metropolitan loyal press had increased or made considerable fortunes, but the same is the case with most of the *employés*, such as the writers of editorials, the reporters, the correspondents and others constituting the personnel of the various newspapers. Gambling in stocks and in gold constituted the principal source of these fortunes.

For this reason the owners and leaders of the press make their utmost efforts always to appear to be those in whom is condensed and concentrated all the political and statesmanlike wisdom of the country. They try to make the people consider them as the central suns around which the people revolves, and from whom all the eminent men in the country's politics and service borrow light, lustre and ideas.*

The metropolitan press connects this country with Europe. For Europe that press is the only exponent of the American events. But for reasons above mentioned, that press is very chary in giving their due to really eminent patriots ; above all, during this struggle. Thus in Europe public opinion knows no names of American patriots except those hackneyed years ago—the names of those whom their official position necessarily, unavoidably brought or brings into the foreground. By the immense majority throughout Europe, Mr. Lincoln, Mr. Seward, Mr. Chase, Mr. Sumner, Mr. Greeley, etc., are considered as exclusive incarnations of the great cause and principle. The names of the best men in both Houses are wholly

---

* The editors of some few papers became wealthy by the immensely increased circulation occasioned by the war. To my knowledge not one among the leaders and *employés* lost a cent by the war. But whatever may be Mr. Greeley's heavy political sins, the *Tribune,* as represented by him, jobbed neither in gold stocks, nor false news.—*Note August,* 1865, *in New York.*

unknown to Europe, although those men and not the above-mentioned hackneyed ones, are the genuine incarnations. Nay, thanks to the "impartial," "enlightened" and "loyal" American press, Europe is not yet put in a condition to understand and appreciate, that the masses, that their dauntless devotion, patriotism and sacrifice, alone save the cause which the hackneyed names so often gave up or dragged to the verge of an abyss. Europe is not aware that the people's virtues almost exclusively animate those men in Congress whom the leaders of the press try to push into the background, or ignore, or criticise in their small, mean, envious way. And some names of such patriots have been repeatedly mentioned in this Diary.

Are the parliamentary labors and the character of a Fessenden, Wade, Grimes, of the Morrills, of Boutwell, and scores and scores of others, held by the "loyal" press before the people at home, or gratefully transmitted to the knowledge of Europe? No. And the reason is that the leaders and owners of the press are conscious that to render justice broadly and largely to those patriots, would in equal measure lessen their own glory. These great leaders believe that to be just to others would be their ruin. If the people were told the truth about others, the sham beacons would be the losers, and *accipere detrimentum in aliqua re.*

The country press, with few and rare exceptions, answers to the tune of its masters, or licks the hands which throw to it *pap* (Americanism.) And of that press :

> *Quid immerentes hospites vexas, canis,*
> *Ignavus adversus lupos.*

One must not expect much character and dignity in the small country press, and therefore its local influence is mostly fatal. Thus I am told that a so-called influential country paper called the Springfield (Mass.) *Republican*, during this war has changed front three or four times. *Pap! pap!*

January 13.—I had an insight into the new batch of *State Papers*. Very, very voluminous. The correspondence concerning the Peterhoff will not add any laurel to Seward's goosequill crown. But in justice to Seward it must be acknowledged that his strain of brains is astonishing. Bad or good, these State Papers are the fruits of a certain mental labor, and the mental labor is of one single individual. In his Department Seward has not one to help him. The Department of State is even below Halleck's staff, and that means a great deal of ignorance.*

---

* In proportion as the heroic sacrifices of the people beat off the waves of rebellion, Mr. Seward became bolder and more imperious in his diplomatic correspondence. His last productions evidence a fully exhausted intellect. The dispatch to Mr. Adams in London in reference to the rebel loan in England is very poor in its legal argument and altogether poor in its statesmanship.—*Note Sept.* 23, 1865.

January 13.—The Administration, Congress, the West Point wiseacres and the press, all of them are pothering about the draft. As customary with the press, it confuses everything by the "thorough information" which it brings to bear upon the question. Admirable!

As made by the law, the exemption is an injustice and an absurdity, and never will enable the Government to find substitutes. The Government ought not to be an exemption broker. *Everybody* ought to be drafted, and with the drafted ought to rest the *onus* to find, at any price, an *acceptable* substitute. When some European Governments, and especially the French, acts the broker, and procures a substitute, the reason is, that almost every year a certain number of soldiers, who have served out their time, leave the service, and the Government, who prefers to retain old soldiers instead of receiving green recruits, offers to, and allures these old *grognards* with, the premium which the drafted pays for a substitute. Here the draft bears heavily and exclusively on the poor, as the three hundred dollars are easily found by those well off. If every rich man, when drafted, were obliged to find his own substitute, or serve, then the poor man hired *by the rich* would be in position to make his own terms, and thus secure the future of his poor family at the cost of the cowardly and unpatriotic rich. O, great press! why can you not see it?

January 13.—Hancock and Burnside are to recruit 50,000 men each, for special purposes, and for separate operations. That is Lincoln's and Halleck's plan to *subdivide* forces, and to operate in parcels on the whole circumference. It is the continuation of Scott's imbecile anaconda, and McClellan's cowardly fears in the winter of 1861–62, and in the following spring. And such a desultory warfare, without any possibility of unity, is to be continued; and few protest, and their voice is drowned in the general *amen.*

January 13.—The President, the Cabinet, and the dignitaries run after the lectures on the Glacial Period. That is the fashion. Oh! those men have already enough of a glacial period in their brains. What innocent sheep to listen to this old rehash, which an academician serves to them as being the latest and newest scientific dish. How one class of dignitaries is humbugged by that other class, the dignitaries of a sham academy!

January 14.—After having been for months wandering in the little desert, the army, between eighty and ninety thousand strong, subsides into quietude. Oh, Meade beats into a cocked hat all the generals *à la Pompadour!* but very likely such have been the orders which Meade received and receives from McClellan.

In any European army, such a general as French would have been court-martialed, and

expelled from the service, but here Halleck and
Meade hush up, and Mr. Lincoln helps them;
and Stanton, poor Stanton—is silent.   Shame!
And senators are humbugged; re-election must
not be jeopardized.   General French is, perhaps,
from Pennsylvania; and Lincoln will be re-
elected; and by the united efforts of the Hallecks, of the Meades, and of the McClellanites in
the army, more of the people's children will be
murdered.   Oh, Stanton, you stand all this!
Where is your patriotism and energy?

January 15.—They blundered and procrastinated, procrastinated and blundered, until Charleston became wholly impregnable to any navy
whatever.   It seems that since the winter
1861–62 (see Diary, v. 1) Lincoln and McClellan,
then Halleck and Welles, rivalized as to who
would make the greatest blunder, and give the
longest time to the rebels to make Charleston
impregnable.   My accusation of the imbecility of
the administration, (not of Stanton,) made in the
winter of 1861–62, stands unshaken, as are many
similar accusations.   Thus with all the modern
inventions, iron-clads, monitors, etc., the old
question of earthen walls against wooden or iron
walls remains either unsolved, or when solved it
is in favor of the earthen fortifications.   That
such is the result in the present struggle, the
earthen walls and the rebels are to be exclusively
grateful, as said above, principally to McClellan,

then to Seward-Lincoln's hesitating policy in 1861–1862, and to Welles' *big wig.*

But for them the rebels would not have had time to cover the shores with batteries, and fill the channels with *chevaux-de-frise*, torpedoes, etc., and now the siege—or whatever you may call it —of Charleston drags; it almost covers the North with ridicule, and is to the credit and the profit of the rebels.

Neither are the land operations more successful than those by sea. After all, this Gillmore seems to be only a very second-rate lieutenant of artillery, and nothing else. With more or less precision, he may have calculated the force of ballistics at Fort Pulaski, and we, (I among others,) in our craving for superior men and capacities, took him for one.

January 17.—The Committee on the Conduct of the War* again hard at work. Well, such

---

*The Committee has terminated its work, and the several volumes of the report, with precious individual evidence, constitute a primordial historical light and source. The past events, wars, revolutions of any other nation and government are deprived of similar documentary evidence. The rage and the objurgations showered on the Committee by all the open and secret traitors, by copperheads, by McClellanites and by their various organs in the press, such as the *Boston Post, Boston Courier*, the *World*, the *New York Herald*, the *National Intelligencer*, (Washington,) and other of the same ilk unknown to me, constitute the best evidence that the laborious, stormy work of the Committee was paramountly needed, that in the highest degree it was patriotic, and that it was thoroughly done.

Senator Wade, of Ohio, was the Chairman of the Committee,

names as Wade, Chandler, Gooch, formerly Wright, Andy Johnson, are *in terrorem* over those most criminal military malefactors. But the beneficial consequences which ought to have resulted to the present from the labors of this committee, are neutralized, paralyzed, and amount utterly to nothing. To be salvation to the country, the committee ought to have published the results every fortnight, and thus on the spot exposed the criminals. Now secrecy, like night, shields the most terrible crimes perpetrated against the people by generals and by their supporters. Secrecy was forced upon the committee by the cowardly considerations of the Lincolnites, Sewardites, McClellanites, Halleckians, etc., as if the exposure of military and administrative crimes could have endangered the cause of the people. It is the darkness, the thick, heavy veil thrown upon all misdeeds, and thrown in behalf of the murderers and the thieves, that creates and magnifies the danger. So far as I know, Stanton favored not secrecy, but many senators and members of the House did, and do. And not the copperheads alone, but the tender, the half-and-half, the Doolittles, Harrises, Dixons, Collamers, Footes, etc., etc., in both the Houses.

---

and this fact alone explains all. I hate comparisons, but as there exist certain names and terms consecrated by usage, and which, therefore, most completely render a meaning, I will say that never in my life have I met a man who is such an old Roman as the patriot, Ben. Wade.

January 18.—The Neptune of the Navy Department and his office holding, pacific pseudo Tritons, Lincoln and the rest, are *now fully satisfied* that Charleston cannot be taken, but will be destroyed piece-meal by a bombardment day by day. If so, it will neither be ever taken, nor destroyed. But the administration, and the pacific naval heroes in the Department, their compeers, are satisfied, and—subside.

This siege of Charleston, etc., costs more in money alone than all that nest of beggars, traitors, and robbers is worth, or was ever worth, not to speak of the men, and the best of them, lost on our side. And all this, thanks to the treasonable cowardice of McClellan, who could have taken Charleston and Savannah in 1861, and who was backed in his cowardice by Seward, both bemuddling poor Lincoln.

January 20.—Re-election! re-election! it is sickening to mind and body. Why has not Congress the pluck to assert its power; crush the politicians; take Lincoln, Seward, and Blair by the collar; shake their scheming, sham souls from them; and throw into the deepest dungeons of Fort' Lafayette all the tribe of the Weeds. How meanly and flatly the press cringes! Look to the press for truth! The hope of the people ought to turn to the generals in the western armies, to those who have not been in contact with Washington, and with that McClellanism, so devouring, so corrosive in the Potomac army. Sometimes the awful question rises before my mind, if this seemingly inexhaustible vitality of the people will be able to resist and to overcome, not the rebels, but all the various mismanagements.

January 20.—General Gillmore has received powers to organize into an army the Africo-Americans from South Carolina, Georgia, and Alabama. At last! And why not sooner? why not a year ago? If this measure is good to-day, it was even better a year ago. But such is Mr. Lincoln's policy. Always behind time at the cost of the people's blood. Seward and Blair all the time have been holding Lincoln by his coat tail. It is not the fault of Stanton, not even that of Welles, that this measure is so belated.

January 20. — *A little business of the White House's political little ones!* A Mr. Hay, the President's private secretary or his *ame damnée*, was last year nominated a Colonel by General Hunter; this year he is re-created a Major; as a proof of a special favor, *tambour battant* he is confirmed by the Senate, and goes to General Gillmore to prepare in Florida a delegation for the re-election, to become a delegate and a member of Congress himself, in accordance with the one-tenth principle of the *Oukase*. The confirmation was hurried through the Senate as if the salvation of the country depended upon it. O Senators! It recalls to me how in 1861, two or three days after the inauguration, Senator Sumner, as chair-

man of the Committee on Foreign Affairs, on the
plea of *public good*, hurried through the Senate
the confirmation of that Sandford, so accomplished in making money on guano, sewing-
machines, shoddy, and worthless carbines. One
is at a loss what to think of such *patres* who
throw dust and ignorance into the eyes of their
too confident colleagues.

January 20.—At the New Year's reception Mr.
Lincoln paid special attention to the representative of the Mexican Republic bleeding under the
talons of the *Decembriseur's* buzzard.   But all
was done by Lincoln in a peculiar way.   Stealth-
ily and *sotto voce*, Lincoln asked the Mexican
about the news from his country.   "It is good,"
said the Mexican.   " Oh, I am very glad," said
Lincoln ;   " I wish you may have the best of the
invaders."   All this was done in a manner as if
Lincoln was afraid of the other diplomats, and
above all, of Seward's ferule.

January 20.—Two volumes, in 750 pages each,
are the last emanations from the State Department, and all is not published.   European chan-
ceries, tremble and vail your inky faces! You
never could be so prolific. Seward has the best
of you.

January 22.—Rumors that certain rebel chiefs
en second are trying to negotiate on their own
hook. Events press upon events, and no human
power can arrest or avert them ; not even the
political crimes (as Talleyrand called mistakes)

6

of the Sewards, the Lincolns, and of other evil genii. This indomitable people will triumph over all traitors on both lines, and over criminal incapacity. This most infamous rebellion may end, as end all the rebellions made in the interests of a caste. In this rebellion the caste of the planters holds the power; it commands the army, and is seated on the neck of the poor whites, as it is seated on that of the enslaved Africo-Americans.

In this or in any other way and time, this rebellion will break down, and all the Northern copperhead democrats, all McClellanites, all Seymourites, cannot save treason from its doom. And when the rebels are crushed, will Lincoln have the credit for what is not his work? Perhaps. But if so, at any rate not for a long time.

January 22.—I am always disagreeably impressed when I judge Seward as a political man, and on account of his fatal influence on the policy of our country. Otherwise, Seward has excellent private qualities. He is a true and devoted friend, *when he is a friend.* He is easy and off-hand in intercourse, and, in my opinion, honest out and out in money affairs. I never heard anything of him to the contrary. Why has Seward meddled with politics, and begun under the tutorship of such as Weed, of whom I saw, observed, and learned only the worst, with not an atom of good to atone for the evil?

January 22.—The McClellanites in and out of the army make capital for their fetish, from the fact that Meade could not move beyond the Rapidan, and that the whole country between the Rapidan and Richmond is one uninterrupted Torres-Vedras. The McClellanite sham heroes assert that now the Administration finds that the Chickahominy route, as struck by McClellan, is the only true and possible one.

(1*st.*) Meade's unmilitary wanderings are only McClellanism in a worse edition. (2*d.*) The regions between the Rapidan and Richmond became Torres-Vedras in the last two years, and became so, thanks principally to the cowardly incapacity of McClellan. No fortifications existed there when the rebels escaped from Manassas, leaving after them——manure to fertilize McClellan's brains. A little, very little pluck at that time, and our pursuing army could have entered Richmond almost together with the flying rebels. But pluck, courage, dash and McClellan never housed together.

January 23.—General Hunter shelved now; may be not a great or any tactician, but his bull-head was the next after Fremont to break the wall by which Union men *a la* Seward, surrounded and defended Slavery. Hunter's name will in history be interwoven with emancipation, confiscation, and the arming of slaves. Hunter inaugurated; Lincoln, like Peter, denied him and then took other people's feathers. The statute book will bear evidence in favor of General Hunter.

January 24.—How shabby look the sham horseguards before the White House! *Tel maitre, tel valet.* These horseguards are the invention and creation of the White House's flatterers, and of Halleck.

January 24.—The confiscation is now on the *tapis.* Babel confusion adrift without a steady aim or a firm, clear comprehension. One wishes this, another that, and the " loyal" press, as is its wont, increases the confusion. The press far-fetches evidences from history, and of course seizes them at random ; and they amount to nothing. It is not the fault of history, but of those who attempt to dabble in historical evidences. The American press, loyal or disloyal, always mercilessly maltreats history. The Romans, and after them all nations and governments of Europe down to our day, confiscated the lands of conquered or of revolted foes, with the aim to weaken and to break them, to implant the victor, and thus to create a homogeneous and friendly population as owners of the conquered and confiscated soil. Everybody forgets that in *law*, the rebels are—first criminals and then public enemies.

January 25.—Mr. Lincoln insinuated to Major Halpine to write and publish a pseudonym letter against Fremont on account of the Missouri campaign in 1861, and principally on the affair at

Springfield. Halpine served under Fremont. A brigadiership was put in perspective as the prize of what was to be *an indiscretion committed by a friend.*

January 27.—The next presidential election is ominous not only for the American Union, but its influence will powerfully affect the destinies of Central and South America, and therefore also influence Europe. If the next President be a man of energy, of farsightedness, and of decision, then not only will the rebellion soon be crushed, but the power and energy shown by the American people will make Europe cave in and give up her infamous and arrogant diplomatic intrigues in Hispano-America. Such results will be obtained even without coming to blows. If the American people show a decided and stern purpose, the *De-cembriseur's* liberticide schemes will be checked; Maximilian may not come; and if he comes, he will pack his trunks and return to his Bourg as soon as the American people emphatically de-clare that his Hapsburg rags must no more pol-lute this continent. Spain will come to her senses, and give up her appetite for Peru and for San Domingo. Spain will find that for her it is best to stay at home, to administer well and to work out her almost inexhaustible domestic re-sources, abandon the old rickety policy of the Dons, and not listen to the incitements of the *Decembriseur.* Spain ought to absorb, or to unite with, Portugal. The differences between the two

parts of the ancient peninsula Yberica are rather
artificial than normal or ingrained. When again
united, the peninsula will easily become at least
the second maritime power of Europe.

Let European powers, nations, and governments quarrel, or make Congresses, or intrigue
among themselves in the old world as much as
they please and as long as their people bear it;
but away, away from the American soil, or their
punishment will be terrific!

January 28.—This 38th Congress works slowly
but steadily. It has good elements, and may
nobly continue the work of its predecessor, and
earn similar misrepresentations at the hand of
the " enlightened press."

January 28.—Ben. Butler would make an excellent President. He has all the capacities of a
statesman. Butler can destroy and build up, organize and administer. He is bold, with keen
insight, and with prompt, unerring decision.
Could only Butler make some *coup d'éclat* before
Richmond! The masses unhappily believe that
a military man ought to have the preference to a
civilian. Butler's capacities as a civilian are
superior, are all that are wanted to save the
cause. If President, Butler would easily select
good generals, and not Meades.

January 30. — The not fighting West-Point
military wiseacres explain and justify the former
and recent bloody military blunders by *internal
and external lines*. The Hallecks, etc., in our

military councils, probably recently learned all about it from Schalk's books. It is a *Eureka* for the wiseacres. When they touch anything, these West-Pointers pervert it at once. Such lines have and had their bearing, but now they are to be the key to all solutions! Oh! first was the anaconda, then stategy at every street corner, now these lines! Napoleon's greatest battles, those which almost upturned the world, were fought on rather external lines. Members of Congress eagerly and devotedly crave truth, but they are confused, befogged by these sham Mars's uttering with empty gravity certain would-be sacramental words.

The same with the organization of the army. Wiseacres talk much and big, but do little or nothing, and deceive Congress. The armies will become organized very systematically and very scientifically any few days after——the war is over. And all this is done by the old Washington clique of the first graduates, and by the remains of Scott's favoritism. I am certain that the Western army has men who understand all military matters far better than the Washington, or Scott, or McClellan, or Potomac cliques.

January 31.—Many of the best men think of Butler as I do; Butler would have good chances for the White House if leading and influential men would speak out their convictions.

FEBRUARY.

February 1.—A call for 500,000. They call to
fill up the quotas. Of course, they always find
an excuse. Certainly troops are necessary for
the "external lines," and the people will come
up to the mark, and not grudge its blood. But
you, oh, you who so recklessly, and mostly so
stupidly, dispose of the people's blood, will you
ever learn anything? Mr. Lincoln, Mr. Lincoln,
take the people's children, but trust them not to
your Hallecks, Meades, and the like, to be
dragged—and stupidly, too—to the slaughter!

Nincompoops say that immigration will compensate for all these losses in men. Such trash,
gravely asserted by Senators, is enough drive
one mad. It is well for a light-headed, gaseous
Seward to make such assertions. The most
intelligent and the best part of the population of
the North, the mechanics, the operatives, the
farmers, the men of all industrial pursuits and
inventions, the men who alone give character to
America, the genuine and only children of the

American spirit and of the American institutions, they constitute the bulk of the Northern armies.   Not such ignorant barbarians or semi-savages as are the planters of the South, and their tools, the poor whites.   And these Northern men, offspring of a high civilization, by scores and scores of thousands mown down on fields of battle in the cause of humanity—these men are to be replaced by immigration!   Such an utterance is absurd, nay, almost sacrilege. This, the most valuable capital of the country, accumulated by the peaceful, orderly, and genuine development of man, is to be compensated and replaced by rough, uncouth immigration! Never any age, any country, possessed or contained such accumulated intellectual wealth as was spread over the free States, and as is now devoured by the war.   Are the Irish to compensate for the destruction of the native-born Americans?   The Irish, who scarcely in the third generation begin to become genuine citizens of the American polity—and nearly the same is the case with the rough material immigrating from all other European countries.   No! not even the numerical loss can be compensated by any, the most numerous, immigration!

February 2. — Governor Andrew's message. He forbodes that war will exhaust in New England that intellect which it took generations to nurse, to develop, and to accumulate.   The Governor advises the finding of a way to fill the

quota without destroying to a man the *best*
population that ever existed on this planet.   The
Governor is always the truest American statesman.*

February 3.—If such mighty interests were not
at stake, it would be almost amusing to witness
and to observe the molework by which the Lincolnites try to secure their master's, and therefore their own, re-election.   The State legislatures are agitated, pushed by various influences,
to take a stand for Lincoln.   These influences
are the contractors, the politicians, the office
holders, the office expectants, and finally the
mass of honest country people, who have strongly
taken into their heads that as, in 1860, Lincoln was elected to be President of the whole
Union, the people owe it to themselves to keep
Lincoln in until rebellion and treason are
crushed.   It is positively asserted that Weed,
the prince of dark deeds, is the secret manager
of the Lincoln pronunciamentos that are made
by various State legislatures.   The knowing
ones say, that as such a move is premature,
Weed purposely instigates it to kill off Chase by

---

* Even a Boston McClellanite, copperhead, and conservative,
also the most venomous being in creation, said recently of Governor Andrews, that " he is the biggest and the broadest man in
New England." This is the best recognition of Governor Andrew's superiority.   He is the product of this epoch, of this war,
and as such he has no equal among his civil compeers.—*Note
September* 20, 1865.

Lincoln, to use up Lincoln by the prematurity, and then to bring out and raise Seward on the *debris* of the two former. We shall see how much truth or probability is therein.

February 3.—The House is awake, and makes a decided step; a bold and patriotic one. The House emphatically declares its wish to have Grant made lieutenant general. A bitter pill to Lincoln, to Halleck, etc., but not to Stanton. At any rate, Halleck disappears, or will be prevented from doing mischief. A man and a soldier is woefully needed at the head of our armies. I hope Grant will have pluck enough to crush the various evil influences.

February 4.—Everybody says that the country at large is decidedly for Mr. Lincoln. And I have not yet met one single earnest and clear-sighted man, from whatever State he may come, that avows his preference for Lincoln. How strange !

February 4.—Look wherever one will and can, always and everywhere the same story. The impulse of the people creates, invents, brings sacrifices of blood and time, pushes on, on ; the Administration mostly impedes, drags, by itself does precious little ; leaves much undone. (I except the War Department, or rather Stanton, when not hindered by Lincoln or Halleck.) Take the Navy. The people are boiling over with capacity for inventions, for industrious constructions ; the people are full of activity and ardent wish to carry out almost wonders. The Navy Department—probably honestly administered, but slow, undecided, behindhand—in many ways impedes the expansion of the people's enterprising genius. If the rebel chiefs had good mechanics and builders to understand and to carry out their chiefs' plans and drawings; if, in one word, the rebel chiefs were backed by a Northern people, our navy would have been lost long ago, and our ports destroyed, notwithstanding all the bravery of our naval heroes, led on by the Farraguts, the Porters, &c.

February 5.—The most thorough and radical measures in relation to slavery and war, that is, measures regulating emancipation, confiscation, &c., have mostly originated in the House, and were not originated by rhetors. In this, as in many other things, the metropolitan and the country press never fully, honestly recognized the services either of Congress or of the various Congressmen.

February 5.—The diplomatic correspondence contains many commonplaces about the finances of the country; and justify my assertion recorded some time ago, that even the best among our diplomats abroad lose the domestic scent, the perception, and the appreciation of domestic affairs. What nonsense about loans, currency, credit. Foreign bankers and the foreign notions inspire all these disquisitions; but these bankers will not have the pleasure and the triumph to be listened to, nor to be asked for loans. We will make greenbacks and loans at home, and again play a trick upon European notions of political economy.

February 5.—Among the best Senators the impression prevails that a poor man when a thorough honest republican, but not backed by powerful influences, has in general very slim chances to be sustained by the administration, and above all, by the Smiths, the Ushers, etc. So said in my presence Grimes and Foote to a poor man. And Foote is not very radical.

February 5.—Ill-omened influences prevail and hover over the military appointments. Many, many genuine capacities are smothered by the combined efforts of patronage, red-tape, and prejudice.

February 5.—A member of the House wishes to immortalize himself, and make himself agreeable to Seward. The member made and carried a proposition to throw away money for the printing of 10,000 copies of the State papers. The plea, "to enlighten public opinion in Europe." Does that honorable and his compeers class the Europeans so low as to believe that they will squander their time in reading the State Papers?

But what is this wagon in which Seward dreams of riding into the White House? Why are the State Papers garbled? I miss there certain correspondence with Barreda, Minister for Peru, in relation to a Peruvian vessel with guano, burnt by the rebels in the Chesapeake. In that correspondence, Mr. Seward, for the sake of dodging the responsibility, advises Peru to look for redress to Richmond. As answer, the Peruvian minister asks Mr. Seward, if following or acting on his advice, Peru is to recognize the rebel government? Thus recalled to his duties, Mr. Seward backed out.

February 7.—I have it from unerring authority that Lee has at the utmost 25,000 to confront Meade. Mr. Lincoln knows it, Halleck knows it; they know that Lee's army is scattered, part of it before Knoxville, part in North Carolina. But we will wait until Lee again gathers around him his scattered forces. That is our mode of warfare. Halleck and Meade improve even on McClellan.

February 7.—Jomini-Corinth's-Halleck's staff was and is busy at translating books, at reviewing proof-sheets, etc. In the summer and fall of 1862, when Wadsworth was Governor of Washington, and looked in the city for spacious houses to use them for hospitals, Halleck and his staff were busy watching over the property of Corcoran, the wealthy rebel sympathizer and emigrant.

February 7.—Senator Sumner is for re-election, and expects to be Secretary of State. Oh, not yet! Wendell Phillips comes out against Lincoln, asserting *that honesty is in a ruler when he is apt to do his duty.* Sentimental reviewers, hero

seekers, lecturers, and all that crowd, come out
strongly for Lincoln.

February 7.—Blair informed various diplomats
that his object is to bring the democrats over to
anti-slavery notions, to make them support Lincoln, and to thus break the hateful republican
party.   Precious trio, these Blairs!

February 7.—Commissioners from St. Domingo.   Very intelligent Hispano-Americans.
The commissioners' wish and beg that their people be recognized as belligerents. ·Seward
refused to offend Spain, although Spain recognizes the Southern rebels as belligerents, and the
Dominicans are no rebels at all.   With the
assent of the Spanish government and of the
Captain General in Cuba, Havana is the principal depository and store-house for the Southern
rebels.   Seward brought the case before the
Cabinet.   The Cabinet kept mute, Mr. Lincoln
told a joke about a black advising his massa to
take to the woods, and there was an end of the
matter.

February 8.—In proportion as Congress pro-
gresses in its labors, the press misjudges and
misrepresents, and confuses the people's judgment.   Whoever will write the history of this
epoch ought to eliminate the press from his
sources and authorities.   The Statute-book and
the *Daily Globe* will furnish to the historian the
truest information about the labors of the 37th

and 38th Congresses, and then he must use his own critical and discriminating powers.

I wish every American would read and learn J. S. Mill's book on *Liberty*, in the same way as most of them learn the Scriptures. Many, very many verses of Mill's gospel are more full of life than some of the worshipped Hebrew hallucinations.

Although many and very honorable exceptions can be made in relation to the small or country press, the average is even *below mediocrity;* and is in every way. The better part of the country press is drowned in the current, or over-awed by the great masters in New York, Boston, etc. This feature of the American press is unknown to Europe, as by reasoning alone, aside from facts, the European writers arrive at conclusions, which so often are either above or below the reality.

And this condition of the press and its relation to the public is the more distressing, as the average of the reading public in America is mentally superior, and by far generally better informed, than are nine-tenths of the editors and leaders in the great and the small press. Generally the contrary is the case all over Europe, and above all in England. But the pursuits of life create certain habits and customs of mind; the newspaper is not read critically by the always *hurrying* American reader, who thus rather *lazily* accepts the opinions of newspaper writers, although he feels well his own superiority to the latter. John Mill's book explains partly a similar phenomenon in England.

February 9.—This war acquires proportions more and more gigantic, and in its character and nature has almost no precedent in the world's history. A great people fighting against each other, with a tenacity so unrelenting as was never yet witnessed by God and man. The nearest analogy is the great Peleponesian war, Greeks against Greeks, as here Americans, divided into various States. The Amphyctions may compare with a Constitution of the federation. The intelligent, quick, enterprising, industrious, commercial, maritime, free democracy of Athens, is New England, is the North. The heavy civilization-hater, and exclusively-on-slavery-relying Spartan is the slaveholding South. Copperheads are the aristocracies in Athens and in the Athenian league. Many other analogies can be pointed out. To crown all, Alcibiades has his caricature in McClellan. Analogy: both relieved from command. But the Athenian was full of talents, military, and statesmanlike; his caricature and counterpart, McClellan, is an opaque, spiritless mass of flesh. A Pericles we have not. It is not so easy for mankind to produce a second one. As a *pendant* to Thucydides, we have the State papers, and—Greeley advertises a history.

February 9.—Another of those infamous wan-

ton slaughters, which only Halleck's and McClellan's school can commit, and, of course, Meade
committed them. Two or three brigades sent
across the Rapidan, into Lee's jaws, to make a
so-called *reconnoissance*. Of course, when the *reconnoissance* came upon Lee's whole force, it was
impossible to support it across the river. Of
course Lee almost surrounded our troops; of
course our officers fought desperately, were
slaughtered, and the enemy justly claims a victory, above all a victory over the stupidity of our
commanders. The official bulletin says: *the object
of the reconnoissance was accomplished.* Of course
it was: several hundred men murdered by you,
Meade; that was the object.

February 10.—The trial of Captain Wilkes
shows that Seward-Sandford understands how to
carry his point. The country's navy was obliged
to go and execute Sandford's private claim
against Venezuela; this at a time when every
nerve was strained to catch the Rebel pirates.
And Mr. Seward was the man who urged it on
the navy. How is it to be called?

Poor Seward! he once compared himself. At
any rate, there is some similitude when he is
between Weed and Sandford. Only not one of
them "*shall be in Paradise.*"

February 10. — Ambulances bringing the
wounded from the last wanton slaughter. A
blight sits on the brains and on the intentions of
these Potomac Generals. Whatever they under-

take turns to murder. No holy enthusiasm
warms and inspires them; what they touch by
their unholy hands turns to a curse. The
Western Generals seem to be inspired. They
ought to come here and reinvigorate the spirit
of the Potomac army.

February 11.—*The object of the reconnoissance
was accomplished.* How? What knows Meade
more to-day than he knew previous to that
butchery? He (Meade) has learned that Lee is
behind the Rapidan. Well, Meade knew that
before. Lee is watchful, and ready to profit by
Meade's blunders; well, this everybody knew
long ago; above all, the bleeding people have
learnt it, paying terribly for the experience. Oh,
for Grant or for somebody to put an end to
Meadeism, re-election or no re-election!

February 12.—The Congress patriotically votes
men and money, and this in any quantity. But
at this time of the revolutionary day it would do
no harm if the Congress would ask a more rigid
account from the military Cains; what have they
done with the people's children? Therein this
Thirty-eighth Congress ought to be more stringent than was its predecessor; and the more so
as this Congress has almost greater responsibil-
ities. *But re-election will be in danger*, say the
Lincolnites. Well, what of that? Is the people's
wantonly spilt blood to secure the re-election? It
is terrible to think that only a great disaster will
cure the people at large from this *Lincoln* infatu-

ation. And still more awful, more terrible it is to foresee, that if a disaster smashes Lincoln, the Copperheads, the traitors, the McClellanites may come into power, and, worse than Judas, they will betray mankind's cause. The dilemma is too terrible, and almost no issue: because even the best Democrat is an offspring of darkness and crime. Blinded by Halleck and other traitors, blinded by his own short-sightedness, Mr. Lincoln seems to be dragged by furies to the abyss; he opposes any change in command, and opposes Grant's nomination. Of course, the Sewards and Blairs support Lincoln. For months Stanton promises to Senators and to others that the Potomac army shall be torn from the clutches of Meade and of his clique, that a great reorganization is to be carried out; and nothing is done.

February 12.—Some artist ought to immortalize himself by a tableau of crucifixion:

1st Tableau. Lincoln between Seward and Halleck. The two 'ma . . . —head down. 2d Tableau. Seward with Sandford and Weed. (See above.) All three head down.

February 13.—George Thompson, old, good natured Englishman, says Washington founded American independence, and Lincoln is the founder of American liberty. It is an ingrained notion to attribute to Washington everything. As a character, Washington stands unique in history; but Washington did not summon the

American people to conquer their independence! the people rose without Washington, and called on him to be a leader after the days of Bunker Hill, Concord, Lexington, when the flame of independence was already burning in the valleys and on the mountains. But Lincoln is only a very second-rate executor of the lofty and ardent aspirations of the unrelenting will of the people; and if Lincoln, as now surrounded by Sewards, Blairs, etc., had been left to himself, and not whipped by the radicals, not much of liberty would have consoled mankind.

Already, in this Diary, I have pointed out this crook in the European mind. European rhetors, etc., always look for an incarnated initiator, and I have shown how the American press sustains that ungracious fallacy, thus, in reality, depriving the people of its due.

Washington believed in final success when the masses desponded and despaired; but Lincoln was, and is, always behind the onward march of the people, and is rather dragged by the people than beckoning it to follow him.

February 14.—I hear that Fremont's chances increase in proportion as Lincoln's chances decrease. I shall not wonder. Fremont is high-minded and progressive; he has ardent, noble convictions, and has the manhood to act on them. All the aspersions against Fremont are merely Chinese shadows. If only Fremont had a better, clearer, insight of men and of their character !

February 14.—More and more dissatisfaction in all directions with the administration of the Navy—that is, with the Department. Welles has excellent intentions, but is not the man. He is slow, undecided, unfamiliar with all matters, and thus, in the hands of his various boards of advisers. In all cases of capture, of prizes, of blockade, of neutrality, in all cases where the State Department breaks down, either by too much absence of mind, or absence of knowledge of laws, or by inborn gascousness, Welles firmly and bravely defends the interests of the sailors, and the true honor and interests of the country, against the encroachments attempted by England. But there seems to end Welles' fitness for his place.

February 15.—Bah! I finished reading that accumulation of after-thoughts, of screams, and of thoroughly unmilitary and unmanly reasonings—called the McClellan report.

Hard work to go through such a heap of confusion and assumption. And I find telegrams omitted which were made public the day when the events took place. I am almost certain that many other telegrams, very damning for McClellan, are expunged by his coadjutors. How easy to pulverize all this laboriously concocted disquisition! In his report, McClellan has the effect of a man sound in limb and body, but whom his shirt prevents from walking.   And this McClellan, this race-runner to a gunboat during the battle at Malvern Hill, (see Diary, vol. 1,) this McClellan writes impertinent despatches to Lincoln and to Stanton! If it were from a victorious field of battle—but from a skedaddler!

The introductory chapter of this unmilitary disquisition smells of the Ketchums and Marbles, although an attempt is made to show that it was prepared in 1862, after the first Manassas battle. How smart!

In the first pages of this self-laudation, one can find the key-note of McClellan's military mis-operations, and McClellan's unmilitary brains; it is the *over-estimation* of the material forces, of the numbers, and of the moral qualities of the rebels, (no wonder in a member of the Lone Star, and a fawner on slaveholders,) the *under-estimation* of the qualities of the loyal Northern volunteers, and the uninterrupted demand for larger and larger numbers, for scores of hundreds of thousands—and he got them, and never understood how to move and use them.

The distasteful impressions of the Lilliputian operations carried out by McClellan in October, November, and December, 1861, operations which long ago disgusted the country, and which must be loathsome to read by any one, who, if only once in his life, served under even a third-rate commander, is not improved by the report. The lock-jaw expedition is even worse when now detailed; the willful massacre of our troops, as now explained, is altogether Mc-Clellan's, and not Stone's work. The massacre is wound up by an apostrophe, written at least eighteen months after the event. The report shows that McClellan was afraid to take Charleston and Savannah, after our success at Beaufort and at Port Royal. Events proved that *unwise* and not *wise*, was the plan of general operations as summed up in the report, and which operations were to be carried out some time in the course of the war. The report justifies that high appreciation paid to Stanton by the best men, by the truest patriots. Stanton *urged* the poor little Mac to action. How dreadful and cruel of Stanton! The memorandum addressed by McClellan to Stanton, February 3d, 1861, was a fair warning to the new Secretary of War, how timidly the Commanding General intended, if ever he intended, to operate, and that his delays would be interminable.

The everlasting, the ever-branding shame of the conquest of trophies, Centreville and Manassas, (March, 1861,) and the worse than unmilitary conduct of McClellan, *at the time of*, *before*, and *after* that victory—these disgraces burn through his own explanation, (p. 54.)

"The history of every former war has conclusively shown"—(p. 67,) that you, O General! that you know nothing about history. Every history shows conclusively that the case is as you assert, when armies are commanded by counterfeits of soldiers. Look at Napoleon's campaigns. Any corporal who served under him would have done with Johnson and Beauregard at Manassas what Napoleon did with Mack in Ulm. Look at Smolensk. Torres Vedras alone makes an exception. But O, great General! You alone may compare Manassas and your campaigning to Torres Vedras and Massena; nobody else will. All this twaddle in the report shows that McClellan tortured his brains to find ways how to push away as far as possible the bitter day, when in person he was to face the enemy. That is the secret of all his more or less anaconda-like expeditions. (Pp. 62, 63.) Schemes and no execution; talk of prompt success on paper—a sloth, and worse when it becomes necessary to act.

What have disquisitions—very poor in themselves—to do with events which occurred months and months hereafter? Oh, I did not believe that this report would so fully justify what I said in the second volume of the Diary!

"Instant assault on Yorktown would have been simple folly."—Page 78. Of course, folly in a General who dreaded fighting, and allowed a handful of enemies to so completely fool him at Yorktown as they fooled him at Manassas. One can imagine the utter despair of Stanton, obliged to read such a lucubration as McClellan's letter, page 79. General Keyes' letter to

Sen. Harris proves that Keyes was just the man to serve under McClellan. This shameful siege of Yorktown shows that when the commander is a McClellan, his spiritlessness, like a plague, infects most of the men around and under him.

"The enemy was compelled." — Page 87. Compelled by what? by your slow demonstrations? The enemy was weak, and after having fooled you during four weeks, withdrew on account of his immeasurable inferiority.

All the elaborate *ex post* reasonings cannot wash off the disgraceful personal conduct of McClellan when the heroic Hooker fought at Williamsport.

A strain of the most glaring incapacity runs throughout all the statements, telegrams, and reasonings contained in this Report. All is blended, and harmonizes; his actions in 1861—'62 with what his coadjutors wrote for him in 1863. On the Chickahominy he continually sees double and treble the number of his enemies, and woefully, pitifully whines. The letter on page 94 is disgraceful to read, disgraceful even to a McClellan, if anything could disgrace him. Nowhere, in the whole report, the feeblest spark of any soldier-like notion or comprehension whatever. The enemy was not *superior* in *numbers*, but the rebel commander had an immense, immeasurable superiority over McClellan in intellectual force, and in courage. Then the poor, wincing General makes guesses as to the *rebel policy*. In proportion as McClellan approaches Richmond, his uneasiness, his fears, his despondency increase. He seems to feel conscience-stricken at raising his hand against his masters, the treacherous slaveholders, and against Jeff. Davis, his special master. His communications to the administration are an uninterrupted chain of fear and trembling. For the first time I admire Lincoln and his nerve, to have resisted such contagious emanations as came from McClellan's daily communications. The fiery Stanton chafed; his patriotism, his manhood was horribly tested when he was forced to bear so long with a McClellan.

Three or four times a report or the telegrams forebode a *last, supreme struggle;* a great, final, decisive battle; and after all such prophecies a mental and shaking chill seizes upon the General. His brain and his hands quake like his pen.

The administration is upbraided for not considering the victory at Hanover Court House so great and decisive as the melancholy condition of McClellan's mind represented it to be. Lincoln this time reasons like a general, and McClellan like a child beside itself with joy to have found a victory.

"It has entirely relieved my right flank." (May 30.) And two days after, the rebels, from the same direction, from Mechanicsville, pounce upon Casey, and McClellan and his staff are perfectly, totally ignorant of the rebel movements, but all of them strong in multiplication of the rebel numbers.

That was the way the Hanover Court House victory, so prized by McClellan, *relieved his right flank*. Less than a fortnight afterwards, that right flank was wholly turned by Stuart's raid, although McClellan was reinforced by McCall's division, and had cavalry; but he had not the first notion how to hold or distribute his troops, how to use them, or how to lead them. Therefore he neither held them well in hand, nor put them well in positions, but misused them, never led them himself; forever expecting what might turn up; and it turned up in the wanton murder of 80,000 men, and in disgrace, not for the army, but for the general. Some more insolent, impudent, ignorant letters to the President and Stanton fill the report. On page 130 the confession escapes: "*And even if Richmond had fallen before our arms, the enemy could still have occupied,*" &c. Who ever heard of a general afraid to strike the decided and deadly blow on his enemy and justify his fear by such unmilitary, namelessly unmilitary considerations! Fitz John Porter, that victim of his infatuation for McClellan, vainly entreated him to march on Richmond, (see Diary, page 2;) and that was the advice of a soldier, of a general, and of a friend. Richmond taken, the gunboats and transports would have arrived by the James River. But *Richmond taken!* this idea frightened McClellan beyond comprehension, and made him speculate what the beaten enemy might do. McClellan never comprehended the natural results of a victory, as he never felt inspired to win one.

The letter to Stanton (page 132) dated June 28, 1862, is an effort to throw on the Administration, and above all, on the Secretary of War, the nameless disasters of the 26th and 27th; disasters absolutely brought about by the unsoldierlike conduct of McClellan in that whole campaign. Events are always concatenated; they do not spring up isolated, but one mistake generates a progeny; and McClellan's military mistakes, equal to the most criminal crimes, are exclusively, absolutely his own; he is their focus and their father; the bleeding country and army are the sufferers. By this effort, for which the human vocabulary has not a name, McClellan cannot wash his gory hands: "*Had I twenty thousand or even ten thousand fresh troops to use to-morrow, I could take Richmond,*" (page 132;) for on page 130 he confesses that it would have been a disaster to take Richmond. No words can say more. What fresh troops? His own record proves that on June 28 he had more than 10,000 troops who had not been in the fight—troops belonging to various corps. Such troops have been thought *fresh.* But it seems that on the precise June 28, McClellan wished *fresh troops,* that is, freshly arrived, freshly landed from vessels or balloons, or stamped out from the earth. This thrust at Stanton means the McDowell corps, that apple of contestation. But if that corps had joined McClellan's army weeks or days previous to June 28th, they would have marched, fought, lost men by fevers, &c., and on June 28th would not have been more *fresh* than any of the other corps then in McClellan's command.*

Then came the Prætorian-Franklin conspiracy, by which Pope was victimized, the country almost murdered; but the victorious Prætorians restored McClellan to command. Enough! heart and mind sicken anew when data or memory brings back that man and his doings.

Horrenda late nomen, in ultimas
Extendat oras.

February 16.—If Seward had a little of a Webster or an Everett or a Marcy, he would not suffer some of the talkative European diplomats to continually offend public decency and the national feelings. When these diplomats make their *obeisance* to the President and to Mr. Seward, they on every occasion rival the most abject

---

* The report on the Chickahominy campaign, as made by the rebel commander Robert E. Lee is now published. It is short, concise and soldierlike. Lee says that in the seven days fighting, his troops captured fifty-five guns, McClellan asserts that he, Mac, lost only one or two. Veracity and probability are on Lee's side.—*Note August* 20, 1865.

copperheads in picking at the Administration, as well as at the principles represented or carried out by the Republican party. Any other Government whatever would long ago have sent home such enemies. Let any diplomat in Paris dare to take sides with Carlists or Orleanists. Twenty-four hours would carry him out of France. I am sure that if Cassius Clay would make his house the headquarters of Polish malcontents, studiously ignoring Russian patriotic and influential men, Cassius Clay would be sent away from St. Petersburg and from Russia, whatever might be his personal obsequiousness to Prince Gortschakoff. But here certain European diplomats assume that all is permitted to them. (Diary, vol. II.) It is certain that the best men, the truest patriots in Congress, rather prefer not to be besmeared by diplomatic gravy, and only very, very few Senators seek that honor. However, the Minister from England is remarkable for his tact and discretion, and certain of his colleagues ought to imitate him. The Minister from Italy, by policy and conviction, is loyal and true to the cause of the North, to the cause of humanity.

February 16.—Every day this 38th Congress shows itself to be up to its mission. Among the new members, Winter Davis of Maryland, is undoubtedly the first genuine orator in Congress, and has few equals out of Congress. He is bold, and his mind is broad and statesmanlike.

This Congress does not hesitate and dives to the bottom of every question, however thorny the question may seem. It does not hesitate to take any amount of responsibility, provided the Union be radically saved and preserved. But how below and behind Congress is the daily and periodical press!

And, nevertheless, the daily press is carried on by a number of more or less talented men; that is the subordinate collaborators. Their fitness and capacity is often remarkable, but they have no individuality. They carry out instructions; are overawed and neutralized by the special leaders or principal owners of a paper. Generally, if not always, nameless contributors build up the glory of the principal sponsor or owner of the newspaper. To such a chief representative of the paper the people at large credit the best articles, when in truth the one thus laureated is generally unable either to conceive or write such varied and often instructive articles.

February 18.—The McClellan party—that is, the partisans of the South—try to make immense capital out of that disquisition miscalled the McClellan report. Mr. Lincoln ought to issue an order to collect all the figures, the facts, and status of the army as commanded by McClellan; collect the maps and charts of Virginia, and of his, McClellan's campaigns, and send all to any *Etat Major,* either in Paris, or Berlin, or Petersburg, or Vienna. I would risk my head that the verdict thus obtained would amply corroborate what I say about it.

February 19.—The struggle is going on. What law, what basis or principle is to be laid down for the eventual reconstruction and reorganization of the rebel States? Congress has the soundest and truest statesmanlike preception of the whole question. Of course, what Congress intends, differs *toto cœlo* from what Lincoln attempts; the press sides with Lincoln. The common politicians appreciate the whole question in view—of the re-election.

February 20.—About a week or ten days ago, the patriots, Wade, Chandler, Harlan, Morrill, Wilkinson, and a few others, personally urged on Lincoln the patriotic necessity of changing the commander of the Potomac Army and some of his coadjutors. Mr. Lincoln emphatically sided with the patriots, approved their views, and promised to adopt them — and as yet nothing is done. At once I doubted Mr. Lincoln's word—and I shall be proved right. Further: To that deputation Mr. Lincoln held out the expectation, and almost the wish, to be surrounded with radicals. We shall see when it will be done. It seems as if Lincoln, advised by Halleck or Seward, would rather not have an able general at the head of the Potomac Army. A victorious general may become dangerous to the—re-election.

February 22.—Sumner spoken of as candidate for the Presidency. Spoken of by some devotees and by—himself. He believes he will be the candidate of the eleventh hour, and that Chase and Fremont will transfer to him their votes. Oh!

February 23.—Whatever may be the real or supposed (by his enemies) deficiencies of Stanton, he has shown qualities not easily found in a man entrusted with power, not easily found in an administrator of the most complicated machinery during this war. In my life I have met eminent administrators, and have been myself at work in complicated administrative machineries, but I have never met one so free from personal, mean, petty influences, so happy in the selection of men around him, as Stanton. He surrounded himself and filled his Department with men whom he selected on account of their proven capacities; not one of them (Watson excepted) has he ever known or met in private life. General Canby has his confidence, because General Canby fully answers to all the requirements looked for in a man, in a general, and in an administrator. Stanton never knew Canby previous to the war. So he never personally knew Dana, but knew *of him*, and made the best choice that a Secretary ever can make.

February 24.—The Lincolnites maintain that Lincoln's slow policy has saved the country and

the cause, by giving time to the people at large
to arrive at the sound comprehension of the necessity of emancipation.

This assertion is very plausible, and in my
opinion altogether misses the point. If inaugurated at once, if carried with firm purpose, with
energy and decision, in Stanton's or Butler's
manner, emancipation would have made itself
comprehended by the most obtuse brains, and
certainly would have economized streams of
blood, thousands of millions, and—time. But
admitting even in full these claims of the Lincolnites, it justifies not their claims for re-election. The virtues needed in the next President
are the power, the capacity of organization.
Admitting that, thanks to Lincoln's slowness,
the people is fully ripe for the question of emancipation, now comes the necessity to carry out,
to give an organic body to those convictions of
the people. The Lincolnites themselves find no
administrative or organizing capacity in Lincoln.

February 24.—I hope the mighty and intelligent German element in this country will remain true to itself, true to its noble origin, will
not be Irishized—*ne s'en canaillera pas.* Germans
are the offspring of an enlightened, scientific
rationalism; they are radicals, and radicals they
ought to remain on this liberty-consecrated soil.
I speak of the various Doctors *utriusque,* as well
as of the masses, those besmeared with Romanism excepted.

February 25.—This political and social confusion or conflagration evokes into daylight the worst compounds of human nature. The fight for offices is carried on with the fury of savage animals. The fighters tear each other to pieces, not minding their own kind.

The Lincolnites are furiously arrayed against the supporters of Chase. The true question is, what *genus* of politicians for the next four years is to skin the people. Between the two parties are the true patriots, ashamed, confused, impassible yet, but feeling that they will be forced to yield to one of the currents. And as to the simon-pure politicians in the two camps——impossible to decide which of them are worst.

Why! oh why! for such a lofty, noble mission, why cannot the people select a new and young apostle? If Lincoln is tested and found base, Chase's record is not better. From March 4th, 1861, Chase has never openly recorded any protest against that sinister and nefarious Lincoln-Seward policy. Chase never boldly defended a radical idea or measure, when such a measure was kicked by Lincoln-Seward. In 1863, Chase saved Seward, and only now, when the presidential race is to begin, Chase makes a show of energy as a radical.

February 26.—Some weeks ago Seward published a certain letter to Lord John Russell, whose menacing tone agreeably tickled the American public. The press of course struck up an immense flourish, and paid incense and admiration to the Secretary's pluck. It comes out now that the letter was never communicated or even read to any English Minister. All this was done for the home market. The "honest" and "loyal" press does not tell the truth to the people, but mightily assists in humbugging the public opinion.

Mr. Lincoln dabbles in foreign affairs as he dabbles in the conduct of the war, although Lincoln was right against McClellan. Mr. Lincoln wrote a private letter to Mr. Adams in London, instructing him to warn the English Cabinet that the American people will not stand the construction of rams for the rebels. What an illogical step! Adams is to mention to the English Cabinet the contents of Mr. Lincoln's private letter. How this officiousness lowers the elevated position of a President of the greatest people in history. A Mr. Evarts, Seward's man, was the bearer of the letter. This Evarts is again sent to England to——dine, and thus to influence favorably the public opinion. Meanwhile, the Queen's Bench, etc., went against us in the Alexandra case, and Evarts has not enlightened the English courts. An Evarts will be shy about penetrating to a John Mill, and John Mill alone has turned the current in our favor.

February 26.—The good men in both Houses painfully feel now how wrong it was not to have long ago told the people the truth about Lincoln's administration; not to have publicly, officially, warned the President, and with earnestness and decision attempted to put the administration on the right track. Now it is too late to disabuse the people.

February 27.—Every one in the War Department, Stanton, Holt, the young colonels, etc., shudder in disgust at Meade's inactivity. Grant fights, Lee's army is reduced to twenty-five or thirty-thousand men, and our Potomac army looks on. But Lincoln is firm as a rock in his support of Meade.

February 27.—How can Lincoln look into General Hunter's eyes! Lincoln twice disavowed Hunter, and subsequently adopted Hunter's emancipation's policy. And Lincoln struts now before the people, wrapped in Fremont's, Hunter's, and Butler's actions.

February 27.—Repulse in Florida. Wanton butchery of our men. And all this the work of Mr. Lincoln's omnipotence, and done over the head of Stanton, through such a tool as General Gillmore. Butchery to bring into Congress that Hay, Lincoln's hireling and *private* servant. Senator Grimes attacked in Congress this bloody, shameful transaction. The *good* press almost attacked Grimes.

February 28.—The disaster in Florida more horrible than it was supposed. The greatest efforts are made to hush up the infamy. Mr. Lincoln has in hand a full report from his agent,

Hay, a report reeking with blood, but, of course, Mr. Lincoln does not show it. Everybody is exasperated.

> *Tacent and palor albus ora inficit,*
> *Mentesque percussæ stupent.*

February 29.—It is refreshing to the mind to witness how simple and quiet is the mode of life of most of the Republican Senators and Congressmen. Most of them live here as they do at home; and they live simply, rather avoiding noisy parties. A few fops only try to be fashionable, or to become familiar with the diplomatic gravies.

February 29.—Were I a man of wealth I would spend a great deal to have for President a Wade or Grimes, or some one of that character. Grimes would make a model President. But it belongs to *pia desideria* to see such men brought before the people, either by the politicians or by the press.

February 29.—Unwillingly I must record the New York *Herald's* words on the Florida crime: *Price of three votes for the Presidency! One thousand lives!* The "loyal" press condemns not.

MARCH.

March 1.—Senator Sherman said in the Senate that the various Virginia campaigns cost 100,000 lives. The figure is too low. If strict account is made it will reach more than 150,000, and half at least by sickness, and McClellan is directly or indirectly responsible for all. Directly, McClellan is responsible for those murdered, or who died during his campaign; indirectly, for having put at the start the campaign on such a false track, that subsequently it became and becomes wholly impossible to correct the false direction. If McClellan had not through cowardice allowed Beauregard to escape from Manassas, the Virginia campaign, nay, the rebellion, never could have acquired such gigantic proportions. A deviation from a direct line, imperceptible even by the strongest microscope, when continued misses the point by an indefinite distance; so it was with the Virginia campaign, nay, with most of the administrative actions under the tutorship of Scott, Seward, McClellan. Already in 1861 Mr. Lincoln deviated from the aim, and the gap between the straight and the deflecting lines is now filled by the people's blood.

March 2.—Many persons familiar with international law, wonder that, as early as 1861, the State Department started on the wrong foot the whole question between the Union Government, the rebels, and the neutrals, and that until yet the Department continues to blunder. I wonder not. One fact will explain. When in June, 1861, I was appointed to the State Department, I found, to be sure, Phillimore's great work in the Department library, but not even the volume containing the international laws had been touched, and its pages were uncut. In general that library is well furnished, but no students.

March 3.—The New York leading press continues to lead astray public opinion in reference to the wanton Florida butchery. Instead of ascending to the head it deals with the tail, with secondary blunders. Now it is a General Seymour who is the perpetrator of the crime, and not those who originated the whole plan. The press knows better; but one newspaper's pet would be hurt if truth were spoken, and another paper willfully strangles it on account of availability. All this paves the way for re-election. And being thus befogged by everybody, the people is for Lincoln—the worse for those who ought to have told the truth in Congress and out of Congress, and did not.

Tu nisi ventis

Debes ludibrium, cave.

March 3.—The reports of battles officially published by the rebel government give the number of their forces at above 40,000 when Grant's army was attacked at Shiloh. Grant had only a part of his forces over the river. The onslaught made by the rebels was a surprise, and they attacked in thick columns our distorted lines. The more glory for Grant and his army to have resisted, and the next day, when reinforced, to have beaten off the rebels, who, in various ways, had about 11,000 men put *hors du combat.* And when Beauregard shut himself up in Corinth with 30,000 men, Halleck—immortal Halleck *of Corinth*, at the head of 100,000 men—repeated McClellan's Centreville, Manassas, and York-town victories.

March 3.—Better and better. *The Florida crime is only the result of a misconstruction made by General Gillmore of the orders given by the President.* So says the ultra-loyal press. The bearer of orders is Hay, a member of the White-House household. Also Gillmore and Hay showed too much zeal. They ought to have known Talleyrand's warning.

If these constructions of the press are not generated by a stubborn purpose to hush up and deceive, then in this case, as in numberless others during this war, the average of the great masters—the *Pontifices maximi*—of the American press justify my opinion expressed in former pages. These great masters have no penetrating eye, no comprehension of details, no insight of men and events. Under the leadership of these *magnati*, the press mostly deals in generalities, and drifts into the dark, into the unknown. During this war the press has very seldom filled the duty of the watcher on the tower. Never yet has it been a beacon, throwing light into darkness. Still less has it been like the astronomer, who, by his material and mental telescope, penetrates space and *tenebræ*. The intellectual telescope of the press is very short, and tightly screwed up by an opaque cover. And this press aims not only to lead the people, but to make the people offer incense to the *Pontifices*.

March 4.—Some of the periodicals already prepare their readers to strike up a hallelujah for Lincoln. Well, the writers and editors of the periodicals are twin brethren of the dailies. Brownson's powerful mind almost alone makes an exception. In force and breadth of conception, in logic and in penetration, *Brownson's Review* towers over all others. (This, my opinion, relates only to the American, and not to the Roman Catholic productions in *Brownson's Review*.)

The London Quarterly Review says: " The Americans are now in a court of trial for nations, where size of country, length of land, breadth of waters, and height of mountains will not count for much, if greatness of soul be wanting. One human spirit, dilating to its full stature, may be of far more avail," etc.

Listen, oh, American press!—is thy Lincoln that *dilating spirit?* The collective people alone, the unnamed, the Many, have the *greatness of soul!*

I have not the slightest right nor capacity to criticize the mastery of the English language as shown by the American reviewers, etc., and compare it with that of the English writers. But when I read an English review, my mind is generally pleased—dilated; what I may not understand, I feel; but when I read American reviews, (with very few exceptions,) I feel—sleepy. I always learn something from the English, but seldom from the American reviews.

March 4.—The sentimental, and the soft-brained, and the small Church, and the optimists through thick and thin find no fault with, but rather applaud Lincoln for having condemned in Fremont and Hunter what he himself afterwards took up and carried out. All the above-mentioned *lumina* see in this act of Lincoln, a deep foresight of events. The truth is, that when Lincoln disavowed Fremont and Hunter, he had not even the slightest notion of afterwards taking up what he disavowed. At that time Lincoln was not thinking of—re-election.

In 1861–62, neither Mr. Lincoln nor his evil genii, Blair and Seward, had any foresight of re-election. Mr. Lincoln palsied the cause in Fremont and Hunter, exclusively to please the border-State politicians, all of them violent pro-slaveryists; he did it to please and to conciliate all the dark, reactionary elements in the North—to please the *Herald,* the *National Intelligencer,* and others of that stamp. I doubt if at that time Mr. Lincoln made even the Jesuitical, mental reservation to take up the emancipation measure himself, if in the course of time he should be cornered by public animadversion.

March 5.—Many genuine, radical, rational Democrats, Democrats not by party name and discipline—also not brainless—but Democrats by philosophical comprehension, assert that Lincoln's re-election will demonstrate the utter failure of self-government. It is not at all so. The immense majority of the people is infatuated with Lincoln, because the mass earnestly and sincerely believes him to be able and true. The masses err, or may err—*errari humanum est;* but no mean, selfish aims and purposes direct or inspire the masses. The people is led astray by those whom it is accustomed to consider as beacons and as leaders; (as repeatedly said in this Diary.)

Neither the press nor the honest or dishonest politicians point out to the people any transcendent, or even half transcendent capacity. The alternative laid before the people is: either Lincoln, *one of themselves*, credited by the people with certain capacities and virtues which he in reality has not, or some Democrat who is a worshipper of slavery, a man without a heart, and without any noble convictions. In such a dilemma the people sides with Lincoln. The people's unwillingness to put in the White House any successful general shows that the masses have sound sense, and that their self-governing sound sense warns them against any such mistake. It will do for a perverse newspaper, or for as perverse a politician, or for that most nauseous and disgusting American social excrescence, *the would-be gentleman, the would-be well instructed, the would-be better classed, the would-be well connected*—it will do for all such to advocate the election of any military man whatever, but it is not what a truly self-governing people ought ever to do. Washington was the military god-father of the new-born nation, Washington was the noblest of characters, and those two criteria made him dear, and deservedly dear to the people. Jackson, the result of pacific party struggles, grandly justified the people's predilection; but the sound sense of the self-governing people feels that such exceptions must not be repeated, and that still less ought they to be repeated now, during or after a civil war. I trust in the genius of our race that no general will be President.

March 5.—The Democrats and the Conservatives, for years and years henchmen to slavery and furious eaters of southern dirt, are as criminal authors of this civil war as are the Southern rebels themselves. Northern Democrats and Conservatives tenderly nursed the pro-slavery creed and all the pro-slavery falsehoods. Northern, that is Boston Conservatives built up a pro-slavery science, and perverted Agassiz to become one of the high priests of this temple. Northern Democrats and Conservatives tenderly and submissively nursed the Southern arrogant ignorance. But for such Northerners, the Southern slave-breeders never would and never could be so overbearing; never would have combined treason and relied on its execution. The contempt with which the South treated the North, the belief in northern cowardice, a belief so general among the Southerners, originated principally in the cowardly submission of Northern Democrats and Conservatives. Nay, these false men in the North are virtually the principal originators of treason, and they are as much fratricides as are the Southerners.

March 5.—Poor Wilhelm III of Orange! poor Macauley his historian! A sentimental reviewer, a lecturer and hero-seeker, who invented the name of *the national man* for a Seward, now compares Lincoln to that keen, far-sighted, stubborn, unyielding Anglo-Dutch statesman.

The Carlylian, erroneous, false, perverted comprehension of history, (so far as American wise-

acres have any notion and comprehension of it,)
the unhappy example given even by an Emerson,
who in imitation of the "hero-worship" invented
"representative men" all these and similar semi-
scientific pranks took hold of the American intellects, and they tell now on that generation
which is presumed to represent the progress and
the unfolding of the American mind. These
scions of Carlyle want a hero to sing, to lecture
about; they cannot appreciate, comprehend, nay,
even feel that collective hero, THE PEOPLE!
From such a stand point, Carlyle denationalized
some of the best American intellects. A hero
they wanted, and gave incense to—in McClellan,
and now they anxiously look around for another.

Walt Whitman, the incarnation of a genuine
American original genius, Walt alone in his
heart and in his mind has a shrine for the nameless, for the heroic people.

March 5.—To witness the loss of life and time
once at the hands of McClellan, and now of
Meade—McClellan's faithful disciple and contin-
uator—is painful; but almost more painful is it
to witness the degradation of human nature in
the preparatory Presidential canvass. One can
swallow it as a bitter pill, when, for reasons mentioned above, the re-election of Lincoln is represented to be a dire necessity; but these canvassers, politicians, contractors, shoddy office-
seekers, sentimental reviewers, give to Lincoln
all the virtues, all the intellectual and mental ca-

pacities of all the heroes of all the times! That is worse than an emetic.

March 6.—Seward and the Sewardites continue to build Spanish castles. I have it from the best authority that Seward and his men still believe that Seward will be the candidate of the compromise between Chase and Lincoln. Well, even the most contemptible shoddy will not stoop so low.

The combinations are musing. Chase flags in the race to become eventually a compromise candidate between the Lincoln and Fremont men. Sumner keeps himself ready to gently, gracefully, and by force of his irresistible rhetoric, conciliate on his person—*a la* Henry VII—the deadly hatred and antagonism of all the above-mentioned parties. Five Richmonds in the field, and to say that the presidential growth is scarce!

March 6.—To help him, Mr. Seward in distress sends for Sandford of Belgium. Sandford of the rotten blankets and worthless cloth, of bursting muskets and saltpetre speculation, and of Venezuela guano, etc., etc., etc.; Sandford, who knows Europe, and is on the most intimate terms with everybody, from the *Decembriseur* down to the doorkeeper in the royal palace at Brussels—Sandford will tell to the native American politicians, statesmen, and to all the world, that only Seward's name corruscates over Europe; that that great name is venerated by every European; that but for the veneration paid to Seward, we would long time ago have had a whole swarm of coalitions against us; the South would have been recognized; offensive and defensive alliances against us concluded; and that, in one word, worse evils than the Egyptian ones have been averted by the necromancer Seward.

If all this will not bring the people to the feet of Seward-Weed-Sandford, then the obtuse American people may perish.

March 6.—So with his *valetaille*, the Nicolays and the Hays, the Lamons and many others of the same tribe, Mr. Lincoln is to earn the results of the sacrifices made by the people! He is to reap what he not only has not sown, but has even attempted to crush out. Undoubtedly Lincoln is the youngest emancipationist, and perhaps even now, even to-day, not of strong faith and convictions.

In 1861, after the attack on Sumter, every Governor in every free State has shown more energy than Lincoln did with the whole crew around him. The Governors forced energy upon the desponding administration. But for the energy and activity of the respective Governors, who were urged and pressed by the people, the administration would have been utterly lost. Then, the Governors showed administrative capacity, and not the administration. Seward was its inspired mouthpiece; and Seward is the prophet of sixty days. Have the Governors and the people worked in 1861 to secure Mr. Lincoln's re-election in 1864?

March 6.—Seward's papers and the loyal papers generally take up the debate in the House of Peers between Lords Derby and Russell, on account of the correspondence concerning the pirate Alabama, and attempt to give all the credit to Seward. But that bold dispatch never diplomatically existed; its existence was most thoroughly for buncombe.

Americans attribute too much weight to these debates in the English Houses, and to all kind of utterances made by the leading Tories. The Tories crave power, and make *flêche de tout bois*, as oppositions always do. Our contest and civil war proffer and open a rich arsenal of weapons for attack and debate. Of course, an opposition attacks what is done by those in power, and advocates contrary or opposite measures. But when the opposition gets into power—and above all the English Tory opposition—then it is as cautious, as undecided on all foreign questions, as the Whigs. Look at the history of the last forty-odd years. If the Tories should come into power, they will do nothing more for the South than is done to-day in England. The Tories would be bound by precedents, by treaties, by international laws and comity, and above all, the Tories, more even than the present English cabinet, would be kept in very respectful respect by the demonstrations of the people, by the armaments of the States and cities of Boston and New York, by the monitors, and above all by the heroic sailors of all classes.

March 7.—Whoever suggested to Chase the gold bill was either his enemy or had only a shaver's notion of finances. To throw ten or even twenty millions on the market signifies less than to throw a glass of water into the ocean. Such a sum will be absorbed in New York in a shorter time than I write these lines, and the *agiotage* will run as it ran, only the treasury will be weakened of as much as it will throw, and never will be able to repeat this absurdity. The treasury will be at the mercy of the speculators, who will play with Chase as cats with mice, and devour him.

March 8.—Since the question of the next presidency is on the *tapis*, Washington's name is desecrated *a toute sauce.* Washington reduced to the littleness of a Lincoln! But it is still more degrading (for those who do it) that the Lilliputian chief, that compost of imbecility and cowardice, McClellan, is put side by side with Washington. However, it is the Democrats', copperheads', doing, and this explains all.

In their admiration, and above all in their Carlylian thirst for a hero, our American heroseekers, our fiery preachers take cunning for force of character.

March 8.—In the last cavalry raid, (concocted between Kilpatrick and Lincoln,) Colonel Dahl-

gren, a heroic youth of 22 years, fell, not in a
battle, but murdered from behind a hedge by a
Virginia coward; but of course an F. F. V. Oh,
for a war of extermination against this whole
Southern breed of robbers!

March 9.—The question of making Grant a
Lieutenant General—urged by the patriots in
Congress, urged by the people, urged by Stanton
—is hanging fire because Lincoln cannot get rid
of his incubus Halleck, and wishes to save him.
Grant will have a hard time with Lincoln's pets.

March 10.—What heavy nonsense these self-
appointed beacons, these teachers of public opinion spread among the reading public through
their newspapers and reviews, and through their
lectures, sermons, speeches, orations, addresses!
How they confuse the people's sound judgment!
Happily, as yet little harm is done by the ebulli-
tions of these luminaries, and they only serve to
more firmly assert the right of the genuine people to self-government. The people show that
they possess the ample sound reason and judgment needed for self-government. Almost all
those who try to bring them light, show that by
their studies, their notions, their judgments of
events and of men, and their appreciation of
history, they belong rather to the past, and have
little perception of the spirit of the age as
manifested in sound historical criticism, and in a
philosophical comprehension of history. They
grope in search of "representative men," and

have under their noses a Representative People, the grandest spectacle in the life of mankind. They put history on the rack and establish the queerest analogies. They are not aware that the great life of a people is the most sublime phenomenon, and to it the "representative men" are incidents, and scarcely even corollaries.

General Scott was " a representative man," a hero without parallel, an idol! To Scottolatry* is to be traced the origin of the whole military mismanagement and military misfortunes, from March 5, 1861. If General Scott had been appreciated for what he was—that is, as a distinguished general in certain given conditions, and not as *the* oracle:—the military side of the ques-

---

* In October, 1860, that national idol published his *Views*—(see the *National Intelligencer*)—wherein the sham patriot advocated a division into four republics. He traces the respective frontiers, points out the capitals, and nevertheless an idol he remained. He bungled in the Fort Sumter-Anderson affair; worse than bungled when Virginia was to be invaded in 1861; and facilitated the defeat at Bull Run or Manassas. (See Diary vol. I.) God and General Scott alone know how far *Mr. Seward's advice prevailed upon the idol* during that fatal spring of 1861.

What Thiers, in his History of the Consulate and the Empire, vol. II, Book XXV, page 172, says about the Duke of Brunswick emphatically applies to General Scott:

"There are established reputations which are sometimes destined to ruin empires; the command, in fact, cannot be refused them; and when it has been conferred, the public which perceives the insufficiency under the glory," (in relation to General Scott unhappily the public perceived not the insufficiency,) etc., etc.— *Note November 26, 1865.*

tion would not have received a false impulse,
which has cost the best blood of the people, and
brought the country to the verge of an abyss.
Oracle Scott generated oracle Halleck; true
military science—not that according to West
Point classification—true soldier-like capacities
and qualities were pushed aside. The men in
power in the Administration in Congress became
befogged, and looked for captains to the laureled
graduates of West Point. Grant would never
have been selected by Scott; Grant was not
among the *first* graduates of West Point. The
war, his own brains, his devotion, graduated a
Grant, as they graduated a Thomas, a Sherman.
This war will be finished by men whose reputation will be due to the field of battle, and not to
the number of their patent of examination as
recorded in West Point. The Potomac army was
ruined and will continue ruined by engineers or
first graduates; whenever it passes into the hands
of self-graduates, and into the hands of field
officers, of artillerists, of officers of infantry and
of cavalry, then the mettle of that army will
show itself. Pure engineers seldom if ever become tacticians and manœuvrers, and tacticians
and manœuvrers alone win battles.

The war has lasted three years. It is more
than is necessary to make a good soldier and a
good commander from any one endowed with
capacity, even if he has not made any prelimi-
nary studies. Three years of practice in the field

are better than any number of years spent in engineering.

March 11.—It seems that Lincoln finds a pleasure in snubbing all the radical measures, and baffling all the wishes and expectations of radicals. Well, well; the time will and must come, when either you will go.overboard with all your varlets and advisers, or you will go on your knees to my friends the radicals, to be saved by them from Gehenna's fire. We will wait and see.

March 12.—Hallelujah! All overcome! The Hallecks, the Sewards, the Blairs, etc., and Grant is made the Lieutenant General of the Armies, that is, *Generalissimus, Connetable* (Fr.,) *Wielki Hetman*, (Pol.,) more than a Marshal of France, or a Field-Marshal of Prussia, Russia, and Austria. Grant commands, who up to to-day has been always successful. And Halleck? Well, as Mr. Lincoln cannot spare his pet, who wound himself around Lincoln's heart, Halleck will be chief of the—not existing—staff; he will be a kind of a General *du-jour*, (daily on duty,) to receive orders, despatches, and to forward them. Halleck will do no more mischief, say Stanton and others; but I am certain that he will find an outlet, and in some way or other repeat his former accursed tricks. I am certain.

March 14.—Sen. Gratz Brown—a man boiling over with indignation, and in the *curulæ* speaking out boldly and patriotically what rankles in the hearts of others. If the radicals had been like Brown, either Lincoln would have been forced to change his bad *entourage*, or he (Lincoln) would not now be forced upon the radicals.

March 16.—Sumner becomes Seward's-Sanford's mouth piece in the Senate. Sumner again lends his back to be a stepping-stone for guano-shoddy-saltpetre, etc., Sandford, and in his enthusiasm, Sumner humbugs his colleagues in the Senate, and displays—at the best—a courier's knowledge of Europe, and utter ignorance of European policy, and of the relations between governments and cabinets.

*Sumner's conduct confirms my often expressed opinion: 1st. That to be a genuine American statesman it is not necessary to be instructed in the windings of European policy. If Everett is familiar with them Marcy was not. 2d. That a by-half and superficial familiarity with a subject is more mischievous than utter ignorance.

March 17.—How tender the President is to his pets. In the order creating Grant Lieutenant

---

* Senator Sumner wrote a letter to the *Evening Post* concerning the Constitutional Amendment. This letter is Sumner's best production. Simple, to the point; no affectation, not over-burdened with heavy and commonplace rhetoric.

During this recess, that is since the adjournment of Congress, Sumner's actions and speeches—as at the Convention in Worcester—are firm, determined, and the speeches, above all, greatly sobered in rhetoric. Never has Sumner been so really dignified, and one can only deeply regret he has not always been so.— *Note October* 2, 1865.

General, Lincoln interpolated that at his own request Halleck is relieved from the duties of a commander-in-chief. Public opinion says, and the whole country knows, that Halleck was kicked out by Congress.

March 18.—Grant published an order in six lines and refused three dinners. If that is not significant of a man then nothing is.

March 18.—In relation to Congress, the press of both sides is untiring in confusing the people. In the appreciation of the members of Congress, of the character of that body, and of its various legislative and administrative labors, the "loyal" press is as opaque as always, and as unjust as always. If the leaders of the "loyal" press were to be just to Congress and to Congressmen, they would detract from their own *editorial statesman-like splendor.* That is the truth in a nut-shell. To the character and to the boundless vanity and egotism of the leaders of the press it is more congenial to befog the people at large, and mislead the people in the appreciation of the services and daily labors of the Congressmen. Men like Fessenden, like the Morrills, like Clark, like Fenton, and generally all the working members of Congress, in one season accomplish more labor in their respective committees than any one of the leaders of the press performs in three years. Most of the editorials are rather mechanical, are done in a kind of routine. For years I saw the newspapers at work, and I witness now the labors of the Congressmen.

March 19.—For the first time I met to-day Captain Worden, of the first Monitor celebrity. He bears on his face marks of that struggle. Simple, unassuming, Worden and his crew in shutting themselves in the unknown, untried Monitor, and going out to sea to fight the terrible Merrimac, did what—to be classic—beats Hercules entering Tartarus (hell.) But Hercules found poets to sing him, and Worden was soon forgotten, even by the newspapers.*

March 19.—The question of the crossing of races, or as the newly invented sacramental word

---

*In March, 1861, Worden was sent as bearer of orders from the Government to Pensacola. On his return from Florida he passed through Charleston. The South Carolina chivalry, headed by Pickens and Beauregard, arrested him, and for nearly eight months during the hottest season he was kept in a slave pen, and his fare corresponded to his prison. He lost his health and is to-day a total wreck.

The nameless horrors of Andersonville were but a carrying out of the firm purpose of the rebel chiefs either to murder our prisoners, or, at least, to disable them for life. As the treatment of Worden shows, that plan and aim date from the first days of the rebellion.

The Andersonville murders have been perpetrated under the eyes and with the knowledge of the whole rebel supreme military hierarchy. Besides, the Winders, Howell Cobb, Jefferson Davis, and his secretaries of war, have been acquainted with the crime. Neither can Robert E. Lee put in the plea of ignorance. It cannot be believed. Robert E. Lee was too high in command of the armies to have ignored the treatment experienced by the prisoners of war.—*Note September* 8, 1865.

says, of *miscegenation*, agitates the press and some
would-be *savants* in Congress, bringing out of
course an immense display of arrogant ignorance on both sides, and in both the arenas.
The worshippers of darkness and of ignorance, as
are the worshippers and defenders of slavery all
over the world, but principally in America, are
in their element when they utter falsehoods and
lies, or when in the most approved democratic
manner they back their bad faith by the grossest
ignorance.   But the other side, the so-called
defenders of the negro or African, pitch into the
contest as empty-headed as their antagonists;
and by high-sounding generalities and phrase-
ology try to make up for their thorough want of
scientific information.   Neither the one nor the
other know in the least anything whatever of the
scientific researches and discoveries of the last
forty years; and thus neither the one nor the
other know how far the ancient continent in
Europe and Asia was once occupied by the
physiological negro; nor do they know where in
Asia are still to be found living remains of the
primitive negro race.   Oh, these lecturers, these
leading editors of dailies, weeklies, monthlies,
etc.! oh, these Demiourgos, Thaumaturgos of
public opinions! oh, these tonsured or not tonsured, anointed or not anointed, consecrated
by Calvin, or by Thomas, or by Andrew, or by
Paul, and preaching in small or broad churches!

Oh, these empty headed rhetors and sham scholars and legislators!

Second. Neither the assailers or defenders are aware how the successive disappearance of the negro has been brought about. They could learn that absorption probably acted more powerfully than did destruction or extermination; that a change of climateric and physical conditions of animal existence or life works and worked slowly to such an end during countless centuries. They could know that "*it is an acknowledged fact that the color and features of the negro or European are entirely lost in the fourth generation, provided that no fresh infusion of one or other of the two races takes place.*" (Lyell.) And the newly baked Academicians come not to the rescue of science ! Poor souls, still entangled in Blumenbach, and under the leadership of an Agassiz, wailing against Darwin.*

Third. Science in hand, how easily it could have been shown to those swarthy-haired and black-souled Seymours, Marbles, Saulsburys, etc., that the difference is only in quantity and not quality of the *melanine* which blacks their eyes, hair, etc., and blacks the whole African ! And perhaps if dissected their *cerebella* would be found to have less convolutions than those of the negro.

---

* Excepted Professor Henry, of the Smithsonian, who is a *genuine savant.*

March 20.—Halleck issues military orders as he did of old before a Lieutenant General was created. Halleck is the exclusive military mischief doer, that is, adviser, of the President. It remains to be seen if Grant will allow himself to be absorbed and neutralized by the President.

March 21.—Oh, how they thrive and swell! All these leeches have been thin, thin before the the war; what circumferences now! But

Fortuna non mutat genus.

All around here, and in wider and wider circles, the busy makers of money at work, and with more than an eagle's eye for any "main chance"! Of course, in regular pursuits, occupations, in working and toil, man ought to make money; and when he makes it he fulfills his duty as a citizen, as a member of a community, as a member of his own and as a member of the whole human family. But it is not a matter of course to grow fat on others' hard labor, as do the cheating contractors or officials, as do shoddy and lobby, who like blood-hounds never lose the scent of the "main chance." And those traffickers in human blood and health, giving poison instead of medicine in hospitals! Their number is legion, and if one is detected, hundreds escape detection. The press mostly writes with a squint at the "main chance," and understands how to make " something out of it." As far as Congress is concerned, I have no doubt about the honesty of the republican majority. I see and observe;

many and various things come to my knowledge;
but I have not yet heard of a republican Congressman running after "making something out
of it."

Neither to change, nor flatter, nor repent
wish I, when speaking of the majority of the
good patriots in both Houses. I wish that the
names of the republican members of the 37th
and 38th Congress might be preserved in every
record, in every history, in every family, and in
every household.

March 21.—The love of routine, and the conceit of officials and of many influential men, have
done as much mischief, and made almost as
much havoc as all the accidents of a war. Pre-
eminently mischievous was the still lingering
conceit of the West-Point classification and patent
for military incompetency.* Then the respect for
West-Point obsolete routine in military instruc-

---

* As the war is finished various disclosures are now semi-offi-
cially made, to explain the faults, nay, the crimes which so pre-
eminently stamp the administrative incapacity in the first stages
of the rebellion. (See I and II, No. 1 of the Diary, 1861–63.)
As to the source of some of these revelations the would-be wise
speak of some secret, mysterious history of the acts of the administration, especially at the beginning of the war. Such a
secret history is exclusively a lamentable, disgusting, degrading
record of double-dealing, vacillation, turpitude and colossal
ignorance—after all, not of Lincoln himself, but of Seward, General Scott, Weed and some others, on whose advice, judgment
and sense the inexperienced Lincoln principally relied.—*Note*
Sept. 14, 1865.

tion, respect which not even Congress is yet able
to shake off, prevents preparation for the future
of genuine military men, not mere engineers—
prevents Congress and the administration putting the artillerist, etc., in the first rank of the
school, and thus having good commanders for
the army. All almost unanimously believe that
the world has nothing to be compared to West-
Point. The world may not have anything to
compare, but—in what sense? Then the conceit
of the press, which takes no trouble to thoroughly master any subject, and speaks of all.
Then the conceit of red-tape, and of routine
ruling in the medical department, prevailing in
the organization of hospitals, and in the treatment of sick and wounded. I know and see that
the hospitals in Washington are well organized.
An intelligent not red-tape, nor conceited director and doctor is at their head. *Nulla regula
sine exceptione*, and I heartily wish the exceptions
may be multiplied. But, alas, there are still
many other conceits to be enumerated; but

Nuper solicitum quo mihi tedium.

March 21.—The *good* press still makes the
utmost efforts, and tenderly attempts to whitewash Lincoln from the Florida massacre. But it
will not do, it will not do.

March 22. — Poor commissioners from St.
Domingo, and poor Monroe doctrine! Seward
in his cowardice gives both up. Seward refuses
to recognize the Dominicans as belligerents, on

the plea that we fight our own rebels. What confused notions boil in Seward's head. Dominicans are not rebels, but citizens of a republic fighting for independence which she enjoyed scores of years, but of which she was of late robbed by the Spanish invasion. Seward almost forgets that the invasion took place since he mismanaged American affairs in general, and those of the Union in particular, and that he himselt once protested against that invasion. Good Seward! before the *parcæ* in some way or other cut the thread of his official misdoings, he will entomb the Monroe doctrine, that arch of this continent.

But blunders and prophecies are Seward's congenial and natural element. The history of Seward's international blunderings* must be studied among the commanders of our vessels and fleets—then volumes of international *Sew-*

---

* A few days ago the United States District Court at Springfield, Illinois, threw out of court the claims of a certain Frenchman, Le Moore, and of his associates, for cotton seized by our Navy on the Mississippi. This fillibustering association led by Le Moore provided the rebels with cloth and other commodities, receiving in payment the so-called confederate cotton. More than a year ago, Mr. Seward peremptorily ordered the United States Marshal of that District to return the captured cotton to the rebel agent. Happily the Marshal did not cave in at the *dictum* of the premier, but answered: "that he could obey only the orders of the Court"—thus giving to the Secretary of State a lesson upon the knowledge of laws and statutes and the paramount duty of conforming to them.—*Note Nov.* 18, 1865.

ardiana can easily be gathered together. The only glory of Mr. Dick (David Copperfield) Neptune is, to have opposed Seward; but Mr. Dick did not do it at once, only when he got at his elbow a certain familiar spirit who has more international and constitutional law in his fingers than Seward and his lawyers and other lawyers put together have in their brains.*

March 22.—Well, well! Under the inspirations of the *Decembriseur*, Spain takes airs and will try to Mexicanise Peru. Those Franco-European intrigues have now full swing, but their time is limited, and all this European rubbish will be swept out from here, and will be thrown into their European royal sewers.

March 22.—Governmental England mends her ways, because her own best people side with the right, because the governing lords see that treason and secession must go down, and that England's better interest is to be friendly to a true and loyal nation and people, and not to robbers, highway murderers, thieves, pirates, and slave-breeders, as are all the rebels. That is where it is, and not in Seward's charming despatches, or his Weed's and Evarts' chat *entre la poire et le fromage.*

March 22.—As yet the best men, nay, the whole republican majority are sullen and taci-

---

* In the second volume of the Diary the name of Charles Eames was mentioned.

turn on Lincoln's re-election.   But the people at large, stirred by politicians, bears heavily for him!

March 23.—On account of Mexico, Spain, etc., one again reads and hears heaps of clap-trap concerning the Latin race—its incapacity for self-government, and similar splendidly ignorant assertions.   O history! how impudently art thou handled by the raceologues and by their counterfeiters.   And of what race—if of race we are to speak—were the ancient Romans?   And municipal and communal institutions, and even the limitation of the royal power were cradled in the south of Europe, and passed therefrom to the north.   The free cities did not originate in Germany, or among any Anglo-Saxons, O raceologues!   And the Athenians and other Greeks had more in common with what you miscall the Latin race and its derivatives, than you or any Anglo-Saxons are aware of in your great familiarity with the world's history.

March 23.—Lloyd Garrison comes out for Lincoln on the ground that we must please Europe. Good, old Lloyd Garrison becomes *un bonnet de coton.*

March 24.—A young patriot urged me to write a special history of internal treason.   He is right.   Internal treason extends over the country like a diabolical net.   The government, the administration are surrounded by and swim in its poisonous atmosphere; internal treason is at work daily, hourly—nay, every minute and second. Many and many times I pointed it out in the pages of this Diary. Since the Democrats, copperheads, and the partisans of McClellan have thrown off the mask, internal treason has acquired gigantic proportions in the press, on the stump, and everywhere. The departments are still filled with the poison, some of them very strongly. But Lincoln and Blair prevent a thorough cleansing, and Lincoln always expects that the stricken with plague will *soon turn the corner.* Burnside was right in saying that "if about one hundred were hung it would do a great deal of good." Of course the *World* was terrible upon Burnside. One thing is certain, that the rebels are better served and more promptly obeyed in certain numerous quarters in Washington and New York—not to speak of the West—than is our government.

March 24.—Grant will not be intoxicated with flattery as was McClellan and Meade, McClellan's poor imitator. I never met with a man of so much simplicity, shyness, and—decision.

McClellanites from the Meade clique thrown overboard. The Sykes, the Frenches, and some other principal originators of those "outmanœu-verings" so "brilliantly" and so "successfully" carried out by Meade.

March 24.—Wadsworth, the patriot of patriots,

again to the front. Wadsworth is always in the front as citizen, as patriot, as soldier, and as a man of the truest and most humane aspirations.

March 24.—Senator Sumner has made a careful study of the Almanach de Gotha (see his speech) to help Sandford. I rely upon the common sense of the good men in both Houses to defeat that mean scheme. *Nous allons voir.*

> *Quel bonheur, quel honneur,*
> *Ah, monsieur le Sénateur !*

March 25.—At any rate, Mr. Seward no more runs all the Departments as he did in 1861. At that time Seward was the all powerful *premier*, nay, the *major domo*, trying to make a *Merovingian* out of Lincoln. Chase was pliable and taken in by Seward's subtleties; Cameron was pliable for his own reasons; Bates and Welles were subdued and frightened. All this has changed since Stanton first politely bowed out the Secretary of State from the Department of War. Emboldened by the good example, and by good advice, Welles began to give the Minister of Foreign Affairs lessons in *international law*, and Bates, leaning on Coffey's broad shoulders and strong mind, asserted his rights as Attorney General; and thus, little by little, Seward was reduced to his own limits, and had more time to deluge the world with his diplomatic oracles. Then Lincoln began to assert himself, and to less dread the Secretary, or be awed by the Secretary's omniscience. At times Lincoln still caves in, but the more foolish acts Seward makes Lincoln commit, the quicker the final emancipation is at hand.

March 26.—McClellan's report and correspondence with Lincoln, Stanton, and Halleck, are the best evidences of the conspiracy of the McClellanites for the ruin of the Virginia army under Pope, and by thus ruining Pope, to ruin the country. Any court would act on the evidence drawn from the Harrison's Landing correspondence. On July 30, McClellan received the first order to bring back his army in all haste to the succor of the threatened capital. On the 2d August, a new order, more urgent than the first was given, to which McClellan replied by a long letter of protestation. On the 4th August the General-in-Chief, Halleck, gives him the definitive order to obey and be silent. On the 5th August, McClellan, instead of obeying, demands reinforcements. On the 6th, the General-in-Chief, Halleck, resolves to send a direct order to embark on the instant such and such regiments, which he designates. McClellan replies: "*I will obey the order as soon as circumstances permit.*" In any country whatever, under any government whatever, despotic or monarchic, republican or constitutional, and above all, in Constitutional England, a General disobedient to the extent McClellan was here, would have been court-martialed, cashiered with infamy, and shot.

The reading of such facts, at times makes me say *mea culpa,* to atone for my severity towards

Lincoln. Poor Lincoln was in a terrible fix,
(Amer.,) seeing clearly McClellan's utter worth-
lessness, and being frightened by the McClellanized generals and officers, who corrupted the
spirit of the army, and falsified and poisoned
public opinion. But the worst is, that Lincoln
seems not to have profited by the lesson received
from McClellan. In the same procrastinating
manner he sustains and keeps Meade, who is no
better than McClellan. I almost withdraw my
mea culpa.

March 27.—The copperheads and the Jeff.
Davis pensioners already attempt, in the interest
of McClellan, to undermine Grant, and already
attribute to him that ridiculous " on to Richmond!" Of course all the ideal military roads
converge to Richmond, which is to-day the heart
and the focus of the rebellion. A victory won
anywhere in the Gulf, in the Rio Grande, or in
Alabama, in one word, a victory won anywhere
on land and sea, is the road to Richmond.
Therefore Grant taking Vicksburg, or vanquish-
ing Bragg in Tennessee, was going " on to Richmond." When Grant moves the Potomac army,
probably he will push it on Lee, wherever Lee
may be, and if he whips Lee, then he has carried
out " on to Richmond," as Richmond then will
be easily taken by a squad of Invalids.

March 27.—General Grant wishes to put General Baldy Smith in command of the army of the
Potomac. Mr. Lincoln wishes to preserve

Meade, and from other parties a stupid opposition is made to Smith. It is a bad sign and a bad beginning. Grant has an immense responsibility, and ought to have his own men and do as he pleases. Grant has his own estimate of generals, and no opposition to him ought to be made, either in Congress or in the White House.

March 28.—How easily Sr. Sumner could put down the pro-slaveryists in the Senate! How easily the Davises, Cowans, Saulsburys, Richardsons, etc., could be answered, when they utter those stale absurdities about the negro race, and attempt to speak wise! But unhappily the Senator, and almost all the so-called "classical scholars" and "accomplished," "well-informed" gentlemen of his generation are wholly unfamiliar with the last results in physiology, unfamiliar with all the strictly modern sciences, such as ethnology, comparative philology, comparative and microscopic anatomy, and the like, which all bear so powerfully and luminously on this question of difference between the so-called races. How easily could the Senator expose the shams uttered by his antagonists in the Senate! What a pity that these "classical scholars" and "highly learned," etc., gentlemen are about forty years behind the actual scientific stand-point of the human understanding!

March 28.—Wadsworth commands his former division of Gettysburg. I hope the division will again behave nobly. Although Meade in his report mentions Wadsworth and the men under him, true justice never was done to Wadsworth and to his men.

March 30.—The Congress slowly hews its way, but its principles are as strong and as good as those of the 37th Congress. I speak of the patriots. But for the numerous traitor-copperheads, the labor of this Congress would be quicker and more satisfactory.

March 31.—Lincoln's and Halleck's partisans give out that Butler is to be put in command of New York, as any reverse of Grant may occasion riots in that Jeff. Davis mob city. How complimentary to Grant, and how wise! what forethought!

APRIL.

April 1.—Boutwell—than whom there is no better and more clear-sighted patriot—said to me, that if Butler were nominated for Presidency and elected, the rebels would at once give up as the raccoon did with Captain Scott. Such is the feeling and the conviction of all the best men in Congress and out of Congress, and I heartily share these convictions. But I begin to see that it would be useless for the patriots now to oppose the current set in motion by politicians and by the press. The patriots have let the time pass by, and now they must yield.

April 2.—One is driven out of both the Houses of Congress, not only by the copperheadism of the Coxes, Voorheeses, Pendletons, Brookses, Davises, Saulsburys, etc., but by the still more nauseous and insupportable display made by those gentlemen of the most shameless ignorance of almost all and everything for which a little study, nay, a little reading, is required. And

154

nobody would or could accuse them of being so ignorant if they only would abstain from arrogantly parading their ignorance, which the organs of Jefferson Davis, such as the *World* or other papers, and the organ of coarseness and vulgarity, such as the *Herald*, applaud.

April 2.—God grant that the Lieutenant General may not bitterly regret having kept Meade in command of the army! Grant ought to have been more self-willed. Meade's hesitation, if not worse, will defeat the best plans, and may defeat the whole campaign.

April 2.—The best patriots maintain that, to enlighten the people, events must be relied upon. I bow to this principle, and shall bow to the will of an, *ad hoc*, enlightened people. But events themselves, *in concreto*, are the results of men's actions, are the actions themselves; events are men. Men, therefore, ought to enlighten the people; could only the people at large see to-day the event or events pushing onward Mr. Lincoln! When the best men decide to support the re-election, it will be only to avoid a greater evil.

April 2.—The radicals and all the enemies of slavery, all who crave its extinction—in one word, all the decided, *truthful* Republicans are called by their haters and enemies fanatics, narrow-minded, men of one idea, and similar names — names intrinsically rather honorable than otherwise. It is true that among those who ardently work to see slavery abolished, there is a certain number constituting the *small church*, whose mental horizon is neither much expanded nor clear. But these constitute that very small minority, known under the party name of *abolitionists*. The immense majority of those who work to-day for the radical destruction of slavery, are men as pure and broad-minded as ever worked in mankind's cause. Nevertheless, it is curious to observe how events more or less similar bring forth or reproduce similar phenomena. The pagan writers and philosophers representing the putrefaction of a sinking civilization, decried the primitive Christians as fanatics, as men of a single idea. The fossils of all times recur to the same terminology.

A man in his normal condition, a man when not besotted by egotism and by prejudices, a man whose powers of mind are not eaten up or dissolved in vile and abject passions—is essentially an abolitionist in the loftiest and purest comprehension. Such a man has the consciousness of progress, as the healthiest condition for his beneficial and multifarious activity. Such a man changes, ameliorates, mentally and materially; he clears his way through marshes, through stagnant waters and stagnant prejudices; he abolishes and destroys whatever impedes the free and healthy activity and impulses of his mind, his heart and his social life, and its normal conditions. In this American struggle,

the copperheads, the conservatives, the fossils,
are like many stagnant pools, from whose poisonous effluvia the American polity must be
liberated and purified—and this on condition of
life and death.

April 3.—Day after day I expect, but vainly
expect and look for the advent of young men.
Where, O, where is the youth? The armies
have not absorbed it all! Not all the youth of
the country spills its noble blood against that
darkest of treasons, against traitors whose infamy
is unparalleled in world's history. Those who
fight give evidence of being inspired and animated with a faith in the higher destinies of
their country, and of the people. But in its
gory embrace this war has not absorbed all the
American youth, and it is perhaps for the first
time in the history of great upheavals and of
national convulsions, that a younger generation
has so little, so imperceptibly impressed the roll-
ing events. Nowhere here the youth asserts its
fresh and lofty inspirations or activity. Not in
the press, not in the popular gatherings, not in
the various councils of the nation, not in Congress, not in the State legislatures. In one
word, nowhere. The leading radicals in Congress, Thad. Stevens, Wade, and others, have
more freshness, fire, and youth in their ideas
than have the young in years but senile in everything else, writers, lecturers, and generally the
young generation between the age of twenty and

thirty-five years. Most of them are formed on
Greeley's model; and like the model, many of
the copies had their ups and downs during this
contest. Model and imitators have shown no
indomitable courage and confidence in the people and in the cause; model and imitators
repeatedly gave up the cause as lost, caved in
before the seemingly victorious treason, and
cried for peace, postponing the final emancipation to some future indefinite time. And thus
Greeley, and the editorial-writing youth mod-
eled after him, although intrinsically faithful to
the great truth and principle, often and often
doubted its victory, and in this way beyond comprehension confused the masses of the people
who confided in them.

In the darkest days the republican majority in
Congress was firm and unrelenting; it never lost
faith in the cause, in the people, and in themselves. And in the darkest days the republican
majority showed mettle and youth, showed faith
and undaunted purpose. The writing, the newspaper editing American youth seldom stood by
Congress; never did any of the Greeleyans rise
to the height of the patriots in Congress, many
of them not young in years but young in soul
and mind.

April 4.—Under the guidance of Halleck, Mr.
Lincoln still continues to influence Grant's military dispositions. Of course, not by giving
direct orders, but by friendly suggestions and

sauvity. In this manner Meade is retained in command, and some other appointments are made, contrary to Grant's better judgement.

April 4.—The re-election ! The re-election overawes and submerges everything, even sound common sense. This people, so quick, so wide-awake in almost every other respect, is easily bamboozled, humbugged, thrown off the track by the lowest stratum in its political life. The people, that is, each district, sends to Congress a man in whose brains and integrity it seemingly has confidence, and nevertheless, in such a grave, mighty question as a Presidential election the people—carried away by all kind of influences—pays no attention to the opinion of its Congress-men, of whom it is to be supposed, that as they had had so much to do with Lincoln, they are better acquainted with his good and bad quali-ties, his capacities and incapacities, his peculiari-ties, his character and the want of it, as can be the politicians, newspaper editors and reviewers, living at a distance, and who only occasionally, and, so to say, on state occasions, come in con-tact with him. And with all this, the people is for re-election, and the majority in Congress is against it.

April 5.—Grant has lost nothing of his fresh-ness of mind and ingenuousness. He avoids Washington and its various corrupting allure-ments, nay, he runs away from them. And Grant is right; his good genius inspires him.

Grant is essentially a soldier for the camp and field. All Grant's predecessors in the command of the army of the Potomac — several commanders of corps, divisions, brigades, and regiments — in one word, many, many officers, and even the rank and file, came to grief, and were ruined by Washington influences. Even McClellan was ruined by his sojourn in Washington, provided that there was anything whatever to be ruined in McClellan. When with the army, the thought and the mind of Grant's predecessors were not in the camp, but in Washington, in its various attractions and intrigues. The commanders and generals, etc., visited and visit Washington when they can; its various attractions ruin them.

Grant told me that Butler pleases him more than any one among his new acquaintances.

April 5.—Oh, how I wish that in some way Grant may reorganize the fated army of the Potomac; reorganize its spirit; reorganize its commanders and order of battle; and finally, change many, many men. From what I hear and read of accounts of battles fought by that army since 1861, few, if any of its commanders and generals understand the use of artillery. The artillery is organized in corps—a colossal absurdity. A brigade, a division, has no artillery; the soldier sees no guns; is not lovingly attached to them; relies not on his own brigade's or division's batteries; they are strange to him,

and he considers it not his honor and duty to
defend them. (I spoke of it in the 1st volume.)
Then, about the use: I read in reports of battles,
and hear in relations by mouth, that one, two,
three, at the utmost four guns were used at this
or that point during the battle. But I never yet
have read or heard of a concentrated fire of several batteries of artillery during a battle. Perhaps the Western army use its artillery better.
I hear, too, that we have a scarcity of good officers of batteries. Well; if so, then do not subdivide batteries in sections, and thus scatter good
commanders. Have batteries of at least eight
guns. So officers will be economized. General
Griffin is a first-class artillery officer, and in the
broadest sense, besides being a thorough soldier
and good general. Perhaps even in France,
Griffin would be considered a prominent organizer and officer of artillery.

April 5.—Fremont's movement for the Presidency has in it too much of the foreign element,
and it does not seem that men of real weight
care to enter into it. Fremont's organ, *The New
Nation*, is violent, conceited, arrogant, and abu-
sive of Grant. The editor of that paper *is reckless, but not a Carnot or a Napoleon.*

With all his noble, lofty, and generous aspirations, Fremont has no luck—and it was luck, as
Mommsen says, that definitively made a Cæsar.
Then Fremont can have no knowledge of men,
as he is always most unhappily surrounded.

But, nevertheless, if I cannot get Butler for a President, I prefer Fremont to Chase or Lincoln.

April 6.—I confess the sin of suggesting to Grant to exclude *all* the newspaper correspondents from the army. Their relations, at the best, are worth very little; their letters confuse public opinion, as their judgment on men and on movements is only indiscriminately picked up, or is prepared to puff this or that General who pats them on their backs. Recollect Wadsworth's case. Many "glorious" Generals owe their glory to such letters. Grant has a well organized military bureau, and the bureau ought to correctly publish the military news.

April 6.—Very likely the amendment to the Constitution, forever blotting out slavery from the polity and from the soil of the Union, will not pass the House. And if not, the cause is to be looked for in those criminal intrigues which in 1862 contributed to defeat Wadsworth, as well as many true members of Congress, and filled that body with copperheads. But I do not despair; the people, stunned by intriguers, will recover; and the next (Thirty-ninth) Congress will complete the great work started by its two predecessors.

April 6.—Even an eye-witness can scarcely realize the inexhaustible vitality of this people, its almost boundless moral and material wealth. Three years of a most terrific civil war, three years of a reckless squandering and waste of all the national wealth, and this as much by administrative inexperience as by stubborn incapacity and conceit, and yet no signs whatever of exhaustion. Manufacturers and mills at work, furnaces smoking, productions and consumption daily increasing. Hundreds of thousands fallen or crippled, and nearly a million of men under arms. New States and new Territories formed and peopled; immigration pouring in and peopling the base of the Rocky Mountains. Such, amidst the most terrific tempest, is the triumph of freedom and of self-government. No other country, nation, or government ever showed such a life, such a power; and no other country, nation, or government ever can show it.

April 6.—Meade, his staffers, and several other Generals, etc., of the Potomac army, tip-top military McClellanites, everywhere spread and insinuate that it was easy for Grant to win renown in the West, where he had to do with a bad army and with poor Generals, but he "*soon will find what Lee and his army are.*" Lee is an eminent General; but he and his army are almost exclusively indebted for their eminence to the incapacities and want of soldierlike qualities of the McClellanites, to the faults of Burnside and of Hooker, and to the worse than faults of Meade. Lee will not inspire a cowardly terror in Grant, as he inspired it in McClellan, this even more in his quality as a slaveholder and rebel than as a good General. Grant will not be awestruck by Lee and the rebels like the Williamsport heroes. But these malignant and cowardly insinuations demoralize the army, and that is the only aim of the clique.

April 7.—I attempt to dismantle the strongholds of shams, and disrobe false gods. I dare to say that blue is blue; pinchbeck not gold; politicians and shifters not oracles; a rhetor not an inspired orator, nor a statesman. I speak out what many think but dare not publicly assert. I offer no incense to idols. I point out those great criminals whose imbecility or cowardice cost the people the lives of scores of thousands of its best children. I dare to shake to the foundations the clay pillars of the sham temples. I am a bad man, but I cannot help it—and I shall continue to record doings and to call things by their right names.

April 8.—How fond this Grant is of violating the easy military regulations! There! Grant establishes his headquarters *ten miles* nearer the army than Meade had his. Grant's headquarters are almost amidst the soldiers. That is a Western, and not a Potomac army custom. Bad precedent, and certainly an anti-McClellan one. Then Grant travels with the simplicity of a Second Lieutenant; without fuss, with a small trunk, which he forgets in his room, and to save time goes off leaving the trunk behind. McClellan, although not a Lieutenant General, had splendid traveling equipages, carriages, etc., all this for a campaign of 120 miles space, and in a country with railroads. *That was commander-like.*

If Grant fails, then a curse is on this Potomac army. Grant is a soldier to the core, and a genuine democratic (not in the party sense) commander of a democratic army from a democratic people. Further: Grant sends off his wife to the farm of her father somewhere in Missouri. If all this—to be classical and highfaluting—is not Roman, Cincinnatus and matron-like, then I am at a loss for precedents and for historical illustrations.

Per contra: McClellan tried as much as he could to ape aristocratic Europe. Brilliant receptions, representations, servility surrounded him, and he thrived on them.

The final question is: Will Grant remain a diamond, resisting the dissolving Washington acids?

April 9.—The re-election makes the best and the not very laudable passions boil, surge, and struggle; it upturns men, turns them inside out. Purity, sternness of principles are assailed, stormed by the sham of expediency, by self-interest, by availability, by selfishness, by civic cowardice and imbecility. A muddy current may at any time overflow the whole country—and who will say: *Stop and rise no higher ?*

April 9.—The dissatisfied attempt to undermine Grant by the outcry that he puts his Western Generals everywhere. He knows them, has proved them, and is certain that he can rely upon them—that they will fight and not intrigue. Grant composed his staff from tried men, not from green-horns, not to please this or that political or social influence. If he only could remove Meade, whom most of the patriotic Senators, like Wade and many Congressmen, consider to be even worse than McClellan!—— The copperheads, the echoes of Jeff. Davis, such as the *World*, tease Grant with "on to Richmond." But Grant knows well that Richmond is in Lee's army. Several times Meade had Richmond thus in his grasp—after Gettysburg, at Williamsport, etc.

April 9.—Some of the press—this time not the *Tribune*—not the *Cincinnati Gazette*—worship Lincoln as if the country, the people owed everything to him. The press is mute, as it is always, about Congress. But the two Congresses, the 37th and 38th, have saved the cause. They and not Mr. Lincoln did all the good that was done.

April 10.—Slavery has so deeply eaten into this American polity that even the courts are full of its mephitic influences. Themis holds not the scales justly when slavery or its interests are concerned. Even now, some Judges of the Supreme Court can not lift themselves to the dignity of a judge. Not to go back to the Dred Scott case, (that stain of infamy on the Democratized Supreme Court of the United States,) but now, during this war, men like Taney, Nelson, Clifford, do their utmost to draw Themis upon the side of the rebellious slaveholders. Sitting in court over prize cases, these copperhead and Democratic sham judges twist and martyrize international and prize laws, to make them favorable to malefactors and to blockade-runners, friends and allies of the rebels.

April 10.—In Pollard's (rebel) history I read that on the third day of the battle of Gettysburg, a panic seized upon the rebels, and their whole artillery remained unprotected. If Meade had sallied out, the artillery would have been ours, and Lee totally routed, destroyed. General Hancock wished to strike the blow, but Meade opposed. Pollard's account squares with the investigation going on before the Committee on the Conduct of the War. That investigation fully establishes what a *pauvre sire* Meade is. And what a psychological phenomenon! Brave when commanding a brigade, a division, a corps, as at Fredericksburg or at Chancellorsville, at the head of the army, Meade becomes worse than worthless.

April 11.—How tiresome and disgusting is the sham erudition, paraded in both Houses by the copperhead orators, the Coxes, Davises, Voorheeses, Pendletons, that coarse Powell, and the like! However this display goes hand in hand. with that made by certain *fine* rhetors and *fine* classical scholars. When my radicals speak in both Houses, Kelley, Winter Davis, Wade,

Clark, Brown, Morrill, Grimes, etc., etc., one is electrified by nerve, by earnestness, and by vigor.

The men of faith and of principle say to-day what they said yesterday. They have nothing to comment upon or to explain. Earnestness and faith in principles are the best logicians; they alone are consequent.

April 11.—I hear from all sides—excepting from the honest radicals—that the Potomac army is, or ought to be, Lincolnized, as a counter-poison to that despicable McClellanism now eating it up. But what signifies to Lincolnize? The worship of one idol for another? Certainly nothing is more degrading for the army than the McClellan worship; but to represent Lincoln as an incarnation would not lessen the evil. The Potomac army in its majority is composed of true, intelligent American citizens, who feel and understand the sacredness of the social and political principle of which they are the armed apostles. They ought to feel that the principle is incarnated in them, and their choice ought to be of such a constitutional leader as is the best standard-bearer of the principle. As for the chaff in the Potomac army, and for those eaten up by old corruptions, nothing will or can save them, and their opinion or choice is of no account.

Mr. Lincoln as a President, as an individuality, did very little for the Potomac army. As commander-in-chief, he provided that fated army with not very enviable or reputable generals. Never on a single general has Mr. Lincoln avenged the wanton slaughter of soldiers. Mr. Lincoln had an unlucky hand with that army; he kept too long in command that scourge McClellan, and keeps Meade, who is even worse than McClellan, not to speak of Burnside and others. From a pure military standpoint, the army of the Potomac has nothing to be grateful for to Mr. Lincoln, and the only weight or signification which Lincoln may have for the soldiers of that army, is not in their character as soldiers, but exclusively in their character as citizens.

April 11.—There is no doubt in my mind, that from the first day of the *Decembriseur's* (L. Nap.'s) intrigues and schemes in Mexico, Mr. Seward, by his commonplace generalizations, by his confusing conversations and insinuations, made Louis Napoleon believe that neither the feeble protest made in Seward's despatches had a serious meaning, nor that the people was *decidedly* opposed to a Mexican empire. Now that Congress has spoken, Mr. Seward declares to the diplomats that Congress has no right to meddle with such questions, and that all the declarations made by Congress have no weight and no signification. I shall not wonder to hear or see a Sewardiana, in the shape of a despatch disparaging Congress, officially sent to Europe.

April 11.—An English blockade-runner is captured in the Rio Grande, one-third of the steamer in Mexican waters. It seems to be a clear case of prize, and if not, the courts are to decide why not. Lord Lyons, as is his duty, claims the *immediate* restitution of the steamer, and Mr. Seward, as is NOT his duty, tries to comply with the Lord's request. A tyro knows that if Mexican neutral waters have been violated, it is for Mexico and not for England to protest against the violation.

April 11.—From what I learn from and of Grant, he is no more afraid to take the responsibility of a million men than of a single company. This is a very praiseworthy feature in his character, and the more so as it is not generated by conceit or indifference.

April 11.—Witnessing most of the various appointments as made by Lincoln and Seward, one must conclude that either they have a very unlucky hand, or that the country has nothing better to show. It would be a very sad result of self-government if the above were true. But it is not. The best men and intellects are pushed aside; the selected ones realize the proverb— *similis simili gaudet.*

Already I have observed in these pages that Stanton, when not hampered from above, makes good and even excellent selections. Neptune Welles—whose good intentions, at least, must be accounted to him—at times selects well, principally when he is free from certain corporate influences around him. But Neptune's power of discernment is not sharp enough.

April 11.—Lincoln wishes to drop McClellan from the army, but has not the courage to do it. So underhandedly he stirs up Congress to do the work.

April 11.—Most probably Mr. Lincoln will harvest what the earnest and patriotic radicals have prepared by their ardent patriotism, by their steadiness of purpose and by their devotion. The radicals in Congress have initiated, pushed through, worked out, all the good measures, all that saved the country. Mr. Lincoln was dragged and *dragooned* into action, the radicals charitably drawing a veil over the defects of his mind, intellect, and character. It is the work of the radicals that Mr. Lincoln stands to-day before the people and before the civilized world as the incarnation of the sacred Northern cause. Lincoln snubbed the radicals, snubs them now, and if re-elected, he will snub and repay them with a kick for having erected a pedestal for him. Lincoln must *fatally* remain true to his own nature, which is far from being a lofty, high-minded, or broad one. The radicals have been always bold and uncompromising, *à la Grant*, always ready and prompt to take any responsibility whatever. But as for Mr. Lincoln

*   *   *   *   *   *

And when I take a survey of what was done to save the people, and how it was done, and by whom it was done, I wish I could see the names of the patriotic members of the two Congresses preserved in indelible characters in the abode of every American citizen, as the ten commandments are venerated in the dwelling of every Israelite.   The names of those patriots will forever shine in the heavens of human liberty.

April 12.—I recommend to the future historian of this epoch to closely scrutinize Mr. Lincoln's public utterances since his inauguration down to the end of his administration, whenever that end is to come.   It is a record of hesitations, indecisions, contradictions, and of an absolute want of statesman-like foresight.   Lincoln is almost never aware, and still less never certain to-day what he will do to-morrow—and, nevertheless, he may be re-elected.

April 13.—The aspirations of my whole life are finally fulfilled; they have become a fact.   The Polish peasantry or agricultural population, than which I have not found a better, worthier, more honest, more intelligent in any country in the world, the peasantry of ancient Poland is finally and emphatically *emancipated.*   It is emancipated as man and as laborer; it receives land—that is, homesteads, and is only subject to the laws and to the power of the sovereign.   This is a progress. Whatever else Alexander II may have done, his name be blessed ! *

---

* In the world's history Alexander II stands as one of the greatest and noblest initiators and reformers.   His heart, as well

I was about ten years old when I began to believe in this emancipation, and to agitate for it.
Half a century I spent not only in hope, but in
working for it, at times attempting to accomplish
it.   And now it is done, and whatever I suffered
or shall suffer is, at least in part, healed.

In the name of those restored to the fullness
of human rights, the Romanoffs are forgiven for
all the misfortunes and evils heaped by them on
the Poles.   Alexander II almost more than
atoned for the sins of his Czarian lineage and for
his own—sins committed against the nation as
well as against single individuals.   The last
bloody drama in Poland had two authors—the
Poles and the Czar's advisers.   In the course of
the last fifty years Alexander I, Constantine,
Nicholas, Michael, Alexander II, his brother
Constantine, six Romanoffs in all, each specially
has wronged and hurt me; but now all is forgotten.

April 13.—The echoes of Jefferson Davis, such
as the *World*, and the champions of the deepest-

---

as his clear insight and patriotism, is the fountain of his actions,
or, as the vulgar call it, of his policy of emancipation.   When he
ascended the throne, Alexander II attempted to conciliate the
Poles by broad concessions and by changing the Russianizing
policy vigorously established by Nicholas I.   Successive events
turned against the attempt, and the violently excited public
opinion in Russia forced, so to speak, Alexander II to return
almost relentlessly to the policy of his father, nay even to go beyond it.   In relation to Poland, fatality baffled the heart.—*Note
April* 19, 1865.

dyed copperheadism, such as the *National Intelli-gencer*, all of them most unrelenting foes of human freedom, and of all that is endeared to humanity, now take high ground in defence of what they are pleased to call *free speech*, which in simple prose signifies an untrammeled utterance of the most treasonable and darkly infamous sentiments, made by some copperhead and pro-slavery members of Congress. Is it *free speech* to defend treason and encourage murder, as did the accused members, and as do, more or less, the copperheads and their organs? No political body would stand it, or ever stood it. Look at history. The House is too mild; an English Parliament would have sent such sympathizers to the tower, and a French Assembly, to the public executioner. The "loyal" Republican press of New York, with its chilling poet at the head, *of course*, turns against Congress, bravely stands by the *World* and the *Intelligencer*, and shows its wonted perspicacity and true appreciation of the principle of *free speech*.

April 13.—How this Sumner more and more becomes a toy in Seward's hands, and an echo of European diplomacy, flavored by dinners. Every day brings new and stronger evidences of this. Sumner caves in before Seward, and carries out Seward's biddings. The House passed noble, patriotic, resolutions dictated by a true American spirit, on Mexico; but Sumner chilled the Senate, stretching across it his ponderous ignorance of statesmanship, his leaden, heavy brains, and all this to gain time and to——receive instructions from the State Department.

In this way the joint resolution is palsied, stripped of its grandeur, and the French schemer fully encouraged. Sumner swallows too much, and his digestive powers are too limited. Sumner is out of place as Chairman of Foreign Affairs, for he is completely *foreign to affairs*. To read the French petty literature, and to have dined with some European statesmen and celebrities, is not an initiation into the windings of European policy and statesmanship, but rather creates confusion in a not too stern and well-balanced mind. To forward speeches, orations, and thereby evoke a correspondence and receive polite answers, does not make one a statesman. I repeat again what I have so often mentioned in these pages: a genuine American statesman has no need of being familiar with the labyrinths of European policy, but he ought to be exclusively the embodiment of American principles and of the American spirit.*

. * Mr. Seward recently published a correspondence between the State Department and our generals, General Herron and others, who command in Texas and near the Mexican frontier. In this correspondence Mr. Seward asserts that Mexico is at war with France, and that the United States are under an imperative international obligation to observe a strict neutrality. Never was humbug more unblushingly asserted, and never was the most absolute ignorance—if nothing worse—so tinctured with untruth.

The Senate has many members, true American statesmen, who would manage the foreign ques-

---

In 1861 –'62 there was some plausibility in considering the Napoleonic invasion as an international war between France and Mexico. But with the establishment of Maximilian's usurpation, the war wholly changed its character. It is a civil war between a usurper and the rightful government of the Mexican people represented by Juarez. Napoleon takes sides with the usurper, and no international obligation forces a neutrality upon the United States, the old allies of the Mexican people and of the Mexican Republic. I challenge Mr. Seward to find any authority whatever among writers on international law by which he can sustain his false position; or to show for it any precedent in the world's history. Mr. Seward may find it expedient to allow Napoleon to slaughter a sister republic. Then he had better say so, instead of perverting the principles of international law and leading astray the administration and the country.

If the United States should attempt to establish a republic in Belgium or on any spot of Europe, no European power, and Louis Napoleon less than any other, would for a moment hesitate to meet force by force. It is likewise preposterous to say, that by opposing with arms Maximilian's usurpation, the United States *recklessly* provoke a war. It is Louis Napoleon who provokes a war in galling the patience of the American people, by establishing his French pickets along our frontiers. Mexico is already a French sinecure; French custom house officers are scattered along the Mexican frontiers, a Frenchman is the Secretary of Finances, and French drumcourts murder Mexican patriots. Recklessness and provocation are on Napoleon's side. Mr. Seward's behavior is nameless. The best that can be said in Mr. Seward's favor is that his diplomatic comprehension became confused by the alacrity and apparent unanimity of the European cabinets in recognizing the usurper. And in this Mexican-Maximilian question the cabinet of St. Petersburg alone among all European cabinets, and the Russian Legation at Washington, have shown consummate diplomatic tact, and a true, statesmanlike foresight. Paris and Vienna pressed the

tions better than Sumner. Such are Fessenden,
Grimes, Wade, Clark, Morrill, and several
others.

April 13.—Brownson, in his *Review*, almost
alone upholds the dignity of the American mind.
Brownson attacks Lincoln from the patriotic
standpoint, the copperheads from that of treason.
Mr. Lincoln does too much against the rebels,
say the conservatives and the copperheads;
Brownson and the radical patriots, in and out
of Congress, upbraid Lincoln for not doing
enough, for being undecided, hesitating, procrastinating.

April 14.—The Catos, the Cincinnatuses, the
Reguluses, etc., of the press are merciless against
Congress for having censured two of its members
for their treasonable speeches. This virtuous indignation would be excellent if this press had
made the slightest sacrifices for the cause, either
by free speech, or otherwise. What right has the
press to speak authoritatively to anybody, still
less to upbraid the members of Congress? The
"loyal" press devotes nothing to the cause of the
country, runs no risks, either material or others;
the press speculates on subscribers; generally
makes money in the most approved fashion.

---

complete recognition of Maximilian, but better advised, St.
Petersburg politely avoided getting entangled in any diplomatic
intercourse. When the hour of exodus strikes, Russia alone will
not be represented in the *cortége* of flying diplomats.—*Note
October* 2, 1865.

The so-called "arduous labors" of the proprietors, of the chief editors, are well, very well remunerated by the public. And what is that merchandise worth?

April 14.—Three years ago the rebels began the war, and began it at once with terrible earnestness. They *were* and *are* menacing, undaunted, and their words and acts are the same to-day as they were April 14th, 1861. But three years ago, if the North was earnest, its constitutional leaders and advisers were confused and not earnest. In that awful emergency, Mr. Lincoln was upholding a legal and constitutional fiction. Mr. Lincoln declared (see his proclamation) that he was to *defend* the property of the Union. Mr. Seward declared to the world that there was no rebellion, no civil war in America. General Scott spoke conciliation, anaconda, and strategy; but if strategy has any meaning in a war, it has it almost exclusively for a defensive war. To-day Lincoln and Seward would be glad if they could eat their own words of 1861, etc. The people has wasted torrents of blood, and millions upon millions of money and of money's worth, because the leaders dared not, wished not, and understood not how to be earnest.

April 14.—This time Congress makes *a faux pas*, but of course the press aids and even persuades Congress to venture it, and at the head of the blunder stands the dauntless Seward, who urges Congress to legislate for the foreign immigration to America. The Government and Congress had better leave immigration to itself. Liberty, wages, space and homesteads are the allurements which attract emigrants from all parts of Europe. At the utmost, Congress should only legislate that upon reaching America, the poor emigrants be preserved from sharks, and from thieves of all sizes and kinds; but to send commissioners to Europe, for the organization or encouragement of immigration, is to meddle with and confuse a social evolution, which emphatically depends upon free will and choice. Such agencies will end in creating trouble, disorder; and God grant that they may not contribute to cheat the emigrant!

April 14.—Gold rises, and of course all the imbeciles are highly alarmed. The *wise* press ditto. This rise is generated by some natural causes, such as the inborn tendency in man to hoard precious metals, and by artificial causes, such as the love of gambling, and of *agiotage*, both in this special case strongly stirred up by the treasonable sympathies of certain New York bankers, Christians and Jews, natural-born Americans and foreigners. Finally, the rise in gold—as I am positively informed—is created, or at least helped, by the operations of certain bankers to whom Jeff. Davis gives money with orders to break down, or at least to undermine the national credit and confidence. Poor fool, and poor fools! The country and the people are not exhausted, and all the combined efforts of Jews, traitors, and bankers will not bankrupt the people. Another rather natural cause of the rise is the littleness of brains in the highest governmental and administrative regions; this generates a certain want of confidence—not in the capacity of the nation—but in the capacity of her leaders. Congress is comparatively self-possessed, impassible and unmoved by the whoops and cries of imbecility and of *agiotage*, and Congress is right. The fever will abate or pass. A part of the "loyal" press is interested in Wall street and in the exchange; another part, influenced by inborn cowardice and narrow-mindedness, attributes the rise of gold to the attempt of Congress to expel a treacherous member; and of course Congress is lustily abused by these little, noisy, frightened barkers of the newspapers.

April 15.—Every time I come in contact with Grant, I admire his truly Republican simplicity. He must have the sacred fire in his heart and brain.

April 15.—The Government has in its hands all the threads of a most perfectly organized treason, by which direct, prompt, uninterrupted communications are almost daily established between Washington and the chiefs in Richmond. A plot was started in Richmond and Washington to bribe a commander of our cavalry, who was to give up his whole brigade to the rebels. The Government knows the names of persons who carried the treasonable negotiations, knows that money was spent, and knows where the money came from and who were the direct bribers, and notwithstanding, no serious proceedings are begun, no steps taken.

The supineness of the Government can only be explained upon the theory that very likely the gang of individuals who trade in treason in Washington on behalf of Richmond, occasionally betray Richmond to Washington. If such is the case, then the only *taken in* is our more than innocent Government.

April 15.—The boundless vitality, the relentless energy of the people alone keeps the country together, and but for the people and Congress, the Lincoln-Seward policy would have long ago shattered all to splinters. But Mr. Lincoln gets the credit for all, and the people is not conscious of its own virtue, and politicians cheat the people of its due and—*hurrah* for Lincoln!

I am afraid that Grant will be dragged down by the Lincoln-Halleck weight. This Halleck is utterly unfit for the duties of a chief-of-staff, or rather a general *du jour*, and his unfitness is intensified by his ill-will and envy. If any body, General Casey ought to have the place so unworthily filled by Halleck. Any sensible Government would give it to Casey, who has forgot more than Halleck ever knew of genuine military science and of organization. But incubus-

Halleck weighs down Lincoln, weighs down the army, weighs down the country.

April 16.—The partisans of Chase and Chase himself are blown up sky-high by the Lincolnites. But nobody dares to say to the people what Lincoln himself is, and how much of the mishaps are due to him and to his special favorites and predilections. Whatever success we have had is due principally to the people in towns, in villages, in the camps and in the armies. Success is due to some few Generals and naval officers, of whom not one is Mr. Lincoln's special choice; success is due to Stanton when Stanton is able to act without being trammeled by Lincoln. And to-day, when every nerve of the people, when all the energy of the Administration ought to concentrate in the army, the bickerings for re-election absorb the vitality of the Administration, throw disunion and disorganization into Congress, and palsy everything. Such is the true and sad story; such is the general and sorrowful feeling of the best men; and I record not only what I feel and judge myself, but I record, so to speak, the groans of the truest patriots.

April 16.—In the question of the sham free speech, the *Tribune* came to its senses, stopped short, and turned in the right direction. The *Times* continues to earn the applause of the most rabid organs of the copperheads, such as the *National Intelligencer* and the *World*. These various organs of public opinion—oh! oh!—are genuine institutions; one may do what he will, but it is impossible to avoid mentioning them or recording their opinions.

April 16.—The Congressional Committee on the Conduct of the War is unanimous in the opinion of Meade's utter incapacity to command any army whatever. Some of them class Meade even below McClellan, and I doubt not that this classification is just.

April 16.—The rebels ahead in inventions with large and small rams, and our Navy Department makes poor economies and paralyzes the active, inventive industry of private enterprise. The Navy Department does not understand that in the present circumstances mean economies are crimes. The people has a contempt for such; the people wants and clamors for vessels, batteries, iron-clads, and rams; the people wishes to pay well, provided the work is well done. An honest contractor ought to have all facilities open to him, instead of being hampered, trammeled, and even impoverished by red-tape. Small avarice—a profit to nobody. I accuse not Neptune-Methuselah-Van Winkle of any ill-will; he has the most honest intentions, but a rather slow convolution of the *cerebellum*. Time is always everything, and in the present circumstances time is even more than everything. But Lincoln and Neptune seem to have no comprehension, no consciousness of time. Look at

Charleston. By squandering *our time*, we gave *their time* to the rebels to make the bay of Charleston impassable and impregnable. (See vol. I and II.)

April 16.—With few exceptions, the diplomatic European *corps* here would be glad to see the Republicans expelled from the administration, and the old friends of the diplomats, the gambling, dining, chewing Democrats again there. *Pas encore,* dear diplomatic gentlemen, *pas encore.* To console themselves, these diplomats—monosyllabic Lord Lyons excepted—hobnob with copperheads and traitors, and are now in great glee on account of the *fait accompli* in Mexico. When the Northern Boreas once blows in that direction, easier than any cobweb the *fait accompli* will be swept away, and with it the European meddlesomeness. Maximilian may find his way to Mexico easy, but I hope he will never be able to return with a whole skin to Europe.

April 17.—Mr. Lincoln's and Seward's* apprenticeship in statesmanship, McClellan's and Halleck's in soldiering, cost this people hundreds of thousands of lives, and thousands of millions of money. And neither of those four, either

---

* Since 1861 Mr. Seward's political activity is an uninterrupted concatenation of false prophecies, blusterings, blunders, mistakes and misconstructions. Never and nowhere did a public man stand on such a *macedonic* pedestal, and the more mistakes and bad arguments, the greater Seward's glory.—*Note August,* 1865.

Lincoln, or Seward, or McClellan, or Halleck, show that they have learned anything.   And one of the four is to be the next President.

April 17.—In the case of the expulsion, the fiery, patriotic eloquence of a Winter Davis, of a Kelley and others, is opposed by the New York *Times* and the *Evening Post.*   Bats against eagles.

April 18.—The great drawback in the American mind is the religious respect and almost childish craving for a precedent.   Daring, adventurous, in the operations of the intellect, nevertheless in most emergencies the American anxiously looks around for a precedent.   He seems unable to decide between right and wrong and act upon it, until he believes he had found a precedent for his judgment and action.   Of course, exceptions are to be made to this generalization.   Some radical patriots, and some writers and thinkers, constitute these exceptions; but the general rule stands fast.   This respect for precedent rather denotes senility and weakness. Events do not look for, are not shaped after precedents, and mental vigor and self-consciousness originate, but neither copy nor imitate.   Happy for the salvation of the cause, of the country, and of the people, that the leading patriots in the two Congresses have been among the exceptions of which I speak; happy for the people that the radical patriots in the two Congresses have been independent of the all-confusing influence of the great metropolitan "loyal" press, which always leans on precedents; happy for the people that the struggle in the West seems to·have evoked to day-light Generals like Grant, and like Thomas, Sherman, McPherson, etc., who, to fight the enemy, look around and before them, and not backwards to precedents, and to the sham axioms of a petty school. All this is happy, or the cause would have been lost long ago.

When discussing military movements, the press generally makes an immense display of *strategical* knowledge and precedents—always wrongly selected and wrongly applied. Cyrus, Alexander, Epaminondas, Cæsar, Frederick the Great, Napoleon, did not imitate, but created, and, so to speak, established precedents. Again, when traitors are to be expelled from Congress, the press tries to overawe the patriots by an array of sham precedents, and innocently runs to the rescue of treason.

April 18.—The Committee on the Conduct of the War has published its report on the Florida crime, but nothing is elucidated; all remains smoky and cloudy. The principal agent, the *familiaris* of the White House, Major Hay, was not before the Committee at all; the Committee is taken in, and the whole bloody intrigue will remain hushed up. I emphatically assert that the affair was concocted between Gillmore and Lincoln, previous to the correspondence between Gillmore on one side, and Stanton and Halleck

on the other, as published in the report. I have
the best authority possible for this assertion.
General Gillmore is evidently an overrated man.
He may be, or even is, a good second or third
rate artillery officer, as he showed at the shelling
of Fort Pulaski. I learn positively that some
influential Irishmen from Brooklyn found means
to make Greeley enthusiastic for Gillmore's
transcendent capacities; Greeley communicated
his enthusiasm to Lincoln, and so Gillmore was
entrusted with the command before Charleston,
and succeeded in —— nothing. (See vol. II,
about the plans of Gillmore being submitted to
Mr. Lincoln and approved by him.)

April 18.— *We are in a state of transition,* say
many Americans, and 'some of them the loftiest,
the most original and genuine American hearts
and minds. Such a one is the poet Walt Whitman. But what is a state of transition? when
and where does it begin, when and where does it
end? Man as an individual or as a *concreto,* as
mankind, as race, as humanity, is uninterruptedly
growing, developing, progressing. Stagnation is
death, and *per contra* nothing is done by leaps.
Nature labors uninterrupted by growth and
decomposition; nature uninterruptedly combines
and produces. So does man; all is change and
transition, from yesterday towards to-day, from
to-day towards to-morrow. All that grows and
lives, grows and lives through an uninterrupted
chain of formation and transition. The cells in

us are formed, grow, are used up, destroyed and recreated every second of our life, and thus our body, our brains, our senses, our apperceptions and appreciations are an endless transition.

April 19.—Of what kind are the original germs of good in human nature? Man is a living, thinking and moral being. Organic nature constitutes *animalism;* the union of the living and reasoning nature constitutes humanity; the union of reason and of morality constitutes an individuality. When our will is ruled by our moral nature, when duty is the absolute rule of our actions, and when pure reason lights these actions and directs them in a straight line, then the man, the individual is good, and fulfills his mission or apostolate among men. O, Lincoln-ites! how is it with Lincoln?

April 19.—What airs the "loyal" press takes towards Congress! Let pass the *Herald,* or Washington *Intelligencer,* or *World,* or *Boston Courier,* or similar! All these offer incense to false gods; one to the god of lies and humbug, the others to the demon of copperheadism and treason, so of course Congress must be nauseous to them. But the "loyal" Press seems to consider it to be its special calling to roughly handle Congress.

The "loyal" press is below Congress in patriotism, in devotion, in sacrifice, in intelligence, in wisdom, in knowledge, and in culture. When the "loyal" press attempts to play Draco,

Solon, Lycurgus, Cato, or any such consecrated characters, that press ought to be like Cæsar's wife in the tragedy, or *sans peur et sans reproche,* like the chivalric Bayard ; besides, the press ought to have some scientific ballast. Such a press I have seen at times in Europe. The virtuous press in America oscillates between interest and principle, looks to subscribers *of course,* and to office or patronage from the Government, or simply speculates in stocks, etc., etc., etc., like any other *sharp* mortal, and then takes an *apodictic* tone with the public at large, and in particular with Congress.

———— Namque,
Neglectis urenda felix innascitur agris.

April 19.—It will forever remain unknown, and no investigator, no historian will ever be able to discover and bring to daylight the fact to what an immeasurable extent Mr. Lincoln's meddling and personal willfulness fatally influenced events in general, but above all the military operations. Most of the great, small, and smallest disasters are generated by the inefficiency of commanders; and Mr. Lincoln's personal willfulness has always presided over the choice of most of the Brigadier and Major Generals.

April 19.—The various moral, intellectual and animal qualities and characteristics of the African excite to a great heat the press, the pulpit, and Congress. The pro-slaveryists make the most incongruous, the most daring, and the most ignorant assertions, and along the *whole line* they are answered with stale generalities, sentimentalities, and common-places. The economists like H. Carey alone constitute an exception. If the anti-slavery Reverends and Doctors would only mix a little of real science with their studies of the Pentateuch, of Genesis, of Deuteronomy, etc., what easy work they would have with their opponents.

April 19.—At the Baltimore fair, Mr. Lincoln makes an out and out abolition, woolly-head, anti-slavery, and radical speech. Bravo! But it looks a little like a bid for the Presidency. Nevertheless, bravo!

However, one can not forget that the circumstances, the emergencies are the same to-day as they were three years ago, and tutored by Seward

> *Stultus and improbus hic amor es*
> *Dignusque notari.*

Where was Mr. Lincoln then? The radicals stand to-day where they stood three years ago; it took Mr. Lincoln three years to limp after them, and perhaps if not stimulated by re-election, Mr. Lincoln would not yet have reached that position. *Better late than never,* says the proverb, but that "late" cost the people torrents of blood, millions of money and—time; and Mr. Lincoln does not seem to comprehend the value at least—of time. If Lincoln be re-elected, and his Sewards and Blairs retained—then, judging from the past, the people will be always in advance, with Lincoln and his crew heavily dragging in the rear.

The next four years will evoke new and momentous emergencies, and generate events and complications; but in harmony with Mr. Lincoln's so admired, slow and procrastinating policy, solutions which emphatically may be required to be given in 1865, will find Mr. Lincoln *ready for the question* some time about 1867.

In that same speech in Baltimore, Mr. Lincoln threatens and promises retaliation for the infamous massacre at Fort Pillow. I hope Mr. Lincoln may keep his word—but—I doubt—nay, I am sure that it will end in words. The best men in Congress, above all, in the Senate, Wade, Chandler, Wilkinson, Wilson, Morrill, Trumbull, etc., a year ago urged him to make a declaration of retaliation; but Mr. Lincoln did not. Perhaps he is aware that the rebels know him well, and would have disbelieved his words; or that the Sewards, Blairs, Weeds, and such ones, would have found means to inform the public that he was not at all serious about retaliation.

April 20.—As the Washington winds raise clouds of dust filled with atoms of offal putrified in the streets and alleys, so in all parties, among copperheads as well as among Republicans, election and re-election fill the air with all kinds of fœtid miasma. All the worst and meanest passions are stirred, and they rise like gases to the surface. And pre-eminent in all this are the princes of corruption on both the political sides. And their name is legion. And since I see what I see here in Washington, I conclude that the administration or Government proper is not the focus, the seat, the generator of intrinsic corruption. Therein consists the difference between the corruption as I witnessed it prevail in certain European Governments and as it is here. Thus in Bourbonic Naples, or in Russia before Alexander II, the officials of all grades were the generators and disseminators of the governmental and administrative corruption. Here, in the immense majority of cases, the official is approached, is tempted, is tampered with by a corrupter who belongs to almost all the various social strata and gradations. For this reason, when the election winds begin to blow, the air becomes filled with corruptors belonging to the various parties, the *ins* and the *outs* being equally eager at work.

During this whole period of the civil war, a period so propitious to administrative malfeasance, millions upon millions have been squandered, partly by recklessness, partly by inexperience, partly by incapacity, and partly by corruption; but few, very few, are the cases of officials at the center of Government to whom public animadversion points as corrupt. And such ones are detected. Congress likewise stands rather unstained. But the administration and Congress are both surrounded with all kinds of Weeds, of lobby-men, etc., etc., who come to Washington from all parts of the country, and belong to almost all social, commercial, and professional pursuits and occupations, such as bar, press, doctors of divinity and medicine.

April 20.—The present and coming generation, and above all the future historian, ought conscientiously and carefully to study the acts and doings of the 37th Congress and of the terrible complications which surrounded that political body. The 37th Congress laid out the work of salvation for its successors, and did it itself; it toiled amidst such complications as almost never surrounded any political body whatever. Only the historian must not look to the press of the day as a source of information on the character of that Congress, the immensity of its labors, and the difficulties which it had to overcome.

April 22.—For more than a year the papers and the reports of various military commanders are filled with records of murders committed by cowardly bushwhackers roving all over the Southwest, and above all, in Virginia. These cowardly murderers desecrate even the name of guerrillas. Of course, *southern gentlemen* and Virginia F. F. V.'s are the leaders of these murderous gangs. When Halleck-Lieber published their scientific disquisition on guerrillas, in the name of common sense I protested, asserting that energy and force, and not disquisitions,

13

would strike with terror the murderers, and stop their cowardly *saturnalia*. Events side with me. Not one guerrilla has been punished. When one is taken, the oath of allegiance is administered, and then the murderer is let loose, and continues his murderous work. It seems that either Lincoln, Seward, Blair, or Halleck are more interested to spare the murderers than to spare the lives of their loyal and brave victims. And so the murderers have it their own way.

April 22.—The Lincolnites of the Seward-Blair gang begin to distrust Grant. They are afraid to find in him a rival for the Presidency. But Grant is a patriot, a soldier, an honest man, and spurns all such suggestions. Nevertheless, the gang of the White House is terribly frightened, and those of them near the helm may attempt to play tricks and hinder Grant's success. Such accusations are made, but I rely on Stanton. Still, I am certain that in some way or other Meade will palsy everything and ruin Grant.

April 22.—Good and honest men arriving from the interior of the various States, almost unanimously assert that the re-election of Lincoln can not be avoided, and that the net as woven by office-holders and by patronized contractors is so thick that no ray of truth can penetrate it. All these good men sullenly submit to what they consider to be an unavoidable evil. Oh, why have the Fremont men begun a flirtation with the Democrats, the copperheads, and the *World?*

All this has immensely increased Mr. Lincoln's chances.

April 23.—The strength of nicknames. The people is taken in by the nickname, *honest Abe.* I impeach not the honesty of Mr. Lincoln, nor even the honesty of his political intentions. But was Mr. Lincoln honest with Lyon, with Fremont, with Hunter, when he used them up and then adopted their initiatory measures? Was he honest—politically—when he made assertions and promises to the conservatives and the radicals, well aware that if he kept word with the right, then necessarily he humbugged the left? Was he honest to the people's blood when he appointed Generals for political purposes, or when he yielded to the suggestions and the influence of a Seward, or when he made a compact with the Blairs against the radicals? Was Mr. Lincoln honest towards Wadsworth during the canvass of 1862? Is he honest towards the Africo-Americans when as yet the murders at Fort Pillow are not avenged?

I wish I could say of Lincoln's political honesty :

> —————— *at ingenium ingens*
> *Inculto latet hoc sub corpore.*

But——I can not. .

April 23.—The Africo-Americans enlist no more as ardently and with such a good will as they did six months ago. The Africo-Americans can not be blamed. Mr. Lincoln retaliates in words and not in deeds, and the rebels act worse than cannibals with the colored prisoners. Then the arrogant stupidity of many commanders must have necessarily scared and disgusted that population. When the officers understand how to handle and lead them, the Africo-Americans fight like men, and stand and fall by their brave and humane officers. Many among the best officers would prefer that the African regiments should form separate divisions, or even a separate corps, and that of course the like corps, division, or brigades, etc., should be exclusively commanded by such officers as have confidence in the men. Such was my original plan, (see vol. II,) and now experienced men confirm my suggestions.

April 23.—Fearful disaster on the Red River. Banks has no luck notwithstanding his good, earnest will, and notwithstanding that he has the "first" West-Point graduates with him. After all, Banks ought to give up soldiering; he is a patriot, an excellent administrator, but war seems not to have taught him much. To put his wagons in front when marching in an enemy's country—to have his van-guard or cavalry miles off! Of course disaster, fearful disaster was inevitable. But Banks had with him Franklin, and Franklin is synonymous with disaster. Besides, this Red river expedition had no meaning, no sense; this expedition looks like a separate, reckless episode among the general

warlike operations.   Texas is not subdued, nor is
the interior of Louisiana conquered.   It will tell
very hard against the unfortunate Banks.   But
it will be interesting to know who originated this
cursed expedition.   Is it cotton?   Or has Lincoln-Halleck assented to it, or is it Banks's own?
Fearful loss in men, and material; and shame,
not on the brave, devoted soldiers and their commanders, but on the originators, on the concocters!   I regret Banks's miscarriage.

April 24.—Mr. Lincoln's reconstruction* proclamation—(is it or is it not a statute law?) works
rather muddily.   In Louisiana Banks carried it

---

* Mr. Seward's *pronunciamento* at Auburn.   North and South
the country has to learn that the reconstruction policy is not
Johnson's own, but belongs to the precedent Administration,
that is to Lincoln-Seward, and as Mr. Lincoln is no more, Seward is the creator and inherits the credit for it.   This, above all,
the grateful South has to bear in mind until the presidential
election in 1868.   To secure the South Mr. Seward outherods
Calhoun in the States-rights theory.   Did not Seward inform
Adams and Palmerston of the character of that policy long before Mr. Johnson's advent?   *Ipse dixit.*   Then in substance: "I,
Seward, discovered Johnson's qualities and I made him a patriot
and a Governor of Tennessee, and a Vice-President, and of
course a President."   I forego comment on the decency of
passing in review the President and the Cabinet; decency and
blind egotism never house together.   Mr. Seward condescend-
ingly and paternally pats on the back the President and all the
past and actual members of the Cabinet.   Benevolence, forgiveness, love, not merely ooze but pour from every word.
Perfect, perfect Christian gentleman and *the* candidate for 1868!
The patriarch sends his hearers home and blesses them with the
scriptural *cresite et multiplicamini.*—*Note October* 24, 1865.

out, and—it seems that the confusion is at its climax, and there is no end of complications between the action of the new semi-civil Governor, and the half civil half military proconsular power; add to the last the full military power of General Canby, who is to take the command of all that *cis-Mississippi* region.

April 24.—I record what I have certain reasons to believe to be true. It is commonly asserted that Mr. Lincoln has sent a certain Lewis or Louis on a secret mission to the Arkansas slaveholders of dubious or of vacillating loyalty, to assure them that for the present they may use their slaves as before. The Union military commanders in that region are instructed in conformity with that liberticide permission. General Thomas, who heartily and with great devotion organized the Africo-Americans on the Mississippi, was instructed not to arm the laborers on liberated plantations. This order to Thomas had in view not to frighten the —slaveholders. It smells Seward-Blair. The arming of laborers was suggested by Wadsworth, (see Wadsworth's report.) So the liberated Africo-Americans on plantations will remain defenceless, and be easily slaughtered by the white murderers. O, small church! *hurrahing* for Lincoln!

April 24.—A rebel ram, the Albemarle, sinks three gunboats, makes general havoc, sweeps our vessels from the Sound, and we lose men, a fort, vessels, and a strong position. Further. The rebels organize a full torpedo corps and our men perish. We have no rams to meet the Albemarle, but Mr. Secretary Welles is very active to ——secure re-election, and takes a very high ground against those who wish to postpone the Baltimore Convention. Well, the losses in men and material occasioned by the rebel rams and torpedoes must be credited to Mr. Secretary Welles.

April 25.—I wonder that the marble of the White House does not sweat blood on Lincoln, Blair, Seward, Welles, Halleck, and on all the familiars and henchmen!

April 25. — Copperheads, Southern sympathizers, Democrats, surround Grant with all kind of blandishments to induce him to give McClellan a command in the army. But Grant will not disgrace himself and the army by such an act; Grant has the true estimate of McClellan's capacity, and would not trust him with a *platoon* of twenty-five men.

April 25.—Butler's activity creates great uneasiness in the White House and among the most ardent Lincolnites. Butler's genuine availability for the Presidency is recognized by all, and any, even the smallest *coup d'eclat* before Richmond, would carry him into the White House. *Of course,* the Lincoln crew in power will take care that Butler has no success.

April 26.—The Sewardites, the Lincolnites,

call "factious" everybody who prefers to uphold his convictions above expediency, or above self-interest. "Expediency" is the great sacramental word. Every day I meet good, earnest men cursing the expediency which forces them to support Lincoln's re-election.

April 26.—This week may be decisive. The army is on the move, or perhaps is already moving. Grant has the cursed inheritance of all the bloody, criminal faults and mistakes committed by his predecessors in command, and above all, the inheritance of the more than accursed McClellan's and Meade's ungeneralship. All the former commanders in some way or other built up the military halo surrounding Lee, and what is worse, their almost treasonable imbecility has virtually fortified all the strong positions occupied now by the rebel army.

Grant has no free choice for his movements and for the way in which he may inaugurate the new campaign. He is fatally chained to what was done before he took command. And between here and the rebels, and all around the rebel army, the configuration of the country favors the rebels and wars against him. He cannot move freely and by his choice; not easily, or rather almost not at all can he flank Lee, and flank him by such rapid movements as to come in the rear of the rebels, press Lee north, and take a position between Richmond and the rebel army. If Grant had had the command of the army in

February or March, 1862, he would have been in Richmond before even the then hastily retreating rebels could have reached it. But McClellan was afraid even of the shadow cast behind by the flying rebels. Lee is to-day entrenched, and Meade has given to Lee all the needed leisure to do it. Lee never will abandon his entrenchments and come out for a free fight. Finally, Grant cannot make a too large circuit with his army, and leave Lee within three days of forced marches from Washington. And the worst fatality pressing on Grant is to have a Meade to execute his orders; Meade fully McClellanized, and with a strong faith in Lee's invincibility.

April 26.—When they captured Plymouth, the rebels indiscriminately massacred the whites and the Africo-Americans.*　I am never astonished

---

* To palsy the efforts of the confessors of right and justice, the copperheads and all the Southern rebels maintain that the Africo-American is wholly unfit for free labor, that with free labor the emancipated race will die out, and several other equally malicious, false, illogical and inhuman axioms. To strengthen their assertions, all these confessors of darkness, lies and violence point to some local disturbances and to the fact that the emancipated are at present unwilling to work, and that they crowd into cities. It is not so generally. But accepting such exceptional facts to be even more or less general, the unwillingness of the emancipated to work now on plantations generally results from the confusion created by the half measures of emancipation, and by the dread of the freedmen to become again the prey of planters and of rebels. And if this whole generation of freedmen should find labor repulsive, and be unable to work otherwise than under compulsion, the fact would prejudice

at any cannibalism and infamy whatever perpetrated by the rebels; it is their natural, congenial element. I should be astonished to find them acting like honorable, humane, or even half-civilized beings. Mr. Lincoln makes menacing speeches, promises to "take into consideration, etc.," and all this time the rebels murder our men. Poor Lincoln! He is not familiar with precedents, with the logic of events, and with the reasons justifying retaliation, and it is not the brains of a Seward, of a Halleck, of a Blair, or of a Florida Hay that can throw any light—even the dimmest—to enlighten and to direct him.

It is absurd to assert that retaliation is to be applied to the person or persons who especially committed a murderous act. An abyss separates the appreciation of a private and of a public crime. The murderers at Fort Pillow, at Plymouth, and all the highwaymen or pseudo-guer-

---

nothing. This present generation of Freedmen is the summing up of centuries of most atrocious degradation. It is the fruit of slavery and of slaveholders. This generation of freedmen is such as the "patriarchal institution" made them under such patriarchs as the planters, the slavebreeders and all kinds of similar chivalry. Those patriarchs equally degraded and brutalized the poor whites, who are *Anglo-Saxons*, (Amer.) If by no other stimulus, *necessity* will soon make a good laborer from the freedman. THE STRUGGLE FOR LIFE, this great law of Nature discovered by the immortal Darwin, will decide the condition of the Africo-American; but the *struggle* will only be decisive when liberty, civilization and laws give to the emancipated intellectual arms at least equal to those now in the hands of their oppressors.—*Note October* 16, 1865.

rillas do not act as private individuals, but represent a complete policy of their chiefs, and murder under orders. Retaliation, therefore, must be applied to every one constituting a part of the gang of revolters, and not to those especially and exclusively who committed the murder. The only way to retaliate with success would be to select by lot from among the rebel prisoners—the superior officers, and not the rank and file—an equal number to that murdered at Forts Plymouth and Pillow, and to shoot them. Such is the true retaliation, and it is the only way that it ever has been or can be logically applied. Look at history.

The disaster in Albermarle Sound * is deeply felt by our naval officers, although it is not at

---

* Lieutenant Cushing, with a crew as heroic and as devoted as himself, has blown up and destroyed the rebel ram Albemarle. But Welles and his Department are as innocent of this glorious action as any unborn babies.—*Note August*, 1865.

a I read in the papers that Commodore Craven, commander of the wooden frigate, the Niagara, is to be court martialed for not having attacked in the Bay of Biscay, the rebel ironclad and double-ender, the Stonewall Jackson.

Every one recollects that the Stonewall was considered the most formidable ironclad craft on the ocean, that it moves on its pivot, and thus could turn on the spot; when the Niagara requires at least half a mile to perform the same manœuvre. Then the metal of the Stonewall was heavier than the metal and armament of the wooden Niagara. To attack the Stonewall would have been the same as to attack the rocks of Gibraltar. The Niagara would have been butted and sunk in no time, without in the slightest preventing the Stonewall from pursuing its

all their fault that the rebels are ahead of us in
naval constructions.　It is not the fault of Golds-
borough that the rebels had a Merrimac, and the
first day we had nothing to oppose to them.
Farragut, at New Orleans, with his wooden vessels, fought against rams and ironcased floating
batteries.　Farragut overpowered them, not by
the aid of any superior material means furnished

---

course.　If the Stonewall was to enter a harbor put under the
defense of the Niagara, then Craven might be blameable for not
persisting in the defense.　But in the Bay of Biscay no honorable or any other necessity existed, and Commodore Craven
would have acted like a madman if he had exposed his craft and
his crew to unavoidable destruction, thus procuring an easy but
resounding triumph to the rebels over the flag of the Union.

No government in the world has on record such a malicious
and cowardly prosecution as this of Commodore Craven by the
Secretary of the Navy and his associates. men, all of them, who
have never smelt gunpowder, never scrambled through a man-
of-war, or up a mast.　If any one is to be tried it is Mr. Secretary Welles and his red-tape crew for having *always* and everywhere obliged our heroic sailors to meet the rebel ironclad
batteries without any other resources than their own bravery
and such scanty means as they could procure themselves.　The
first day of the Merrimac, the rebel ram Arkansas, the naval
battle in the mouth of the Mississippi in 1862, the ram Albemarle, even the fight in the bay of Mobile, are so many evidences
against Mr. Welles.　Farragut and the heroes under him, by their
courage and ready wit, made up for the material deficiencies and
administrative shortcomings of the Navy Department.　If the
Secretary of the Navy court martials commanders of wooden
ships for not fighting and destroying the most formidable iron-
clads, then the Secretary implicitly recognizes the superiority of
wood over iron.　Why then spend millions in the construction of
monitors and other ironclads?—*Note November* 6, 1865.

to him by the Navy Department, but by the indomitable bravery of his officers and men, and his own heroic, dauntless devotion. All the victories and successes of our navy are exclusively due to the officers and crew, and not to any administrative foresight, not to any fertility in resources, or capacity of the naval administrative clique in Washington.

April 27.—Burnside goes with his corps to the army of the Potomac. I pity him. He is good, honest, devoted, but has no capacity whatever for the field. He will lose in the field whatever there remains of him, and of the good name won at the defense of Knoxville. But Burnside is a General after Lincoln's heart and brains, and Lincoln virtually will deal him the finishing blow.

April 27.—A would-be serious periodical called the *Atlantic* gravely asserts that the country cannot find a more experienced pilot than Mr. Lincoln. Experienced in what? in blundering and shifting? Mr. Lincoln has not yet proved in any act whatever that he has acquired any knowledge and experience of the men around him and in his councils. Events and the decided partiality of the best and most patriotic men sustain Stanton more than any attraction felt towards him by Lincoln. A Seward, a Blair, a Weed, are still Mr. Lincoln's familiar spirits. Lincoln's experience of events goes hand in hand with his experience of men. Has

Mr. Lincoln foreseen any breakers? has he skill-fully untied or solved any of the riddles and knots which daily emergencies evoke before his eyes? Experience in shifting, in delaying, in procrastinating, in pushing away and postponing for to-morrow what ought to be done to-day; experience in always deciding only to act when heavy losses force him to make an onward step, or change and give up his stubbornness. Such experience is rather a curse.

The country has really experienced men, but the scales on your eyes, O! farseeing gentlemen, are too heavy and too opaque; you cannot discern the light from the dark, the right from the wrong, nonsense from common sense. The country, the people are not so poor in sound and luminous brains as you make it out. Besides some names pointed out by the best and most patriotic men, the loyal Governors, as of Massachusetts, Maine, Indiana, Illinois, Pennsylvania, in one word, of all the loyal States, (the disloyal Seymourite of New York excepted,) have all of them shown more energy, far-sightedness, and varied administrative capacities than has Mr. Lincoln in any act during these fatal three years. And I am certain that each of those Governors in his respective sphere is better surrounded than Mr. Lincoln. The Blairs, the Lamons, the Hays, the Nicolays, the Wallachs, cannot be outdone. The country, the people are not so poor in brains as you, O! dark-lantern luminaries, make it out.   Both Houses of Congress contain many clear-sighted, energetic, high-minded patriots, whose steadiness, firmness, and experience in men and in things are of the true metal.

April 27.—The rebel ram has driven us from the Roanoke and has it its own way. Neptune-Methuselah ought to go to the river to butt the rebel ram with his wig.

April 27.—O, could I only condense the vocabulary of all nations, idioms and times, to give their due to the American politicians* and to the American press! The various losses and disasters which so rapidly struck us during this month, Florida included, are discussed by politicians only from the re-election's point of view.

---

* In the pages of volume II I expressed the ardent hope that, the war over, the dirty breed of politicians would disappear, and a new, purer, nobler generation would fill this, in the American polity, so necessary function. But as yet there are no signs of a new era on the nation's horizon. All the same old rotten hacks and corruptors agitate the surface of the political activity. They transform the administration into a sewer whatever may be the efforts of the men in power. Now it is even worse, as the whole Democratic-copperhead offal is *unchained* and let loose on the administrative peristiles. The most venomous opponents and the most billingsgate objurgators of Mr. Johnson pending the presidential canvass of 1864 are now up and at him for favors. Nevertheless I still hope that a few years hence all this corrupt superstratum, composed from the offal of both the parties, will disappear, and a healthier political growth will brighten the people's life.—*Note Washington, Sept.* 27, 1865.

Not a man boldly tells the truth, and thousands upon thousands are ready to lie at the shortest notice.

April 27.—How boldly Lincoln's cronies, above all the Sewards and Blairs, wallow in the mud! The Blairs attack Chase by contract and for a reward; which reward Lincoln—of course—will grant and pay. And the press is mute or indifferent. The mean way in which Chase is attacked, and the public corruption, make me indignant.

Still I hope; I have faith in the people's righteousness; I hope that before long the people will wash off the thick mud with which luminaries and politicians have besmeared its eyes and its consciousness, and I hope that for the Presidential election nothing will be left of Lincoln. .

April 28.—The Italian artists generally complain that Englishmen (alias Anglo-Saxons) applaud an artist always in the wrong time; that is, they applaud, they get excited and delirious with delight when the artist himself feels he has committed a *cuack*, and not deserved the applause. In a certain way Americans assert their pure Anglo-Saxon origin. The American luminaries, wiseacres, writers, critics, classical and not classical scholars, first graduates of first honors, rhetors, etc., etc.—all of them generally are enraptured with a bad idea, a distorted action, a wrong man.

April 29.—Since the rebel ram Albemarle

swept us from the Sound, we lose position after position all along the interior of North Carolina, besides being altogether unable to blockade Wilmington.   During the time that Welles pondered, listening—or not—to his advisers and to the various cliques, composed of academicians and of simple mortals, and while he pedantically cramped the SOAR of the people's inventive and constructive fertility and powers—the rebels built rams.   For one ram that the rebels bring out we ought to have ten of various draft and size; but we have Welles.   I regret that Fox is in the same team.

April 29.—Thank you!   O, thank you!   O, Mr. Lincoln!   I began to doubt my own judgment and conscience.   For the first time in my life I almost began to be frightened at standing alone, and speaking out boldly what many, many feel but dare not utter.   But I was right; and you, O Lincoln! you willingly give evidence and sustain me.

In his letter to certain Kentuckians, or to a Hodges, Mr. Lincoln candidly confesses that he never foresaw any event, but that he always was behind events; and that every time when anybody else, as Cameron, Fremont, and Hunter, was ahead of events, he at once pushed him aside.   It is such a limping statesmanship, such backwardness in Mr. Lincoln that for three years I have recorded in the volumes of my

14

Diary, and therefore, I do not believe him to be the right man in the right place.

Of course the Lincolnites and the *good* press admire this Christian virtue, candidly confessing its own shortcomings and sins. This *mea culpa* may open the doors of Paradise, but it costs blood, life, and money to the American people.

April 30.—Notwithstanding all the villainous intrigues and delays of the copperheads and the partisans of the rebels in both Houses, the Republicans in Congress remain true to the people and to their sacred mission. The laws passed by them during this session secure to these noble patriots the gratitude of history.

MAY.

May 1.—Never was treason more exasperated and consequently more rampant than it was in Washington during the whole preceding month of April. Propped up and sustained by the copperheads in and out of Congress, the numerous Washington secessionists were and are defiant. Copperheads and secessionists spout contempt on the efforts of the patriots, and forebode for Grant worse defeats than those earned by McClellan. If so, it will prove that Grant has not sufficiently purified the army.

May 1.—One is awe-struck when surveying the almost boundless space of the theatre of war. Before its expansion and immensity all the theatres of war as recorded in history, collapse and disappear in nothingness. When Alexander the Great was beyond the pyramids, or almost touched the Indus, he only warred where he was, and peace or at least quiet prevailed at all other points of his dominions. The wars of Republican and of the first centuries of Imperial Rome did not extend simultaneously throughout all the Roman world. When Aurelian pursued Zenobia to the farthest eastern limits of the empire, its western limits enjoyed a comparative quiet. Napoleon's legions once extended from Madrid to Moscow, yet the fight raged rather only on the two extremities of that extensive line. But here blood flows on an uninterrupted line of almost several thousands of miles. Add to it the new element of the strategic points and lines as created by the nets of the central knots of various railroads, add to it many other various direct and contingent elements, forces and data, and all of them such as even a Napoleon had not to encounter and cope with. A mind which has to embrace this immense space with its variety of forces, agencies, and data, might easily become dizzy, confused, and commit mistakes.

. This American war must not therefore be appreciated, judged, reviewed, or criticised with Jomini—or with any other theoretical book—in hand. Mistakes are unavoidable, and therefore pardonable. Thus Grant may commit mistakes. But McClellan and Meade violated all the eternal rules of science and of sound common sense, and such violations always become unpardonable crimes.

May 1.—Mr. Seward makes a speech at the Baltimore fair, which is a last and a desperate bid for the Presidency. Mr. Seward explains how nicely he would have saved the

Union if—he was the President, or if—at least—he could have had his own Sewardian ways. The "I" is the upshot of the whole speech. "Take me; here I am; I alone, capable to save you and to perform wonders; take me at the last, the eleventh hour." This is the key-note of that *Sewardiana*.

May 2.—During three heavy years Mr. Seward has dabbled in international laws and has not mastered even their rudimentary elements. In the case of the Sir William Peel, captured in the Rio Grande, Mr. Seward's knowledge again splendidly corruscates. His statesmanlike · brow reddens not with shame when English admirals—with a *sham* good nature—sermonize our brave and faithful commanders, and lecture them on international laws and on similar questions; when the greedy Englishmen enlighten our navy, saying that England cannot suffer a *would-be* violation of the Mexican waters, and that our navy is to look on quietly when English blockade-runners unload in Texas their contraband of war for the rebels; when the English minister and the English admiral recklessly attempt to insinuate, nay, even to force into practice, a new and for England profitable rule or theory about the right of capture inside or outside of the maritime league. Mr. Seward rebuffs not these arrogant English encroachments; asks not England by what right she pretends to defend the integrity of the Mexican neutrality and waters; asks not England since when she has assumed this strange protectorate over the waters of other independent nations; but like a good Christian, he meekly submits his checks and virtually and in principle delivers our navy to her enemies and espouses the English assumptions.*

---

* During the whole war, nay even up to to-day, when engaged with the English Cabinet in the discussion of various principles of international law, Mr. Seward has been always rather worsted in close, logical argument, and it is because of his unfamiliarity not only with international laws, but with the history of his own country. Further, Mr. Seward has displayed a most astounding unfamiliarity with the bearing, the meaning, the reach and the use of expressions strictly technical in international laws and in diplomacy.

I. When discussing that hasty and evil-intentioned recognition of the rebels in the character of belligerents, instead of resorting to commonplace spreadeagleism, it ought to have been so easy for Mr. Seward to shame England by recalling to the memory of the English statesmen the statutes and the orders in Council in 1775–76 published against the neutrals by the English Parliament and the English government, and which laws and orders in Council forced the neutral European powers to unite and to proclaim the Armed Neutrality.

II. In filing a bill in the English chancery court for the claim of the United States as successors to the rebel or Confederate government as being a *de facto* one, Mr. Seward recognized the *legal* existence of the rebel government, and before the law Mr. Seward may make the United States liable for all the debts contracted by the Confederate government. Mr. Seward seems to accept the inheritance pure and simple, giving up the *beneficium legis and inventarii.*

III. Mr. Seward assured Lord Lyons that it was wholly indifferent if the rebel or enemy's property was transferred on

May 2.—Tax! Tax! Tax! is now the shibboleth, and the men in Congress who faithfully perform their duty are exposed to all kinds of animosities, contumely, and lies. Never, in any, even the most overtaxed country was taxation such a difficult task and question for solution as it is here. The solution given by such practical and honest men, as are the patriots in the two Houses, is given without the aid of professors, doctors and wiseacres, of which the House has none, and the Senate only one, and that in the " classical rhetoric " line.

---

neutral bottoms before or after the proclamation of the blockade. Of course Lord Lyons informed his government of this large concession made by the Secretary of State; the English government informed the English ship owners, who may thus have acted in *bona fide* and carried rebel goods. But our cruisers seized the carriers, and our courts condemned the prizes, the courts paying more respect to the international laws than to Mr. Seward's international fancies.

So repeatedly Mr. Seward by exchange of notes has tried to establish international principles, nay almost to conclude treaties. *Risum teneate amici.*

Then of what use is it to call names when one shrinks from acting up to his words. I consider the Semmes, the Maffits, the Waddells, the rest of them in principle and in fact to have been outlaws and pirates. But Mr. Seward's recognition of belligerents throws over such pirates a belligerent character. And if Mr. Seward considered them to be pirates, why, when they fell into our hands, does the Government treat them as belligerent prisoners? Why the *pirates* of the Florida under Mr. Seward's ægis have haughtily strutted in Washington and paraded the pirate's garb!

Such are a few from among the uncounted evidences of Mr. Seward's deep international mind.—*Note October,* 1865.

To harmonize the so varied, and seemingly so contrary and even inimical interests of the multifarious industries, productions and regions, and then the wants of the producer and the consumer, to fuse into one the agricultural and the industrial interests, and not to sacrifice the one to the other; to take care of the depressed, of the poorer in the community; to reach the capitalist who generally escapes, and in all countries has hitherto escaped all the attempts of a taxer; to overcome the natural repulsion of the native-born and of the emigrant to any kind of imposition; to guard and secure the new law against all the subterfuges and evasions to which the private interest, so fertile in expedients, will recur to cheat the treasury and the people at large—such have been among the prominent solutions which Congress had to give, and it gave them honestly, positively, and with the utmost lucidity and precision. As it stands on the statute-book this law of taxation is one of the greatest victories of a patriotic self-government; it is one evidence more that aggregated intelligent atoms legislate better than any single one or even several of the so-called "representative men."

Excepting Henry Carey and his school, almost all the men considered to be of any practical authority, almost all the wiseacres who here and there have perused some few books on political economy and on finance, the whole pernicious and unpatriotic·sect of free traders as the New York *Evening Post*, all the pro-slaveryists, all the copperheads, all the spurious Democrats outside of Congress and in the community at large, condemn and curse the patriots. No effort is omitted to stir up the vilest prejudices and passions, to throw all imaginable impediments before the progress of the work, and to brand the devoted Congressmen as venders of their honesty and conscience, and almost as traitors to the cause, to the people, and to the future of the country.

Will the prosperity of the country, will the wages of the workman, or the daily laborer increase in proportion to the taxation? are questions for the future to solve. The emergency, the salvation of the country emphatically called for the broadest taxation; the patriots had to fulfill the exigency of the hour. *Advient que pourra.*

The first and necessary commodities increasing in price soon may be no more within the reach of the laboring part of the population; then not only comparative, but genuine, social, economical, old-fashioned poverty—not, however, pauperism—may thus become inaugurated on the American soil.

However, I for one have the fullest faith in the indomitable and inexhaustible vitality of the principle which is to be saved in this struggle.

Freedom, free labor, * self-government,* pruned of excrescences grown upon them by time, will take, so to speak, a new, loftier and broader start, and the deep, almost deadly wounds inflicted by selfishness and treason, as well as by incapacity, and by that cursed flighty, unearnest policy of 1861, (Seward's policy,) will be healed. If not—then the coming generation will know at whose door to lay the crime.

May 4.—In that letter to Hodges and to the Kentuckians, Mr. Lincoln asserts that when two years ago he dabbled in emancipation with the border States, he was scheming and thinking the opposite of what he asserted. Thank you, O Lincoln, for thus justifying and vindicating me!

May 6.—Will Grant be able to dislodge Lee from positions which are strong by nature and have been made almost impregnable by art? All this, thanks to General Meade's over-respectful and un-soldierlike mode of warfare. During the whole fall and winter Stanton could not suc-

---

* This war has emphatically established and illustrated the paramount superiority not only of free labor, but the superiority of the culture of the soil and of its productiveness when divided among yeomanry rather than when laid out in very large farms. In all probability this war has consumed more agricultural products, such as grains, flour, bread, meat, mules, and horses, than were consumed, used, and destroyed in the Napoleonic wars until the campaign of 1812. Three or four thousand acres laid out in middle-sized farms, as in America, produce more than one or two very large farms, even under such high culture as in Germany or in any other part of Europe.—*Note August,* 1865.

ceed in forcing Meade into fight, although Meade stood two to one. And now the bloody work has begun. That bloodless and unmanned Meade ought to earn the fruits of blood and of maledictions.

May 6.—General anxiety about Grant. He is beyond the reach of the telegraphic communications. His move is a bold one, and besides, he could not make another. May only the Generals not Meadeize, not McClellanize!

May 7.—In the whole history of parliamentary debates I never read of or witnessed a position like that occupied by Senator Sumner. He is attacked by political enemies and is obnoxious, nay, at times nauseous, to men of the same party principles as his. He stands alone; is roughly handled by the opponents, who at times expose his arrogant assumptions and superficiality. So did Reverdy Johnson on legal questions; so did Cowan on the French *assignats;* so Senator Howard gave him a lesson on Livy, and in similar ways he is often thus treated by other opponents and political friends. Nay! by his petty schoolmaster-like conceit, and by the everlasting pompous display of his rhetorical superficiality and undigested erudition, he averts from him the best men in the Senate; the truest Republicans and anti-slavery apostles at times are forced to put him down. *Risum teneatis,* when the learned Senator appeals to Shakspeare on the question of a mint for Oregon or Philadelphia, or when doctor-like he utters sentences about finances and political economy. What is perused one evening is rehearsed next morning. An everlasting citer is not necessarily a *savant*.

May 7.—Fremont's manifesto out. It is not a thorough one. Fremont is honest and sincere, but the writers or concocters of this appeal for a convention in Cleveland seem to be of the pure politician *genus*.

May 7.—Patriots agonizing for news from Grant. It will not be believed, and nevertheless it is a fact, that Mr. Lincoln has not taken any measures to organize a line of couriers and to have direct news from the army. The struggle is momentous for the people, and is one of *to be* or *not to be* for Lincoln and for his crew. For three days the slaughter is going on, and the *first positive news* which reached Washington has been brought here and communicated to the Government by an enterprising correspondent of the *Tribune.* What governmental coolness! what serenity!

Meade behaved in his most Meade-like manner. Until May 4, and when our army already moved on the flank of the enemy, he heeded not the warnings of Warren, who said to him, " here we must fight." Meade supposed that Lee would not attack, and therefore, moving the army, he left a gap of four miles, into which Longstreet threw his corps. Hancock's impulsive bravery and the valor of his troops alone prevented Lee from cutting the army in two.

How can Grant abandon to Meade the execution of any military movement of the army? * *

May 7.—Blood flows in torrents, and the re-election intrigues quietly go on. I am puzzled. The same men who in this and in the 37th Congress faced boldly the most desperate emergencies, and by their legislative acts saved the country, now cave in before the pressure exercised by the Lincolnites, by the Sewardites, by shoddy, and by the low *stratum* of politicians.

May 8.—More and more news. Grant sustained his reputation for unrelenting stubbornness, and the troops heroically, nobly sustained their glorious stubborn endurance. It is said that after the first two days' fighting Meade advised Grant to——retreat. I do not doubt that it is true.

Grant forced Lee to retreat or to fall back on another impregnable position. For the first time after having crossed and fought, we do not *recross* the Rapidan.

Wadsworth fell leading on his troops!

May 9.—Dearly-bought victory! Wadsworth fell shot through the head when leading his division to storm a position from which we had been twice repulsed. That is Wadsworth!

Oh, why could I not meet Seward to avenge upon him Wadsworth's death!

Stanton behaves with great and deep feeling on account of Wadsworth. Stanton was always Wadsworth's true friend.

May 10.—Wadsworth was the purest and noblest result of the American political and social life. Not a flaw in him. He was a type, a model generated by the free American institutions, and none of their shadows darkened his character. Devoted to the cause with all the loftiness of a patriot, not an atom of selfishness or of personal ambition marred his patriotism. He was the simple, unsophisticated man of truth. Assumption, hypocrisy, double-dealing, humbug, fuss, were as repulsive to his generous nature as light to darkness, as evil to right and verity. He was all devotion to his conscience and to his convictions; of a devotion as unsurpassed here and now, as in any time, nation and country.

Wadsworth, father of six children, and grandfather of two, possessor of a princely fortune, enjoying an elevated social and political position and the general consideration bestowed on an eminent and true citizen; Wadsworth was foremost among those who, when treason struck the matricidal blow—rushed to arms with the unrelenting decision not to abandon the gory field until treason should be crushed. The devoted, pure confessor of the cause of mankind, he cheerfully, unhesitatingly, unostentatiously sacrificed all that endears life, sacrificed the happiest earthly and social existence.

A poor Africo-American asked me if it was true that Wadsworth fell. Hearing my answer, he said: " I pray to God that my boys may now fight with a greater rage." He had two sons in the army.

May 10.—Some years ago and before the outburst of treason, in an intimate conversation Wadsworth said to me, that he would leave his children well off, but would leave them no *name.* Where all over the world is now a son who can point to a nobler name, to a nobler father?

May 11.—The lick-spittles are furiously at work to make capital for Lincoln out of the massacres in the *Wilderness.* It is maddening to think that a Wadsworth fell, and with him scores of thousands of the best sons of the people, that scores of thousands will remain crippled for life, and that all this sacrifice is appreciated and weighed as far as it will bear on—re-election. Of course it is not so with the true and patriotic men; not with those whose names I have so often recorded as the archetypes of true patriots and Americans.

May 11.—Wadsworth gloriously ended his career, and his name will forever corruscate in the annals of this war, of a war for humanity. His name will forever live in the memories of mankind. He is not a martyr. He sacrificed himself by his free choice. Few, very few such sacrifices and devotions are recorded and transmitted by the world's history.

But I lost not only a friend—I lost a man whom I respected, who more than any one made me firmly believe that genuine Democracy and self-government generate true manhood. My regrets will not easily be healed.

Before all just men, before all true patriots, before the present and the coming generations, before the tribunal of incorruptible history, I accuse

Seward.

Halleck.

In 1862 Weed and Seward counteracted Wadsworth's election. Lincoln was then insincere. He was afraid to have for a Governor of New York a man of such character as Wadsworth. Lincoln virtually played false to Wadsworth and to all the patriots.

Further: Stanton repeatedly wished to give Wadsworth the command of a military department—at one time Missouri, at another Kentucky; Halleck stimulated Lincoln to baffle Stanton's attempts. And for those reasons deliberately and conscientiously I repeat my accusation:

SEWARD, HALLECK, YOU HAVE TO ANSWER FOR WADSWORTH'S BLOOD.

May 12.—This terrible slaughter in the Wilderness pushes the days of Gettysburg into the background. I cannot find a name nor a comparison to it either in antiquity or in our times, either in mythology or in biblical epochs, either in the war of the Titans or in Milton.

I observed somewhere that the condition of the Greek republics and the Peloponesian war alone has any analogy with this American struggle. That analogy holds. When "Greeks meet Greeks" can justly be applied to the seven days' fight in the Wilderness.

Acerba fata Romanos agunt
Scelusque fraternæ necis.

The by-the-Americans murdered Remus is the poor, oppressed Africo-American, once enslaved by all of them, enslaved before a political North and South sprang up in this country, and whom still prejudice, sham science, sham religion, sham philanthropy, degrade and morally enslave.

May 12.—A certain Senator Cowan has made in the Senate a most savage onslaught on human liberty. Cowan spoke as Slidell, Mason, Wigfall, or any other savage Southerner would have spoken. He wound up his ignorant display by an appeal to what he desecrated by calling it science or raceology, and the poor New Zealander was introduced for the sake of scientific illustration.

Humanity O! Cowan, is more desecrated by you, and is daily by such as you, than that poor savage could desecrate it. A New Zealander will not tread under his feet right and justice, and do it to help, to sustain, to excuse slavery. And Sumner sat there in his *curule* and refuted

15

not this sham and worse than sham science.
Here was the time and arena for the display of
real science, for quotations, for genuine scientific
authorities.

May 13.—Step by step Grant hammered and
hammers Lee's army back. Grant the Hammerer displayed high military capacity. The
terrain of this Wilderness, rendered any movement or manœuvring almost impossible and
what in this respect was done by our troops
could not be outdone even by the oldest and best
drilled European. And the fighting was hand to
hand, the fire was of musketry, for the thickness
of the wood absolutely prevented the use of
artillery ! Never a Napoleon or any other European captain or European troops fought under
such conditions.

And when the best of the people's blood runs
in torrents, when mythology and reality, when
the past of all nations is overshadowed by the
present, to witness the efforts, the schemes, the
intrigues of politicians for election or re-election,
etc. !

May 14.—The diplomats—that is, the few
principal European sympathizers with the South
whose names have repeatedly been pointed out
in the pages of this *Diary*—the diplomats are at
their old tricks. They cannot be reconciled to
see Lee hammered back on Richmond. This
time they stretch to the utmost their little brains,
to belittle Grant and his army, and to please the

secesh offal in Washington and in New York. These diplomats have a great will to bite, but are toothless.

May 14.—The correspondence and the news from the army contained in various dailies, say: *Meade's army, Meade ordered, moved, decided, etc.* It is, however, not the fault of these correspondents when they say what is not true; some of them are truthful men and know that they publish a falsehood. The truth is, that having the police of the army under his control, Meade intimated to the reporters that if they dared to speak otherwise, they would be excluded from the army. With all this contemptible effort, Meade does not succeed in bemuddling public opinion. Every one knows that Meade executes orders given to him by Grant, and many, many justly doubt if such orders are well executed by Meade.

May 14.—The stubborn, unrelenting way in which Grant operates and fights makes it the more to be regretted that early in the spring of 1862 he was not in command of the army. Undoubtedly the war would have been over long ago. Of all the generals in the history of war, McClellan in 1861–62 had the easiest task, and fulfilled it in such a way as to richly deserve the curse of the present and of future generations. On his brow, on his name the mark of Cain will burn for eternities.

May 14. — Beyond measure is the moral

degradation of the English and of the French
would-be better or court class, or aristocracy.
Whenever it can do it, that degenerated, degraded aristocracy shows its partiality for the
South. Honor, humanity, and civilization are
outraged by those degraded, degenerated, aristocrats and nobles, who attempt to baptize, or
help to erect into a nation, the offspring of the
most hideous and corrupt social element such as
Southern slavery and Southern "chivalry."

May 15.—Although a pupil of West Point,
Grant shows that he is not permeated with defer-
ence to, and fear of slavery or slave-bred Generals. Nothing in Grant *a la* McClellan, Meade,
Franklin, etc.

Night and day fresh troops pass the city *en route*
to fill the gaps made by daily slaughter. The
soldiers are cheerful and martial. Boundless is
my admiration and veneration for this great
people, but boundless also are my regrets to see
how the same people is childishly confident in its
legal nurses.

May 15.—The *bank bill* or *national bank bill*, so
good for the West, may prove ruinous to the
Eastern States. This bill will destroy the small
capital and capitalists, and may prove ruinous to
the prosperity of States. It increases the paper
currency, and I look upon it as an attempt to
centralize the capital in the hands of large capitalists, doing it at the cost of the States.

In 1861 the country was saved by the energy,

the devotion of the respective States and of their respective Governors, and not by the energy or capacity of the central administration, who even in many cases did its utmost—unconsciously, of course—to palsy or at least to impede the patriotic energy unfolded by the States.

May 16.—Senator Sumner's great aim is to be considered as having left the imprint of his mind on the legislation of the country. A noble ambition, but rather indiscriminately carried out. It would have been better for him if Sumner had exclusively restrained himself to the *role* of a Wilberforce and had given up the attempts to lecture his colleagues on each and every subject.

May 17.—In this struggle in Virginia Lee has almost all the moral and geographical advantages on his side. Lee's army is in impregnable positions. For reasons mentioned above Grant was forced to enter a *genuine* Wilderness, where he could not or cannot with facility manœuvre or deploy. Lee has fought for two years with the men under his command, and is deified by them. Grant is obnoxious to many of the Generals, who must consider his victory over Lee as their most bitter condemnation, Generals and officers who at the start surreptitiously slandered Grant and undermined his influence over the soldiers. Lee is supported by an infuriated population, among which conviction or fear prevent treason. Grant, with Washington for his base, is literally in an enemy's country. Washington is filled with thousands and thousands of enemies and spies, kept and nourished there by the leniency of the Government; spies and traitors whose eyes and ears penetrate every administrative and governmental fissure. Grant's preparations and movements are communicated to Lee and known to him as soon as almost mooted. With difficulty or not at all can Grant discover what Lee and Richmond are about. Seldom, if ever, had a General to overcome similar difficulties.

May 17.—"Out of friendship for the Union" Petersburg and Russia advise moderation, forgiveness, and mutual forbearance.* If Alexander II and his advisers think so and preach to us leniency, then why are the Poles punished and persecuted?

Some diplomatic saloons and the diplomatic, principally English, *attachés*, do their utmost to discredit the rebel atrocities at Fort Pillow and the rebel cruelty toward our war prisoners. Such diplomats turn up their noses at the War Committee. I wonder not. Certain diplomats here are too much below the average of manhood, and thus cannot appreciate *the men* who sit in that committee.

May 17.—Wendell Phillips asserts that supported by Seward, Blair, and the like, Lincoln has almost ruined the country; that secession

---

* I am told that this advice was insinuated through the American legation in St. Petersburg.

could have been crushed in 1861 and 1862; that the vitality of secession increases with every year of its duration; that slavery could have been destroyed at the beginning of the war, etc. These statements made by Wendell Phillips confirm what I say and what I said in the first two volumes of this Diary, and I am proud to have the support of a Wendell Phillips. Besides the traitors, somebody else is responsible for more blood than was spilt by Marius and Sylla put together.

May 17.—Lord John Russell's last speech in the House of Lords on American affairs is that of a true and honest man. True and honest is likewise Lord Lyons. Both Lords to the utmost of their powers defend such private interests as they judge to be hurt by certain measures or occasionalities generated by this war, and to do it is their duty. But when great principles are in question, both Lords as yet have been on the side of right and humanity.

May 17.—I wish that whoever undertakes to write the history of this war, may do it before the present generation, or at least before many eye-witnesses and actors pass away. Their evidence will be as the small rills and streamlets at the sources of a great and powerful river; by such evidence alone many facts and events can be understood and explained. But as yet no written record gathers and preserves such evidence.

May 18.—General Meade and his crew complain that the country gives no credit to Meade for the last deeds of the Potomac army. The country knows well and cannot forget that for months Meade had a by far easier work before him; that he missed it, fulfilled it not, and did his utmost to strengthen Lee. The country knows her men.

May 18.—The stubbornness with which the rebels resist at all points is one more among the many evidences recorded in history how easily perverse but skillful chiefs can fanaticize ignorant masses. The South is ruled by certain master minds of such intensity, that thereby almost the whole material, intellectual and industrial superiority of the North is met, counteracted, kept in check and often neutralized. These Southern chiefs almost repeat the wonder of the loaves and fishes. It cuts one to the quick to witness such powerful, manly qualities devoted and wasted to sustain a social lie, and the most degrading moral and political perversion ever recorded in the history of man.

The grand, Satanic figures of Jefferson Davis, of Lee, together with the group of their coadjutors and henchmen, will for eternities overshadow the records of American history, the records of man's progress and development.

May 19.—Informal funeral of Wadsworth's body on its passage to New York. The State renders the last honors to its noblest and best son, to the truest and best American and citizen soldier.

May 19.—How these rhetors and would-be classical and other scholars disgust me. Conceit and heartlessness are all that is in and of them. Hearts and minds dried up, and little, very little of superficial and not varied information. *Never* and *nowhere*-have I met with such misproducts of sham learning and of sham civilization. It seems that Harvard University is the special and exclusive soil from which luxuriantly grow up these parasites of the human mind and intellect. The best men in Congress and out of Congress are those who graduated at large and with honors in life, not in Harvard or in West Point. When the heart unites with convictions and with sound sense it warms the brains, and far better illuminates them than the pigmy, conceited, one-sided, narrow and superficial culture acquired by the *graduated*.

May 19.—Whatever was urged on him by his convictions, Wadsworth did simply, without any fuss, not even attempting to have his noble actions credited to him.

May 20.—About *graduates*. Senator Wilson, warm-hearted, impulsive, and generous, has rendered more efficient services to the country's cause, than a cold rhetor, wholly wrapped up in himself.

May 20.—General Hooker again wounded. Hooker belongs to the most splendid fighters ever known in history. What a pity that the camp at Falmouth and some unaccountable psychological phenomena at Chancellorsville, so utterly ruined him as a captain! If a comparison is to be made, Hooker compares with Marshal Ney. Hooker is a devoted patriot, not an intriguer, and has no false pride where the country is concerned.

May 20.—Dr. Johnson said that "patriotism is the last refuge of a scoundrel." Something similar may now apply to abolitionism, and to the many among its newly-converted confessors. Every day I see such new converts, but I more than doubt their sincerity; the creed newly-adopted by them may cover many hard and inveterate sins.

May 20.—Senator Sumner attributes to envy his anomalous position with the best men on the Republican side. He cannot understand that it is his scholarly pretensions which render him unpalatable to his colleagues. His cold rhetoric falls powerless at their feet, and no Senator envies him his fertility in random quotations.

May 21.—When the English contraband and blockade-runner, "Sir William Peel," was captured, the English Government—as is its duty—claimed all kinds of restitutions, indemnities, and above all claimed that the case be decided by the administration, and not submitted to the prize court, the only natural, legal, and logical jurisdiction. Mr. Seward was at once ready to

grant all that England claimed.   Mr. Seward
was *befogged* by his masterly familiarity with
questions of a public and international character.   Welles opposed and finally got Mr. Seward to look for light beyond the luminous
precincts of the Department of State.   In a
memoir on this question, Mr. Eames unfolded to
Mr. Seward's astonished mind what is the reach,
the bearing, and the difference between the
administrative or governmental and the judicial
management of prizes in accordance with English and American precedents, laws, and statutes.
Eames explained to Seward wherein differ the
power of a king and of a President, together
with other points relating to international ques-
-tions.   As the English claims and demands. are
based on English laws and English constructions,
and as Mr. Seward ignored certain cardinal
differences existing in both the international
jurisdictions, Mr. Seward was befogged by the
display of English would-be authorities, and confused the English and the American principles
and polity.

May 23.—I am astonished that Democrats and
copperheads can take up McClellan.   Even for
them and in their hands McClellan will burst
and prove a failure.   He will not even be a good
tool for a peace or for any other unpatriotic aim.
McClellan is a most perfect nonentity.   This
spurious or true enthusiasm for him is and will

remain an inexplicable psychological and monstrous phenomenon.

But it likewise is and will be a phenomenon, that stern, honest, intelligent patriots are forced to take up——Lincoln.

May 24.—Grant the Hammerer, twenty-five miles from Richmond! And what a powerful hammer is the Potomac army! All of them are the people, Grant is of the people, the true people, and of different cast from the "great" press, the *pap* press, and the politicians.

May 24.—From ten to twelve days ambulances cross the streets in all directions. The sufferings of the wounded must be a hundredfold increased by these procrustean boxes in which they are huddled. It is a shame that the Yankee inventive fertility has not yet created something better than these ambulances. I am certain that the European ambulances are better. Very likely that red tape and the conceit of officials, surgeons, and quartermasters prevent the inborn inventive capacity of the Yankee spirit from substituting better ambulances for those horrible boxes.*

---

* The Circular, No. 6, published by the Surgeon General's Office, Washington, November 1, 1865, is a contribution of the greatest scientific value to general surgical science. For the first time the improved fire-arms have been at their destructive work on such a gigantic scale, and the results of gunshots and of conic balls, studied on such an extensive field as during this protracted war. This publication shows that in the last stages of the conflict the Medical and Surgical Department has made

May 25.—Among the many results of this war it must be counted that the comprehension of relations between the Government or administration and the people at large will for a time be perverted. Almost every day I observe how men in power, not only the intriguers, but even the best patriots get accustomed to consider the Government as being something distinct and separated from the people. I am not at all surprised when a Seward tries to imitate the like bad, old European example, and when he imagines himself in duty bound to appear grand and all-powerful, to appear almost a despotic premier above the people and above the public opinion, and impress European diplomats and European cabinets with his grandeur, etc. Again: upon men such as Stanton and other patriots, unavoidable necessity and rampant treason force many despotic or dictatorial acts, but in recognizing the necessity, one regrets that it is so, as the example is dangerous, and despotism ought to have remained an anomaly in the American polity. Treason bears bitter fruits.

Even financial measures discussed and accepted by Congress, also by the best of the

---

immense progress in the right direction, and that it knew how to improve the opportunities for the benefit of science, and therefore for the benefit of suffering humanity.—*Note December*, 1865.

patriots, are stained by this European tendency to consider the interest of the Government as distinct from the interest of the people, to centralize and to absorb as much as possible of the people's interest. The bank bill will concentrate almost the whole capital of the country. Its greatest condemnation is, that L. Napoleon admires it and would wish to see it adopted in France. Then the Government's securities are to be exempted from taxation; thereby the pre-existing various public securities will become depressed and almost driven out of circulation.

May 27.—Mr. Seward delivers Arguelles to Spain, not because he has any earthly right to do it, but to impress the diplomats and Europe with his power, and to justify what I said above.

This is not the only violation of right, of humanity, and of hospitality committed by Seward. In the course of the last week Mr. Seward returned and delivered to Russia several Russians and Poles, who fled from the Russian squadron and enlisted in our army. To do this Mr. Seward willingly exhumed an old treaty, existing and obligatory only by *sufferance* rather than by a direct, absolute, indisputable tenor.

In his subserviency to the European diplomats and his craving appetite for despotic acts, Mr. Seward violated even the above-mentioned obsolete and into-existence-galvanized extradition treaty. According to the dispositions of that

treaty, when claiming the extradition of a deserter, Russia is to prove, by various positive
written and official documents, the real status of
the man claimed by her as a deserter; in the
present cases not one of these guarantees and
proofs as prescribed by the treaty were given or
shown by Russia, and the magnanimous Department of State did not even think of disturbing
Russia and requesting her to *show cause.*

May 28.—The Northern traitors, the copperheads, the organs of Jefferson Davis published in
New York, in Boston, etc., the *Couriers*, American and French, the *Worlds*, the *Albions*, etc.,
may now exclaim with Tacitus, "*rara temporum
felicitas ubi——quod sentias dicere potes.*" Treason
is not yet so rampant as to not tremble and have
the gallows in prospect.

May 29.—Grant's manœuvre by which he
brought the army across the Pamunkey is almost
unprecedented in military history. This manœuvre is sufficient to immortalize both the captain
and his army.

May 29.—What nauseous nonsense the wiseacres of the New York "loyal" press publish
about the campaign and the fighting in the Wilderness! They rival each other to see who will
display more absurdity in judgment of facts,
more insipidity in speculations. Their appreciation is wide of truth and of sound sense; it would
do mischief as such, but that the people's com-

mon sense and instincts neutralize the evils spread by the press.

May 30.—Wilberforce-Sumner would be glad to impress and persuade public opinion that he alone through thick and thin remains faithful to the anti-slavery cause. By this conduct Sumner offends truth and his colleagues. Morrill, Wade, Wilson, Wilkinson, Harlan, Fessenden, Grimes, Clark, Foster, Hale, that oldest uncompromising anti-slavery champion in the Senate, Gratz Brown, Morgan, Foote, Collamer and others are as unrelenting emancipationists as Sumner. But not one of those true men attempts to absorb all the glory for himself. Likewise not one of the above-mentioned patriots imagines that he will become the man of the last, the eleventh hour, and be nominated for the Presidency in Baltimore.

May 31.—Greeley finds many faults with Congress, is highly dissatisfied with the House, and is highly incensed against Thad. Stevens for his bad leadership of the House. Greeley is himself a public power, and thus he is subject to be held up and judged. I shall not offend that sterling patriot, Thad. Stevens, by putting him side by side with Greeley. Stevens was and is as the immovable rock battered by hurricanes. The *Tribune* is an indestructible record of Greeley's uncourageous inconsistencies, of his unmanly despondencies. Repeatedly Greeley (the whiner)

despaired of success, cried "mercy," "enough,"
begged for peace, and scared by shadows, he for a
time forswore even the principle of general
emancipation.

If during this war the country, the people, and
Congress, had been under Greeley's leadership,
the country, the people, the national honor and
existence would be at the mercy of traitors and
of copperheads.   The people will triumph over
its enemies and override this bloody tempest, but
Greeley has not led them to victory.

For the sake of his own name, and for the
sake of the public good, on March 5th, 1861,
Greeley,* together with General Scott, with

---

* Becoming a politician Mr. Greeley at least marred, if he did
not utterly ruin his splendid and noble qualities of mind and
heart.   The politician obfusticates in Greeley the sentiment of
justice and makes him bitter, partial and unjust.   Thus Greeley
is Stanton's bitter enemy.   Whatever might be the reasons for
this enmity, Greeley ought to bear in mind that when he, in
despair, was ready to recognize the Confederacy in June, 1863,
Stanton organized armies and never despaired, and the results
were: Gettysburg and Vicksburg.—*Note August*, 1862.

a. Greeley, who repeatedly during the war declared the country to be bankrupt, now advocates cowardly economy, and his
quill hovers over the heads of Major Generals.

But most of these Greeleyan nightmares—and above all the
Major Generals of Grant's creation—have faced death and contri-
buted to victory, when Greeley advocated peace and submission.
Where would be to-day all the pacific, reforming, economizing
Greeleyanism without most of the quill-doomed Major Generals!
By dismissing them, economy will be very small and ingratitude

Seward, and with many others, ought to have disappeared from the political arena.

---

very great.   Wade Hampton, deeply,· deeply dyed in Union blood, finds more favor with Greeley than the defenders of the Union.   No wonder that Greeley is to-day the favorite of the blackest rebels.—*Note October* 28, 1865.

JUNE.

June 1.—A colonel of the French army, sent
here by Louis Napoleon to observe or learn,
spends some time with the Potomac army, and
finds that the whole campaign in the Wilderness
was very well conceived, conducted, and executed. *Certain diplomats* are perfectly upset by
this opinion of a distinguished French officer, as
certain *very friendly* diplomatic quasi-saloons have
already given their verdict upon Grant, and
decided him to be a charlatan, and not a
General.

June 1.—Greeley, the historian, is the same as
Greeley, the war leader. The truth is, that notwithstanding his generous impulses, his eminent
intellectual capacities, his devotion to the interests of the masses, Greeley is useful to the people only in the normal condition of society, only
in peaceful times. But these mighty events
upset his *morale ;* they overawe, confuse his intellectual capacities and his judgment, and finding himself no more listened to as of old, not as

influential a power as he was before, his feelings are hurt, and his very, very mighty *amour propre* is bleeding. Poor qualifications for a historian of his own epoch. Will Greeley in his book account for his various tergiversations? The dedication to John Bright is splendid, and opens —the English market. The book, advertised, prepared, puffed before its birth, will sell well; it will richly compensate Greeley for whatever losses he may have suffered (? ? ?) in this war, and it will considerably confuse the people's judgment. The book is swollen with extracts from various country papers—which extracts are to evidence the condition of the public opinion. Poor barometer that, but not so poor before 1860 as since.

Some pages are written with the old Greeleyan power and fire, but many, very many are in the lowest newspaper style. Almost on every page the politician pierces through. I find misrepresentations and omissions, and shall point them out.

June 3.—The Titans fighting again. History is put to shame by this superhuman struggle. Both armies display and bring forth alike fighting qualities—*the same family.* But the Northern army fights under all the disadvantages of position and of *terrain,* which altogether favor the rebels and allow them to concentrate while the Potomac army must unavoidably extend its lines, so that when all this is counted in, the Potomac army, the North, shows fighting qualities superior to those of the rebels.

June 4.—In his so-called history, Greeley is very unjust to many who rendered eminent services, to many who sincerely devoted themselves to the cause. Names are ciphers, and no prominent personality is recognized by the historian, who, of course, is to stand out prominent, foremost, and alone. In the long parliamentary struggle for Kansas the name of Senator Sumner is almost ignored. And Sumner's warm, bold defense of freedom in Kansas ended with the bloody and cowardly assault by a Southern murderer.

Called into the Cabinet by Buchanan in the last days of his administration, and after its traitor members absconded, Stanton,* Dix, and Holt then saved the Union. But for those three patriots, the inauguration of Mr. Lincoln might never have taken place. Greeley ignores these patriotic actions and the names of the patriots. So he forgets to mention the name of Lyon, the great patriot and martyr of the West, an omission which is not honorable to the historian.

---

* A member of the last months of Buchanan's Cabinet, and therefore a colleague of Stanton during those dark days, asserts that Stanton's feelings and advice were ultra-northern THEN. This disposes of all the slanders invented against Stanton by traitors, copperheads, and by his other enemies. The member of the Cabinet above-mentioned is thoroughly a man of honor, and although southern in his feelings, is not a rebel and does not belong to a rebel State.—*Note November* 24, 1865.

These are specimens of the numerous omissions committed by Greeley, omissions which almost seem to have been voluntarily, deliberately made.

Further: As yet, that is, in his first volume, Greeley altogether ignores the foreign relations, which constitute such a great episode in this struggle. The new rules and solutions in international law evoked by this complication do not move Greeley's mind and find no place in the Greeleyan publication. But Hudibras and Beaumarchais are not forgotten; their names head respective chapters in this history, ardently and devotedly palmed on the good-natured people.

June 5.—The practical financiers, that is, the bankers, merchants, etc., do not seem to have a very great opinion of Chase's financial capacity. I know well that great allowance must be made for the judgment of such men, but almost all of them agree that Mr. Chase never comes to the point, never utters a decided and conclusive opinion. They believe that Chase is a recipient of the notions and conceptions of others, rather than their generator.

June 5.—Washington is overrun with politicians, with contractors, and with busy-bodies of all kinds and sizes. The Baltimore Convention is at the door, and the ravens make due obeisance to the White House. Many true patriots, such as Potter of Wisconsin, Grow and Thaddeus Stevens of Pennsylvania, Morrill of Maine, and similar ones are sent by the people to the convention, but they are in a minority. Their communities instruct them to vote for Lincoln, and therefore the current cannot be stayed. The hearts of the patriots are with the army; the politicians turn towards the White House—the army is only for them a subject of speculation, as to how much capital for Baltimore can be made out of the heroes' blood.

During nearly two years the patriots in the two Congresses have been bleeding inwardly for being forced by events not to expose Lincoln's shortcomings and blunders, which almost ruin not only the Republican party, but a noble cause and a noble people. The vilest politicians of the Seward and Blair genus, the Lincolnites, devoted to "the main chance" lose no time and are making capital from that sullen acquiescence of the patriots; the people at large is taken in—and demands Lincoln's re-election.

June 6.—The Mexican question is settling down more and more. Never, never did the would-be statesmen of any country give up a cause so shamefully as Seward-Sumner gave up Mexico. I say Seward-Sumner, for in this, as in all foreign questions, Sumner was a tool in Seward's hands and his submissive echo in the Senate. Seward played on Sumner's conceit and vanity, and with remarkable success used foreign diplomats to influence him. Sumner, who wished to appear wise, was always led by the nose. From

the first day of the Mexican complication until
this, Seward played Mexico into the hands of
Louis Napoleon, and therein Sumner helped
Seward with all his might. Judged by this
Mexican mismanagement, Sumner showed the
most colossal, astounding incapacity for a Chair-
man of the Committee on Foreign Affairs. The
Senate could not make a worse choice.

In 1861–'62 Sumner eminently helped to
shelve the Corwin-Mexican treaty. The ten millions of dollars which by that treaty were to be
loaned to Mexico could not injure our finances.
They would have been a drop in the ocean
added to the current expenses of this war. But
with this money Mexico would have paid off the
spurious Napoleonic reclamations. By this payment the plausible cause for invasion would have
burst in the schemer's hands, and he would have
been forced to withdraw or to unveil his
schemes. The great statesman of the Senate
never could understand this simple logic, and
Corwin's treaty was annulled. Under the same
influences, and always kept in strings by Seward,
Sumner used various parliamentary tricks to
palsy the noble impetus of the House, and to
prevent the Senate from acceding to the joint
resolution as presented by the House in favor of
Mexico.

The name of Sumner ought to be cursed by
every Mexican patriot; as for Seward, not only
Mexicans, but mankind at large, cannot and

never will bless him. Louis, the *Decembriseur*, and the diplomats alone have Seward in grateful remembrance.

June 7.—Baltimore. What a crowd of sharp-faced, keen, greedy politicians! These men would literally devour every one in their way. I pity the patriots, who in this crowd seem isolated like hills in a marshy, unhealthy, desolated plain. Everywhere shoddy, contractors, schemers, pap-journalists, expectants, etc., etc., etc. The atmosphere, the space are filled with greedy and devouring eyes. The moral insight of the convention would disgust one with the people, but I know the various combinations and events which brought this scum to the surface, and I know that it is not the genuine people.

Governor Andrew, elected member for the convention from Massachusetts — absent. Not ready to put his finger in the pie. Senator Morgan made a good speech. He laid great emphasis on the destruction of slavery, and incensed—nobody. I hear that a delegation from South Carolina is to claim a seat in the convention. I hope that delegation will be composed of Africo-Americans, no shoddy and contractors among them.

Even here I witness how reluctant the best men are to go for Lincoln. They know him. The small chips from the country, the sentimental writers, and other ·g**** believe they know Lincoln-Seward better than the good and pure men who during these three years have been in daily contact with the President. The leaders in this convention are Jim Lane and Raymond of the *Times*. This is enough.

The efforts of patriots will carry the point that Mr. Lincoln be admonished by the convention to mend his ways, and change his constitutional advisers. The Wisconsin delegation, filled with radicals, takes the lead in this. Potter, ousted from Congress by the efforts of Seward and of Catholic priests, (see Diary, vol. II,) is a member of the Wisconsin delegation. A German, whose name I forget, once Governor of that State, nobly sides with Potter, that genuine American yeoman. The country has thousands and thousands of such men as Potter. These farmers may be justly compared to the Roman farmers of the times of Regulus or of Cincinnatus. As an antidote to true patriots, Baltimore is filled with the familiars of the White House, Nicolay, Lamon, etc., etc.

Mr. Lincoln will be nominated, but will he be elected?

Good night, O! convention in Baltimore.

June 8.—Thurlow Weed* publishes a stirring

---

* Thurlow Weed lately became the political nurse and tutor of Preston King, and the whole country was awestruck with the death of the noble, simple-hearted and devoted patriot.—*Note November* 24, 1865.

defense of Sandford, the Belgian diplomat, and
* * * * *Honor among,* etc., etc., is splendidly
justified.

June 8.—Poor Fremont! In his letter of
acceptance of the Cleveland nomination, he is
silent on the fact which exclusively endeared him
to the people—the fact that in this war he was
the first to proclaim *emancipation;* to have been
persecuted by Lincoln for it, who now takes up
and struts in his ideas. Fremont asserts that he
is opposed to confiscation, notwithstanding that
the people's sentiment is decidedly for it. He
commits this mistake to conciliate the Democrats,
and it will be a flash in the pan. Then Fremont
indirectly assumes the defense of the *World* and
of other copperheads who roar for free speech
and free press, that is, for the liberty to undermine and destroy, not Mr. Lincoln and his aco-
lytes, but to undermine and destroy the noble,
lofty principle which inspires the Republican
masses and all those Democrats who hate treason
and slavery, and to sacrifice all for the destruction of both. In a word, Fremont's letter is
written with an eye to Chicago and and to copperhead Democrats, and they will cheat him.
How badly advised he has been !

June 9.—Mr. Lincoln is nominated. But what
a chill runs through the best men ! Many, many
have not yet made up their minds to go for him,
and what is still worse, to go for his Sewards

and Blairs. Many of the best Republicans in Congress and out of Congress will be almost indifferent if Mr. Lincoln is not elected. Many look to the Chicago Convention. If the Democrats nominate a man, and not a dunce; if this man—of course, not a McClellan—should be a character and inspire confidence in his manhood, many Republicans will adopt him, and others will remain passive towards both.

It is likewise possible that a new Republican convention may be called, and a new nomination made. This, however, depends upon the events of the war. Lincoln and the Sewardites and the Blairites turned into capital the longanimity of the best Republicans, and the Republicans are now—duped.

Such at this day is the condition of minds. Ominous for Lincoln, but likewise ominous for our principles. A miscarriage now may push back for more than half a century the sacred cause of mankind; the victory of the Democrats, copperheads, and slavery worshippers is a victory won by Satan.

Terrible is the dilemma of the true men and patriots; the issues awful, and black despair at the end of both of them. To swallow a Lincoln dissolved in Seward and Blair, and to try to save the country with that not heavenly compound, or to facilitate the dark, humanity-destroying victory of the Democrats.

I am certain that the division in the party

will be very considerable. I am certain that the
stern men, who number thousands and thousands, will not easily fall in with the Lincoln
ranks. And if they fall in, it will be only yield-
ing to the pressure of an unavoidable, imperious,
life or death deciding necessity. I pity the
honest and conscientious patriots. Their lot is
to be misunderstood, misrepresented. Many,
many of them will struggle, and then submit to
the dire fatality.

*Tout être laisse quelque chose aux buissons de la route,
Le troupeau sa toison, et l'homme sa vertu.*

June 10.—*Rara temporum felicitas* is at hand for
all the Weedites and Sewardites, for the expectants, the contractors, the leeches, etc., etc. They
will enumerate their services in the cause of re-
election and of—their own. All who impudently
swelled from toads to elephants will be safe.
And all of them will strike at once *hosannah in
excelsis*—and expand their pockets.

June 10.—It would be interesting to make
analytical statistics of the Baltimore convention.
Then it would be found out how many office-
holders, postmasters, contractors, lobbyists, expectants, pap-editors composed it. Then find out
how many bargains were made in advance, how
many promissory notes were delivered, and similar facts, and the true character of that convention
would be understood, and the people would see
how it was cheated out of its trust. As it stands
now neither Weed nor Greeley, nor any other of

that kind of politicians is master of the situation created by the convention. The true master is Raymond of the *Times*, and, as it is rumored, with the promise of the legation to France in his portfolio.

June 11.—That Meade ought to be very grateful to Grant. He basks in Grant's glory, gets credit for what he did not do, and no blame for the mishaps and difficulties which have befallen Grant's operations and which are almost all to be traced to Meade. It seems that Meade spent all his fire when he commanded a brigade, a division, and a corps. I expected that he would be a good Chief of the Staff under Grant, and execute Grant's combinations well, but he is not even good for this.

June 11.—Ambulances cross the city in all directions; crippled, lame, wounded in all the streets; thousands and thousands under the sod in the cursed Virginia soil, and all this sacrifice seems to have been made for the glory of the politicians. They disgrace the air and render it pestilential with their rejoicings, hurras, promenades and serenades—and prostrate themselves in the dust before their newly-gilded idol.

June 11. — Like a dying scorpion, Seward stung Hamlin, the Vice President, and had his name dropped from the new ticket. Hamlin was always opposed to Seward's flighty, gaseous, worse than half and half, untrue, unmanly, un-

American policy. So Seward intrigued and humiliated Hamlin.

June 11.—Many otherwise good patriots admonish me that I ought to submit to the people's will, and oppose Mr. Lincoln no more. There may come a time for it, but not now. I oppose not; I record actions, characters and events. I do not see that the people at large has ratified the nomination. Of course, I shall not separate from men with whom I am in the communion of faith and of principles, and go over to the enemies of light, truth, and progress, the copperheads and the Democrats. But I shall go on recording what I see and hear, and contribute to explain what otherwise may remain forever unexplained: how such an intelligent people could re-elect a Lincoln, and by what combinations and workings of events the best and the most clear-sighted patriots will be, or are already, obliged to adopt him. Unavoidable necessity forces many patriots in both Houses, and out of Congress all over the country, to swallow the bitter pill; the same unavoidable necessity may in time break or bend even the sterner ones. I shall observe and relate what I witness for their and for history's sake. I wish to throw an independent and unadulterated light on men and events which work out the destinies of this noble people in its gestation of solutions for the mightiest problems of social polity.

June 12.—Senator Hale is dropped from political life. His State sends on another man for the next Congress. Hale has drawn upon his head many enmities. He unrelentingly attacks the abuses of men in power. He shakes Neptune Welles by his beard and by his wig. Hale is the oldest anti-slavery champion in Congress; he spoke out boldly at a time when others were mute. By his talents and by his sturdy courage he has rendered eminent services to the cause. His speciality in Congress will not easily be replaced. He retires poor, very poor, and thus puts to shame all the mean inventions of his powerful enemies. If the party abandons Hale it will serve as one more evidence how ungrateful political parties are.

June 13.—Congress is unrelenting in its prosecution of treason, and in its uprooting of slavery. I mean the Republican majority. The statutes will bear evidence of the value of this 38th Congress—press or no press. Unrelenting are the copperheads in their hatred of loyalty to human rights and eternal principles, and unrelenting are their efforts to save the fact and the *prestige* of treason and of slavery. The democratic-copperhead treasonable minority in Congress throws all impediments allowed by parliamentary tactics to delay the final emancipation, and to delay the expurgation from the Constitution of slavery, that Cain's stain. But if not carried to-day it will be carried to-morrow, and the more opposition and hatred shown by the copperheads inside and outside of Congress, the more infamy and curses they accumulate on their names and on their heads.

Both Houses of Congress contain many members who, as characters and capacities, would be of mark in any public body. Some of their names have been repeatedly mentioned in the pages of this *Diary*, and I regret that I have not been able to do justice to all those honest, devoted, intelligent patriots, whose efforts and labors—next to the people's devotion—alone saved the country. The names of those devoted workers in the noblest cause are scarcely well known and appreciated throughout the Union, and totally unknown to what is called public opinion in Europe. I have already pointed out how the crotchety, narrow-minded, egotistical Press deludes public opinion here and abroad; I have pointed out how the hierophants of the press try to assert themselves as the seminal minds of the American life, but are not. To deal in generalities is the best that these hierophants and their crew know how to do; but generally error lurks in generalities.

Every slipshot, every imbecile, every quill-driver, every nincompoop, every ignoramus and snob believes it to be his duty to speak with contempt of Congress and of the Congressmen. So do broken-down politicians, treasury thieves, corruptors and lobbyists, and all that is mean or ignorant or corrupt in any society. So do also

17

those would-be respectabilities who look for
speeches instead of for records on the statute
books, and so do all those senile fogies, those
worshippers of the past who believe that grass
was greener when they were younger.

June 15.—The infamy of the fugitive slave bill
is blotted out from the statute book and from the
political life of America.   That bill was conceived in throes of despondency, subserviency,
and in the moral prostration of men whom the
public opinion considered to be almost the demi-
gods of the American mind, of American polity.
Webster, Clay, passed to posterity having the
Cain's stamp of that bill on their brows.   They
both fell and prostrated themselves before the
mammon of slavery.   My first step on American
soil was greeted by that bill, concocted · by selfishness and treason, by moral and physical
cowardice.

Humanity, duty, right, even dogmatic Christianity were spit upon and outraged by that bill.
Humanity was still more outraged in the high
intellectual standing of its concocters.   To-day,
in solemn national council, men comparatively
without names, without any high-sounding and
clarioned political or oratorical standing, simple-
minded men, but inspired by truth and justice,
inspired by the purest and loftiest feelings and
urgings—men, atoms among the self-governing,
atone for the crime committed by their predecessors.   Such men rehabiliate the purity of the

American name, muddied by what public fallacy considers and stamps as the glories of the American social and political life.   Often, very often names present clearly a condensed meaning. Daniel Webster, Senator from Massachusetts, was the godfather of the fugitive slave bill; Henry Wilson, Senator from Massachusetts, a—so-called —uneducated cobbler, and at whom "classical scholars," "high-toned conservative gentlemen," (without anything gentlemanlike about them,) turn up their noses; this Henry Wilson is one among the foremost destroyers of that bill.   O conservative fossils! which name of the two will be recorded with love by the genius of our race and of history ?

The destruction of this bill transmits to the gratitude of posterity the names of the members of this Congress.   Those names will be dear to the memory of their co-citizens, dear and honorable to their children.   Even the weaker vessels in the Republican majority nobly performed their duty and wavered not.   In this, as in all vital questions, this Congress, as did its predecessor, wavered not amidst the infuriated breakers. The Republican Congressmen wavered not when the national pilots confused everything, confused the conscience of the legislators.

The initiative for the repeal of this bill was not Lincoln's—quite the contrary; under the influence of the Sewards, of the Blairs, and of such like, for more than two years Mr. Lincoln opposed the repeal.

June 16.—Grant marched the army from the northern side of the Chickahominy and reached James river without giving Lee a chance to attack him. Compare this with that fatal change of base in 1862 commanded by Mc-Clellan.

The ignorant as well as the treasonable partisans of McClellan triumphantly exclaim, that Grant was obliged to imitate McClellan's great foresight and follow in his footsteps; and that instead of crossing the Rapidan, Grant ought to have at once embarked for the James river. In former pages of this *Diary* I explained the reasons which peremptorily forced Grant to march on Lee; and as to the change from the Chickahominy to James river operated by Mc-Clellan and by Grant, the difference is that McClellan was beaten by Lee and by the rebel army from one river to the other, while Grant has hammered back Lee and then moved freely —almost undisturbed.

Whatever might have been the awful loss in men during the fights in the *Wilderness*, Grant was forced to redeem the crimes and the criminal mistakes committed by his predecessors in command; by them Grant was fatally bound. Whatever may be the. future developments of this campaign, up to this day Grant has not committed mistakes, excepting that cardinal one of keeping Gen. Meade in his present position.

June 17.—As furious hurricanes, as geological as well as social upheavals always do, so this civil commotion here brings from the bottom to the surface many and various dregs and impurities. These *weeds* are most active and agitating, and spread their rottenness all around with uncommon velocity. If the Lincolnites maintain that these dregs find no affinity in Lincoln, at any rate many among the most intimate of Lincoln's familiars are of that kind. The enemies, not only of Lincoln—this I should not mind—but of our principles, profit by the above-mentioned affinities, and point them out to the public as corruptions inherent to the Republican party. Then comes the comparison with the bygone times, and the regrets for the former rulers, the "high-toned" slaveholders—or cavaliers.

Certain domineering and arrogant manners, this peculiarity of the "high-toned"—are neither true chivalry, nor do they constitute genuine good manners. The "chivalrous" Southron is virtually as low and vulgar as are the dregs and their affinities. But the court at the White House, together with its familiars, does not represent truly the country, or even the society. The simple, and in their manners natural and intelligent, unassuming, unaffected Senators and Congressmen, and their gentle families, these constitute the genuine social representatives of the Republican party. They are as superior in polish and culture to the dregs and to the familiars as they are superior to that sham gentility so admired in the slaveholding society.

June 18. — Grant, the noble and patriotic schemer, schemes how to crush Lee and the rebels. The radical Senators, Stanton, Dana, and others of that stamp, join with Grant. But Seward, Blair, and the host of politicians behind them, and the "good" and the bad press, all scheme how to re-elect, and Mr. Lincoln's heart and mind are deep with these last schemers.

June 18.—Some newspaper gives an account of Wadsworth's earnest, cool, and indomitable bravery before the enemy. As if Wadsworth could have been otherwise! Even now I cannot realize that he is gone, and that nevermore shall I see his honest face.

June 19.—One after another Chase's partisans fell into Lincoln's ranks. They do it because the small group of people who wished for Chase, has given him up.* Then the danger of a victory to

---

* Chief Justice Chase takes now a very decided stand in favor of the Africo-Americans and of their equal political and civil rights with the whites. The question of suffrage is daily more and more complicated. Equity, humanity, even gratitude is on the side of those who demand an immediate extension of suffrage to the loyal Africo-Americans. Such an immediate extension can only be made now by Congress, that is by the central, federal power. If however human wisdom could find a way to confer the suffrage to Africo-Americans by the special districts and communities—that is by those principally and immediately

be won by the Democrats spurns Chase's politicians. The radicals are sullen, and most of them hold back and hope that the bitter pill of adopting Lincoln will be spared to them. God grant it!

June 19.—The triumph of McClellanism will be *peace and the recognition of the rebellion.* All the bloodshed, all the sacrifices, made by the people will be thus frustrated, and the people's sacred, fiery enthusiasm condemned. Then will come the time of infamies, of repudiations, of despair, of giving up national integrity, of a general breaking up into splinter-like States and sovereignties, and of the reign of Satan all over this world.

June 20.—Nothing is more discordant, more rending to the mind and every feeling, than to listen to the copperheads and McClellanites speaking of human rights, of progress, and of eternal justice.

June 21.—Almost all over the country, but principally in New York, some of the wiseacres of the press now lustily tear to pieces McClellan and shake before him and before the public the long litany of his bloody crimes. But at the time when the crimes were perpetrated, many of the same wiseacres roared themselves hoarse

interested, then of course the principle of Self-government would thereby be fully preserved in its immaculate purity. But I am afraid that as events now run, the last may have to count among the *pia desideria.*—*Note October* 16, 1865.

with hosannahs for McClellan's great strategy and bloodless victories. Some of those who to-day tear him down, only yesterday recognized in him eminent and soldierlike capacities. Such are the great military writers in the *Times* and the other military sham critics. O, ignorance, ignorance and conceit! your nest is in the American press. Exceptions are few and rare. How unanimously the "good" press condemned that brave and indomitable patriot, Senator Chandler, for his anti-McClellan speech in 1862, during the perpetration of the Chickahominy crimes. How the wiseacres were then after the patriot, and how they defended the criminal!

June 22.—Every day I stumble over men who complain of and curse some acts of the departments, but principally the procrastinations and slowness in the Navy Department. Almost every day I hear complaints of arbitrary dealings with what is called the contractors. It would not be objectionable if only the thieving contractors *a la* Belgian blankets and rifles, were struck, but it is the honest, patriotic contractors who mostly suffer from the deeds of red tape.

June 23.—Arrests for thieving and for malversations increase daily. When such enormous sums are lavishly spent, of course, thieves will be attracted. The temptation is too great, and perhaps even honest men could not resist it. *L' occasion fait le larron* but——

June 23.—Governor Boutwell, M. C., of Massachusetts, would make a perfect President.   Not a flaw in him.   Earnest, warm-hearted, clear-sighted, broad-minded, he is one among the genuine incarnations of the people.   The people would certainly elect him; but the politicians, the leaders, the press will never put before the people men of Boutwell's caliber.

June 23.—The papers state that Farragut, the great naval hero, is in danger of having his wooden vessels destroyed by the rebel ironclads or rams in the bay of Mobile.   I tried to ascertain if this report is true, and unhappily it is. The only variation of it is that at least some ironclads are *on their way* to join Farragut.

Everywhere the Department of the Navy is laggard, and with their, at the best, one-hundreth part of our material resources, the rebels everywhere are in advance.   But as compensation for want of materials the rebels have decision and energy; we have Neptune-Van Winkle-Methusaleh-Noah Welles.   He ought to be daily stimulated with the whip of snakes in the hands of furies.   After all, Hale is right to shake him out of his bones, and to cut to pieces the red tape of the boards and cliques so all-powerful in the Navy Department.   But Fox ought to have more promptness and decision, or more power.

June 24.—The task of Grant and of his army daily becomes heavier and more complicated. Will it be possible to Grant and to the army to correct now and make up for that criminal imbecility paramount in the conduct of the war which began with Scott, and culminated in McClellan and in Meade?

Since 1861 all the rules of logic and of sound sense have been violated by those twin-brothers: Mr. Lincoln's generals and his special war policy. What Scott or McClellan did, after all emanated from or was the result of, that large and comprehensive Sewardian oracle in 1861–62, by virtue of which in sixty to ninety days all was to be over. Such violations of logic and of common sense were for the rebels like the heavenly dew which makes the trees in the forests take deep root, grow and expand. And now the rebellion is so firmly planted that superhuman efforts alone will uproot it. The people is equal to such efforts, but how is it with the galaxy in and around the White House?—Stanton excepted.

June 25.—Several Senators as anti-slavery as Sumner assert, that Sumner *really* believes he has the slavery question in *fee simple* to himself, and that no one has the right or understands how to deal with it. It is Sumner's fault if he makes such an impression on his colleagues.*

---

* On February 5 and 6, 1866, pleading for absolute right and for absolute justice, Sr. Sumner took a stand in the foremost rank of champions of all nations and of all times.

The petty, affected "classical scholar" and the rhetor receded. The thinker, the MAN spoke and stood on true American ground, on ground consecrated to mankind.—*Note Feb.* 8, 1866.

June 27.—If Lincoln is re-elected, then in the next four years the people will pay dearly, very dearly for its infatuation.

June 28.—The rebel sharpshooters make great havoc among our best men in the army. It seems that the rebels have perfected this mode of warfare to which the modern improvements in fire-arms are so especially adapted. At the beginning of the war we had a corps of sharp-shooters far better than the rebels, but McClellan began to disorganize it, and under his successors the corps wholly disappeared. And now it seems that our best men are at the mercy of the rebel marksmen.

June 29.—In a few days Congress adjourns, and again the destinies of the country will be uncontrolled and at the mercy of Lincoln's *bon plaisir*. After all, Congress at least kept in order a little Mr. Lincoln and his Sewards and Hallecks and Blairs. But now those worthies will kick up a dust like horses let loose from a corral. The best members are not yet converted or perverted to the Lincoln creed. Events may bring forth strange complications, although Lincoln has in his favor the powerful administrative organization, and many, many good men subside and bend under the clamor, and the thus created necessity to support him. But the *to-morrow!* the *to-morrow* may play Lincoln a trick. Patience!

June 30.—Chase resigned. He could not

honorably remain with Seward and Blair, and with Lincoln himself. With all his short-comings, Chase is better, far better, than the best in that triad. If Chase's resignation is to be the beginning of the breaking up of the Cabinet, and if it could upturn all the seats except Stanton's—then it would be a blessing. But it is impossible.

The Senate has shown a bold front; the Senate instantly returned to Mr. Lincoln the silly choice of Chase's successor.

The nomination of Tod shows that Mr. Lincoln has learned nothing; that he does not intend to mend his poor, small country politician ways and that he dreads to call a *man* into his Cabinet.

This nomination is an awful foreboding of what, if re-elected, Lincoln may dare to do. The people ought to comprehend the signification of this "Lincolniana," but it is not the "loyal" press who will speak the truth about it.

The good side of this nomination is, that it stirred up the Senate and the House to a sense of manhood in their relations with Lincoln. It showed Lincoln, Seward, and Blair that Congress is no more in the mood to allow them to trifle with the people's destinies; that Congress knows how to use the curb in its hands, and may now oftener apply it against the *bon plaisir* appetites of Lincoln, acting under the advice of the Sewards and the Blairs.

JULY.

July 1.—At last a MAN forced upon Mr. Lincoln. Fessenden enters the Cabinet. With his whole might he is opposed to going in; he wishes to avert the bitter cup, but he is pressed by the best men in the Senate and the House, and, what is more, he is demanded by the wish of the people in all the States, and by the honest bankers and financiers. Seldom is such an homage paid to the character of a public man. Few have received such proofs of confidence. Fessenden is a patriot of the truest steel. His whole time and health are devoted and sacrificed to his patriotic duty, and the only reward which he claims is the consciousness of having fulfilled his duty towards the country—towards the people. That is the only way in which Fesssenden courts public opinion, and he has never in any way courted the press. The press (the "loyal") would never have found out Fessenden, but the people and public opinion are more clear-sighted and sound.

Fessenden is the head of a noble, devoted family. He had three sons and the three responded to the country's call. One fell in Virginia in 1862, the other lost his leg in the fighting in Louisiana, the third is still in the field. A nest of patriots.

July 2.—The most glorious and vivifying result of this war and of the destruction of slavery will be the thorough purification and elevation of the American polity, and its thorough adaptation to the lofty principle incarnated in America and represented by her in the ascending development of mankind. Further, the political development and life will become purified from the former bickerings, compromises, and shiftings, in which grow up and thrive the contemptible race of American politicians. "Availability" will no more be the test presiding over the selection of men for high duties and functions. The mass of the people will become schooled and its mind disciplined and tried by the terrible earnestness of the times. The people who sacrificed so much for a principle, and so sternly faced terrible emergencies, will henceforth honor principles; will scorn availability, and for its own use will bring up and educate a higher set of politicians.

Such is the horoscope drawn by me.

July 2.—Weed, Seward's henchman, furiously and ignobly attacks Chase's reputation. That attack and the underhand stabs aimed at Chase

by Seward, honor Chase.   Thus Seward repays
Chase for having stood by him when Congress
made an effort to free the country from the official Sewardism.

July 3.—Stimulated by, and envious of the
laurels won by a Lorenzo de Medici, by a Riche-
lieu, by a Frederick the Great, and by his colleague Wilson, Sumner made an attempt to be
the founder of an academy of moral and political
science.

To be serious.   The natural sciences (Wilson's
academy,) have at least eminent representatives
in America, and possess some well established
names in the scientific republic of the world.
The names of the academicians presented by
Sumner are as new to moral and political science
as to any other science whatever.   In all probability some of them even ignore the existence of
such branches of science.   A few rhetors, editors
of newspapers, lecturers, compilers, literary bara-
tors, translators, etc., and Halleck, (Halleck!) at
the head!   Just the man to be an academician
in an academy of Sumner's foundation.   A few
speeches, orations, even on " the grandeur of
nations," editorials and paltry compilations do
not stamp one as a scientific man and a scholar
in the field of moral and political science.   The
true object is, to parade the new academy before
Europe, to send to the real savants nominations
signed "Sumner," to make one's self immortal,
to appear ridiculous, and to be laughed at by

genuine science. In the confusion prevailing during the last days of a session, Sumner attempted to smuggle through his academy, but the sound judgment of his colleagues saved them from ridicule. One Senator told me that in the general hurry and confusion, many of his colleagues did not really understand what was the matter. But they voted the project down because Sumner presented it.

July 3.—The unremitting efforts of Governor Andrew have blotted out one stain more from the people's escutcheon. At least as to the pay, the Africo-Americans are put on equal footing with their white compatriots in the army.

July 4.—Congress adjourned, and the great labor of the day will be to secure the re-election of Mr. Lincoln, considered by many true and good men as being the final victory, *not* of an individual, but of the principles which brought his name into the political strife. But the principle could as well have had a better and fitter standard-bearer. Perhaps we may have such a one yet.

July 4.—Whatever might have been the gaps separating the good patriots from the copperheads in the two Congresses, at least on one subject both parties sincerely united. Patriots and copperheads, the last only with a few exceptions, have been unremitting in their care of the soldiers, above all of the wounded in the Washington and in the army hospitals. Members of

Congress have been indefatigable in finding out the soldiers of their respective States. Such repeated visits to hospitals must not be confused with others made for effect, for incense, and for the sake of being heralded in the press.

July 5.—The gunboat Kearsarge sinks the pirate Alabama in the sight of Europe. The Kearsarge, Winslow the commander, and his heroic crew fought single-handed—it can be said —against Europe, as the two great maritime powers, England and France, fitted out, armed, coaled the steamer, furnished crews, and stood by the pirates. But Winslow ought to have sunk that officiously treacherous English yacht in the pay and in the service of the confederates. But for the operatives of Lancashire, but for a John Stuart Mill, a Goodwin Smith, a John Bright, and others like them, you English upper classes, you English snobs—and you are legion— you English sham-nobles and gentility, would make England and dishonor synonymous.

July 5.—English snobs, making their pious journey to Mecca and Medina, that is to the secesh region, when returning home, publish the relations of their unholy pilgrimage. Their reasonings, their opinions, and judgments are not much, but facts and data furnished by them deserve some credit. The facts and data furnished in this way almost in every point confirm what, since 1862, I have said concerning McClellan's visions of double numbers of the enemy,

and concerning McClellan's unsoldier-like qualities.

July 6.—Too good to be passed over. The
Blairs—(the whole family)—speak of Lincoln as
a " good Blair man ! "

Acheronta movebo.

At this Seward ought to hang himself; he is
distanced by the Blairs.

July 6.—Mr. Lincoln spites Congress and
pockets the bill for reconstruction as passed by
both Houses. Mr. Lincoln finds the bill
good and finds it not good; exactly the Lincoln
shilly-shallyness. The bill pushes aside Mr.
Lincoln's fussy *one-tenth* reconstruction. Wait,
wait, Mr. Lincoln! you have not yet heard the
last on account of this *escamotage.*

July 6.—Whoever wishes to have a genuine
measure of the *first-class* power of the " loyal "
press, should read attentively a leader in the *Tribune* (Greeley) of this day. It speaks of this
Congress's session. All the arrogant presump-
tion of a disappointed, nay, of a deposed leader
of a party, pours from every line. It is very
natural, however, that a Greeley cannot comprehend and appreciate to its full value the majority
of Congress. The majority did not idolize
Greeley, and laughed at his peaceful propensities and shameful inconsistencies. *Jude iræc.*
Well, the Congresses will be curiously handled
by that Thucydides of this war.

July 6.—The rebels spread over Maryland. Is

it a raid or an invasion? Our frightened
Jomini-Halleck is invested with command and
cannot yet find out. Of course not; it is far
easier to find a word in a dictionary than to find
out the numbers of a roving enemy.

If it is an invasion, then it is a brave and desperate attempt of Lee to escape Grant's jaws or
to divert his attentions and his forces. Halleck,
the brave powder-eater, has doubled the pickets
around—his house.

July 6.—Congress adjourned, and the contumely thrown on Congress by Seward and heralded by him all over Europe is not avenged.
Seward could impudently tell European governments that the opinion of Congress amounts to
less than zero. No English minister, not even
the most powerful, would ever have dared in
such a way to kick an English parliament. The
fate of such a premier would have been sealed:
impeachment, the tower, and the block. The
noble patriot Winter Davis did his utmost to
save and avenge the honor of Congress. Senator
Sumner did his utmost to degrade the Congress
and—succeeded. To be inspired with the dignity of a political body, one must have the feeling of personal dignity.

July 7.—The Government calls out militia to
meet the raiders. The day when Grant took
position south of Petersburg was the time to call
out the militia and to be prepared for any and
every emergency.

July 7.—Here is a proof what a good police
the secessionists have in Washington. Mr. Lincoln asserted to-day that the 6th Corps would
land at Baltimore; a secesh tells me that it is
coming to Washington. I ascertained that the
secesh is right.

July 7.—Seward in his rocket-letters proudly
asserts that Lincoln's renomination is his work.
Well, if so, what a fall for Lincoln from the
King-Maker Warwick-Greeley to the King-
Maker Warwick-Seward.

July 8.—It would be amusing were it not so
saddening, to witness how the myriads of ants
are busily engaged in screwing into Uncle Sam's
belly their big and little screws and drawing
greenbacks therefrom. The honest men in the
Departments, such as Stanton, Dana, and a few
others, vigilant to the utmost, as they are, cannot
prevent this phlebotomizing and are often im-
potent against the myriads.

The secesh in Washington are rampant, jubi-
lant, and forebode wonders from this raid in
Maryland.

July 9.—Gen. Wallace defeated by the rebels.
So far as I know, Wallace is Lincoln's pet and
choice. Gen. Wallace is a stern patriot, good to
keep under the heel that villainous, treacherous,
Baltimorean sham aristocracy of beggars' lineage; but he is not for the field.

July 9.—I am certain that Seward must have
sent some grandiloquent despatches to Europe.

We suffer small disasters and a big disgrace; they always follow when Seward lifts himself on the Pythonessa's tripod.

July 9.—What blunderings, and ignorance and shame! The military powers, the commanders, the Jominis are ignorant of the whereabouts of the rebels, of their number, and allow them to promenade undisturbed from one end of Maryland to another and all this under the noses of our mighty ones and within reach of a good telescope! And their commander's blood does not boil to be thus slapped in the face and on both cheeks.

July 9.—It is impossible to decide what is most revolting to witness here. Is it cowardice —is it imbecility? The powers are scared out of their senses. We are taken by surprise, like monks, nuns, or chickens. Eagles we are not, and not bulls. We dare not show either talons or horns, and not even our faces. Oh! what a shame! A man with only the smallest courage would confound these rebel marauders. It is impossible that they number scores of thousands. Fear sees double.

July 10.—The Spanish Republics, Peru, Chili, show their teeth to Europe even when virtually abandoned by our Cabinet. In this embroglio between the Southern Republics and certain European courts, Russia could and ought to be the moderator, the pacificator, the umpire, and the balance-holder. "*La Russie pourait jouer un beau role,"* said I to a diplomat from one of the Hispano-American Governments. " *Oui,*" he answered, " *mais la Russie joue aux cartes.*"

July 10.—Impotency and incapacity rise in proportion as the rebels spread, maraud, burn, and approach Washington. I am certain that the poorest farmer in the country is not as terror-struck by the approach of these robbers and marauders as are our Jominis and Carnots commanding now in Washington.

The Washington traitors and secessionists are active as bees; rampant and bold as if Early and Breckinridge were already in the Capitol. It is certain that numbers of them crossed over to Frederick and joined the rebels; others urged the rebels to march on Washington, *comparatively* defenseless two or three days ago. But only *comparatively* because a nightcap commands here. These Washington secessionists and traitors are indefatigable in their treacherous activity. But it is an old game. It began even before the day of Sumter, and has been openly carried on until to-day, and Lincoln-Seward shut their eyes and always expect that the traitors will turn the corner. It is said that more than anybody the Blairs contribute to mollify Lincoln's retributive justice. When a Washington traitor is caught, then all of them play the lambs, and swear to the traitor's innocence. All the traitors here have so many ramifications by men and women, and have so entangled certain men in power, that it can be said there is no help against treason; that it can no more be repressed, and the Government is forced to suffer it with eyes open.

July 11.—What a genius is this Halleck! The rebels drive in the pickets around the fortifications, burn, and play pranks within gunshot of our batteries and bastions, rebel bayonets glitter around, rebel cavalry gallops across the fields in all directions, and Halleck, the impurturbable translator, who directs our *defensive* movements, literally has not yet put his nose out of his office. If General Augur had his hands free, this shame could not have befallen us. Augur and his staff are tried in fire; they all know how to fight, and how to whip an enemy. But Augur cannot even place a picket, but must receive Halleck's orders.

Halleck and his Staff are familiar with oysters, champagne, and cigars, but the glitter of the enemy's bayonets hurts their eyes; dry and burnt powder is very distasteful to their *delicate* nerves and frames.

July 11.—It would be curious to ascertain if our Æneas and Anchises (see vol. II) had again a vessel ready and under steam to convey them away from this fated city. Certain it is, that a mail steamer filled with flying crinolines— among them one eminent Senator—left the city in a hurry.

It seems that the rebels are not in strong force and not strong in artillery, which they virtually

have not yet used against us. Neither have we
dared to fire even our 100-pounders. O, Halleck!

Hannibal ante portas, the danger is not very
great, but the shame nameless for us, and the
glory for the rebels in proportion to our shame.
The rebels do not attempt to storm, but knock at
the defenses, and we dare not kick them. "The
rebels have surrounded Washington *with a ring
of iron and fire*," said to me one scarred brave.
This ring is composed of dismounted cavalry,
and *we* are still in the dark about the number of
their infantry. They cannot be much, perhaps
ten to fifteen thousand in all. Not enough even
for a *coup-de-main*, even with a Halleck commanding inside of the fortifications.

July 11.—All the incapacity, all the blunderings
are exclusively Halleck's work. It is positive that
when the rebels crossed the Potomac Grant tele-
graphed to Halleck that he might ask for troops
from the Potomac Army, if he judged it necessary. Halleck found out—nothing, and asked
for—nothing. Maryland was set in flames, and
then only Halleck, the great, the equable, called
on Grant for troops. The 6th corps could have
been here ten days ago, but for Halleck.

But how can Stanton have any confidence in
Halleck, who cannot command even three broom-
sticks. As for Lincoln, he must consider Halleck
to be his military clown.

July 12.—During the Peninsular campaign,

Wellington complained of newspapers. What would he have said of these American mosquitoes the reporters?

July 12.—During more than a week the rebels approached Washington. For the last five days they shook their fists in our faces; and now when we have troops enough to take them all, the Government calls out the Washington militia. Wonderful courage, and more wonderful foresight! Had this been done in time, the militia could have manned the forts, and the troops could sail out and give battle. But Jomini Halleck gives no battles.

Now I understand why Halleck did not fire on the rebels, who quietly at from five hundred to fifty yards deployed before Fort Stevens. The first scare over, Fort Stevens became the object of fashionable promenade. Our highest men, our Secretaries, and ladies pilgrimed to the fort to gape at the rebels. Halleck was too polite to fight seriously, having *such a public* for spectators. The stern patriot, Ben. Wade could not stand this mockery, and vehemently protested against the crowd of d—— f——s who presided over those unsoldierlike exhibitions.

July 13.—The audacity of the rebels deserves the highest admiration. They keep us hemmed in, awe us with bold and active demonstrations, and we cannot pierce the veil which covers their real numbers. But the rebels know well that

Halleck is in command, and they can dare every thing.

July 13.—The rebels retreat. The damage done by them amounts to very little, but the disgrace on our side is unspeakable. I doubt if the history of war records any campaign as disgraceful, as shameful as this campaign in the defense of Washington has been for us. Never and nowhere have I read of a government being so slapped in the face as ours has been by this rebel raid. History has not on record military conduct so below any honor and manhood as that of Halleck in this campaign. I pity Stanton for being carried or dragged in that whirlwind of fear and mud. I cannot turn my eyes on the War Department.

The rebels disappear and retreat, and we—of course—know not in what direction. We do not follow. Halleck is *too wise* to do it. Best to give the rebels a start of at least twenty-four hours, then they can concentrate better, and even incidentally crush Couch, or Hunter, or anybody, before Halleck can send troops after them.

If Lincolnism survives the indelible shame of this Washington campaign, then it can survive everything.

The generalship shown on our side during this decade of shame almost borders on treason. I never would have imagined that imbecility could be so gigantic.

July 14.—Fort Stevens, the theatre of our

shame. O heavens! the whole area around increases a hundredfold the criminality of our
commanders. For more than two miles around,
the land is open; the movements of every single
rebel, and not only those of larger bodies, were
perfectly visible from the fort! And how the
rebels could have been allowed to approach so
near, and pick off our men in the fort! Every
soldier thus killed, was virtually murdered by
Halleck and by those who keep Halleck in command. Any other Government would cashier
and tear off publicly the insignia from the
shoulders of such a commander, who so mortally
dishonored the soldiers and the Government.

July 14.—In pompous and empty generalities
the great New York press explains the shame
of Washington. Even if it were through ignorance that the press thus confused and led astray
public opinion, it could scarcely be pardoned.
But the press deliberately wishes to blind the
people; it shields the real authors of this criminal disgrace, and the plea for this treason to
public opinion is, that the administration must
be sustained.

July 14.—The criminals, the imbeciles, and
cowards try now to authentically, authoritatively
establish that the rebels before Washington were
30,000 strong, with a large park of heavy
artillery. But their encampments at Silver
Springs show traces of *scarcely* half that number.

If the rebels had 30,000 men and heavy artillery, they would have swept us out of Washington.

The hide of the biggest bull in the world, nay, the hide of an elephant, would not suffice to record on it all the military stupidities committed from the first day of the invasion of Maryland to this hour. And those who come in contact with Lincoln—the good Senators—assure me that Halleck becomes endeared to Lincoln in proportion to the amount of imbecility and of cowardice shown in this last dishonorable performance.

July 14.—I learn from a highly reliable source that Grant saw with pleasure the invasion of Maryland by the rebels. Grant was certain that not one of them would be allowed to recross the Potomac. I pity Grant for putting any reliance on Halleck and his military coadjutors.

Thus ended the siege of Washington; ended in shame, humiliation and disgrace for the Lincolnites.

It seems that the rebels faltered. Doubtless during the night of last Saturday they could have pierced through and burned Washington, provided they were as strong as our frightened commanders believe. If so, then Washington was saved by a moral terror in the hearts of the rebel matricides.

Whoever is connected with the fact or the action or the something else by which Halleck is kept even on the outskirts of the War Department, should never be pardoned by the people.

July 15.—Banks *reconstructs* Louisiana. I wish he may succeed. I shall deeply regret if his attempt miscarries, and any blame whatever befall him. In reconstructing Louisiana on the principle of the Proclamation, he undertakes a very difficult task; his sincere, devoted, patriotic efforts deserve success, and certainly he ought to be heartily supported by Mr. Lincoln, whose notions he attempts to carry out. Perhaps, likewise, it may be time to try against the slaveholders men of firm but conciliatory ways and methods. The attempt will fail, but let them make it. At any rate Banks is true and honest, and if he has made faults or mistakes—who has not?

July 15.—The country, the people at large, will swallow the worse than humbug concerning the great rebel force which appeared before Washington, mainly before Fort Stevens. The "loyal" press will aid and the distant population will be taught to firmly believe that the capital and the country's honor were miraculously preserved, and that the miracle was performed by the skill, the caution, and the high courage of Halleck-Lincoln and of other braves commanding supreme in Washington.

Already the "loyal," the "good," the sincere and truth-seeking press FALLS IN. The siege and the disgrace " are the fault of nobody except the impudent, daring rebels." The rebels impudently promenaded in Maryland, and sacrilegiously put their fists under the noses of the powers in Washington. Oh, these rebels! The press absolves Lincoln-Halleck of all want of foresight!

July 15.—What a pity it would be, if even after the nomination at Baltimore, "sacrilegious" men should raise their voices, appeal to the sound sense and patriotism of the people, and put them on the track to discover that there have been enough of incapacities at the helm, enough of wanton slaughter, enough of shifting and of sticking in the mud; teach the people that there is no *real* danger in annulling the decision of Baltimore, and in looking for and selecting a man with firm and large brains—a *man in himself;* and not by the help of Seward, or Blair, or Halleck, etc.

What a pity if it should come to that! and the nice little arrangements made beforehand should thus come to grief, and so many greedy "patriots" become disappointed, and lose the fat accumulated already and the expectations of more and of a new fattening lease, etc., etc., etc. What a pity, what a pity, should it come to that dire, that accursed extremity!

The rebels having gone, the gunboats arrive on the Potomac to defend the city. Always and everywhere foresight and *apropos.*

Zadnym umon krepki.

July 16. — The relations, the details, the accounts coming from various different sides and

sources confirm the truth that in sight of Fort
Stevens the rebels were at the *utmost* 8,000,—if
so much.   The *official measurements* of the rebel
camps at Silver Springs and around, establish
that a large army bivouacked there.   But a large
army would have destroyed more, and left at
least considerable—manure.   (The reader must
forgive.)   The rebels having space at their command took it comfortably and leisurely; their
encampments were not crowded, but spread out.
A wise cunning may have prompted them to do
it; seen from a distance and by frightened men,
a large space occupied by the encampments
would induce belief in immense numbers.   So
much for the *official survey*.   The rank and file of
the soldiers disbelieves the story of large numbers; the panic which raged in Halleck's and in
his coadjutor's bosom did not touch the hearts of
the rank and file.

July 16.—Grant's campaign is the bloodiest
known in history.   It is so on both sides.   Our
heroic soldiers cover the cursed and treacherous
Virginia like grass mowed by the scythe.   Hancock and his corps are considered the prominent
heroic fighters of this campaign.   Hancock cannot be an engineer, or from among the West
Point "first graduates."   But so far as I can
judge, every corps and its commanders, generals
and other officers have each their days of glory
in this merciless slaughter.   Meade has the

glory of being the only dead-weight of the glorious and fated Potomac army.

July 16.—The reasons for this last national disgrace before Washington at Fort Stevens are explained. To-day's newspapers announce the issue of *Jomini's Life of Napoleon,* translated and annotated by—Halleck. Of course, during the last five weeks, Halleck could not watch such earthly things as the movements of a bold and. a desperate enemy. His mind soared in higher spheres than the national honor.*

July 16.—Now the storm and dust are over, *we* are active, grand; we organize, arm, drill the poor clerks, and get ready to scare off any future attempt on the honor or safety of the capital.

All the efforts of the Washington military big night-caps are directed to make the people firmly believe that the masses which attacked Maryland and Washington amounted to more than 40,000 men. I observe that since the rebels retired, the governmental sources increase their number at the ratio of at least 5,000 men per day.

When the rebels crossed the Potomac, Halleck, entrusted with the supreme command, for more than a fortnight considered it below his dignity or not worth his while to pay any attention to their pranks. It was, in his authoritative opinion, "a cavalry raid which would soon disperse and disappear." His confidence and self-

---

* See Appendix II.

possession were at the least—admirable. After the defeat of Wallace at Monocacy, from an unbounded equanimity and security our Jomini rapidly passed into the condition of fears and trances. When the rebels approached Washington, then instead of beating them off, he and his martial associates strained their bellicose and strategic brains to invent a theory about the further movements to be made by the rebels, and to speculate what more they would invade and destroy. The wings of imagination spread and fearfully expanded the capacities of our strategians. The presumed operations of the rebels bordered on the gigantic, the marvelous. Early, Breckinridge rose to the stature of Merlin the magician; the rebels were to march on Point Lookout, free the thousands of rebel prisoners kept there, and carry out similar undertakings!

The war of debate whether the rebels numbered 12,000, 24,000, 54,000, continues. The Administration plays *chorus* for the largest number. It believes in this way it will incur less shame. But it will not do. If the rebel host in Maryland was 50,000, then the greater the incapacity on our side to have considered it at the start an insignificant raid, and taken no precautionary measures until they spread over Maryland, and turned upon Washington. An army of forty or fifty thousand can easily be scouted out; its movements are not the movements of raiders. Poor-brained Administration! stupidity

19

on one horn of the dilemma, on the other an un-
nameable disgrace.

July 17.—For the hundredth time during this
war, the many, the nameless, the people pay
with their blood for the imbecility of pet commanders; the nameless alone rescue the national
honor. Under Halleck's command the army
marches, countermarches, in heat, dust, and
thirst. The enemy flies and escapes; and escape
he would not, but for immortal Halleck's combinations. And now by hard fighting the
soldiers will again be obliged to correct the proof
sheets—dipped in blood—of Halleck's generalship.

July 18.—A new call for 500,000 men. Lincoln ought to make his *whereas* as follows :

Whereas, my makeshift and of all foresight
bereaved policy—

Whereas, the advice of a Seward, of a Blair,
and of similar etc's—

Whereas, my Generals, such as McClellan,
Halleck, and many other pets appointed or held
in command for political reasons, have occasioned a wanton slaughter of men; *therefore*

I, Abraham Lincoln, the official Juggernaut,
call for more victims to fill the gaps made by the
mental deficiency of certain among my commanders as well as by the rebel bullets.

July 18.—Halleck's masterly combinations tell
upon Grant. Two army corps withdrawn from
him, and for an indefinite time. The blun-

derers in the Shenandoah valley, and the blunderers in Washington may occasion, if not the
loss, at any rate the procrastination of the campaign before Richmond. As early as April the
blunderers began; they were marked by keeping
incapable Generals in command in the valley.
It is an absolute and a general military rule, to
put a separate command in the hands of the
most experienced and the best tried General. In
the relative positions of armies at the beginning
of this campaign in April and May, the operations in the Shenandoah valley were second in
importance only to the operations of the main
army. And those operations in the Shenandoah valley were full and complete mistakes, if
not worse, equal only to the ability displayed by
Halleck against the RAIDERS in Maryland and
before Washington. The Government will
assert the contrary, so will the "loyal" press;
Grant, inspired by politeness, may be silent, but
common sense contradicts the governmental assertions.

July 18.—The White House is showered with
denunciations and accusations. The Blairs are
rabid for the burning of their houses by the rebels,
and for some other small losses. As if the losses
suffered by such as the Blairs deserved to be no-
ticed! The Blairs will be compensated in some
way, but these Halleckings impoverished hundreds, if not more, of small owners of land and
houses, of laborers, and of honest workmen and

operatives, and nobody speaks on their behalf, nobody thinks of compensating them. The conspirators in the cabinet, Seward and Blair, seize this occasion to try to crowd out Stanton from the councils, although they know very well that it is not Stanton's fault if a Halleck and other deadweights are entrusted with commands. Stanton did not command the defensive operations in Maryland and before Washington, as he never meddles with the manœuvres of armies. Stanton is however accusable for having subdued his sound judgment to other influences, and suffered certain men and actions which he blamed or blames. But it is not for this mistake that Seward and Blair condemn Stanton.* Seward attempted to

---

* I can most thoroughly understand the bitter, poisonous, unrelenting, never-to-be quenched hatred which infuriates all the copperheads, all the McClellanites, all the peacemen, all the Democratic politicians, and all the northern traitors, against Stanton. But for the energy, the prompt and daring decision, displayed by Stanton during the presidential canvass, *undoubtedly* McClellan would have been elected. If he is sincere, the future historian of that ominous epoch will establish the above assertion beyond doubt or cavil. It is not the place here to give the various details and facts that irrefutably confirm my statement. All the stumpings and speechifyings, all the battered enthusiasm and all other etceteras, would have proved powerless to elect Lincoln, had not Stanton grasped the matter. The copperhead intrigues and money would have been too much for the Republican politicians. Stanton saved them, and with them the national honor and the nation's existence. Every one knows that with McClellan, peace, sympathy with the rebels and with slavery, and the gallant martial galaxy of McClellanites, Meade included, would have been paramount. Grant, Sheridan, Sherman,

get into the Cabinet a man more after his own
heart.   But the fullness of time of the Sewards
and Blairs is not *yet* at hand.   *Proh pudor* O,
Lincoln!

July 20.—The life of Lincoln written by Raymond.   A campaign document, and therefore of
no intrinsic value, but nevertheless it reveals new
facts brought out as exculpatory of faults of which
Lincoln is believed to be the perpetrator.   What
extenuation for Lincoln, if with eyes open on
McClellan's incapacity he nevertheless kept him
in command?   What exculpation for having
appointed Burnside, or for keeping Halleck?
Among the many exculpations attempted in this
biography is the justification of General Pope,
corroborated by evidence given before the Committee on the Conduct of the War.   What
months and months ago I recorded, (see I and
II vols.,) is confirmed by these revelations and
investigations.   Pope was betrayed by McClellan
and by his pets.

July 21.—A new, dirty, confused, clownish attempt at patching up a peace.   Smart, cunning
rebel intriguers on one side of Niagara Falls, and
on the other a monomaniac, if not worse, a certain Colorado Jewett, Greeley *of course*, Florida-
Hay, and at a distance Mr. Lincoln, dragged in
by Greeley, and probably pushed or tickled into

Thomas, would have been pushed aside, the people's glory tar-
nished and trodden in the mud. *Jnde iræ et lacrymæ.*—*Note*
July, 1865.

it by Seward and Blair. Fessenden and Stanton wash their hands of all this dirt. I wish the negotiators might meet on that plank or bridge over the Falls, and then be shoved into the foam. These peace meddlers sacrilegiously attempt to cheat the people out of its sacrifices, out of its blood. So Wadsworth and hundreds of thousands of heroic Northern confessors laid down their lives, that a Greeley, or a Seward, or some such one may patch up a peace.

The *Independent*, the *Observer*, and very likely other weeklies and monthlies, edited by divines, at times appreciate the events and men from a standpoint by far higher and clearer than that of the common press. At times these preaching and writing divines and their coadjutors are the genuine apostles of the spirit of our age.

July 24.—Lull interrupted by Sherman's distant thunder. What a combination of brilliant, rapid manœuvres is Sherman's campaign towards Atlanta! Well, I am certain that Sherman is not an engineer.

Grant has now on hand a work before whose magnitude disappear all the other sieges known in history, from Troy to Sebastopol. Grant has not men enough for such a work, and with Meade to execute his combinations, he is in danger of being baffled.

The prevailing lull is likewise interrupted by the wranglings in the Cabinet. Blair still attempts to upset Stanton, and Seward pats Stanton on the back, and underhandedly supports Blair's efforts.

July 25.—The so-called *money market* is very heavy for the Government. No wonder. The money bags, the leaders of such markets in New York and Boston, the presidents of the various banks are mostly copperhead-Democrats, or Mc-Clellanites, or open partisans of the South. Add to it the facility with which many administrative acts can easily justify assertions establishing the incongruity and the incapacity of our rulers, and those who wish to break the money credit of the Republican party have very easy work.

I pity Fessenden if the above-mentioned combination should frustrate the fruits of his financial activity. He will be sacrificed and atone for the faults and crimes of others. But he is a true man and patriot; he looks to his duty and wavers not.

July 25.—Washington covert secessionists and open spies are unscared and defiant. They predict a new invasion of Maryland and various other events. These secessionists are hand in glove with the Democrat-copperheads, and the McClellanites. Jefferson Davis would crush in Richmond and all over the South every Union man who would behave like the Washington secesh and their twin brothers the New York copperheads. But Lincoln's make-shift leniency is inexhaustible. And the organs of Jeff, Davis,

such as the *World* and the *National Intelligencer*,
talk of poor Lincoln's tyranny!

July 25.—Mud and dirt accumulate in and
around the White House and nobody to clean it
up.

July 25.—Speculators in Cabinet-making already draw their horoscopes for the eventuality
of re-election. Already they decide who will go
out, who shall be kept in. Away with all of
them, except Fessenden and Stanton! Bates*
will be eaten up by the Missouri radicals. All
that is good in Bates can be resumed in this
single fact, that he sincerely tried to have under
him young, intelligent, thorough men. ' Such
was Coffey, such is now Ashton of Philadelphia.

After all, by his "to all whom it may con-
cern," Lincoln smartly escaped part of the ridicule into which he was dragged. But it will
always remain on record that Lincoln used underhand agents, and selected men who must
throw ridicule on all such attempts and proceedings. Lincoln ought to have been warned by
Greeley's past, by his Switzerland *umpiro-mania*,
and above all by his almost criminal association
with an obscure adventurer, and through the adventurer with the French *Decembriseur*. Gree-

---

* James Speed succeeded Bates. The country, the cause of
justice and of a thorough emancipation have gained, and gained
considerably, by this rotation.

ley's conduct in 1862 and since ought to have been a warning for Lincoln not to touch even with a stick whatever came from that quarter.

July 26.—The Sixth Corps marches, counter-marches, and the invaders are altogether—safe. Of course Halleck commands. Halleck's written orders are remarkable—not for their clearness and precision, but for the cunning of a petty lawyer. The Generals who receive these orders cannot find out their meaning, and Halleck's responsibility is *a couvert*. I regret that Stanton puts his mantle over the Halleckings and Lincolnings, and assumes such a responsibility.

July 27.—Ben. Wade says: "*Put Halleck in the command of 20,000 men and he will not scare three setting geese from their nests.*" To be sure this Halleck—one of Sumner's miscarried academicians—never saw a cartridge burnt, and never had even the curiosity to see one.

July 28.—The want of reserves is now deeply felt on account of the merciless consumption of men. But it is too late. The difficulty ought to have been overcome in the first year of the war. (See v. I.)

July 28.—One may daily assist at the Falstaffian organization of the various clerks in the various departments. The ridicule is overpowering, and among the high and the low the parts are distributed with a Shakspearian perfection.

July 28.—Republican papers, and above all the grave, sedate *Evening Post*, clamor that McClellan be used in the field. This gives the measure of the consistency of the American press. The press accused McClellan of incapacity. If he was incapable six or twelve months ago he is now. If his unsoldier-like qualities generated disgraceful defeats, has his sojourn in New York developed any new or latent martial spirit? Either these worthies of the press have been utterly ignorant of what they spoke when they attacked McClellan, or are worse than ignorant now.

July 28.—"Cotton is king!" was the arrogant war cry shouted against human liberty by the pro-slavery Southern and Northern conspirators. "Cotton is king!" was the animus of the treacherous and matracidal undertaking. What is cotton now? No more a king in the South, but the temptation now to dirt and vileness for many, even once tolerably honest men in the North. Cotton licenses, cotton contracts, cotton speculations, and anything whatever connected with cotton, is the bait held out by Satan to ruin men's souls and drag them with hurricane velocity into perdition.

July 28.—Lincoln-Halleck and their bellicose strategic coadjutors proved to their own satisfaction that the brilliant incapacity displayed by them in the defense of Washington, is to be recorded as the *ne plus ultra* of high military qualities. These heroes have subsided into a self-admiration before which vanishes even the celebrated Harvard-Boston circle!

July 28.—This defense of Washington, or rather this nameless disgrace, is one more evidence how Mr. Lincoln sacrifices to his whims and pets the best blood of the people and the country's honor. He keeps up Halleck against general contempt and curses, as he keeps Meade to ruin Grant's campaign.

July 28.—The *Atlantic Monthly*, a g-r-e-a-t review, is enraptured with Seward because in all his State papers the Secretary of State emphatically asserts that a disintegration of the Union is utterly impossible. But O great statesman of a great press! what else could Seward say? Could he, in his official capacity, admit the possibility of disruption? And the gallows, eh? It would have been high treason. Seward is not a traitor in the strict sense; but the various ups and downs of his policy since March, 1861, his sixty and ninety days' prophecies, his utter want of earnestness, his offers of seats in Congress to the rebels, his diplomatic, official assertions in April and May, 1861, that there is *no war*, that *slavery will be preserved*, and numberless similar pranks, made him the laughing-stock of European statesmen. Add to it his Mexican policy, his utter ignorance of international laws, customs and processes; add to it his intrigues, his enervating influence upon Lincoln, etc., and then it will be found that Seward has done mischief almost equal to that of any one who joined the rebels, and all his easy spread-eagleism cannot atone for the evil which he has already perpetrated.

July 29.—The same periodical has fears and forebodings about foreign intervention, recognition, and God knows what. Since the breaking out of the war, if not daily at least monthly, the like trances have shaken the busybodies and the politicians, etc., and my answer is the same to-day as it was in May, 1861, and since: *whatever be its liberticide appetites or hatred of America, no European power will dare to interfere or to recognize the rebels.* At times Seward underhandedly stimulated and stirred up such fears, to be able to appear as Virgil's Neptune "*quos ego,*" and calm the excitement and be the saviour of the country.

The European press, paid by the rebels in France or England has often asserted, and will continue to assert, that now or at some *not distant time*, the European powers will interfere. That press must earn its wages; that is all: and the worse for our diplomats abroad if they are caught by such articles.

A new nation to be in position to beg a recognition must at least exist in geographical conditions, must be able to show at least approximatively positive geographical boundaries. Certain sovereigns and despots of Europe, certain rotten aristocracies and corrupt, dishonored, mercantile classes may overflow with sympathies for traitors and for slaveholders, and hatred of freemen; but the Governments are no fools and know well what is possible and impossible, what is feasible and what is not.

The sympathies shown in certain quarters to the Southern traitors, are neither so general nor so intense as was, and even is, the deep interest Europe felt in the fate of Poland and of the Poles. Poland periodically shakes Europe, evokes lively sympathies, even half-armed demonstrations, but never a recognition. And Poland is not a newcomer, not an offspring of dastardly treason to God and man like the South. Poland had geographical frontiers well known to Europe. For more than ten centuries Poland has had a large page in the world's history. Poland is a nation who can show an Elective Government which was in operation five or six centuries ago—a nation who nearly seven centuries ago had more thousands of free electors than England had then hundreds of them; and Poland is no more, and the principal cause of her non-recognition now-a-days is because old Poland has no longer positive, geographical, well-established frontiers.

This is one from among the reasons why the South cannot be recognized. Other and more stringent reasons are on the surface of events. Neither in England nor in France are treason and slavery popular with the great mass of the genuine people, and neither the *Decembriseur* nor his cronies' can stand against the genuine popular current. And the rest of Europe is *en corps* for the North.

July 30.—Wiseacres, theorists, schemers, etc., are very uneasy that the public debt has no steady principle of amortisation, no sinking fund. To sustain their declamations they appeal to European precedents—which in themselves are rather stale. These financiers are very uneasy about the European capital invested here. But first, the bulk of the loans is not made in Europe, not contracted with any Hopes, Rothschilds, Barings, Hottinguers, etc. If European capital is invested in American bonds, stocks, and funds, such investments are not made because of confidence in any sinking fund, but European capitalists are glad to get a high interest, and above all, they trust in the inexhaustible, in the *unsinking* vitality of the people. All these petty, soreheaded financiers are ridiculous with their petty schemes for regularizing the debt, when events are unsettled, and therefore the amount and the character of the debt remain still beyond the possibility of a positive settlement. The true American financiers are the members of Congress who feel that the debt is secured in the resources, the youth, the vitality, and the future of the people; they feel that *the future* will pay off the debt by ways, means and resources not yet dreamed of to-day; they know that it is useless to speculate and speak of amortisations and of sinking funds at a time when the amount of the debt cannot be fixed, and when *all* the resources and means are wholly absorbed by the war, and absorbed to an extent that makes it impossible to divert therefrom the smallest fixed national income. When the expenditures are reduced to a steady and normal condition, then will be the time for amortisations.

August 1.—From almost all points very bad news in relation to Mr. Lincoln's chances of re-election. The people at large seems not at all so enthusiastic for him now. The question is not about him, but about the principles of the party of which he is a poor, very poor instrument, and not a representative. If our principles succumb, then at least for half a century mankind is thrown backward, and a heavy up-hill work again begins. I am accustomed to such ups and downs in the life of confessors, but nevertheless rage and despair seize one to witness that a glorious victory was and is yet within grasp, and that the interference of a few bunglers prevents us from cleansing the path of progress from the most fœtid and corrosive obstruction left by the remotest ages and incarnated in the Southern traitors and slaveholders.

If the Democrats nominate a *man* at Chicago then Mr. Lincoln's fate is settled, and the Republican party is upset for perhaps a long time.

But have the Democrats a *man* in their ranks?
I know none. The Democratic party-creed is
base and degrading; a *man* cannot be inspired
thereby.

August 2.—A mine sprung before Petersburg,
and—a disaster for us. The reverse of what
generally happens ·in such cases. The mine
seems to have been well laid, but badly sprung.
Why use a fuse and not electricity? But the
fault was in the commanders. One or both
lacked heart or brains. Not, of course, the
troops, who behaved well and were slaughtered
to bear witness to the high, soldierlike fitness of
their commanders. Now, or never, for a stern
investigation, for a court-martial, and for an ex-
emplary punishment. Human and divine—if
there is a divine—justice, awake!

It would be almost impossible to admit that a
bad command occasioned the frightful disaster.
Almost any one gifted with an atom of bravery
and of common sense can comprehend how to
use troops when a mine is sprung in the enemy's
works. If the generals entrusted by Grant with
the execution confused all, then they ought to
be reduced to sweep the streets. The execution
and the command have been *a la Meade*, and that
is enough!

I will try to find out the truth. about this
slaughter and this disgrace.

August 2.—Burnside is accused of the miscarriage of the mine operation. It was his corps.

20

But in my opinion the fault and the crime is with somebody else besides Burnside.

August 2.—The Potomac army's wiseacres have found out that the climate, the air, the temperature act on the soldiers, on their muscles; and that on our, as well as on the enemy's side, the troops no longer fight so cheerfully. That may be true to a certain extent; but likewise, at least in our camps, the soldiers may have found out that they have too much Meadeism.

The rank and file, and generally the officers, fight well, fight heroically on all fields of battle in Virginia, as in Tennessee, Alabama, Louisiana, or Arkansas; most of the soldiers are hero-patriots after Wadsworth's type. And if this country should be wrecked, the great and sublime devotion of the many, the heroic sacrifice and death of their children,—these alone will surround the wreck with a halo.

August 2.—The streets of Washington, the bureaus in the Departments, and I am certain that the country at large also is, so to speak, filled with young men who dodge or escape the military service. It is a shame if those in power patronize or yield to such an unmanly practice, and keep as clerks individuals who could well go into the field.

August 3.—The secessionists here assert that Lee and Beauregard were very well informed concerning the mine, and were well prepared to meet the emergency. That may or may not be so, and does not diminish the crime of *our* commanders.　Very likely the secessionists in Richmond and here found it out, as inevitably they always find out everything; and when in their turn such secesh blood-hounds are found out or caught, then leniency steps in, as there are always coats or crinoline who in one way or other plead for the traitors.

August 3.—The Boston slave patriots of the stamp of the Ticknors, the Curtises, the Hillards, etc., men who prostrate themselves in the dust and lick the back of the slaveholders—call Everett a demagogue.　The noble old patriot can stand contumely coming from such quarters.

August 3.—The slaughter was again horrible. The history of the race scarcely has on record such cold, stubborn slaughters as are exhibited and perpetrated in this war.　And to use the stale and unscientific sham, that is raceological definition: all the races participate in those slaughters; *Shem*, (many Hebrews,) *Ham*, (Africo-Americans,) *Japhet*, in all its branches; the whole Indo-European family, and a branch of the Mantschou Mongol in the Indians.　In one word, the whole human "happy family."

August 4.—National fast day appointed by Mr. Lincoln.　Well, the people may fast to propitiate Divine Providence, but what kind of atonement shall Lincoln and his associates practice that God may forgive them?

Perhaps the people's God will have pity and inspire his children to select another leader.

August 4.—The general opinion is that somebody blundered in relation to the mine before Petersburg. They speak of investigation. Undoubtedly some one ought to atone for the reckless butchery. Accounts coming from the army do not say that Meade was in person on the spot. It was his duty to be there.

August 4.—The copperhead and other press clamors for a command for McClellan—says "that McClellan will lead the men." But where has he ever led the troops under fire? McClellan never in person positively was in line with any infantry, neither with a company, a battalion or a regiment; never during any action was McClellan in the front of a genuine field of battle, never under any fire of musketry or grape. And musketry and grape give the baptism of fire.

In the history of military trophies, McClellan inaugurated the enumeration of small arms picked up on a field of battle. (See his report after Antietam.) Of course only a McClellan could do it. Victorious troops either immediately follow up the victory, pursue the enemy, and thus have no time to pick up abandoned small-arms, or after a hard day they repose through the night to again move and pursue the enemy. Neither of the two was done at Antietam, and for a *passe temps* small-arms were picked up.

August 4.—As it stands now, Mr. Lincoln or Seward may be considered as the best canvassers for the success of a Democratic candidate. They divided the Republican party; its best men have no heart in the re-election, and scan the horizon for light and for a hope.

August 5.—The telegram is the ruin of greenhorns· in power. Only matured minds and hands ought to handle lightning. Otherwise mischief and confusion are created. Orders are given at random and over the heads of responsible men; such orders are not registered, recorded, and thus vanishes the responsibility for a misuse of power.

August 5.—The pro-slavery men and newspapers accuse the colored troops of cowardice, and lay on them the miscarriage and the disaster of the mine. I am certain that it is not so. When a corps leaves half its men on the field, such a corps fights and does not run away.

A Court of Inquiry is to be appointed to investigate the truth about the conduct of generals on July 30, (the mine.) If the court elucidates anything, will the truth become public property?

August 6.—Better late than never. Two *men* call the people and Mr. Lincoln to their respective senses. Senator Wade and Winter Davis rise and fulfill the duty of patriots, of citizens, and of guardians of the rights and duties of Congress and of the people. Long ago Mr. Lincoln's mistakes and errors ought to have been checked by an opposition professing the same principles as the Administration, and having the same aims. Such an opposition would have done good to Lincoln; it would have prevented many mischievous blunders, and to-day the future of the party would not be so desperate.

Wade's and Davis's protest against Lincoln's willfulness may constitute a new era in the history of this and the subsequent Congress and in their relation with Lincoln, or with any other President.

August 7.—In the life and the onward march of peoples and of nations, great ideas, lofty aspirations, great aims always have inspired a man for *the work* and for *the hour*—a captain in the sense of Carlyle—in one word, the wants of the hour have been incarnated in a leader. In this great trial of the American people, in its sacrifices for light and right, the incarnation is neither individual nor personal, but the whole people is inspired. This absence of captains is a new phenomenon in the life of mankind, and will constitute a new era in the development and the ascension of man. The South, which rose for the maintenance of all the social offal of by-gone ages and times, is incarnated in a certain number of traitor leaders, who in their turn recognize and are inspired by Jefferson Davis and by Lee, those traitors in chief.

But it is nauseous to hear the Lincolnites assert that their fetish is "the man for the hour," that *he* and *no one* else is the true expression of the people's generous aspirations. A make-shift, never even for once inspired, who never beckoned to the people from any moral or intellectual elevation, one who was and is always pushed and dragged onward by the firm will and by the patriotic aspirations of the people—he may be a true incarnation of the heartless, and the narrow-minded, and the selfish politicians, etc., but not of the genuine and generous people. And if with all this Mr. Lincoln be re-elected, it will be the result of some dire, unaccountable, and inevitable necessity; it will be done under the pressure of those events which so often darken the most glorious hours and days in a nation's life.

August 8.—Surveying, computing, and analyzing all the battles as fought in Virginia during these nearly four years, the average result proves :

1st. That before Lee and under Lee the rebels were most worsted when fighting us in equal numbers and on equal terms, that is, in an open field and not behind breastworks.

2nd. That on the average their manœuvres and tactics in 1861, '62, '63, were superior and more skillful than the tactics of the Union generals.

3rd. During this campaign Lee never dared to fight Grant in an open field, but kept his army in natural and artificial entrenchments from which the rebels were always pressed, crowded, or beaten out by the heroic bravery of the soldiers, and by Grant's daring movements.

4th. Lee had *all* the advantages on his side, and he feels well that if he comes out and gives up his advantageous positions, he, his army, and the rebel cause will at once be lost.

The bugbear of Lee again invading Pennsylvania is a hallucination produced by fear on certain "loyal" and "courageous" presses; the copperheads, the secessionists, and all the partisans of the South use it as a scare-crow, as a ghost story, to frighten the population and to throw them into the hands of the so-called peace McClellanites or any kind whatever of democrats or pro-slaveryists.

Lee knows now very well that what he could dare against a McClellan and against his successors he cannot dare against Grant and his army. He knows well that it would be his own ruin, and Lee will not now, and perhaps *never again*, leave his entrenchments before Richmond.

August 8.—I have the best reasons and the best authority to believe that Grant is disgusted with the Lincoln-Halleck military prowess as displayed in the defense of Washington; but why does Grant keep that Halleck in such a responsible place?

August 8.—The fate of Mexico and the continual complications and explanations which our Government is obliged to give to certain foreign powers on account of foreigners domiciliated here, prove how cautious the American republics ought to be in admitting foreigners to their midst.

Hungry and barefooted adventurers of the worst class have crept into Mexico, cheated the Mexicans, become rich by all, but mostly by unlawful means, then made false pretenses and counts, and finally invoking for their robberies the protection of their former native governments, have entangled Mexico in a war and occasioned the loss of Mexican liberty and independence.

In the same way thousands of foreigners come to the United States without any intention of sharing the destinies of the country and the people, but only to become rich by the aid of the liberal and hospitable American institutions and life. Now, when the crisis comes, they wash their hands and impede the action of the people and of its Government, make as much mischief as they can and then appeal to what they call their native governments.

Such horse-flies would better stay at home and starve there. The American people ought to make a law that henceforth no foreigner shall be allowed to earn even the smallest day's wages, and still less establish any business or work whatever, until he has taken the oath of allegiance to the American people and emphatically repudiated any claims whatever for protection from his former government. It will be the only way to avoid becoming the prey of lawless adventurers.

August 9.—The European diplomatic circle is

highly amusing *in concreto* and *in partibus*. With few, very few exceptions, it is busily devoted to undermining and breaking down the republican party.

Never and nowhere in my life have I witnessed such ill-will towards a Government as prevails among certain diplomats in Washington. Neither have I ever witnessed, and I am certain that diplomatic history has not record of, diplomats so totally ignorant of the condition of the country in general, and so especially, ignorant of the character of daily events passing under their noses as are most of the diplomats in Washington. Sometimes it seems that they must make the most superhuman efforts not to know the true condition of affairs and of things. I pity their respective governments.

August 10, *Long Branch.*—On my way here I passed through Philadelphia. What a difference between now and last year! No enthusiastic populations, no signs of any enthusiasm, no flags; most of the best men gloomy and almost despairing, and the masses almost indifferent. Lincolnites cannot work up and warm the public opinion, and in general few of them can be met. Poor Lincolnites! they must stretch their brains to the utmost to defend, to justify, to explain Lincoln's actions, policy, and make-shifts; and they have no time left for, and no audiences to listen to any prize disquisitions on the Lincoln-Seward policy.

August 10, *L. B.*—In regard to the Wade and

Davis protest, the "loyal" press maintains its character. Of course. High civic courage is above the comprehension of that press.

That "loyal" press does not even understand how to sustain Grant against the attacks directed against him by the Copperhead and by the Fremont press. The Copperhead press attempts to defame Grant for the sake of McClellan; and the loyal press cannot muster enough knowledge, judgment, and courage to throw the dimmest light on Grant's Virginia campaign.

August 11, *L. B.*—To use common parlance: Lincoln's prospects are very blue, nay, very dark. If events do not brighten, the Democrats will have the upperhand, and they may nominate and elect almost any one they choose. The good Republicans will have no time to put up any body —*il est trop tard*, as Lafayette said to Charles X. The Lincolnites-Sewardites and their principal organ, the New York *Times*, are enraged against the true men because they cannot yet swallow their fetish, and because they hope for light.

August 15, *L. B.*—This place is crowded with all kind of honest and dishonest opponents to the principles of the Republican party. I am repeatedly asked to explain the reasons of Stanton's animosity to McClellan. "They were once great friends," say the McClellanites. "So they were," is my answer. "But Stanton ardently wished that McClellan might save himself and his friends, and urged him to begin the campaign, (February, 1862,) and to fight. When Stanton found out how bitter a pill it was for McClellan to draw his sword, how from hour to hour, from day to day, he postponed, procrastinated, and evaded opening the campaign, then only Stanton turned against the unworthy commander and took off one star from his shoulder straps. Stanton's motives were pure and patriotic." Repeatedly I have given the same explanation in the other volume of this Diary.

I meet with comparatively few politicising Americans who admit that in such complications as the country is in now, men like Stanton, or Wade, or Grimes, or Chandler, or Wilson, or any of the patriots so often mentioned by me, can be impelled by sacred, pure, and patriotic motives. The genuine people is more pure and more confiding, and so, also, was Wadsworth, that noble type of a true American Democrat; Wadsworth reluctantly suspected the motives of men.

August 15, *L. B.*—To the great relish of Northern slavery worshippers in New York and Boston, some forlorn Virginian slave-breeder attempts to make a case against that old patriot Everett, because some slave-breeding establishment called Little Brandon was destroyed by the Union soldiers. The Virginian enumerates the hospitalities which were proffered at Little Brandon to Everett, and to many other men of mark. And what of it? Everett and other patriots shook hands with Virginians and with other slave-holders and slave-breeders as long as those Southern hands were unstained with matricide and fratricide blood.　Everett did not drive the slave-breeders to treason and to perjury; but when they deliberately tried to murder the common country, then he acted like a patriot, whatever might be the fate of any Little Brandon, and of that so vaunted, but intrinsically sham, Southern hospitality.

August 16, *L. B.*—The Democratic copperhead convention in Chicago is near at hand.　*Whoever be nominated,* recognition and disintegration are at the end of any copperhead Democratic victory. Humanity will be outraged and trodden down.

And certain European governments or political parties, and certain European diplomats here, ardently wish and agitate for a Democratic political victory!　Those Europeans do not see or understand, that a Democratic peace and eventually two republics, means war against Europe.　The Democrats will be forced to throw a bone to the outraged national honor, and Mexico is at hand.　Both the eventual republics would unite in their hatred against England, France, and Spain, and give an outlet to the hundreds of thousands of veterans created on both sides by this civil war.　But with few exceptions the big and the small, the young and the old European diplomats residing here, live in the foulest social and political atmosphere to be

found in Washington, in New York, or anywhere in the country. No wonder that their
senses and their intellectuality are blunted,
bemuddled, confused, and that they neither
detect, nor see, nor can find out the true condition of affairs and of the country.

August 17, *L. B.*—Lincoln's familiars call
Wintěr Davis a Mephistophiles and say that he
beguiled Wade. As if Wade wanted to be
spurred to do a civic and a patriotic duty. To
those Sewardites, Lincolnites, Blairites, and
above all to the familiars of the White House, a
stern sense of duty is as repulsive as sunlight to
Satan.

August 18, *L. B.*—About this time last year
Wadsworth was here with me. He was full of
life, of hope, of faith in the people and in the
people's destinies. And now—

> *Jak wspaniały zachod słonca,*
> *Takim jest zgon Bohatera;*
> *Choc niknie kraju obronca,*
> *Jednak wiecznie nie umiera.*
>
> *Zgaste słonce sie odrodzi,*
> *By nowym blaskiem jasniało;*
> *Tak Bohater z swiata schodzi*
> *By pickniejszo jasnial chwalo.*
>
> *J ten wyzszy nad mocarze,*
> *Ten goodzien ludow nagrody;*
> *Ktory krew i zycie w darze,*
> *Niesie na ottarz swobody.*
>
> *Like the magnificent sunset,*
> *Is the death of a hero;*

And if a defender of the country is lost,
He is not forever dead.

The extinct sun rises again
To corruscate with renewed splendor;
So the hero falls
To corruscate in purer glory.

And he is above the mightiest;
He deserves the gratitude of peoples;
Who his blood and his life
Lays on freedom's shrine.

August 18, *L. B.*—Among the greatest disgraces in this country, if not the greatest, is that such a man as Thurlow Weed could become a powerful political individuality. Such facts, if multiplied, would disgust one with republicanism and with American citizenship.

August 20, *L. B.*—How many generations will it take for the average of Americans to learn to make a difference between a man's speeches and his actions? In 1860 Lincoln was elected principally on the strength of his stump speeches against Douglas. But speech-making does not constitute a statesman.

August 20, *L. B.*—Neither in the Press, nor in the various legislatures, nor on the stump, in one word, in no one of the arenas opened to mental activity, has the American youth asserted itself. A strange, and in the history of man, above all in the history of the last hundred years, an unwonted phenomenon! I know very well what complicated impediments are thrown in the path

of American youth; but after all, those impediments are not so mighty as not to be easily overpowered. But this youth lacks an impetus. I
speak of that portion of the younger generation
—between twenty and thirty-five years—which,
for various reasons, (some of them good, some of
them not so,) did not rush to arms.

It is otherwise in the army. Certainly this
war will end, and I hope, nay I am certain, it
will end gloriously, under the leadership of a
new and younger generation of commanders, of
Generals, etc. Already in the Western and in
the Potomac army the most brilliant deeds are
the deeds of new men *unknown* three years ago,
some of whom have almost wholly grown up in
the storm of this sacred struggle.

August 21, *L. B.*—Paid a short visit to New
York. The city seems to be owned principally
by Jefferson Davis and McClellan. The principal bankers, financiers, and shavers are all
leagued against the Government, and do their
utmost to break down the Government's credit;
the one for the sake of the rebels, the others to
thereby benefit the McClellan-copperhead-demo-
cratic party, so tenderly disposed towards slavery.

With a few exceptions almost all the foreign
houses established in New York sympathize with
the South, and at times very actively and devotedly operate in favor of rebels. English,
French, Italian, Spanish, German, Irish houses
constitute one and the same category. Many of

them, if not all, are runaways from political, social, and conventional slavery in their respective countries, where they belonged to the lowest strata in stratified Europe, and here in America they believe it to be high-toned to admire and side with slavery, rebellion, and treason.

The above is one of the reasons why the Government is so often entangled in financial difficulties, and explains the rise and the fluctuations in gold and in exchange. Then there is the struggle of partisans of a foreign loan, partisans who wish to become rich on commissions, and those who justly warn against foreign loans and with truth assert that the country can be saved and find all its means and credit within itself. Then the struggle between banks, bankers, and capitalists, holding large quantities of various governmental stocks, who dread any issue of more bonds, and those who wish to own stocks and wish to buy them cheap from the Government.

The genuine patriotic commercial houses, bankers, and capitalists are rather in a minority in New York, but this minority is devoted, and such houses constitute the glory of the commercial and financial metropolis.

The rabid McClellanites in New York and their organs in the press, look for news of disasters from our armies, and such news is a godsend to them. This feature of McClellanism and of copperheadism ought not to escape the attention of the future historian of this civil war. These men hail any success of Lee or of any other rebel chief with a joy equal to that felt in rebeldom. If they decently could, they would, in their Irish and other churches and temples, strike up a solemn *Te Deum* for every success of the rebel arms.

The republicans in New York are comparatively small in numbers; at the present hour they are rather apathetic, confused, some of them hopeless of any good, and the others misled and misdirected. All feel the necessity of having a man of strong action and unbending will at the head of the Republic, and shudder to see a Lincoln with a Seward carried on the electoral waves.

August 24, *L. B.*—Soon the fate of political parties, nay, the fate of the country, may become settled at Chicago. If McClellan is nominated and elected, it is principally because he is the incarnation of a general dissatisfaction with Mr. Lincoln, with his Sewardism, and with his makeshift policy. Thousands and thousands may vote for McClellan, not with any intention of helping the rebels and rending the country, but only to overthrow Lincoln's hateful policy.

August 24, *L. B.*—If our newspapers, etc., are read in Europe even by a half-informed public, the astonishment, and perhaps the contempt, felt there for our luminaries and wiseacres must be gigantic. Above all, when the Jominis of the press parade their knowledge of military history, of *strategy*, and of other warlike paraphernalia. Here is an example from among hundreds of similar ones to be found almost daily in American journalism. One of these wiseacres gravely enumerates the distinguished leaders of cavalry in the Napoleonic wars, and ignores— Murat.

It is as if one writing of the Hannibalian war in Italy had omitted the name of Maherbal, Hannibal's chief of cavalry. The press is at once in its senility and its childhood; and

Peccantem puerum quisquis non corrigit—odit.

August 25, *L. B.*—The rebels, above all the chiefs, inspired by rage, fury, disappointed ambition, show and have always shown almost superhuman force. The chiefs understand how to stir up the most fanatical. passions, and thus almost all the available masculine population is, in one or another way, under arms. If similar mental conditions were to prevail over the North, Grant could have to-day at least half a million troops more, and the cities and the towns would still teem with men. But whatever may be the efforts of the treacherous rebel chiefs, it is psychologically and physically impossible that this furious exaltation, paramount now, could be sustained for a long time. The calm and unalterable decision of the North will and must win, even if the Northern pilots, even if the Lincolns, the Sewards, the Hallecks, the McClellans, should again inflict on the people the whole calendar of their sinful policy, of their deadly mistakes, of their bloody crimes.

From the first hour of this rebellion the rebel chiefs acted despotically as *a committee of public safety*, and carried everything before them. They allowed no neutrality through all the strata of the white Southern population. From the beginning of the war the chiefs literally forced everybody to plunge into the current. In this way they carried with them the indifferent as well as those who, in the first days of the rebellion, were Union men at heart. The protracted war fused all the various elements, and fired up passions and blood; and probably the secession fury is more general and more violent to-day than it was in 1861. Exaltation spreads like wildfire, and with irresistible force the general flame overpowers the sober-minded.

The Southern society is yet half savage; it has not and never had, any of the elements, or at the best a very few only, of humanizing civilization. There is the answer to that ignorant fallacy which concedes to the Southern man a kind of fiery, proud character; a fallacy·by which it is attempted to establish a difference of race between the Northerner and the Southerner. Not the slightest historical or any fact whatever supports those assertions concerning two different races; ignorance and bad faith are the only data and sources for it.

Certain social modes of life, certain various conditions, in all ages and in all nations, produce certain similar characteristics; they transform, or at least modify, they ennoble or disfigure individuals, communities, social strata, and often whole nations.

Turbulence, recklessness, contempt for life, contempt for laws, always characterized that social stratum which, superposed upon the others, lived by the labor of the oppressed. In this respect, little if any difference exists between the Roman patrician and slaveholder of the last centuries of the Roman Republic, and the Anglo-Saxon earl, the Norman baron, the French, the German, the Polish, the Magyar, the Spanish, or any medieval noble whatever. Different by the so-called origin of race, they all, the patrician, the baron, the earl, have a very great social similarity, and certain of their prominent features are moulded after the same common type. So history teaches on every one of its indelible pages.

August 26, *L. B.*—Stanton continues to be the object of hatred for all the McClellanites, for all the partisans of rebellion, for all the open or secret liege-men of Jefferson Davis. This hatred stamps Stanton as the best and noblest of patriots. The "loyal" press—at the best—is very tepid towards Stanton, and the reason is, that he never flirts with the press, never courts its applause, and even at times treats it with rough indifference.

Stanton's greatest enemies cannot and do not impeach his integrity, and certainly he has no selfish interest in serving the people. Stanton occupied an eminent, lucrative, and independent position at the bar. Almost all the lawyers, his colleagues, became rich, while he, true, devoted, and honest servant of the people, ruins his health and increases not his fortune.

August 28, *L. B.*—The McClellanites assert that the victor of Antietam will receive justice at the hands of the people. I hope so.

Victor of Antietam! The records of battles fought through ages have nothing to out-do Antietam as a day full of glory for the soldiers, and for some among the secondary commanders, and full of disgrace for the commander-in-chief. The battle of Antietam is the indelible evidence of the fullest and the most gigantic unsoldier-like capacity of that hero of small-arms as *spolia optima*. McClellan showed no generalship before, during, or after the battle. He who never stood the fire of small-arms lost time in picking them up on the field of battle, instead of following and pressing the retreating enemy. In one word, McClellan wholly neutralized the advantages won at Antietam by the soldiers and by their respective commanders and officers.

August 30, *L. B.*—The type of the American Democrat (not by principles, but as a party denomination) is the Southern slaveholder and rebel. The Northern Democrats are small sprigs of that Upas tree. It is this descent that makes those Northern Democrats—I mean principally the leaders—so subservient to their Southern masters. The Northern Democratic leaders are without courage, without dignity; they are incarnated falsehoods and shams.

August 30, *L. B.*—With their deep instincts, with their ardent love for all that is dark, retrograde, contrary to reason and to manhood, the Jesuits in America, and the Catholic clergy—Irish and not Irish—side with the rebellion. If the Jesuits and other priests appear publicly as partisans of the North, in the confessional they instruct in favor of slavery and of rebels. Of course, there are exceptions, but the exceptions are rare. Archbishop Purcell is almost the only ecclesiastic sincerely devoted to the North; the most of the priests imitate Hughes's double dealing.

August 31, *L. B.*—A telegram from Chicago. McClellan nominated by the Democrats, by the open and by the secret copperheads. Even the few serious and honest Democrats, as perhaps Guthrie and some others are, stand up for McClellan. It is a proof how party spirit can degrade, twist, corrupt even honest men and honest intellects. All again for the sake of availability. But it is to be seen how far McClellan will be available even for the copperheads. It is impossible that the clear-sighted Democratic leaders can ignore that McClellan is a thorough intellectual and moral nonentity, neither a man nor a soldier. He is taken up by the politicians as glue to catch flies, but he may prove not even good for that. It is perhaps better for the Republicans that such a Democratic nomination was made.

August 31, *L. B.*—The Chicago platform. The rebels, traitors, and slavery to be saved. That is the spirit and the letter of that platform. Well done. The people at large can be befogged no more. The people at large will easily make its selection between the two principles. The people at large will not betray itself. Will the people voluntarily, deliberately prostrate itself in the dust before the rebels under this leadership of the Chicago Democrats? I hope not. The Republicans must now rally and fight for their sacred principles. The issue is square and open:

The integrity of the Republic and the destruction of slavery, or the disintegration of the Republic and the preservation of slavery. The people, the many, have now to decide between the two standards.

SEPTEMBER.

September 1, *L. B.*—*Aut* Lincoln, *aut* McClellan is to be the war-cry. I still hope that some better light will rise on the Republican horizon. If the West, if Illinois is to be the breeder of Presidents, they should take Senator Trumbull, who is a thorough man.

McClellan is an incarnation, or at least the leaders of that party present him as such to the people. Those leaders attempt to vail the hideousness of their principles by certain presumable virtues in McClellan. To make McClellan easier to swallow, to his other attributed excellences they add now the freshly-invented character of a "Christian gentleman." Like a genuine Christian gentleman McClellan avoided fighting.

If Lincoln is brought before the people, it is not as an incarnation, but as an incident evoked to the surface by the surgings of events; not Lincoln, but the principle will be preached to the people, and Lincoln's individuality will be veiled by the great aims and the sacred duties of the American people towards itself and towards mankind.

September 2, *L. B.*—Now the arena opens for the press on both sides. The loyal Press of all shades, if in its immense majority extremely insipid, is at least intrinsically honest and is warmed at times by the eternal fire of truth. The loyal Press is now in its congenial element; it treads on familiar ground in the struggle for a Presidency. But the courage, the insight, the knowledge needed for a Presidential campaign are of a far, far lower calibre than the qualities of mind imperatively needed in the men of the Press, who during this civil war have claimed to be leaders of or lights for the people.

All over the country the Democratic Press has not a particle of civic honesty or civic virtue. All over the country it advocates darkness, slavery, and the reign of evil and of Satan over this fated Republic.

September 2, *L. B.*—Farragut is a hero of heroes on the sea. Farragut truly incarnates the American genius.

September 3, *L. B.*—The great Democratic army is organized. First rank: leaders faithless to God and man, intensely bent upon saving slavery, and upon humiliating the confessors of eternal truth and light. Behind the leaders, an uncultivated, ignorant or deluded mass of people.   Then the incendiaries, the perjurers, the highway-robbers, the murderers, and all kinds of social offal.   Then the coarsest, the most opaque Romanism incarnated in the Irishry and the lowest Germans.   Such are the various elements and compounds of the great Democratic host, and McClellan is its fit and perfect incarnation.

September 3, *L. B.*—Almost every day in one way or another I get evidence that the best fighting generals in the Potomac army, and even such as once rather preferred Meade to any Western general, now almost unanimously assert, *that the first condition for a successful campaign before Richmond is to have Meade relieved from command.*   For nearly a year Stanton's opinion has been the same.

September 3, *L. B.*—Atlanta taken by Sherman.   Sherman is *the* general of this war.   And early in 1861 the wiseacres, the great military authorities and luminaries, such as Scott, Buell, such as the great West Pointers, the then foremost oracles in the War Department, and subsequently McClellan and his clique of generals, all of them unanimously declared Sherman fit for the lunatic asylum.   Like Grant, like Thomas, so Sherman had not the reputation stereotyped among the Washington parlors, and among the Scott official clique.   Sherman, Thomas, did not graduate at West Point as "first-class" engineers, but as infantry and artillery officers.   Therefore now they are not only good generals, but almost first-class captains.

September 4, *L. B.*—The meanest and most degraded copperheads, of which the Seymours, the Curtises, and such are the types, are wont to abuse the lofty spirit animating New England— themselves being New Englanders. "Leave New England out in the cold," "leave New England out from the Union," and similar utterances are periodically made by those traitors. "Leave New England out in the cold!" that means: let the soul escape and the clay remain! New England is the brains, the heart, the conscience of this Republic. "Leave out New England," and what remains? Barbarity, *sauvagerie*, clay, automatons, but no soul. And when I say *New England*, I do not think of the so-called "fine scholars," nor of rhetors and phrase-coiners, nor of fine shams and toadies; but for me New England's spirit is incarnated in the laborious, intelligent, daily working, daily daring operatives; in those men who planted and plant States, and who organize them; who erect school-houses, not for "classical scholars," but for barefooted boys and girls. When I say New England, I think of New Englanders, who with their brains and with their hearts touch everything, embrace and understand everything, shape and mould everything, who organize, create townships, cities, communities, and republics.   That New England is the heart and core of this great Republic, that New England is the goal of humanity.*

September 7, L. B.—Few are conscious to-day that the patriots of the North struggle and die for the pure principle of *self-government.*   These Northern patriot-confessors give their life to redeem from eternal perdition the Southern—not Africo-Americans—but the Southern *animalized* whites.   The victory won by the North will mark a new era for those millions of brutish but good-natured whites, perverted, degraded, lowered by the slaveholding aristocracy, and by the Northern so-called Democrats.   As by a charm, the victory won by the North will destroy the "mudsills," the "clay-eaters," and the other similar white skinned products of slavery, elevating them to a superior sphere, transforming them from brutes into civilized beings.   Then only self-government in the South will cease to be a blatant lie, and then only the genius of

---

* The Freedmen's Bureau is a Yankee or rather a Massachusetts notion.   The idea originated among the men of Massachusetts and of New England, and the Massachusetts delegation brought it before Congress.   Stanton heartily joined it and gave his unconditional support.   But for the Freedmen's Bureau, the Africo-American would have been already virtually re-enslaved, to-day, —— six months after the material overthrow of the rebellion.

General Howard most thoroughly incarnates the pure and humane conception which originated this Bureau.—*Note Nov.* 1, 1865.

humanity will not be forced to avert her face from the Southern part of this Union.

September 8, *L. B.*—At Auburn Seward makes an electioneering speech. Seward fights *pro domo*, that is, to remain in the Cabinet during the next Presidential term. Thus he attempts to identify his and Lincoln's case. .The people, he says, is to fight for Lincoln, because Lincoln is the Union. *Excusez du peu.* And " I, Seward, I am Lincoln too." Seward—as usual—insults the people. Never has the people backed out from any sacrifice, but it has forced the Lincolns and Sewards to deal freely with its blood. A Seward attempting to persuade anybody that he has to inflame the lofty patriotism of the American people!

September 8, *L. B.*—I learn positively that some among the European diplomats agitated a great deal in favor of McClellan. Very kind of them, but, at least, very incautious. The influence of diplomats is very low, even with the copperheads, who mistrust them, and have not much consideration for their diplomatic capers.

Among the diplomatic phenomena, and not truly appreciated in this country, is: That Belgium has not recognized the rebels as belligerents when the rest of Europe did it. *Our great friend* Russia did it. If the rebel pirates had reached the Chinese waters, then notwithstanding that China and Japan do not recognize their piratical flag, they could have found refuge in

the Amoor, and done mischief to American com-
merce.

The non-recognition by Belgium must not be
credited to Sandford of guano, shoddy, saltpetre,
and bursting-rifles celebrity, but to the soundness
of the Belgian diplomacy and statesmanship, and
to the sound advice given to his government by
Mr. Blondeel, the Belgian diplomat in Washington.   I hope that this fact will be remembered
by the people, and that the Belgian political
soundness will be rewarded by some good commercial treaty.

September 9, *L. B.*—Poor Stanton, to be puffed
by a Seward.   I am willing to be quartered if
Seward, in any way, knows what was the real
character of Carnot's genius.   All such comparisons are idle; Carnot had qualities which are
wanting in Stanton, who again has characteristics in which Carnot was deficient.   Stanton is
Stanton, and he has to deal with a heavier load
than Carnot.

September 10, *L. B.*—"Lincoln has acquired
experience," say his partisans.   Granted.   But
new events will find him hesitating, shifting, and
instead of grasping them, Lincoln will again be
obliged to "acquire new experience," and the
people be obliged to pay for the apprenticeship.

September 11, *New York.*—To judge from this
city, even to judge from what I hear from
Republicans, Lincoln's chances, and with him
the chances of the party, are very slim.   Some

Republicans will attempt to nominate another candidate, but this effort cannot save the party. The only hope is in how far the people at large are disgusted with the Chicago platform, and how far on account of principles they will prefer to take Lincoln as a *pis aller* with all his shortcomings, and worse than shortcomings, than swear fealty to the Chicago platform with all its copperhead perfections.

September 12, *New York.*—Great fall in gold; great excitement, and some forebode therefrom improvement of the chances of the Republicans.

I am not astonished that gold is falling, but to me the wonder is how gold can so considerably rise. It is not exclusively on account of European exchanges. Forty to fifty millions of dollars in specie exported during the year to Europe ought not to occasion such fluctuations. The gold panic, that is, the rise of gold, is due to artificial causes and to popular imbecility, or to an ingrained fallacy.

Notwithstanding this terrific war, the country is in a healthy normal condition. The two paramount sources of the national life, industry and agriculture, are flourishing, all kind of labor is in high demand, wages are increasing and secured for every operative and laborer.

Iron foundries, coal mines, cotton and woolen mills, have received an impetus unknown in past years. Almost every month witnesses new inventions transformed into lucrative industries. Nothing is disorganized or stagnant, and the North is teeming with highly productive labor. I am certain that in New England, in New York, in the West and in the Northwest, almost every farmer has this year more acres under culture than he had in 1860 or 1861.

The great trouble in the popular mind is about the *greenbacks*, in which imbeciles attempt to see the celebrated French *assignats*, and draw parallels between the two.

I repeat: every kind of labor is in demand, all produce finds a consumer, everything finds a buyer in the domestic markets, and the cost of transportation is thus economized for both the producer and the consumer.

Such was not the condition of France during the reign of the *assignats*. Industry had almost disappeared from France; small was the demand for labor, and small the offer of it. All was in the air; property insecure; the means of communication wholly neglected or wanting; and nearly one-half of the soil of France—the confiscated property of the nobles, of the clergy, the great domains—had no legal owners, no careful hand interested in its culture, and was almost abandoned. How childish the fears here; how imbecile the assimilation of the two conditions, countries, and epochs ! *

---

* The national debt and the so-called inflated currency now justly constitute almost a paramount national question. But to

22

September 12, *N. Y.*—I hear and observe from different sides that the so-called *financiers*, that is,

---

settle or to elucidate it, far-fetched precedents from the old world are mostly dragged in. Undoubtedly there are certain phases in the general question of inflated currency which are ominous and must receive attention. But the pessimists and many of the so-called financiers lose scent of and seem to ignore the positive fact, that very likely one-half of the national debt and three-fourths of the paper currency imperatively evoked by the war, have not been squandered or wasted, but in various ways have been employed to vivify the various productive forces of the country, and therefore have an almost uninterrupted *re-productory* agency and action   The expansion of currency facilitated the expansion of various industries and manufactures. The easily obtained greenbacks fertilized the agriculture. I am certain that notwithstanding the war, far more acres have been laid under culture in 1864 than there were in 1860. The greenbacks enabled the farmer to buy more land, to increase his stock, and thus to meet the demand which the war has made for provisions and animals, and made with an unparalleled voracity. The greenbacks fired up furnaces, worked mills and put in motion various manufacturing establishments. The greenbacks cover and facilitate thousands and thousands of healthy, normal, agricultural and industrial enterprises and healthy normal speculations. The inflated speculators, the shoddies, the stock and gold gamblers, more noisy, more visible, are dangerous excrescences ; but they constitute a minority when compared with the results obtained in agriculture, in industry, in manufactures and in sound speculating operations.

Wherever and whenever European governments ran into debt or inflated their currency, this inflation was used differently and therefore had results almost wholly opposed to the results which are palpable in America. It was so for various special not general causes, broadly recorded in the political and economical history of the European nations ; causes almost impossible to occur in this country. What in various ways I have pointed out in the pages of this Diary, I repeat again, that many so-considered the bankers, shavers, etc., and the utopists, the financial wiseacres, and nincompoops, expect great schemes from Fessenden.   May God avert it!   Schemers in power have entangled, run deeper into the mud, but never restored the finances of any government or nation.   Happily Fessenden is not a schemer, but a sound, firm, and clear intellect.   In times like these, schemers ruin a government and a nation.   History teems with evidences.   A secretary of finance has a different range of action and of intellectual activity than a banker or a merchant.   A secretary of finance ought neither to concoct schemes nor to operate as a speculator.   A secretary of finance has nothing to do with *catching*, with *running after*, or with *regulating* exchanges.   It is idiotic to make such demands on a man directing the finances of a nation.   Was Pitt a schemer, was Colbert or Turgot, or any other great and

---

axioms of political economy, of finances and of taxation give different results here than they gave in Europe.   All the data and conditions of this new country, new society, virgin soil and natural elements and forces, are so vastly different from those of the old world, that great caution and discrimination are required in the appeal to precedents or even to axioms.

Considering as one hundred the aggregate of the various social data and of the natural forces and elements in Europe, scarcely one-fourth of them are yet active in America, when in Europe, England included, the per centage is at least seventy-five to eighty.   America's prosperity has therefore an immense natural, and as yet untouched margin; when, so to speak, the soil, the elements, begin to fail Europe.   Greenbacks cannot yet destroy this margin.—*Note December* 4, 1865.

celebrated national financier?   Order in the
administration and in the finances constitute the
credit of a government and restore it when that
credit is prostrated.   But the credit of the American people is not prostrated, and God grant that
it may not become entangled by financial
schemers!   Pitt taxed everything, taxed light
and air, then borrowed, but never meddled with
exchanges and schemes.   And Pitt did not have
to overcome such financiers and Jews as New
York and Boston bristle with—men who make
all efforts to injure or break down the credit of
the Government and of the Union.   Pitt did not
have to overcome domestic traitors, who, by
exaggerations and lies, frighten and mislead the
people, and generate distrust in the financial
measures of Congress and of the Government.
New York, Boston, and many other spots, have
in their midst numbers of these bitter antagonists of the principles of the party in power.
Hostile bankers are the plague of a nation's
prosperity, of a nation's honor.   It is on record
that when the battle of Waterloo was lost the
stocks in Paris rose on the exchange.   Further,
Pitt did not have to overcome impediments
thrown in his way by a well-intentioned but
ignorant or flighty press.

God preserve this country from a speculating
and scheming financier at the head of the
national finances.   The luminaries of the "good"
press loudly clamor for a schemer, and so do the

numerous *faseurs*, busy-bodies, would-be financial authorities, etc., all of them firm in the
belief that a *good* Secretary of the Treasury will
by a *legerdemain* reduce gold to par and open
new, charmed, unknown sources of wealth,
credit, and everything else. Most, nay all, of
those above-named do not understand the difference that exists between the capacity for the
administration of the resources or finances of a
country, and the capacity of a merchant, of a
banker, of a financial operator, making fortunes
by commercial and other operations and speculations.

I am certain that not even a Rothschild would
make a Secretary of the Treasury for England
·or France, or for any other European country.
Bankers would never do for it. Necker's celebrated *Comte-Rendu* was not the work of a
banker or of a schemer, but that of an administrator of the national fortune. Necker pointed
out abuses and cancers; he proposed no financial
schemes but the abolition of privileges, the taxation of property, the reduction of expenses, the
institution of order and economy.

September 13, *N. Y.*—Wade's and Davis's manifesto stir up some minds. Amidst the noise for
election and re-election, here and there the question of reconstruction is discussed by both the
electioneering parties. Whatever be the result
of the Presidential campaign, reconstruction
will become more and more the order of the day.

The reconstruction carried out by the Republicans must be one from the bottom to the top; it must have as a basis the broadest recognition of *man* as an intelligent, self-governing being, and classify him according to his intellect and not according to the shams of race and of color. The loyal Africo-American ought to be the corner-stone of the reconstruction, and the disloyal white man should become an apprentice to loyalty, to human rights and to intelligent liberty. The time is past and gone to force the loyal Africo-American to be tutored otherwise than by laws of equality with the whites, and whoever legislates differently is a traitor to humanity and to his country.

For at least one generation more, disloyalty will glimmer in the bosom of the great majority of the Southern population. Any reconstruction on the absolute white basis will tell against the minority, composed of genuine loyal men in the South, and give the legal power into the hands of the disloyal numbers. The always loyal Africo-American as a voter at the polls can not only restore the balance, but throw the political and legislative power into the hands of the honest and devoted white patriots.

September 13, *N. Y.*—I meet a great many politicians and political men belonging to various parts of the Union. Many of them emphatically assert, others only hope, that Mr. Lincoln has learned a great deal, or at least something, and that he will be an improved President during the next term.   .

But Mr. Lincoln never yet boldly faced events and emergencies, never seized the hour by the forelock or the bull by the horns. Mr. Lincoln was great in backing out to the last moment. Can he and will he change his nature ?

September 13, *N. Y.*—Good men are scarce in New York—one in twenty or thirty—and above all, scarce in the business part and in the would-be aristocratic and fashionable part of the city.

All over the Union the radical Republicans, whom events force to take the stump for Lincoln—as the party has no other candidate—the radical Republicans will speak to the people of the principles of the party, but not of its accidental standard-bearer. That is honest, and makes the whole affair not nauseous, but supportable.

Sherman's success at Atlanta, the copperhead Chicago platform, and copperhead conspiracies cause a revulsion of feeling in favor of the Republican party.   Fremont recedes — honest patriot that he is—and thus Mr. Lincoln, although not at all wished by the best men, will nevertheless become elected by their votes. Strange and perhaps unique phenomenon on the horizon of an Elective Government !

September 13, *N. Y.*—Great outcry against the Republican party because some officials in Custom-houses have become rich. But the Democrats did likewise, and if they could they would cheerfully commit the same sin. Besides, publicans and Custom-house officers have been the same all over the world. In all nations and governments, in all ages and in all countries, in Egypt as in Judea, in Rome as on the Ganges, Custom-housers have been peculators.

September 13, *N. Y.*—I learn from the *most positive* authority that Mr. Lincoln wished to dismiss Stanton and put in his place Morton, Governor of Indiana.

The reasons *why* give the best insight of Mr. Lincoln's notions of the fitness of men for the high duties of the Cabinet.

Stanton was to be dismissed not because he is incapable, altogether the contrary is Mr. Lincoln's sincere conviction; but on account of a certain geographical balance to be kept up in the Cabinet.

Fessenden and Welles being from the eastern section of the country, and the West after Chase's resignation having only one insignificant representative in the Cabinet, Mr. Lincoln conceived the idea of changing Stanton for Morton, and thus re-establishing the equipoise. O, Oxenstierna, how true is thy axiom!

September 14, *Philadelphia.*—If the population of New York in its immense majority is copperhead, and even open partisans of Jefferson Davis, the majority of the population of Philadelphia is loyal and devoted to the cause of the country. The bulk of this population is more truly American than, and not so adulterated as, the population of New York. One may say that the principles of the Quakers still permeate Philadelphia, and the character and the race of New Amsterdam still predominates in New York.

I met a Methodist clergyman, the Rev. Walker Johnson, a type of his sect—devoted to the cause and radical to the core, and not affected or full of assumptions as are many of the reverend doctors.

Generally the immense majority of reverends from all Christian denominations are patriots, and well enlighten the people about its duties in this struggle; many of them are simple but true confessors. Hopkinses are rare, and most of such apostates to genuine Christianity are found in the Episcopal church.

The copperheads in the North and the Southern rebels hate the good clergymen. But a true Christian cannot and ought not to remain impassible when the highest human morality is in danger of being destroyed by the blackest human immorality, such as is the Southern rebellion and its Northern adherents.

September 15, *Philadelphia.*—I found Carey, one of the foremost economists of our epoch, and an eminent social philosopher—I found him with his mind and heart in this struggle. He appreciates and justifies the financial measures of the two Congresses. Carey believes that the best fusion of the two antagonisms can be effected by constructing a great railroad from the South to the North, through Northern Alabama and Eastern Tennessee, making it an artery for the pulsations of the internal, domestic, industrial, and commercial life. The hills will dominate the swamps and the plains where dwell slavery and cottonocracy, and where all railroads conduct to the sea-shore—that is, to Liverpool and to English influence.

September **17**, *Washington.*—The court appointed to investigate the murder of our soldiers in the mine before Petersburg has not yet *published* the results of its investigations. I hear that Burnside is to be sacrificed, and the truth with him : and the truth is as follows :

The mine was to be blown up at 3 o'clock, A. M. Burnside's corps was to rush in. The fuses missed twice, and only at 5 o'clock, A. M., the explosion took place. The attacking corps was deployed in six lines of battle, one behind the other, and thus prepared to rush. But the first attack took place at six o'clock, one hour after the explosion, and thus was lost in indecision one hour of the most precious time. From 6 to 9 o'clock no fresh troops were sent to support the first attacking party. The enemy, who at the explosion ran away from *all his works*, recovered his senses and positions, and was fully prepared to repel the attack when the Africo-American regiments were sent to be butchered by cross-fires. Then again was paramount confusion, absence of brains, of courage and of unity in action, and a whole brigade, which took a good position and entrenched itself, was forgotten, received no order to retreat, became surrounded, and was made prisoner. All this because the commander of the corps, only about 10 o'clock, A. M., began to notice what was going on. Such are the simple facts of this butchery. On the success of this mine depended the success of the campaign before Richmond. If our troops had been thrown rapidly, without the loss of a minute, into the works abandoned by the terror-stricken enemy, if no time had been given to the enemy to recover and return to his abandoned positions, Petersburg would have fallen that day. It was a sacred military duty for General Meade, as commander-in-chief of the Potomac army, to be on the spot and to direct in person operations on which depended the fate of the campaign, and of the army entrusted to his command. Further: General Meade and his staff never in their lives had a chance to witness the explosion of a mine; military curiosity ought to have kept them awake, and attracted them to the spot.

General Meade is more criminal than Burnside; on General Meade weighs the fullest responsibility for the unsuccess and for the butchery. In any other government General Meade would lose his command and his rank, if not worse; but here *nobody is hurt*, with the exception of the five to six thousand of the best men butchered.*

September 17.—In private and in the public prints Mr. Lincoln is upbraided for not being a scholar, a " classical scholar," therefore not a gentleman and unfit for the Presidency. This is too much. For once I must heartily stand up for Lincoln. One must know these American " gentlemen" and " scholars," and above all the " clas-

---

* Official reports say that Grant's campaign against Richmond 1864–'65, cost 95,000 in killed, wounded, disabled. One-third of this loss must be credited to Meade's executive powers. When all the truth is told, this assertion will be fully justified. If Grant's first lieutenant could have been a Thomas, a Sheridan, a Baldy Smith, or a Hancock, or any brave, prompt, devoted, patriotic officer, and not a pompous, envious, slow, undecided, half martinet, the campaign would have been shorter and the losses less heavy. General Meade is perfectly innocent of the crowning, brilliant actions of the Potomac army, April, 1865. Sheridan's report fully establishes that General Meade did his utmost to thwart all Sheridan's splendid movements and combinations. For this, or probably for a similar reason, General Grant himself directed the movements of the various corps of the Potomac army during the last three days of the campaign, as otherwise most probably Lee would have escaped. The special order was issued from General Grant's headquarters, and this order is on record. Meade only accompanied the headquarters. *The last of General Meade* is an order in the last days of March 1865, wherein he announces that he is on the eve of fighting the most decisive battle in this most brilliant campaign; that he, Meade, found the enemy deployed on the other side of a stream, and that he, Meade, took—"repose." General Meade begged himself into the Major Generalship of the regular army—see the debates of the Senate—and of course has secured to himself a warm " repose."—*Note June,* 1865.

sical scholars," to be highly disgusted with the
breed. A few exceptions like Everett do not
break the rule. I speak not of professional
teachers and professors. As for the others the
general rule is: that the immense majority of the
so-called "scholars," and above all of the "classical scholars," navigate through life under false
pretenses and false colors. Generally they are
superficial; they have a limited, a schoolboy's
knowledge of the classics, and the schoolboy's
ignorance of almost everything else. They are
narrow, dry, very conceited; they generally have
very little mind, and not large, expansive,
elastic intellects. In general appreciation and in
proportion to the variety and the range of
modern culture, the "classical scholars" are
uncultivated; rhetors and not orators. When
they speak they never elevate, inspire, or inflame
their auditories. The genuine American "classical scholar" seldom if ever comprehends or
embraces a new idea; he has no revelation of the
heart, no spontaneity, and it costs him heavy
labor to reach—if he ever reaches—any loftier
and broader standpoint on the scientific or on the
social questions. A "classical scholar" will be a
good lawyer; he will make a good and even a
thorough argument on a given legal question,
'but never, or at least seldom, is he a thorough
jurisprudential mind. The commonly called
American scholar "is a product of that scholastic

and verbal education which prefers words to things, and ancient to modern thought."

For all the above-named reasons I rejoice that Lincoln's mind is not befogged by that limited scholarship; and if the worst comes to the worst, I prefer the railsplitter to any narrow, classical hairsplitter.

September 18.—What an irony of fate to make Mr. Lincoln an unavoidable necessity, when the country and the party has so many men fitter for the place! Almost every Senator and Congressman from among those so often mentioned in this *Diary* would make a better and a fitter President. Then the *loyal* Governors of all States, north and west, such men as Governor Andrew, Coney, Morton and others. In one word, I could name hundreds more fit, more energetic, more clear-sighted, and in every respect more proven and more eligible, and nevertheless the country, the people subside on a Lincoln! But as it is now the only way to escape the disgrace of the rule of the copperheads and of McClellan, then *va pour un Lincoln.*

The angel of mercy seems to have averted his face from this people!——

September 18.—That true and noble patriot, Edward Everett, joins the best men of Massachusetts, or rather joins the great and noble Massachusetts and New England people. Everett has shown a moral courage seldom found, seldom recorded.   At his age he stood up and publicly confessed, confessed to his country, to the civilized and uncivilized world, "that he was wrong, that he committed a mistake in having once stood by the slaveholders."

Everett showed a still greater courage in boldly facing the ire of the political and social intimacies and associations of his whole life; that is, of the Boston "gentlemen" conservatives.   The creation contains no more vile, mean and venomous vermin than are those moral, mental and political Boston eunuchs.

September 18.—The copperheads throw it in the faces of the Republicans that their reckless administration has disorganized and ruined the finances of the country.   But as commander and as organizer of armies, McClellan squandered about one thousand million in round numbers. The Quartermaster's accounts and that of the Navy will prove it.

McClellan was the most recklessly extravagant commander of an army ever known in the history of any country.   For more than a year the administration most lavishly and promptly satisfied all his demands, requisitions, whims, and blunders.   Add to it the loss of precious time, the disasters brought about by him almost with a deliberate choice and will; add to it about 100,000 men crippled and killed during his command, and then sum up the cost and deduct it from the general expenditure.

The perspicacious "loyal" press has not taken the trouble to find out the cost of McClellan's military prowess.

Wadsworth and I were among the first to find out what was in McClellan. In this respect our record dates from October, 1861. Already then we became certain that McClellan avoided and dreaded attacking and fighting the rebels, and that he humbugged the army and the country.

But neither Wadsworth nor I *have ever* attacked, opposed or criticized McClellan on account of his political convictions, or on account of his strong pro-slavery propensities. For more than a year I was not aware that McClellan was a Democrat. The soldier, the officer, the commander of the army alone filled with disgust and distrust Wadsworth's and my mind.

September 18.—Lincoln and Mac. fight for the possession of the White House. Their first seconds and bottle-holders, Raymond and Belmont, fight for the mission to France, such at least *vulgatior fama est.* A regular medieval square fight. But Belmont is the man who bleeds and will bleed the most. No even half sincere and half honorable can hesitate between the two seconds, as he cannot hesitate between the two principals. Whatever Raymond may be, he is *a man* when compared with Belmont.

September 18.—Almost every day I meet with *nouveaux riches,* born in this epoch of civil war, and, of course, the cities and even the country bristle with them.   These new Crœsuses must be classified.   First, that ignoble class of the so-called shoddy, or of cheating contractors, of individuals who made fortunes *a la* Weed or *a la* Sandford the diplomat.   Others have honestly made their small or large fortunes by honorable, lawful, legal pursuits and labor, by honest and skillful operations and speculations.   Again, many who are in a position to turn up—not a penny—but hundreds of thousands and even millions, have done nothing of the sort.   I am certain that Republican Senators and members of Congress have made no money by using their political influence.

Here is an evidence of honor and modesty. The Treasury assigned to Rear Admiral David Porter sixty thousand dollars as proceeds from cotton, etc., captured by him and confiscated by the Treasury in the Mississippi region.   It was the admiral's personal legal profit or remuneration. But as the law gave nothing to his tars, the admiral went quietly and diligently to work to have his sixty thousand dollars legally divided as prize-money between his officers and sailors.

September 18.—The presidential campaign brings out forgotten facts and hitherto unpub-lished documents, such as reports, letters, and various official communications, principally between Lincoln and McClellan.   Most of these publications and revelations brand McClellan for want of veracity and confirm *all*, since 1861, I have

23

said about him in these *Diaries*. More than ever one must be thunderstruck how this McClellan could have been so long kept in command, and why long ago all these revelations and facts were not brought before the people.

This and a great many other incidents in this war prove: that this people is in reality so great that no amount of bad government and misrule can ruin it.

September 18.—The *great Anglo-Saxon race* (as they will have races, they may have them) is likewise the greatest, if not the unique, breeder of snobs. Robt. C. Winthrop, of Boston, is the most thorough-bred snob ever produced by the great Anglo-Saxon race. Winthrop joined the Democrats, whom he has life-long denounced; he stumps for McClellan. In thus crawling on all-four into the Democratic camp, in discovering in McClellan all kind of eminent qualities, in attempting to be foremost among the McClellanites, Winthrop wishes to eventually gain the mission to England, there officially to flunkey to lords and bishops. To do this has been the loftiest goal of Winthrop's life-long ambition.

September 19.—Every day the railroad terminus vomits into Washington crowds of contractors and of every kind of claimants, all—as they say —having unfinished business before the departments. Re-election still seems doubtful; a change of administration is therefore possible, and as says the Teuton: *Jeder will sein Schaeff'chen schaeren;* that is, every one wishes to close his accounts with the administration and part with it, if part he must, with as many greenbacks in his patriotic pocket as it will be possible to pack into it.

September 20.—Yesterday, in a speech, Senator Chandler said that he would prefer descent from Benedict Arnold than from a Northern copperhead. Whatever may be Chandler's shortcomings, he is a devoted, energetic, courageous, clear-sighted, and disinterested patriot, one who never contributed to befog in any way the people, and never hesitated to say the truth and to denounce misrule.

September 20.—The heavy and bloody cloud at last pierced through. Sheridan wins a **victory,** and by what I can judge from all reports, Sheridan understands how to follow up a victory and how to pursue the flying or retreating enemy. Sheridan fights not like McClellan, not like Meade. The era of new generals and of a new generalship is inaugurated by Sheridan in this fated Virginia campaign.*

---

* Sheridan inaugurated the use of cavalry in the line of battle, and this he did in a mountainous country, as is the Shenandoah Valley. Few if any such examples can be pointed out in all military history, and in the great campaigns of Napoleon. At Samo Sierras a battery was taken by the Polish lancers, but this was rather a *coup de main* performed by one squadron. Previous to Sheridan all the Union as well as rebel commanders of armies used cavalry for raids but not for battles. McClellan,

Although Sheridan was not his and Halleck's choice, Mr. Lincoln will have all the credit for this victory. But it is positive that an attempt was made to prevent Grant from trusting to Sheridan the command in the Shenandoah valley. Grant stood firm, and the result is a brilliant victory won by Sheridan, a victory which strengthens Mr. Lincoln in the saddle for the campaign. Sheridan is the child of his own works; he was unknown to General Scott, to the Scott and McClellan cliques; he was un-

nominally an officer of cavalry, was even more ignorant of any use of cavalry whatever than he was generally of everything else.

Previous to the war the paramount idea of the people North and South was, that to the South belonged the martial spirit, generalship and every military capacity. But events showed how baseless and fallacious were these assertions arrogantly maintained by the Southrons and to which the North almost submissively bowed and assented. The rebellion began with Beauregard, the Johnstons, Lee, Bragg, Hardee, Longstreet, the Hills, and it ended with the same names and commanders. The most bloody and straining struggle, lasting four years, has not evoked in the South any new name, any new military capacity of a superior order. The North used up, first Scott and his engineering clique, as the Buells, etc., etc.; then McClellan and his unmilitary galaxy; then Hooker; then various Halleckians; then Meade and his Meadeites; and the war was brought to an end by commanders unknown before, nay even scorned by the West Pointism. These new men are all children of the four years of war. Such are Grant, Sheridan, Sherman, Thomas, then Schofield, Wilson, (the captor of Jeff. Davis,) and numerous other field officers—not engineers, not first graduates in West Point, but first graduates on the battle-fields.—*Note May 15, 1865.*

known to West Point Washington combinations, and therefore he shows the true mettle.

September 21:—The speculative Cabinet-makers are at a loss who shall be the Secretary of State in the future Cabinet. Their great trouble is to find a man *familiar with the European policy.* What in God's name has the American people to trouble itself with about any European policy in Europe? An American Secretary of State ought to be permeated with the American policy; his duty is to uphold this policy in the teeth of Europe when Europe meddles with this continent. An American Secretary of State ought not to meddle with the European policy in Europe, but force the European Governments to respect the American policy on this hemisphere.

September 21.—In a few days Postmaster Blair will be thrown overboard by Lincoln. A victory by the radicals. The best of it is that Blair is Lincoln's innermost intimate, as well as is Seward; and that not one of them knows what hovers above Blair's guilty head. Lincoln begins to be a man.

September 21.—In my small way I must support Mr. Lincoln. Many of the reasons have been already explained in this Diary. I cannot politically separate myself from my best political friends, from men whom I truly respect, and between whom and me not a shadow of difference in principles exists. But this will not prevent me from truthfully and conscientiously recording the events and the "Lincolniana." Therein I am my own standard-bearer, and will try to save the truth from this *bagarre.*

As soon as the news of Sheridan's victory reached Washington, Mr. Lincoln in person, as well as some of his familiars, tried to inspire the correspondents of the various newspapers with the idea that Sheridan was victorious because he executed the plans and manœuvres traced out for him by Mr. Lincoln!——

September 21.—A few days ago in a speech, Seward solemnly promised to the American people at large, *that there would be no draft.* To-day Mr. Lincoln orders a new draft. And this Seward is suffered!

Fixa cœlo devocare sidera.

September 22.—In a letter to me, the upright Grimes gives the best definition or justification for the necessity of helping Lincoln's re-election. "Mr. Lincoln is very far from being a popular man to-day. He will only be accepted because the people is so generously loyal to the Government, and because the people is afraid to trust the men who concocted the Chicago platform, and who will surround McClellan should he be elected." Men like Grimes, Wade, Boutwell, Trumbull, W. Davis, Wilson, Ashley, Kelley, etc., etc., stump for the principles and not for Lincoln.

September 23.—If the Democrats are beaten in this election then they disappear from American

politics, and will no more disgrace the American
history and the lofty name and principle of Democracy. Slavery will be kicked into the abyss,
and it will drag therein its apostle and god-
father, the Democratic party. Events and time
will evoke new issues and broader platforms.

September 23.—What a superb general Sheridan is. The first on record in this war, and this
on both sides, who understands how to win a
battle with artillery and infantry, and to use his
cavalry. The Yankee horsemen sabre to pieces
the F. F. V. centaurs.

September 24.—*Dum cadet elusus ratione ruentis
acervi.* Blair out of the Cabinet. A victory
over Blair and Seward almost equal to that won
by Sheridan. Lincoln behaved splendidly *a la*
Macchiavelli. Blair never expected to have his
boasting letter turn against him. What a wry
face Blair makes in his answer to Lincoln, who
behaved in a masterly, cool, unconcerned, statesmanlike manner. No *porphyrogenus* could have
behaved more sovereign like.

The victory was exclusively won by Senator
Chandler. He fought single-handed and earned
the country's gratitude. I ardently hope that
Blair's name drops from my pen for the last
time.*

---

* The history of the formation of Mr. Lincoln's Cabinet, March,
1861, is yet unwritten. In my first volume I only mention it
in a few passing words. That interval was fraught with the
most momentous results for the destinies of the country during

Great shaking among the other culprits in the
Cabinet; no one of them feels secure.   They

Mr. Lincoln's subsequent administration.   Mr. Lincoln starting
with an energetic, earnest, able, and homogeneous Cabinet, how
much blood and time might have been economized!   In that
struggle for the formation of the first Cabinet, Thucydides-Greeley took an eminent personal part, but he is dumb about it in his
book.   All the best and leading members of the Republican party
united their efforts to secure for Mr. Chase a seat in the Cabinet.
Mr. Seward and Mr. Weed strongly opposed it, as did likewise
Simon Cameron, who himself wished to be Secretary of the Treasury.   In the course, (several days,) of the struggle, repeatedly
Mr. Seward menaced Lincoln with giving up his position in the
Cabinet if Chase should enter it, and thus the loyal and good
Republicans, all opposed to Seward, become victorious.   Wads-
worth's parlor at Willard's was the headquarters of the so-called
New York radicals, and the principal point of operations.
Patronized by Greeley, Montgomery Blair was very obsequious
to the radicals, begging for a seat in the Cabinet from the same
men of whose policy he is now the most bitter defamer.   Mr.
Blair considered himself to be predestined for a Secretary of
War, and bitter was his disappointment when, by the appointment of Chase and Cameron, only the postmastership remained
for him.   It cost even more of a struggle to get Mr. Blair into
the Cabinet than Mr. Chase.   Seward and Weed opposed, and
wished to have Winter Davis.   Several times I piloted to the
doors of Mr. Lincoln's rooms in the hotel, deputations of
Marylanders on behalf of M. Blair.   When in 1862 Simon
Cameron resigned his seat in the Cabinet, M. Blair was certain
he would replace him.   Disappointed again, Blair, Hannibal-
like, swore hatred and revenge on Stanton, and he keeps his
word.

In his recent speech at Clarkesville, Md., M. Blair puffs and
extols General Scott, while in 1861, he was the most virulent
exponent of Scott's imbecility.   In the first days of October,
1861, certain Republican Senators and patriots met General Mc-
Clellan in M. Blair's house, and a few days afterwards General

may be right. *Always the beginning is the most difficult.*

September 25.—How the McClellanites strain every nerve to present McClellan as *a man!*

——— *neque omissos colores*
Lana refert medicata fuco.

September 26.—Splendid is Sheridan; splendid as a soldier and as a General. Always *really* in the front; always in the fire; cheers the soldiers and *effectively* leads them on. A new martial era!

September 27.—The fight for the presidential victory deafens the roar of the cannon. I hope that the impurities accumulated by this campaign will be precipitated into the depth of destruction, whatever else may be the results of victory or of defeat for our side.

September 28.—I am certain that seldom have diplomats showed themselves so useless to their respective governments as did during this war,

---

Scott resigned his duties. M. Blair often asserted that if Senator Wade was President instead of Lincoln, the South and the rebellion would be crushed as if by the spell of magic. M. Blair became a faithful and devoted defender of McClellan in the expectation of becoming Secretary of War by McClellan's cursed influence.

When Chief Justice Taney died, M. Blair believed he would get the Chief Justiceship. Then Blair blandly insinuated to certain radical Senators that it would be for the benefit of the radical cause to have a radical like himself, Blair, at the head of the Supreme Court of the United States.—*Note September* 7, 1865.

certain diplomats in Washington. I am sure that several among the European governments are wholly misinformed about the progress of events, and consider the election of McClellan to be a foregone conclusion. Perhaps the English government is better informed, as Lord Lyons is not passionate, not one sided, and tries to observe well and to be well informed.

September 30.—Never has the Democratic party shown its hand so fully as this year. One can now be thoroughly acquainted with that party.

Of all political parties that ever existed in any nation since nations and parties existed, the American Democratic party is the greatest *abnormality*. It has nothing whatever of a genuine American principle and American spirit.

Democrats denying and treading down human rights, Democrats, worshippers of slavery, Democrats, devoted to building up the most contemptible and villainous aristocracy that ever disgraced the globe! Is all this American principle?

And the numerical strength of the Democratic party has been repeatedly analyzed in these pages.

OCTOBER.

October 1.—Led on by the Grants, the Sheridans, the Shermans, the Thomases, our troops pour their blood in torrents, and behind the backs of these myriads of unnamed heroes, the Democrats, the McClellanites make the utmost efforts to belittle the people, to save their gracious masters, the rebels, and to elevate McClellan on the ruin of the country and of her honor. Such is the symbol of McClellan's election.

October 2.—Everywhere in pacific occupations and pursuits crowds of young men, as if for the last three years no war was raging. The resources in men seem to be inexhaustible! But it is saddening to find that so many young men escape military service. I hope that before many years have elapsed, every able-bodied man under thirty-five years of age, who has not participated in this holy struggle, will be scorned by his country and by his generation; that he will be the black sheep in his township and in his village; that he will never get a wife, and if he does, that she will be the ugliest devil incarnate.

October 2.—No people ever in the world's history paid so dearly for the apprenticeship of war, none waded to manhood through such sacrifices and streams of blood as my American countrymen. And they are not yet at the end of this awful race. The thorough incapacity of the leaders under whom the start was made rendered the task heavier and more sanguinary. When the war began comparatively few dawning capacities were scattered among the army and the people, but the incapable leaders could not, would not, or did not understand how to select and to evoke to action even those few. It was repeatedly pointed out in the volumes of this Diary how, in 1861, fatally governed by cliques, the narrow-minded Scott and McClellan made the most fatal selections and nominations, how the inexperienced Lincoln obeyed them, and likewise obeyed other political influences, and how thus the higher military grades were at once filled with incapacities who subsequently rendered it almost impossible for capacities to assert themselves.

As soon as he came into power, Stanton warred against this fatality, but the evil had taken too deep root, and with it the army of the Potomac was almost eaten to the core.

No commander whatever can do anything in the field if his subordinate officers are incapable.

In the first Italian campaign, the young officers, almost Napoleon's companions, secured his victories by executing his combinations with precision and rapidity. With the divination of enthusiasm they understood their leader. And the immense majority of these lieutenants of Napoleon, of high or low grades, had no other military school than the love of their sacred cause, the camp-fires and the fields of battle.

A new era dawns now upon the military fate of this people. It dawned first in the Western armies, because of their not being so directly subject to the fatal influences of Washington. (See vol. II.) And now new men—unknown to cliques—lead this great people to the glorious goal. All this will be, however, changed if McClellan should be elected. It will be a relapse into the old ways, and any one knows what a galaxy of bad generals, his compeers, etc., McClellan would drag after him.

Lincoln's favoritism and *politicianism* have likewise done a great deal of mischief, but nevertheless he was often forced to do good. Thus under the advice of Stanton, and under the pressure of Congress and of public opinion, Lincoln entrusted with command Grant, who in his turn brought *en relief* the Shermans, the Sheridans, and a whole galaxy of new commanders. Lincoln will still do awful mischief, as he does now by his pertinacity in sustaining Meade, but nevertheless the military fate and honor of the country are thousands of times safer in Lincoln's than they would be in McClellan's hands. This is felt by the people, and is one of the necessities which in this dilemma makes Lincoln an anchor of salvation to escape the curse of such a lee shore as McClellan. And thus, although with bleeding mind and soul, I now *heartily* join in the hurrah for Lincoln.

October 3.—What good boys are those English ill-wishers to our sacred cause and devoted partisans of the rebels! Money is sent from England to secure McClellan's election. I am glad for the poor devils who will get this English money. Most of them will be the Irish, and what a strange coincidence! . The genuine American spirit will soar above this mud, and English gold or no gold, McClellan will not be elected.

October 4.—Winter Davis's speech in Baltimore is one of the greatest patriotic *phillippiques* against his enemies and against his opponents.

October 4.—One of the after-curses generated by this war will be the necessity of keeping a large standing army, and thus nursing the cursed spirit of military caste, that spirit of perdition, which always so easily entangles the human mind. A great many among the subaltern officers, and above all among the pupils from West Point wish for McClellan, agitate for him, and will vote for him because they consider him the champion of a *Marsocracy* against the civic spirit of the people. One reason more for siding with Lincoln.

October 5.—The military Medical Department is highly incensed against the Sanitary Commission. The Commission may have committed some mistakes and nevertheless remain what it is, the noblest offshoot of a free and humane people. The red tape is incensed because at the beginning of the war in 1861 the young activity of the Sanitary Commission stirred up the old fogyism in the officials, swept away venerable spiders and their cobwebs, and indirectly forced a new life into the Department.

The copperheads, such as the *World*, virulently attack the Sanitary Commission because of the good the Commission has done to our armies on fields of battle and in the hospitals. *Inde iræ* of traitors.

October 5.—Last Friday there was a bloody encounter before Petersburg. We lost about two thousand men, because General Meade *forgot* to establish a connection between the two operating corps. The enemy availed himself of the fault, penetrated into the gap and cut right and left. It can be easily established, that since the beginning of this Virginia campaign the various criminal blunders exclusively committed by Meade, cost the life and limbs of at least forty thousand men. Will Meade never be impeached and court-martialed ?

October 6.—The naval heroes do not feel much

flattered to be under the heel of such civilians as preside over the Department of the Navy. Fox, at least, belongs to the Navy, and is of the craft. The *sic vos non vobis* receives the most complete and emphatic illustration in the relations of our naval heroes to the heads of the Department of the Navy.

October 7.—It may be considered curious and interesting to follow, ascertain, and record all the hopes, all the wishes, all the expectations, all the demands, and all the intrigues already on foot to secure positions under the future or eventual Republican administration.

Fessenden told me that he by far prefers the legislative to his administrative duties, and that he wishes to be re-elected to the Senate. Fessenden is a true man and patriot; he prefers political and mental independence.

October 8.—A few days ago Seward said to a dissatisfied Republican, "*that factions rule in revolutions.*" Of course he knows this by personal experience. He and his faction—the Weeds and their consorts—ruled the country for nearly three years.

October 8.—As yet the diplomats have never congratulated the President upon any victory won by our troops. The diplomats accredited by a government or a sovereign in Europe *must* congratulate the sovereign on the success of his arms. Some of them here wait until they will be able to congratulate McClellan, their pet; others would, if they could, congratulate Jeff. Davis. Some lesser diplomats here would heartily congratulate the President, but they are overawed by some of their mighty *confreres;* and seldom, if ever, a diplomat dares to step outside of the diplomatic treadmill in the place where he diplomatizes.

October 8.—Led on by the New England spirit, inspired by the genius of humanity, the American people is fairly under way to come nearer and nearer to that perfect social condition to which sages, such as John Stuart Mill, point as its goal.

Slavery, political Democracy, aided by the Irishry, stopped the way and have thrown *all* off the track. But the struggle will clear the road, provided the electoral victory remains with the Republicans and with the radicals.

October 8.—This civil war has transformed the southern chivalry, and principally the F. F. V.'s, into bushwhackers, cowardly murderers and highway robbers. Virginia swarms with them. Robert Lee authorizes, sanctions such warfare, and appoints the bushwhackers. Lee disgraces himself almost more by this, than he did by treason.

October 8.—Perhaps Lincoln will unfold sterner qualities. I doubt not that if at the beginning of the war he had not fallen into the hands of Scott, of Seward, of Weed, and of the border State unpatriotic politicians, he might have shifted less, and acted with more foresight and energy.

24

October 9.—The enemies of light and of right, (now collectively to be called the McClellanites,) have very skillfully divided the characters to be played by them before the American people. One batch of them deplores the trials of the country and insinuates peace. McClellan himself and certain of his henchmen try to look martial, *a la general* Thumb. Finally, the rebels themselves roar fire and brimstone. The genuine people is thus to be frightened, allured, or whipped in to vote for McClellan. We shall see.

October 9.—Senator Wilson the indefatigable patriot almost daily stumps various parts of the Union, and thus comes in direct contact with the populations of towns and villages, that core of the people and of the cause. Wilson tells me that everywhere the people are for the country and not for the Administration, as incarnated in Lincoln and Seward. So I thought and I never doubted the people. Further, Wilson assured me that Stanton daily gains ground in the people's confidence, and that they are still prepared to make any sacrifices to save their own cause.

The copperhead-democrats are not the people, but weeds scattered in the people's garden. The copperhead-democrats are certain well-to-do and well-dressed *gentlemen*, and with them is the lowest and the coarsest social stratum. Between these two extremes is the laborious, intelligent, orderly, civilized bulk of the American population. This is the people, and this will decide the election.

October 11.—Some electoral victories on the people's side. Satan called together his legions and was worsted. Blindfolded diplomats baffled.

October 12.—Seward speaks loud about the electoral victories, but as he sees that these victories are due to radicals, without whose support the pure-blood Lincolnites would have been beaten, he now becomes the fixed point around which crystallize various floating and loose dissatisfied Republicans, shelved politicians, Weedites and other leeches, and whom he calls the *moderators.* Seward believes he can form thus a faction strong enough to avert from him Blair's fate.

The radicals decided these October elections, and their casting vote will decide the great November election. But Mr. Lincoln once elected may turn and snub off the radicals, and subside into his old ways. I wish to be able to muster up some confidence in Lincoln.

October 13.—Sherman's report. The work of a thorough-bred soldier, as have been his operations and his Atlanta campaign. The report is written as the' operations progressed, and not months, almost years afterwards, in the McClellan and Meade most approved fashion. It gladdens the heart to find in this report how the Western generals work together and do not intrigue against each other, as do in the Potomac Army the remnants of the McClellan and Meade-ites.

General Thomas again prominent. Thomas never failed in any of his undertakings. I know him. He is slow but sure; he does not aim at brilliancy, but never takes a false or a backward step. If a comparison were to be made (although I hate comparisons)—judging from a purely military view, Thomas seems to have something of Washington and of Wellington; he seems to be very surefooted, and most probably he will win a still greater page in the history of this war.

McPherson fell a young hero-captain!

October 14.—The Copperheads, beaten in elections, charge that bribery had much to do with their discomfiture, and that the Central National Republican Committee spent and spends millions. It is, however, peremptorily true that the above-mentioned committee has not spent millions for the simple reason that it has no millions at its disposition. Further: The character and name of a Senator Harlan* who directs

---

* Mr. Harlan, now Secretary of the Interior, in expelling Walt Whitman from a clerkship in that Department for the publication of a volume of poetry, has shown himself to be animated by a spirit of narrow-minded persécution which would honor the most fierce Spanish or Roman inquisitor. The narrow spirit of dogmatism crystallizes priesthood, be such priesthood Roman or Protestant, and persecution is the homage which dogmatism has ever paid to conscience. *Per contre:* the Department of the Interior pays a fat salary to a Swiss adventurer

it, and the names of the other members of the
committee are a sufficient guarantee that mean-
ness and fraud are impossible. But how is it
with the Democratic Central Committee in New
York? The director, the chairman, and the
other parties have political profligacy burning on
their brows.

October 14.—Good-natured, befogged senti-
mentalists unite with Copperheads in denounc-
ing Grant and Sheridan for the wholesale devastation of a part of the Shenandoah Valley.

By weakening the rebels, such a devastation
precipitates the end of the war, and thus will
eventually spare the life of thousands and thousands, and economize the waste of property, of
material and of time, worth hundreds of times
more than what is destroyed in the valley. It
will be thus beneficial for both sides. Grant is
to be admired for despising the petty talk of sen-
timentalists, and he does not shun any responsibility, and strikes boldly in all directions.

---

who conspired against the liberty of his native Canton Neuf-
chatel and attempted to establish the rule of royalty over a sister
republic. When the treasonable attempt miscarried, the conspirator ran away and found a warm berth under the wings of
the republican eagle. Thus the American Republic pays off the
debt contracted by the Prussian king towards a conspirator
against freedom.

But the Swiss is a *mommer*—that is, an intolerant protestant,
Jesuit and absolutist; and intolerance probably constitutes the
affinity between the Swiss and the Secretary.—*Note September*
12, 1865.

The devastation is incomplete. The northern part of the valley, that hive of bushwhackers and freebooters, ought to be rendered uninhabitable. The innocent will not suffer, and if so, they are precious few and can easily be compensated. The families of F. F. V.'s, bushwhacking murderers, deserve no pity.

October 15.—"The great Democratic party," as it calls itself, is to save the country!

Great in what?—in its elements of coarseness, of opaqueness?—in its compound of what is the most corrupt, savage, and ignorant in America?

The integral force of the Democratic party always consisted, and now consists in the perversion of all higher principles, and in catering to the vilest passions; the nerve of the party was and is the slaveholder, the slavery worshipper, the social offal and the Roman Irishry. The incendiaries and murderers in the New York riots, 1863, were the simon-pure Democrats.

October 15.—What will be the fate and the organization of the Africo-Americans when the rebellion is crushed and emancipation fulfilled? Few around me think about it; most of them rely upon the hour which will give its own solution. They may be right. With his purity, with his clearsightedness, and with his great practical sense, Wadsworth would have been the man to direct on a large scale the social and economical organization of the freedmen, and in this respect his loss is irreparable.

Wadsworth's idea was to organize the freed-men into self-sustaining and self-defending agricultural colonies, locating them on confiscated, and on new, hitherto uncultivated lands. Wadsworth was altogether averse to hiring out the freedmen as laborers; he considered it as a perpetuation of slavery, disguised with another name. Of course Wadsworth recognized the necessity of appointing directors, who were to preside, to organize, and to direct the labor of the colonists.

October 16.—It is not correct to assert or to maintain that by his personal magnetism, by his skill, by his power or by his transcendent merits, Lincoln beats out of the field all his antagonists, or that thereby he forces the pure men in the party and the radicals to accept and to sustain him.

Events and circumstances alone, and not his merits, serve Mr. Lincoln. The issue becomes narrow and pointed. Light or darkness, slavery or freedom, honor or dishonor, negation or asser-tion, Ahriman or Ormuzd—must be selected. Vacillating as he is, Lincoln still upholds that *labarum* of mankind, and behind him are arrayed the confessors—behind McClellan are arrayed all the powers of hell.

October 16.—Belmont, of Wall street, the dictator of the "great Democratic party!" What a fall, what a fall even for the Democrats! Belmont issues manifestos, issues orders of the day, and has Marble for his lieutenant. This Belmont is an excellent banker, a luxurious dinner-giver, a polite " gentleman " for the brilliant and the highly "high-toned" Fifth avenue society; he is generally polite when he is not arrogant, but he is ignorant even for one of the circumcised, and that is, perhaps, what makes him a leader and a dictator of the Democrats. And men, such as a Guthrie, a Cass, a Ganson, and some such others, manœuvring under the orders of a Belmont! What a degradation!

I am told that in the event of McClellan's election, Belmont oscillates between the mission to Paris and the Secretaryship of the Treasury. To shave the country at large as he already shaves Wall street! Oh, no! Such as Belmont will not yet take a foothold in Washington. Not yet, O! Joshua-dictator, not yet.

Chase nobly redeems his character. Goaded and deeply wounded by the Lincolnites, abandoned by many of his partisans, Chase forgets all, and supports the people's cause, although thereby his unrelenting personal enemies will be elevated.

October 16.—Some very few European diplomats, and among them Mr. De Geofroy Chargé from France, and de Stoeckl the representative of Russia, have understood the treacherousness of the Chicago platform; they now disbelieve the possibility of its being swallowed together with McClellan, by the people. Some

South American diplomats are a little awed by certain of their European colleagues and empty-headed Colossuses. Frederick Barreda, representative of Peru, must be excepted. He is most loyal and devoted to the cause of the North in Europe now, as he was during his stay at Washington. Barreda is not to be imposed upon by any European diplomatic malignity and narrow-mindedness whatever.

October 17.—If in the next elections the Democratic party is overpowered, then the doom of slavery is settled, as the reason of the existence of that pro-slavery party disappears from the American polity.

October 17.—John Bright, the great and high-minded English Quaker, answers Thucydides-Greeley's dedication by a letter, urging the re-election of Mr. Lincoln. The intentions of Bright are noble and generous, but his manner and style are a little too patronizing. He speaks to Americans as to children. But with all their greatness and nobleness, even the English Brights have to learn much from my American radicals in the Congress and out of Congress. The English have yet to learn what is patriotism, devotion, sacrifice and insight in our own domestic affairs. Bright's letter is out-and-out European; it is based on a very one-sided and limited knowledge of the American people, and of the men who now are in the foreground.

October 18.—Seldom, if ever, Stanton makes a

mistake in his *free, untrammeled* selections of men.   Charles Dana, in the War Department, is the incarnation of integrity, patriotism, and of an almost peerless capacity to run the most complicated and the largest administrative machinery.

October 18.—Men who receive the bounties for voluntary enrollments desert, and attempt to play the same tricks in another district.   They call these wretches bounty-jumpers.   Many of such are Polish and German Jews.   Do these thieves manœuvre under the orders of Joshua Belmont?

October 19.—How the little penny-a-liners in the press are after Stanton!   The loyal as well as the disloyal crew is against him; but as the powerful and noble Newfoundlander minds not the attacks of little curs, so Stanton pays no attention to such presses.

October 21.—Sheridan has put to shame the Cæsarean *veni, vidi, vici.*   Never and nowhere in history was a thorough defeat by a turn of the hand transformed into a most brilliant and decisive victory as was that won by Sheridan two days ago in the valley.   Neither Cæsar, nor Napoleon ever did the like, and it is as stupid as offensive for Sheridan to compare his day to the second part of the day of Marengo.   Never in the history of captains and of battles was the influence of the personality of a chief so manifest, so almost miraculously manifest as in this last battle.   At the sight of ITS Sheridan, the literally destroyed and utterly routed army turns against the enemy. Sheridan brings no reinforcements; he is alone on his horse; at the sight of him running soldiers turn their faces towards the enemy, pick up whatever weapon they can, form and fall into the ranks. No captain had ever such a glorious day! Sheridan, not Meade, ought to be next to Grant in command.

Sheridan is not a graduated engineer, but a graduated captain. Sheridan was unknown to any West Point or Washington clique, but his name belongs to immortality.

October 22.—I hope that the military deeds of the Shermans, of the Sheridans, of the Thomases, and of many other field-officers will finally open the eyes of the people and of the Congressmen. I hope public opinion and Legislators will now find out how defective and even how mischievous are the method and the classification of studies prevailing at West Point. This method and classification are worse than fogyish; they are contrary to logic, to common sense, and to genuine military science. In previous volumes I explained wherein the mistake consists. Stanton understands the matter thoroughly, but the West Point prejudice is too strong, and it has a very extensive ramification. Mr. Lincoln decides; but at the best he is innocent as a baby and about as able to comprehend this West Point question.

October 23.—Young Colonel Lowell of the Massachusetts Cavalry, killed in that last battle. From boyhood Lowell always performed more than he promised.

Massachusetts must glory in such sons; no better, no braver, no more devoted than this young Lowell.

If all the millions of Southern traitors of both sexes were destroyed, their destruction could not atone for the losses of the loyal North's best children.*

October 24.—Winter Davis not re-nominated for Congress. He succumbed to the intrigues of his most bitter enemies, the traitors in Baltimore and the simon-pure Lincolnites. The absence of W. Davis from the next Congress is almost a public, and at any rate, it is a parliamentary calamity. He is an orator without compeer, and a genuine American statesman.

The 37th and the 38th Congresses have yielded too much of their own special constitutional powers to the Executive. The two Congresses yielded in good faith, and because in their lofty patriotism they believed it to be the necessity of the hour, and unavoidable for the salvation of the cause and of the country. Nevertheless thereby dangerous and bad precedents have been

---

* Now will be made the balance sheets of the losses in this war. It will be shown, I am certain, that Massachusetts alone has lost in the war more well-bred, highly educated, and well-to-do young men than have the F. F. V.'s and the whole Southern so-called best blood summed up together.—*Note May*, 1865.

established. (See Diary, vol. II.)   Such precedents
may become a chronic disease, eating up the
public liberties.

Winter Davis is just the man to recall to their
duties the too confident and the indifferent Congressmen.   Bold, eloquent, keen, independent,
Winter Davis was the kernel from which could
grow a patriotic and statesmanlike counterpoise
to the encroachments of the Executive.

To encroach and to extend its power is the
tendency of every Executive, whatever may be
its origin; but subservient political bodies are the
greatest disgrace and curse of nations.

October 26.—General McCall, the brave commander of the undaunted Pennsylvania Reserves,
takes up McClellan's report and convicts him of
misrepresentations, of untruth, and of having
slandered that brave division.   Preparing his belated disquisition, McClellan was forced to slan-
der others, and thus redeem his own unsoldier-
like conduct.   When the other generals in detail
take up whatever concerns them in that so-
called report, then truth will come out, and whatever I may have said against McClellan will be
found below the facts.

October 27.—Judging by the rebel press, as
well as by various other disclosures coming from
rebel sources, the South heartily wishes and
expects that McClellan will be elected, that the
Democrats will come into power, that the Union
will be•divided and sub-divided, that slavery will

be saved, that humanity will be degraded, and the American name dishonored for eternities. Such for the rebels and traitors is the meaning of McClellan's election.

October 28.—The Democrats attempt to put a certain decency and plausibility on their treason to the cause of freedom and of humanity. They maintain before the people, that if Lincoln is elected our liberties are lost.

Poor Lincoln accused of tyranny! He has not nerve enough, not mind enough to be a tyrant, even in a sacred cause. As yet Lincoln has not hung one single robber and traitor, when the rebels and their chiefs in cold blood have murdered thousands of Union men in the revolted region.

Lincoln has not put one man in prison who has not richly deserved to be put there and kept to the end of the rebellion. Domestic traitors freely and arrogantly walk among us, give various advice to the rebels, and thus occasion many disasters to our troops. Most of such traitors are virtually reeking with the blood of our men, and nevertheless Lincoln leaves them unharmed. Such traitors, well known to the Government, are more criminal than their *confréres* in secessia.

Freedom of the press put in danger by Lincoln! I wish Lincoln had the pluck to suppress the treasonable *Worlds, Intelligencers,* Boston *Couriers,* and all such prints which all over the country preach treason to right and to humanity, and poison the minds of the people. If Lincoln has or is to have energy, God grant that he may show and apply it in the right hour and on the right side.

A few days ago Wendell Phillips made a true and brilliant analysis of Lincoln's character. As a patriot, as an apostle, as one of the loftiest minds, Wendell Phillips yields to the necessity of Lincoln's election, and announces what the patriots are justified in expecting from an *amended* Lincoln.

October 29.—True men who approach Lincoln say that his looks are subdued and melancholy; that his former so offensive jocosity has left him. I wish it were so; it would be a proof that Lincoln has the consciousness of what the people is doing for him. Further: that the consciousness of his humility is evoked; that he will make all efforts to atone for the past.

October 29.—The New York Democracy in distress perpetrate the most infamous frauds and forgeries with the soldiers' vote. The dead, the fallen are evoked from their heroic graves, and their names forged and signed. But is there anything vile, mean, infamous enough to make a New York *thorough-bred* Democrat and Seymourite shudder or stop?

October 30.—Of how many major generals, of how many McClellans, Buells, Porters, etc., will

Belmont be obliged to take care after the election?

October 30.—The papers publish a letter written by Lincoln in August, 1863, to a certain Conkling. This letter is firm and noble, the best Lincoln has ever written. But why has he never acted as he writes?

The awful crisis, the fated day of election approaches nearer and nearer. Civilization, humanity, progress are to be endangered or to be victorious.

Will Lincoln respond—even half way—to the expectations of the despairing patriots? Will Lincoln's character become true steel under the hammerings of mighty events? Will he henceforth act with the consciousness of a stern duty upon him? Will he fulfill his duty towards this confiding people, and thus fulfill his duty towards mankind? It is horrible to think that Lincoln may baffle all the prayers and expectations of the patriots, and relapse into his past " Lincolniana."

NOVEMBER.

November 1.—The Presidential campaign approaches its end, and the struggle is every hour more bitter, envenomed, and *desperate.* Accusations and counter-accusations fall thick as locusts in Africa. The Press is pitiless, excited, tearing out the bowels of the antagonists and of their respective candidates.

The copperhead McClellanite press is so utterly shameless, so outrageous in its falsehoods against the administration, that it reconciles one to Lincoln, and so to speak, whips one into his camp. It is certain that Lincoln could have done more towards crushing the rebellion, but it is also certain that the McClellanites in power will do everything to make rebellion victorious.

November 2.—On all sides conspiracies in favor of the rebels, of slavery, and of McClellan. The copperheads rampant, defiant, and threatening to substitute bullets for ballots. New York may repeat the murders of July, 1863.

November 2.—Butler is going to New York to

prevent disorders, murder, and arson.   The Mc-
Clellanites, the Belmontites, and the Seymourites are in a rage.

November 3.—Both parties emphatically affirm
that theirs is the victory.   But the signs seem to
indicate that Lincoln will be elected.   And if
elected, will Lincoln *turn up* what the majority
of the good-natured people believes him already
to be, or will he remain what he really is?

November 3.—The *honorable* the prince-dictator
of the Democrats, the liege lord of Wall street,
Belmont the Great, continues to issue orders of
the day, and to register them; even makes
speeches.   The *honorable* the prince is awfully
bitter against the abolitionists.   The abolitionists disturb his princely rest and—his exchange
operations.   The honorable Shemite forgets that
the generous spirit urging the American abolitionists to action is the same which all over
Europe inspired those who claimed and carried
through the political emancipation of the Jews,
and freed them from political and from social
disabilities which for long centuries crushed that
part of the human family, and which in some
European countries still hang over the children
of Jacob.   The prince-dictator forgets that the
spirit presiding over the abolition of slavery is
the same which introduced a Lionel Rothschild
into the English Parliament, and which in
France utterly destroyed the stupid and degrading prejudices based on any sham distinction of

race. A Cremieux, a Fould, an Alexander Dumas may well give information to our haughty prince-Democrat.

It is a curious phenomenon that the character of the *parvenu* is the same in politics as it is in conventional society. The great European disfranchised, the Jews and the Irish are in America the most bitter and hateful enemies of the Africo-Americans. Both the Jews and the Irish only in America enjoy that recognition of full rights which was and is denied to them in Europe. Politically they become new men or *parvenus*— and they are the most jealous that others, at least their equals, may not become similarly admitted to full freedom and equality.

November 4.—A Presidential campaign is the true element of the loyal press. It is now *sans peur et sans reproche.* Why not always so ?

November 4.—A few days more and *consumatum est.* The strenuous efforts of patriots, I ardently hope, will be successful, and the copperheads under McClellan will be defeated.

I am haunted with a nightmare. Has Lincoln learned something from the past? His hands will be now untied, and if he earnestly wishes, his path will be untrammeled by all those artful border State politicians, or by Sewards, or by Weeds, or by any others of that crew.

Has Lincoln learned and has he acquired the consciousness that it was of no use to him to continually make sacrifices for the sake of conciliating copperheads and sham Union men? to spare Northern traitors who played and play the spies for the rebels? to spare pseudo-guerrillas, bushwhackers, murderers, and their abettors inside of the Union lines?

Or will Lincoln continue to trifle with the blood and the sacrifices of the people?

A very earnest and true patriot told me that if Sewardism and Blairism shall continue to prevail in Mr. Lincoln's policy, then those who voted for McClellan will have more influence and protection than the honest radicals and patriots who will vote Mr. Lincoln into the White House. All is possible in this great world.

November 5.—Lincoln is put up as the agent of the will and of the principle inspiring the Northern people, and that is his signification and his force.

November 5.—Already flatterers, lick-spittles and good-natured imbeciles bedizen Lincoln with all the highest and noblest qualities of mind, heart, and intellect. What will it be when he is re-elected? If Lincoln does not become dizzy, then really he has more manhood in him than I ever believed. But Lincoln's past shows him not to be flattery-proof.

That well-intentioned old English relic, George Thompson, in his good-natured but patronizing manner, already puts Lincoln on the level with Washington. So does Seward and many others.

Before long they will hoist Lincoln above Washington, who thus will become only *second best.*

The only similarity between Lincoln and Washington is, that the one and the other were evoked, were taken up and elevated by the people, and that neither Washington nor Lincoln inaugurated the movement, and called on the people to join or to follow them.

But once at the head of the people, Washington became a rock of salvation, a true leader, almost an initiator and the people's *labarum.* Never did Washington make a false step in his general and military policy. Washington headed the events, and was almost always in the first line; up to this hour Mr. Lincoln has always followed the events; has been pushed by, but never has led on the people.

And mentioning the patronizing airs with which our *genuine* English friends encourage and advise the loyal American people, it is necessary to record that the sage, John Stuart Mill, that ardent and devoted champion of human rights, of the rights of reason and of freedom, and thus a champion of the North, never and under no circumstances *condescended* to patronizingly advise the American people, or to pat it on the back.

November 6.—Beauregard, J. Davis, and Hood conceived the invasion of Tennessee, thereby believing they could draw Sherman away from Georgia. Soon they will find out they have caught a Tartar. Sherman will give them over to the mercies of Thomas.

Sherman is to march through the bowels of Georgia. The plan is his own, and if he succeeds, it will be one of the most daring, most skillful, and most truly soldier-like operations ever undertaken by a captain. Sherman *is* a captain in the fullest sense, and I have full confidence in his definitive success.

Sherman and Sheridan are the heroes of this year. Grant keeps Lee by the throat, and perhaps already some time ago Grant could have strangled the rebel were he not so *ably* and so *efficiently* seconded by Meade.

November 7.—Two days more, and the throes and anxieties will be over. The Copperhead and McClellanite leaders are still defiant. But their defiance may be: *Bonne mine à mauvais jeu.*

Has Mr. Lincoln learned anything? and will the re-election be a plunge in Lethe, and wash out from his mind those mischievous shortcomings so pre-eminently constituting his first term? Has Lincoln acquired knowledge of men? Will he be able to surround himself with strong men? I wish to believe it, but my doubt is stronger than my faith. Lincoln is too old to bend, and may rather break under the weight of his old ways and mental habits.

November 7.—It seems that this time many, many Germans will follow in the wake of the Irish, will vote for McClellan, for slavery, and forswear principles.   These false Germans are mostly Roman-Catholics; then certain *nouveaux riches* and would-be gentlemen; and finally that coarsest element contained in every agglomeration of men, in every community, in every nation.   As neither the German Roman-Catholics, nor the German *parvenus*, nor the German loafers have any intelligent particle of the true German spirit, and as all the three elements combined constitute a minority of the German element in America, so intrinsically the Germans remain true and faithful to the German spirit, and to the cause of light and of humanity.

November 8.—It is all very fine to speak of forgiveness, if at the polls to-day the people will grant the power to the Republicans.   To forgive what?   The crimes perpetrated by the McClellanites and the Copperheads?   Since 1862 the Copperheads and the McClellanites did everything in their power to poison public opinion, to save rebellion and slavery, to degrade the national honor, to palsy the action of the patriots in Congress, to embarrass the Administration. The New York riots, the various conspiracies, are the work of the McClellanites and of the Copperhead-Democrats.   If they pay the taxes for the war it is because they cannot help it.   In many ways the Democratic Copperheads and the McClellanites are responsible for the duration of the war, and thus for the increase of its burdens; the Republicans divide the burdens with the others, although they do not divide the crimes. Perhaps never a political party went to the polls with such criminal purposes as do to-day the Mc-Clellanites.

November 9.—Wadsworth's memory is avenged; the honest country people, the marrow of the State, expels from power Seymour the *friend* of the rioters, of the murderers, and of the incendiaries; the patron of the forging jackals; the unyielding friend of the rebels, and the intended saviour of slavery. The noble people of my adopted State denies you, O Seymour, denies the crew of your friends and Wadsworth's slanderers !

Right, humanity, justice, light are victorious, and the combined powers of hell overpowered! In this victory Lincoln is an *incidental* incident, a collateral *pis aller*. And nevertheless Lincoln's luck remains one of the French proverb : *il est nait coiffé.*

This victory of good over evil is one luminous ray more in the struggles between the two principles, struggles coeval with the existence of man, struggles which alone have generated all the teleologies and all the social organizations of the human race.

Slavery and its devoted henchmen, the American political Democracy, are prostrated and crushed, self-government loftily asserted, and its enemies and slanderers bite the dust. The stain

on the American escutcheon is blotted out, the
sin is atoned, and humanity satisfied.

The people at large atones for the sin committed in 1862, committed under the seduction
of treacherous Republicans. The people sends
back to the Congress not only many sterling
patriots whom electoral treason upset in 1862,
men like Roscoe Conkling, Bingham of Ohio,
but considerably increases the phalanx of patriots
for the 39th Congress.

The next, the 39th Congress, will have a
majority *for good* such as there never was in all
the history of parliamentary and representative
governments, of all nations, the great French
National Convention excepted. In the normal
existence of parliaments and of other representative bodies, overwhelming majorities are found
for the evil, but seldom, if ever, for the good.

The power of the next Congress will be enormous and unprecedented. That Congress will
harvest and carry out what its two immediate
predecessors have so nobly, so courageously laid
down in their respective legislative labors and
records. The 39th Congress will continue and
enlarge the great work of which the two former
Congresses have laid the foundations.*

---

* The true men in this 39th Congress, those high-souled patriots
who, during the past four years, steered the fate of the country,
and whose names have been so often mentioned in these Diaries,
those veterans of the greatest political struggle of our century,
will have now a harder fight than had Grant and his army in

But likewise on account of this unprecedented majority being almost without a counterpoise, the 39th Congress may run among various parliamentary breakers. The 39th Congress will be by far more powerful and in more propitious conditions than its two predecessors to sternly control and direct the Executive.

November 10.—Mr. Lincoln is therefore re-consecrated by the people. But he is re-consecrated only as the incidental standard-bearer of the people's sacred creed. Nothing more.

As all that is great and noble, the victorious people will be magnanimous and forbearing towards those in the North who attempted to falsify and almost to destroy the lofty historic signification of the American life in mankind's progress and development. Forbearance towards the misled Democratic masses is a duty. They will easily return to the patriotic track—but their corrupt leaders—never! never!

Mr. Lincoln ought not even to notice all the abuse with which he was covered by the Democratic leaders. But as the standard-bearer of a

---

the Wilderness. The true men in Congress will have to hammer prejudices, nay, even superstitions, ignorance, and sham-science worse than ignorance. These true men will have to battle against political and against administrative perfidy, selfishness, and narrow-mindedness; against subtle and insidious sham-patriotism in Congress, in the press, in the administration; against copperheadism, and in a word, against all the artifices of hell. But the true men will win, because in them are light and right.—*Note December* 18, 1865.

great and noble principle, Mr. Lincoln ought always to bear in mind that those leaders are corrupt to the core, that they left nothing unspared to disgrace our sacred creed and principle; that they would have rent the Union. Such men may be forgiven but never trusted; their depravity is beyond atonement; their names belong to the pillory.

This election is not a victory of Lincoln over McClellan; but it is the victory of a devoted patriotism over all the impure and disintegrating elements in the American polity.*

---

* Out of the confusion and combustion prevailing during this civil war new parties or new cohesions will emerge.

The conservatives of all hues, the men possessing large, untaxed capitals and stocks, the shoddy, the corrupt politicians, the men used up by holding and by wielding the power, the flunkeys, the men without heart and without convictions, in one word the egotists of all kinds, naturally will coalesce in one party.

To oppose this offal will grow up a genuine Democratic party, a party having its deep roots in the intelligence of the *many*, of the nameless, that is of the people at large, in whose soul and heart are ingrained the pure, eternal principle of that democracy which, during those years of terrible trials, saved the country and saved humanity. It is the people, it is such a democracy which was the hero, the statesman, the emancipating genius, and the financier during this mortal duel with darkness and treason. The future will and must belong exclusively to that party which will be the pure expression of the aspirations and of the lofty tendencies of the genuine people.

The faith in such a democracy and in the grandeur of the American people, the faith in the elevated level, but not in self-asserting eminences, inspired every page of this Diary.—*Note November 29, 1865.*

The people voted for its own duration, for its own life, for its own national integrity and honor. This verdict of the people sounds: *not a State out of the Union, no slavery in the Union.**

The American people has redeemed its pledge given to mankind. Calm, orderly and resolute, it has proclaimed its will. And at the polls thus thundered the people's voice:

"Abraham Lincoln! notwithstanding your short-comings and your bloody mistakes, we elect you because we believe you to be sincerely willing to destroy the rebellion and to destroy slavery. As to this hour we have not grudged, so we shall not grudge men and money, and you, O Lincoln, make up now for lost time!"

That is the voice of the people to the re-elected President.

---

* The newly inaugurated reconstruction policy seems to me to have a rotten basis. As the French proverb says:*peche par la base.* The reconstruction is put in the hands of the citizens of 1860. But since that year, by blood and martyrdom, loyalty has gestated and evoked to life new citizens, and to the loyalist of 1865—color or no color—ought to be exclusively intrusted the work of reconstruction.—*Note October* 8, 1865.

ＥＮＤ.

EPILOGUE.

1865, April 14.—Night.

LINCOLN MURDERED!

More blood. The slaughter at Seward's house and the attempt to murder him increase the horror of this night. Bathed in his own blood Seward becomes purified from almost all his political misdeeds.

Judging from rumors and from various reports, these horrors seem perpetrated by comparatively young men, incited to murder by those fierce, savage, beastly notions forming the gist of slaveocracy.

Under the eyes and by the direction of F. F. V.'s, and of other so-called chivalry in Richmond and all over the rebel region, the press for years incited to Lincoln's murder. For years a part of the Northern press, often mentioned in these diaries, a press which was and is the gospel of Northern Copperheads, slavers, and traitors, pointed to Lincoln as to a tyrant, and to Seward as to his henchmen. Murder and slaughter by infuriated wretches are now the fruits of those stimulating teachings.

April 15.—The immense majority of the population horrified, dumbstruck; only some few ultra secesh and slaveocrats satisfied. Of course.

The pilot of the Government welters in his blood. To-day Stanton's powerful hands seize the direction and transmit it to the hands of the new President. Stanton is equal to every emergency. Abused by the press and by certain republicans, hated by the Democrat-copperheads as well as by traitors of all kinds and latitudes, Stanton serves well the people, the country. The war is virtually over. The great organizer and administrator of the armies of France, Napoleon the Great, had not to cope with such difficulties, had not such a load to carry, had not to deal with such gigantic masses of men and of military materials of all kinds as Stanton has had in the course of these last three years. And Napoleon the administrator, in no way better fulfilled his task than Stanton.

This murder, this oozing blood, almost sanctify Lincoln. His end atones for all the short-comings for which he was blamed and condemned by earnest and unyielding patriots. Grand and noble will Lincoln stand in the world's history.

No crying injustice, not a single inhuman or perverse action stain Lincoln's name; and whatever sacrifices his vacillations may have cost the people, those vacillations will now be forgiven.

His hand and his blood sealed the terrific

struggle.　His end will live in history and in the people's grateful, warm, and generous memory.

The murderer's bullet opens to him immortality.

He disappears in an apotheosis, and disappears with an unsullied name.

He might have become crushed by the gigantic and difficult solutions which he was to give during his further administration.

To-day the regrets and the blessings of mourning humanity surround his funeral pile.

GENERAL GRANT'S REPORT.

This report is the last military page of a bloody episode in the life of a great self-governing people. It reaffirms what has been already elucidated by events, and for which the country has given credit to the General. It proves that he solely conceived that great and glorious campaign which, early in 1864, opened simultaneously from the Potomac to the Rio Grande, against the rebellion. For lucidity, simplicity, comprehensiveness and modesty, this report has few equals in military history. Seldom, if ever have such extensive military operations been conceived and centered in, or issued from, a single mortal brain.

General Grant took the command with the firm purpose to *hammer* the enemy, and this he did without respite, day and night, winter and summer, in storm and in sunshine.

Doubtless certain parts and details of this report will create heartburnings and may evoke refutations. If modesty and simplicity make the General throw a magnanimous vail over some mishaps of his subordinates, others are treated with unwonted and pointed severity. Such especially is the case with General Butler. On the other hand, the report slides good-naturedly over the nameless conduct of those who directed the defense of the country and the capital against the rebel invasion under Breckinridge and Early in the summer of 1864.

The simultaneously published report of the Secretary of War completes the evidence which proves to what an extent, by the victory over Hood at Nashville, General Thomas secured the success of Sherman's splendid march through the South. In his mention of Thomas, General Grant briefly renders justice to that distinguished officer's judgment.

General Meade is the subject of General Grant's inexhaustible magnanimity. But before the testimony of that magnanimity can be received, the voice of many subordinate generals ought to be heard. The evidence of those generals, the evidence of facts, will perhaps show why, during the battles of the Wilderness, the Potomac Army, in the words of the report, "*has not accomplished as much as I had hoped.*" That evidence may show that the cause was the same which, in the fall of 1863 and the winter of 1864, characterized Meade's warfare—that "masterly generalship" which forced Mr. Lincoln to yield to Stanton's advice and the country's will, and invest Grant with the title of Lieutenant-General and the charge of the campaign against Lee and Rich-

26

mond. The true culprit of the disaster of the mine before Petersburg, is also magnanimously hidden. If the *special* commander of the Potomac Army had been in person on the spot, where it was his absolute duty to be, perhaps the *disaster*, at least, could have been avoided. Magnanimity, likewise, leaves out General Grant's order, by which, during the two or three days previous to Lee's capitulation, the Lieutenant-General, and not Meade, directed the movements of the various corps of the Potomac Army. Sheridan's report, elsewhere mentioned in this Diary, points out how Meade might have baffled Sheridan's efforts to cut off and surround Lee. It is, however, wholly established by General Grant's report that, but for Sheridan, Lee might have accomplished his junction with Johnston, and that at that *finale* Grant found, in Sheridan's unsurpassed soldier-ship, a fit executor of his own masterly plans and combinations.

General Grant's four years' military career finds few precedents or parallels in history. No clique supported him; the pure West-Pointers turned up their noses and shrugged their shoulders; and as soon as he appeared upon the horizon, he was assailed by and almost became a victim of the most venomous calumny, spread by many of his former colleagues. When he captured Fort Donelson, the success was claimed by McClellan, and for him by his worshippers. The press assented. It was asserted, and the assertion was accepted, that Mac. directed Grant's movements by telegram ! Few, very few, at that time, protested against such an absurd assertion. My own humble protest is on record. From the day of Fort Donelson to this, I have recorded with admiration Grant's splendid military career.

"THIS GOVERNMENT IS FOR THE WHITE MAN."

NOTE JANUARY 12, 1866.

In Congress and out of Congress, North and South, in a word all over the country, the worshippers of darkness and of the most degrading prejudices, the sworn enemies of human rights, proclaim that the Africo-American cannot be invested with political rights on account of his "intellectual inferiority." Now, in philosophy, in anthropology, as in the Bible, the paramount criterion of sound reason and intellect is the power or faculty to discriminate between right and wrong, between good and evil. Treason is a form of evil; loyalty to the Union is a form of good. North and South the Africo-American is loyal; and while he proved his loyalty with his life-blood, on what side was the main portion of his inveterate white-skinned enemies?

The objurgations of the pro-slavery Americans of to-day, and all the falsehoods to which the enemies of right appeal, are nothing new. I hear them repeated parrot-like and by rote by the enemies of emancipation here, as for more than

half a century I heard them in Europe.   I heard
them in Poland and in Russia; years and years
I read such arguments in various languages, in
all the writings of the retrograde, oppression-
preaching fraternity abroad.   These perfidious
fallacies, these flagrant offenses to the sense of
humanity, have been uttered over and over again,
against the emancipation of the slaves, of the
serfs, of the *ascripti glebæ*, of the villeins, of the
peasants and laborers of Europe.   Oligarchs,
privileged persons, oppressors in Europe, argued
precisely in the same manner against the manhood of the "white man" as their twin brothers
here argue against the Africo-American.

APPENDIX I.

Names of Members of the House in the Thirty-Eighth Congress who blotted slavery from the Constitution and from the polity of the United States.

YEAS.

Alley,
Allison,
Ames,
Anderson,
Arnold,
Ashley,
Bailey,
Baldwin, Mich.
Baldwin, Mass.
Baxter,
Beaman,
Blaine,
Blair,
Blow,
Boutwell,
Boyd,
Brandegee,
Broomall,
Brown, W. Va.
Clark, A. W.
Clark, F.
Cobb,
Coffroth,
Cole,
Colfax,
Creswell,
Davis, Md.
Davis, N. Y.
Dawes.
Deming,
Dixon,
Donnelly,
Driggs,
Dumont,
Eckley,
Eliot,
English,
Farnsworth,
Frank,
Ganson,

Garfield,
Gooch,
Grinnell,
Griswold,
Hale,
Herrick,
Higby,
Hooper,
Hotchkiss,
Hubbard, Iowa.
Hubbard, Conn.
Hulburd,
Hutchins,
Ingersoll,
Jenckes,
Julian,
Kasson,
Kelley,
Kellogg, Mich.
Kellogg, N. Y.
King,
Knox,
Littlejohn,
Loan,
Longyear,
Marvin,
McAllister,
McBride,
McClurg,
McIndoe,
Miller, N. Y.
Morehead,
Morrill,
Morris, N. Y.
Myers, A.
Myers, L.
Nelson,
Norton,
Odell,
O'Neill, Penna.

Orth,
Patterson,
Perham,
Pike,
Pomeroy,
Price,
Radford,
Randall, Ky.
Rice, Mass.
Rice, Me.
Rollins, N. H.
Rollins, Mo.
Schenck,
Schofield,
Shannon,
Sloan,
Smith,
Smithers,
Spalding,
Starr,
Steele, N. Y.
Stevens,
Thayer,
Thomas,
Tracy,
Upson,
Van Valkenburgh,
Washburne, Ill.
Washburn, Mass.
Webster,
Whaley,
Wheeler,
Williams,
Wilder,
Wilson,
Windon,
Woodbridge,
Worthington,
Yeaman—119.

The unflinching Allies of Darkness and of the deadliest social crime.

NAYS.

Allen, James C.
Allen, W. J.
Ancona,
Bliss,
Brooks,
Brown, Wis.
Chanler,
Clay,
Cox,
Cravens,
Dawson,
Denison,
Eden,
Edgerton,
Eldridge,
Finck,
Grider,
Hall,
Harding,

Harrington,
Harris, Md.
Harris, Ill.
Holman,
Johnson, Penna
Johnson, Ohio.
Kalbfleisch,
Kernan,
Knapp,
Law,
Long,
Mallory.
Miller, Penna.
Morris, Ohio.
Morrison,
Noble,
O'Neill, Ohio.
Pendleton,
Perry,

Pruyn,
Randall, Penna.
Robinson,
Ross,
Scott,
Steele, N. J.
Stiles,
Strouse,
Stuart,
Sweat.
Townsend,
Wadsworth,
Ward,
White, C. A.
White, J. W.
Winfield,
Wood, B.
Wood, F.—56.

APPENDIX II.

HALLECKIANA.

Jomini's Life of Napoleon, translated by Major General Halleck, adorned with Notes and a Red Cover.

Jomini's work is not in question. In itself it is of a very secondary value among the productions of that eminent author. It had some celebrity at the time (1827) when it was published, as one among the first attempts to cast the Napoleonic era into a literary unity. But since then the Napoleonic era has the most complete and the most multifarious literature of its own—a literature crowned by Thiers' immortal *History of the Consulate and of the Empire.*

The above are the reasons of the difficulty *of procuring a copy,* as stated by the translator. French publishers had no inducement to reprint it, and Englishmen had no longing for it; and not much gain will accrue to-day to the English language and literature from the more than decennial labor of the present translator. The work itself is a good hand-book (*compendium*) for the use of dabsters in literature.

Now for the so pompously advertised *Notes.*

The Notes are two-fold: *Notes*, translations from Thiers, from a few others, and from Encyclopedias. *Notes* concocted by the translator, and constituting his personal intellectual property in the four volumes. This property is the object of these lines. It scarcely amounts to three or four pages of printed matter in the whole work. But it is increased by several scores of mistranslations, by which the original meaning and the facts are perverted and falsified.

The *North American Review*, October, 1864, points out a large number of these mistranslations.

The translator's preface, page 26, says: "*The Commentaries of Cæsar are of no great military value*," etc., etc., and that at that time "*strategy*" *was very little understood*."

Napoleon, who did not talk of strategy, thought otherwise about the Commentaries, and after all Cæsar may be consoled.

"*Josephus, Herodotus, Thucydides*, and some twenty historians down to our times, are called *military historians*." This classification, so new, so original, by which the all-embracing comprehension of a historian is contracted into the specialty of a *military historian*, would mightily astonish all the living historians and students of history: but happily for the inventor, his invention has no chance of becoming known to that class of men.

Page 26, Vol. I. "While Jomini stated," etc.

The paragraph is very wise; but facts and logic oppose and weaken it. To be sure "*Napoleon solved problems,*" but not simultaneously, "*while Jomini stated,*" etc. When the latter established his theories, the solutions had been long previously given by Napoleon.

Page 22, *Vol.* I. Disquisition about the grade of a General-in-Chief in the Russian army, and the assertion that, as Prince Gortschakoff, the defender of the Crimea, never won a battle, he was not created a Field Marshal.

The immortal defender of the Crimea died about four years ago, and died a Field Marshal of the Russian army, having been made so a couple of years previous to his death.

The Russian army has no such special grade as a General-in-Chief. It existed in the eighteenth century, and perhaps a few years at the beginning of the present century; but it exists no more.

The Russian army has, 1st, Brigade Generals; 2d, Lieutenant Generals; 3d, Full Generals; 4th, Field Marshals. Full Generals are of infantry, of cavalry, of artillery, of engineers. The number of the *Full* Generals is, proportionally, rather considerable, many in the active service or in the field, others filling various other duties.

A Lieutenant General commands a division, and at times a *corps d'armée;* a Full General commands a *corps d'armée* and likewise a whole army. A Full General may be a Chief-of-Staff of an army, or may be attached to the staff or to the person of the commander himself.

Page 45, *Vol.* I. The father of Catharine II, of Russia, the Prince Anhalt-Zerbst, never served in Russia, and never could have been a Russian Field Marshal, as *the note* makes him.

Vol. I. Excursion into genealogy of the family d'Este. The d'Estes will not be flattered by it. The pride of the d'Estes consists in tracing their legend back to Hercules, when Hercules visited Italy. For this reason the name Ercole was almost hereditary in that family.

Page 119, *Vol.* I. Tribute of admiration paid to Napoleon's activity. Very well. The once Commander-in-Chief of our armies might have shown his admiration by following the example; but when in command he never hurt under him a single horse.

At times, Halleck, the translator, refers to Halleck, the internationalist. Cheap advertisement.

Page 286, *Vol.* II. About Talleyrand and a certain *Bernese* fund or stock. What fund or stock? At that epoch no such fund or stock existed, in which Talleyrand or any private individual whatever could in any way have been interested. There existed a celebrated treasury of the city and oligarchy of Berne, a treasury containing from five to six millions of dollars in gold and silver, and the whole interest of Talley-rand might have been to dip his fingers therein.

Vol. II. A note as a squint at political influences on military appointments. Napoleon is admired for having resisted them. The allusion is very transparent, and points home to the White House. But here, during this war, the political influences have torn away the country's fate from the claws of a Vampire and from the strangling pressure of an incubus—the one and the other in the shape of a Major General of the active army, and both once commanding the whole army of the United States—McClellan and Halleck.

Page 15, Vol. IV. Sixty thousand French, Italian, Jewish inhabitants, followed the retreating army from Moscow. Immense numbers for that time, and how did they get there? Certainly even to-day no sixty thousand Frenchmen and Italians inhabit Moscow. As for Jews, it is doubtful if even fifty of them lived in Moscow in 1812. It can safely be asserted that not one thousand Jews lived then in all Russia Proper, or the Great Russia. The laws forbidding Jews to live in Russia were very stringent, and very stringently executed. They were only abolished by the present sovereign, Alexander II. Jews are very numerous in such parts of the empire as once formed Polish and Turkish dominions.

Vol. IV. A note as an inference from the events of 1830 in relation to France and the other European powers as to what might have happened in certain eventualities after Napoleon's escape from Elba. All that can be said of this note and inference is, "Oh, Halleck, *thou art a great diplomat!*"

Such is the bulk of the notes and of the intellectual property of the translator of Jomini's Life of Napoleon.